# A PRISONER OF MEMORY

### AND 24 OF THE YEAR'S FINEST CRIME AND MYSTERY STORIES

EDITED BY ED GORMAN & MARTIN H. GREENBERG

PEGASUS BOOKS

NEW YORK

PRISONER

A PRISONER OF MEMORY
AND 24 OF THE YEAR'S FINEST CRIME AND MYSTERY STORIES

Pegasus Books LLC
45 Wall Street, Suite 1021
New York, NY 10005

Collection copyright © 2008 by Tekno Books

First Pegasus Books edition 2008

Interior design by Maria Fernandez

Library of Congress Cataloging-in-Publication Data is available.

ISBN: 978-1-933648-80-4

10 9 8 7 8 6 5 4 3 2 1

Printed in the United States of America
Distributed by W. W. Norton & Company

*This volume is dedicated to*
*the memory of our friend and colleague Ed Hoch*

# COPYRIGHTS

# CONTENTS

# THE MYSTERY IN 2007
*By Jon L. Breen*

C all 2007 the Year of the Stage Mystery. In the early twentieth century, mystery and detective plays were a mainstay of the American theater, but they spent several decades in relative eclipse. The Mystery Writers of America have offered a best-play Edgar Award since 1950, when Sidney Kingsley's *Detective Story* was honored, but only two more were awarded in the '50s, one each in the '60s and '70s, four each in the relatively fruitful '80s and '90s. When there was a theatrical winner in these years, it was almost always the sole nominee, the only exception being 1962, when Frederick Knott's *Write Me a Murder* won from Harry Kurnitz's *A Shot in the Dark*. In the twenty-first century, though, things are looking up. Best-play Edgars have been awarded in 2000, 2003, 2005, 2006, and 2007; in each case, there was more than one nominee.

In June, the International Mystery Writers' Festival, held in Owensboro, Kentucky, presented 48 performances over six days, including premieres of plays by Ed McBain, Robert S. Levinson, Stuart Kaminsky, William Link, and others. The second annual event is scheduled for June 2008 and is to include *Chimneys*, a play by Agatha Christie never before performed in the United States.

A history of crime on stage by Marvin Lachman, one of the field's most learned and reliable critics and historians, is being serialized prior to book publication in the periodical *Give Me That Old-Time Detection*, edited by Arthur Vidro. The most recent segment as of this writing, in the summer 2007 issue, covered sensational melo-dramas of the early twentieth century in the United States and the Grand Guignol school in France. (For information on the magazine, write Vidro at Post Office Box 313, Williston Park, NY 11596-0313 or at oldtimedetection@netzero.com.)

The year 2007 might also have been called the Year of Stephen King, though why award a year to someone who's already dominated at least three decades? The Mystery Writers of America's decision to give King their Grand Master Award was greeted mostly with approval but with mild grumbling in some quarters, based on two arguments: first, that King is not really a crime or mystery writer; and second, that several very important writers (Bill Pronzini, who will be named a Grand Master in 2008, and H.R.F. Keating, to name two) had not yet been honored. The second point is hard to argue with, but the first won't hold up to scrutiny. While King's usual generic pigeonhole is horror, he commonly mixes popular categories—mystery, fantasy, science fiction, even western—in a way that only a perennial best-seller can get away with. Even if you throw out all his supernatural fiction, the substantial number of books and stories that remain are surely about crime, indis-putably involve suspense and mystery, and occasionally even include detection, though his closest approach to a classical detective novel, *The Colorado Kid* (2006), was missing the essential element of a solution.

Early in his career, King was regarded in literary circles as an author of entertaining but disposable popular fiction. Over the years, his reputation has advanced to the point that he is now a frequent contributor to that highest-browed of well-paying fiction markets, *The New Yorker*, and in 2007 became (after Walter Mosley) only the second "genre" writer to edit Houghton Mifflin's prestigious annual *Best American Short Stories*.

The first novel King published under his at-first-secret pseu-donym Richard Bachman was *Rage*, a book he now apparently dis-owns: a footnote in the 2007 Bachman title *Blaze* (Scribner) notes it is "[n]ow out of print, and a good thing" and it is not included on the same volume's "also by Richard Bachman" list. Its subject matter, a crazed teenager taking over a classroom, may bring it too close to scary reality after Columbine, but it is an extraordinary crime novel.

*Blaze*, nearly as good, is a affecting portrait of a simple-minded crook, in acknowledged homage to Steinbeck's *Of Mice and Men*.

The most important scholarly book of the year, *Arthur Conan Doyle: A Life in Letters* (Penguin), edited by Jon Lellenberg, Daniel Stashower, and Charles Foley, represents a genre threatened with extinction: collected correspondence. Throughout the twentieth century, public life was recorded in greater detail than ever before, while the day-to-day record of private lives both great and obscure declined, an erosion accelerated in our telephoning, text-messaging age. As technology changes every few years, will blogs, e-mails, and other ephemeral electronic communications be preserved, and even if they are, will they prove as satisfying and enlightening as the letters and journals of the past?

Literary figures are virtually guaranteed to be interesting letter writers. In the crime fiction field, we already have collections of the letters of Raymond Chandler, Dashiell Hammett, and Dorothy L. Sayers, and there are many worthy subjects left to explore: Ross Macdonald, Ellery Queen, Agatha Christie, Jim Thompson, Cornell Woolrich, Anthony Boucher. All we need is scholars ready to do the labor for limited economic return, estates willing to let them, and publishers prepared to make the works available.

## BEST NOVELS OF THE YEAR 2007

It was tougher than usual to narrow my best of the year to fifteen titles, which could mean one of three things: I'm getting to be an easier grader (not likely); I did a better job of choosing what to read and review (could be); or it really was a banner year for crime fiction (maybe so). For the near runners-up, see titles by Boris Akunin, Richard A. Lupoff, Lisa Scottoline, Reginald Hill, Dean Koontz, and Jan Costin Wagner mentioned in the sub-genres roundup. The standard disclaimer applies: I don't pretend to cover the whole field—no single reviewer does.

Richard Aleas: *Songs of Innocence* (Hard Case Crime). Like two other writers below, Aleas topped an Edgar-nominated debut with an even better second book, featuring the disillusioned New York private eye John Blake.

Anne Argula: *Walla Walla Suite* (Ballantine). The Spokane police-woman Quinn of the Edgar-nominated *Homicide My Own* is now a Seattle private eye in a case less supernatural but just as offbeat.

Gianrico Carofiglio: *Reasonable Doubts*, translated from the Italian by Howard Curtis (Bitter Lemon). The third novel about the Italian advocate Guido Guerrieri is one of the best courtroom books of recent years.

Michael Chabon: *The Yiddish Policemen's Union* (HarperCollins). A Jewish refuge in Alaska is the unlikely setting for an alternate history cum police procedural by one of America's most celebrated living novelists. For all its literary ambition, the novel delivers the goods as a genuine detective story.

Deborah Crombie: *Water Like a Stone* (Morrow). Once again, Crombie proves she is the best American writer of British police novels.

Margaret Frazer: *The Traitor's Tale* (Berkley). A first-rate historical of fifteenth-century England features nun-detective Sister Frevisse and actor-spy Simon Joliffe.

Steve Hockensmith: *On the Wrong Track* (St. Martin's Minotaur). The second case for Gustav ("Old Red") Amlingmeyer, a wild west Sherlock Holmes acolyte, is even better than his Edgar-nominated debut.

Åsa Larsson: *The Blood Spilt*, translated from the Swedish by Marlaine Delargy (Delacorte). With sidelights on the state of religion and gender politics in Western Europe, this was one of the year's top three for me.

Dick Lochte: *Croaked!* (Five Star). Set in 1965 Los Angeles, this satirical workplace detective story reminded me of Dorothy L. Sayers's *Murder Must Advertise*.

Walter Mosley: *Blonde Faith* (Little, Brown). The remarkable saga of Easy Rawlins, African American private eye of late 1960s L.A., continues in a novel rich in psychological and sociological insights.

Arthur Phillips: *Angelica* (Random House). A spellbinding and complex multiviewpoint novel of a troubled Victorian family may be a ghost story or detective story or psychological study, or all of the above.

Bill Pronzini: *Savages* (Forge). The creator of San Francisco's not-quite-nameless private eye belongs in the top dozen or so greatest living mystery writers.

Ian Rankin: *The Naming of the Dead* (Little, Brown). Edinburgh's John Rebus confronts multiple cases at the time of the 2005 G8 economic summit. This one was my book of the year.

C. J. Sansom: *Sovereign* (Viking). Most mystery novels aren't worth 600 pages. This third sixteenth-century historical about an English lawyer, Matthew Shardlake, wears its heft well.

Martin Cruz Smith: *Stalin's Ghost* (Simon & Schuster). Arkady Renko returns in an outstanding mystery of post-Soviet Russia.

## SUB-GENRES

*Private eyes.* Ed Gorman's *Fools Rush In* (Pegasus) marked a welcome return for Sam McCain of Black River Falls, Iowa. Marijane Meaker revived her Vin Packer byline after thirty-eight years with *Scott Free* (Carroll & Graf), introducing a transgendered detective. Other shamuses worth a look included Parnell Hall's New Yorker Stanley Hastings in *Hitman* (Pegasus); Mark Coggins's San Franciscan August Riordan in *Runoff* (Bleak House); Loren D. Estleman's Detroit veteran Amos Walker in *American Detective* (Forge); and Peter Spiegelman's Manhattanite John March in *Red Cat* (Knopf).

*Amateur sleuths.* Among the not necessarily cozy non professionals in commendable action were Kit Ehrman's horseman Steve Cline in the Dick Francis–like *Triple Cross* (Poisoned Pen); Deborah Donnelly's wedding planner Carnegie Kincaid in *Bride and Doom* (Dell); Lyn Hamilton's Toronto antiques dealer Lara McClintoch in *The Chinese Alchemist* (Berkley); and Aaron Elkins's skeleton detective Gideon Oliver in *Tiny Little Teeth* (Berkley).

*Police.* Two long-standing series illustrated the turf war between everyday law enforcement officers and terrorism specialists: Reginald Hill's Dalziel and Pascoe novel *Death Comes for the Fat Man* (Harper-Collins) from the British viewpoint, and Michael Connelly's latest about L.A.-based Harry Bosch, *The Overlook* (Little, Brown), from the American. Jan Costin Wagner's *Ice Moon* (Harcourt), translated from the German by John Brownjohn, offers a fresh variation on the overly familiar cop-vs.-serial-killer situation. Lee Goldberg's very funny and cleverly plotted *Mr. Monk and the Blue Flu* (Signet) will challenge those with a prejudice against TV novelizations. Other series cops in good form included Garry Disher's Australian team of Hal Challis and Ellen Destry in *Chain of Evidence* (Soho); Paul Charles's Ulster-bred Londoner Christy Kennedy in *Sweetwater* (Brandon/Dufour); and two Italian crime fighters, Andrea Camilleri's Sicilian inspector Montalbano in *The Patience of the Spider* (Penguin), translated by Stephen Sartarelli, and Carlo Lucarelli's Commissario De Luca, displaced in post–World War II Italy in *The Damned Season* (Europa), translated by Michael Reynolds.

*Lawyers.* A young law professor is featured in Lisa Scottoline's typically excellent *Daddy's Girl* (HarperCollins). Richard North Patterson's *Exile* (Holt) has fine courtroom action and evenhandedly illuminates the Israeli-Palestinian dispute. Harlan Coben features a New Jersey prosecutor in *The Woods* (Dutton). Among series lawyer in commendable action were Margaret Maron's North Carolina judge Deborah Knott in *Hard Row* (Warner); the late Mercedes Lambert's Whitney Logan, making her third and final appearance in the unusual *Ghost Town* (Five Star); and Jeffrey Miller's Canadian appellate judge Ted Mariner (whose cases, I must warn you, are narrated by a cat called Amicus Curiae) in *Murder on the Rebound* (ECW).

*Historicals.* Richard A. Lupoff's *Marblehead: A Novel of H. P. Lovecraft* (Ramble House) is a treasure for fans of the *Weird Tales* master, of pulp magazines generally, and of American history between the world wars. In Boris Akunin's *Sister Pelagia and the White Bulldog* (Random House), translated from the Russian by Andrew Bromfield, a nun-detective in nineteenth-century Russia fronts a novel that is old-fashioned in several good ways. A young Oliver Wendell Holmes appears in Tess Gerritsen's *The Bone Garden* (Ballantine), mostly set in 1830s Boston but including a disposable contemporary story as well. Max Allan Collins adopted the pseudonym Patrick Culhane for *Black Hats* (Morrow), a 1920s adventure of Wyatt Earp. Two other potential new series characters operate in 1940s New York: that same Collins's newspaper syndicate troubleshooter Jack Starr in the Queenian-Wolfean *A Killing in Comics* (Berkley), illustrations by Terry Beatty; and Kathryn Miller Haines's unemployed actress Rosie Winter, making do on the home front in *The War Against Miss Winter* (Harper). Peter Tremayne's seventh-century Irish advocate Sister

Fidelma in *A Prayer for the Damned* (St. Martin's Minotaur) was joined by a sister lawyer of several centuries later, Mara, Brehon of the Burren, who debuts in Cora Harrison's *My Lady Judge* (St. Martin's Minotaur). Also in action: Michael Jecks's fourteenth-century team of Sir Baldwin Furnshill and Bailiff Simon Puttock in *The Malice of Unnatural Death* (Headline/Trafalgar); Rosemary Rowe's Longinus Flavius Libertus, of second-century Roman Britain, in *A Coin for the Ferryman* (Headline/Trafalgar); Joan Druett's 1830s seafarer Wiki Coffin in *Deadly Shoals* (St. Martin's Minotaur); and two sleuths created by Kathy Lynn Emerson, the sixteenth-century British Susanna, Lady Appleton in *Face Down O'er the Border* (Perseverance), and the 1880s American Diana Spaulding in *No Mortal Reason* (Pemberley). Would a Wall Street analyst pronounce me overweighted in historicals? I'm unrepentant.

*Thrillers.* Few writers can involve the reader on a gut level as well as Dean Koontz, whose two 2007 books were *The Darkest Evening of the Year* (Bantam), especially recommended to dog lovers, and *The Good Guy* (Bantam). For a scholarly adventure in the tradition of *The DaVinci Code* but much better written, try the best first novel I read in 2007: Jennifer Lee Carrell's *Interred with Their Bones* (Dutton). Lee Child's Jack Reacher novels are generally classified as thrillers, but the former military policeman is a real detective, too, as shown again in *Bad Luck and Trouble* (Delacorte). The late Philip R. Craig's J.W. Jackson and William G. Tapply's Brady Coyne join forces for presumably the last time in a case that ultimately proves more thriller than detection, *Third Strike* (Scribner). The characters in Saskia Noort's *The Dinner Club* (Bitter Lemon), translated from the Dutch by Paul Vincent, may not be likeable, but this suburban adultery story will hold your attention.

*Juveniles.* I don't know if mysteries for kids are better than ever, but the ones that come my way tend to impress: e.g., Robert B. Parker's 1940s-era basketball story *Edenville Owls* (Sleuth Philomel); Donna Jo Napoli and Robert Furrow's *Sly the Sleuth and the Food Mysteries* (Dial), a collection of genuinely clued puzzles for readers seven and up; Eric Berlin's *The Puzzling World of Winston Breen* (Putnam), another that will help create a new generation of classical mystery buffs; and Nancy Springer's *The Case of the Left-Handed Lady* (Sleuth Philomel), the second book about Enola Holmes (Sherlock's sister) with a vocabulary to challenge and delight young readers.

## SHORT STORIES

Though fewer single-author collections appeared than in the past few seasons, what was offered was choice. The major book of the year was Ross Macdonald's *The Archer Files: The Complete Short Stories of Lew Archer, Private Investigator, Including Newly Discovered Case Notes* (Crippen & Landru), adding to all the previously published stories eleven tantalizing unfinished cases that were remarkably polished and had no false-start aura. The Macdonald scholar and editor Tom Nolan's introduction is a surprisingly detailed biography of Archer. The same publisher's Lost Classics series added Lloyd Biggle Jr.'s *The Grandfather Rastin Mysteries* and Max Brand's *Masquerade: Ten Crime Stories*, edited by William F. Nolan.

At least two volumes of pastiches belong in every Sherlockian's library: Donald Thomas's *The Execution of Sherlock Holmes* (Pegasus) and Richard A. Lupoff's more playful *The Universal Holmes* (Ramble House). Lupoff's parody collection *The Compleat Ova Hamlet* (Ramble House) is mostly science-fictional but has some criminous crossover interest.

Other notable collections included James Lee Burke's *Jesus Out to Sea* (Simon & Schuster); Joyce Carol Oates's *The Museum of Dr. Moses: Tales of Mystery and Suspense* (Harcourt); Jeffery Deaver's *More Twisted* (Simon & Schuster); and a regathering of some of Marcia Muller's previously collected stories, *Somewhere in the City* (Pegasus). Russell James's *Underground and Collected Stories* (Stark House) combines a 1989 novel new to U.S. publication with five short stories.

Jorge Luis Borges's 1962 collection *Labyrinths: Selected Stories & Other Writings* (New Directions) appeared in a new edition with an introduction by William Gibson. *Arsene Lupin, Gentleman-Thief* (Penguin Classics) gathers thirteen of the best stories about Maurice Leblanc's great early-twentieth-century rogue turned detective, in vintage Alexander Teixeira de Mattos translations, selected and annotated by Michael Sims.

Turning to multiauthor anthologies, Akashic's city-centered noir collections of original stories are becoming almost too numerous to keep up with. Some of the 2007 titles, with editors in parentheses, were *Los Angeles Noir* (Denise Hamilton), *Bronx Noir* (S. J. Rozan), *New Orleans Noir* (Julie Smith), and *Wall Street Noir* (Peter Spiegelman). Other all or mostly original anthologies of more than passing interest included the Canadian Christmas-themed *Blood on the Holly* (Baskerville), edited by Caro Soles; *Dead Man's Hand: Crime Fiction at the Poker Table* (Harcourt), edited by Otto Penzler; *A Hell of a Woman: An Anthology of Female Noir* (Busted Flush), edited by Megan Abbott; *Chicago Blues* (Bleak House), edited by Libby Fischer Hellmann; *Hollywood and Crime* (Pegasus), edited by Robert J. Randisi; and *Sisters on the Case: Celebrating Twenty Years of Sisters in Crime* (Obsidian), edited by Sara Paretsky. A late-2006 item deserving of special note was the Detection Club's *The Verdict of Us All* (Crippen & Landru), stories in honor of H.R.F. Keating, edited by Peter Lovesey.

The biggest book of the year among reprint anthologies, both literally and in terms of significance, was surely *The Black Lizard Big Book of Pulps* (Vintage), a massive gathering edited by Otto Penzler. Mike Ashley's *The Mammoth Book of Perfect Crimes and Impossible Mysteries* (Carroll & Graf) combined originals and reprints. In *Passport to Crime* (Carroll & Graf), *Ellery Queen's Mystery Magazine* editor Janet Hutchings selected stories from that magazine's mysteries-in-translation feature. Two scholarly anthologies from Penguin Classics, while not entirely criminous, have considerable crossover interest: *Dashing Diamond Dick and Other Classic Dime Novels*, edited by J. Randolph Cox, including an appearance by the original Nick Carter, and *American Supernatural Tales*, edited by S. T. Joshi.

The annual best-of-the-year volumes went their separate ways in their 2006 coverage. *The Best American Mystery Stories 2007* (Houghton Mifflin), edited by Carl Hiaasen with series editor Otto Penzler, gathered all its twenty stories from original anthologies, literary magazines, and *The New Yorker*. The present volume's predecessor, *The Deadly Bride and 21 of the Year's Finest Crime and Mystery Stories* (Carroll & Graf), edited by Ed Gorman and Martin H. Greenberg, actually offered a mix of 2005 and 2006 stories.

## REFERENCE BOOKS AND SECONDARY SOURCES

Two reference volumes had their points but caused some readers to gnash their teeth over their assumptions, emphases, and omissions: Barry Forshaw's *The Rough Guide to Crime Fiction* (Rough Guides), a good job of writing albeit very biased toward the hardboiled and contemporary and regrettably error-prone; and Patrick Anderson's *The Triumph of the Thriller* (Random House), which offers some useful reading tips but distorts history in its attempt to prove that the contemporary thriller is something new and superior to what has gone before.

A worthy addition to the Chandler shelf was Judith Freeman's *The Long Embrace: Raymond Chandler and the Woman He Loved* (Pantheon), offering new information on the somewhat shadowy Cissy Chandler. A pioneering Dashiell Hammett study, George J. Thompson's *Hammett's Moral Vision* (Vince Emery) appeared in book form for the first time. One of their contemporaries in a slightly different medium was the subject of family biography in Jean Gould O'Connell's *Chester Gould: A Daughter's Biography of the Creator of Dick Tracy* (McFarland).

John Williams's *Back to the Badlands: Crime Writing in the U.S.A.* (Serpent's Tail) updated his earlier combination of travel book and interview collection *Into the Badlands* (1989). Also of regional interest was the unusually meaty *Florida Crime Writers: 24 Interviews* (McFarland), edited by Steve Glassman.

Books on TV shows were prominent, including *Reading CSI: TV Under the Microscope* (Palgrave Macmillan), a collection of professorial articles edited by Michael Allen that was informative if sometimes heavy going; and *Neptune Noir: Unauthorized Investigations into Veronica Mars* (BenBella), a livelier treatment of the teenage private eye series edited by the show's creator and executive producer Rob Thomas (but it's unauthorized?) with Leah Wilson.

Dr. D. P. Lyle followed up on his earlier Q&A with the entertaining and informative *Forensics and Fiction: Clever, Intriguing, and Downright Odd Questions from Crime Writers* (Dunne/St. Martin's Minotaur).

## A SENSE OF HISTORY

Among the most notable current reprint projects is the revival of Lawrence Block's Evan Tanner series, mostly published in paperback original in the 1960s. Harper's paperback reprints include entertaining afterwords by Block. Meanwhile, Hard Case Crime reprinted a pseudonymous Block novel, *Lucky at Cards*, originally published in 1964 as *The Sex Shuffle* with the byline Sheldon Lord. In addition to its program of paperback originals, Hard Case also reprinted (with evocative '50s- and '60s-style girl-art covers) such writers as Gil Brewer, David Goodis, George Axelrod, Cornell Woolrich, and Robert Terrall.

Penguin's reprinting of Georges Simenon's Maigret novels continued with *The Madman of Bergerac* (1932) and *The Friend of Madame Maigret* (1950; also published as *Madame Maigret's Own Case*), in translations by Geoffrey Sainsbury and Helen Sebba, respectively.

For old-timers, as well as younger readers with classical tastes, the best news generally comes from Rue Morgue Press, which revived Catherine Aird's scarce nonseries novel *A Most Contagious Game* (1967); Morris Bishop's academic comedy *The Widening Stain* (1942, as by W. Bolingbroke Johnson); and two early novels by Michael Gilbert, *Close Quarters* (1947) and *The Danger Within* (1952; British title *Death in Captivity*). Rue Morgue also added titles by previously featured authors Stuart Palmer and the team of Constance and Gwenyth Little. All of the above include informative introductions by the publishers Tom and Enid Schantz.

Millipede, a similarly classy reprinter with darker tastes, revived David Goodis's *Nightfall* (1947) and *Street of No Return* (1954), with introductions by Bill Pronzini and Robert Polito, respectively. Felony & Mayhem launched a reprinting of Reginald Hill's Dalziel and Pascoe series with their 1970 debut, *A Clubbable Woman*, with a new introduction by the author. Albuquerque's Sidewinder Press, having reprinted late in 2006 Tony Hillerman's *The Blessing Way* (1970) in a handsome new hardcover edition, introduced by Ernie Bulow and illustrated by Ernest Franklin, added in the same illustrated format the second novel in his Navajo series, *Dance Hall of the Dead* (1973), introduced by Margaret Coel.

Southern Tier offered reissues with new introductions of several novels about Richard Stevenson's gay private eye, Donald Strachey, including *Icy Blues* (1986), *Third Man Out* (1992), and *A Shock to the*

*System* (1995). O'Bryan House's edition of W. R. Burnett's Dillinger-inspired novel *Dr. Socrates*, a 1935 magazine serial made the same year into a movie vehicle for Paul Muni, is, remarkably enough, its first in book form.

*A Trio of Gold Medals* (Stark House) is an omnibus drawn from the heyday of paperback originals: Dan J. Marlowe's *The Vengeance Man* (1966), Fletcher Flora's *Park Avenue Tramp* (1958), and Charles Runyon's *The Prettiest Girl I Ever Killed* (1965). Stark also reprinted in a single volume two early nonseries suspense novels by the versatile and prolific Bill Pronzini, *Snowbound [and] Games*, from 1974 and 1976, respectively, with introductory comments by Marcia Muller and Robert J. Randisi. In the most unexpected and surprisingly enjoyable reprinting project of the year, Ramble House brought "sleaze" novels by Jim Harmon to a new audience, two to a volume: *Vixen Scandal*, pairing the 1962 novels *Vixen Hollow* and *The Celluloid Scandal;* and *Maniac Siren*, consisting of the 1961 titles *Silent Siren* and *The Man Who Made Maniacs.*

Finally, a new edition of Laurie R. King's 1994 first novel about Mary Russell and Sherlock Holmes, *The Beekeeper's Apprentice* (Picador), included that odd new feature of some trade paperbacks: discussion questions for book clubs.

## AT THE MOVIES

In this volume's predecessor, I deemed 2006 a poorer year for crime films than 2005 "at least through its first three quarters." Of the three releases still to come that I noted as promising, one proved a total dud (*The Black Dahlia*); a second was only so-so (*Hollywoodland*); and the third (*The Bridesmaid*) never came to a theater near me. What I didn't see coming was the Oscar and Edgar winner *The Departed*, directed by Martin Scorsese from a screenplay by William Monahan, based on the 2002 Hong Kong film written by Siu Fai Mak and Felix Chong. It's a great gangster movie, if not quite enough to raise 2006 to banner-year status.

That 2007 might be better was suggested by three outstanding films that appeared in quick succession early in the year. *Breach*, suspensefully dramatizing the exposure of FBI agent turned Soviet spy Robert Hanssen (masterfully played by Chris Cooper), was directed by Billy Ray from his screenplay with Adam Mazer and William Rotko, based on their story. Also fact-based was *Zodiac*, about the unsolved Bay Area serial killings of the 1960s and '70s, directed by David Fincher from James Vanderbilt's screenplay based on the book by the San Francisco reporter Robert Graysmith. The purely fictitious *Fracture*, with Anthony Hopkins as a murder suspect, may be the most Edgar-worthy of the three, a trickily plotted legal thriller directed by Gregory Hoblit from the screenplay of Daniel Pyne and Glenn Gers, based on Pyne's story.

Through the middle of the year, 2007 proved not especially notable. A couple of franchise entries were okay if not quite as good as ballyhooed: *The Bourne Ultimatum*, directed by Paul Greengrass and written by Tony Gilroy, Scott Z. Burns, and George Nolfi, from Robert Ludlum's novel; and *Live Free or Die Hard*, directed by Len Wiseman from a Mark Bomback script based on his screen story with David Marconi, an article by John Carlin, and (distantly) Roderick Thorp's original characters. Exploring fresher ground were *You Kill Me*, a comedy in which Ben Kingsley sympathetically portrays an alcoholic hitman, directed by John Dahl from the script of Christopher Markus and Stephen McFeely; *Shooter*, an action political thriller about a plot to kill the president, directed by Antoine Fuqua from Jonathan Lemkin's screenplay, based on Stephen Hunter's novel; Louise Osmond and Jerry Rothwell's documentary *Deep Water*, about an out-of-his-depth amateur sailor's daring and ultimately tragic attempt to cheat in a 1968 round-the-world yacht race; *The Hoax*, an enjoyable account of Clifford Irving's notorious Howard Hughes autobiography scam, directed by Lasse Hallström from William Wheeler's script based on Irving's book; Mark Fergus's *First Snow*, written with Hawk Ostby, which proves once again that cold conditions are a great plus for thrillers (see also *Fargo, Road to Perdition, Insomnia*, et al.); and Jonathan King's wonderfully straight-faced horror movie send-up, *Black Sheep*, in which normally placid New Zealand farm livestock turn into mutated killers.

The late-year Oscar rush brought a series of strong crime films. *Eastern Promises*, a chillingly expert (and incidentally extremely violent) tale of the Russian mafia in London, was directed by David Cronenberg from Steven Knight's script. Russian organized crime, this time in New York, also figures in James Gray's *We Own the Night*, an effective variation on a familiar situation: brothers who begin on different sides of the law. Tony Gilroy's excellent noncourtroom legal thriller *Michael Clayton* was notable for its sympathetic and nuanced view of mental illness. An updated reimagining of Anthony Shaffer's classic play *Sleuth* was scripted by none other than the Nobel Prize winner Harold Pinter and directed by Kenneth Branagh. The NC17-rated World War II espionage film *Lust, Caution* (Chinese title *Se, jie*) was the director Ang Lee's atmospheric and erotic tribute to film noir, from a screenplay by James Schamus and Hui-Ling Wang, based on a short story by Eileen Chang. Sidney Lumet, a specialist in hard-edged crime films, directed *Before the Devil Knows You're Dead*, about an all-in-the-family robbery gone horribly wrong, with a well-crafted script by Kelly Masterson. A superb late-year gangster saga that could run the Oscar-Edgar table like last year's *The Departed* is *American Gangster*, about New York police corruption and the Harlem drug trade of the late 1960s and early 1970s, directed by Ridley Scott from Steven Zaillian's script, based in turn on a nonfiction article by Mark Jacobson. Another strong contender for Edgar honors might be Joel and Ethan Coen's suspenseful and thematically complex thriller *No Country for Old Men*, from the Cormac McCarthy novel.

Final verdict, with the possibility of still more late-year triumphs (how about Johnny Depp as *Sweeney Todd*?): 2007 was an excellent year for cinematic crime.

### AWARD WINNERS

Awards tied to publishers' contests, those limited to a geographical region smaller than a country, those awarded for works in languages other than English, and those confined to works from a single periodical have been omitted.

Awarded in 2007 for Material Published in 2006
EDGAR ALLAN POE AWARDS
(Mystery Writers of America)

**BEST NOVEL:** Jason Goodwin, *The Janissary Tree* (Farrar, Straus and Giroux)

**BEST FIRST NOVEL BY AN AMERICAN AUTHOR:** Alex Berenson, *The Faithful Spy* (Random House)

**BEST ORIGINAL PAPERBACK:** Naomi Hirahara, *Snakeskin Shamisen* (Delta)

**BEST FACT CRIME BOOK:** James L. Swanson, *Manhunt: The 12-Day Chase for Lincoln's Killer* (Morrow)

**BEST CRITICAL/BIOGRAPHICAL WORK:** E. J. Wagner, *The Science of Sherlock Holmes: From Baskerville Hall to the Valley of Fear* (Wiley)

**BEST SHORT STORY:** Charles Ardai, "The Home Front" (*Death Do Us Part*, Little, Brown)

**BEST YOUNG ADULT MYSTERY:** Robin Merrow MacCready, *Buried* (Dutton Children's Books)

**BEST JUVENILE MYSTERY:** Andrew Clements, *Room One: A Mystery or Two* (Simon & Schuster)

**BEST PLAY:** Steven Dietz, *Sherlock Holmes: The Final Adventure* (Arizona Theatre Company)

**BEST TELEVISION EPISODE TELEPLAY:** Matthew Graham, *Life on Mars*, Episode I (BBC America)

**BEST TELEVISION FEATURE/MINISERIES TELEPLAY:** Ed Burns, Kia Corthron, Dennis Lehane, David Mills, Eric Overmyer, George Pelecanos, Richard Price, David Simon & William F. Zorzi, *The Wire*, Season 4 (Home Box Office)

**BEST MOTION PICTURE SCREENPLAY:** William Monahan, *The Departed* (Warner Brothers)

**GRAND MASTER:** Stephen King

**ROBERT L. FISH AWARD (BEST FIRST STORY):** William Dylan Powell, "Evening Gold" (*Ellery Queen Mystery Magazine*, November)

**RAVEN:** Books & Books (Mitchell Kaplan, owner); Mystery Loves Company Bookstore (Kathy & Tom Harig, owners)

**MARY HIGGINS CLARK AWARD:** Fiona Mountain, *Bloodline*
(St. Martin's Minotaur)

## AGATHA AWARDS
### (MALICE DOMESTIC MYSTERY CONVENTION)

**BEST NOVEL:** Nancy Pickard, *The Virgin of Small Plains* (Ballantine)

**BEST FIRST NOVEL:** Sandra Parshall, *The Heat of the Moon* (Poisoned Pen)

**BEST SHORT STORY:** Toni L. P. Kelner, "Sleeping with the Plush"
(*Alfred Hitchcock Mystery Magazine*, May)

**BEST NONFICTION:** Chris Roerden, *Don't Murder Your Mystery*
(Bella Rosa)

**BEST CHILDREN'S/YOUNG ADULT:** Nancy Means Wright, *Pea Soup
Poisonings* (Hilliard & Harris)

**LIFETIME ACHIEVEMENT AWARD:** Carolyn Hart

**POIROT AWARD:** Douglas G. Greene

## DAGGER AWARDS
### (CRIME WRITERS' ASSOCIATION, GREAT BRITAIN)

**DUNCAN LAWRIE DAGGER:** Peter Temple, *The Broken Shore*
(Quercus)

**INTERNATIONAL DAGGER:** Fred Vargas, *Wash This Blood Clean from
My Hand*, translated from the French by Sian Reynolds (Harvill
Secker)

**IAN FLEMING STEEL DAGGER:** Gillian Flynn, *Sharp Objects* (Wiedenfeld & Nicholson)

**BEST SHORT STORY:** Peter Lovesey, "Needle Match" (*Murder is My
Racquet*, Mysterious)

**NEW BLOOD DAGGER:** Gillian Flynn, *Sharp Objects* (Wiedenfeld &
Nicholson)

**DIAMOND DAGGER:** John Harvey

**ELLIS PETERS AWARD (FORMERLY HISTORICAL DAGGER):** Arianna Franklin, *Mistress of the Art of Death* (Bantam UK; Putnam)

**DAGGER IN THE LIBRARY (VOTED BY LIBRARIANS FOR A BODY OF WORK):** Stuart MacBride

**DEBUT DAGGER (FOR UNPUBLISHED WRITERS):** Alan Bradley, *The Sweetness at the Bottom of the Pie*

## ANTHONY AWARDS
### (BOUCHERCON WORLD MYSTERY CONVENTION)

**BEST NOVEL:** Laura Lippman, *No Good Deeds* (Morrow)

**BEST FIRST NOVEL:** Louise Penny, *Still Life* (St. Martin's Minotaur)

**BEST PAPERBACK ORIGINAL:** Dana Cameron, *Ashes and Bones* (Avon)

**BEST SHORT STORY:** Simon Wood, "My Father's Secret" (*Crimespree*, Bouchercon Special Issue 2006)

**BEST CRITICAL/BIOGRAPHICAL:** Jim Huang and Austin Lugar, eds., *Mystery Muses* (Crum Creek Press)

**SPECIAL SERVICES AWARD:** Jim Huang, Crum Creek Press and The Mystery Company

**LIFETIME ACHIEVEMENT AWARD:** James Sallis

## SHAMUS AWARDS
### (PRIVATE EYE WRITERS OF AMERICA)

**BEST HARDCOVER NOVEL:** Ken Bruen, *The Dramatist* (St. Martin's Minotaur)

**BEST FIRST NOVEL:** Declan Hughes, *The Wrong Kind of Blood* (Morrow)

**BEST ORIGINAL PAPERBACK NOVEL:** P. J. Parrish, *An Unquiet Grave* (Pinnacle)

**BEST SHORT STORY:** O'Neil De Noux, "The Heart Has Reasons" (*Alfred Hitchcock Mystery Magazine*, September)

**THE EYE (LIFE ACHIEVEMENT):** Stuart Kaminsky

**HAMMER AWARD (FOR A MEMORABLE PRIVATE EYE CHARACTER OR SERIES):** Shell Scott (created by Richard S. Prather)

## MACAVITY AWARDS
### (MYSTERY READERS INTERNATIONAL)

**BEST NOVEL:** Nancy Pickard, *The Virgin of Small Plains* (Ballantine)

**BEST FIRST NOVEL:** Nick Stone, *Mr. Clarinet* (Michael Joseph/Penguin)

**BEST NONFICTION:** Jim Huang and Austin Lugar, eds., *Mystery Muses* (Crum Creek Press)

**BEST SHORT STORY:** Tim Maleeny, "Till Death Do Us Part" (*Death Do Us Part*, Little, Brown)

**SUE FEDER HISTORICAL MYSTERY AWARD:** Rhys Bowen, *Oh Danny Boy* (St. Martin's Minotaur)

## BARRY AWARDS
### (*DEADLY PLEASURES* AND *MYSTERY NEWS*)

**BEST NOVEL:** George Pelecanos, *The Night Gardner* (Little, Brown)

**BEST FIRST NOVEL:** Louise Penny, *Still Life* (St. Martin's Minotaur)

**BEST BRITISH NOVEL:** Ken Bruen, *Priest* (Bantam)

**BEST PAPERBACK ORIGINAL:** Sean Doolittle, *The Cleanup* (Dell)

**BEST THRILLER:** Daniel Silva, *The Messenger* (Putnam)

**BEST SHORT STORY:** Brendan DuBois, "The Right Call" (*Ellery Queen Mystery Magazine*, September/October)

**DON SANDSTROM MEMORIAL AWARD FOR LIFETIME ACHIEVEMENT IN MYSTERY FANDOM:** Beth Fedyn

## ARTHUR ELLIS AWARDS
### (Crime Writers of Canada)

**BEST NOVEL:** Barbara Fradkin, *Honour Among Men* (Rendezvous Press)

**BEST FIRST NOVEL:** Anne Emery, *Sign of the Cross* (ECW Press)

**BEST NONFICTION:** Brian O'Dea, *High: Confessions of a Pot Smuggler* (Random House Canada)

**BEST JUVENILE NOVEL:** Sean Cullen, *Hamish X and the Cheese Pirates* (Penguin Canada)

**BEST SHORT STORY:** Dennis Richard Murphy, "Fuzzy Wuzzy" (*Ellery Queen Mystery Magazine*, August)

**THE UNHANGED ARTHUR (BEST UNPUBLISHED FIRST CRIME NOVEL:** Phyllis Smallman, *Margarita Nights*

## THRILLER AWARDS
### (International Thriller Writers, Inc.)

**BEST NOVEL:** Joseph Finder, *Killer Instinct* (St. Martin's)

**BEST FIRST NOVEL:** Nick Stone, *Mr. Clarinet* (Michael Joseph/Penguin)

**BEST PAPERBACK ORIGINAL:** P. J. Parrish, *An Unquiet Grave* (Pinnacle)

**BEST SCREENPLAY:** Eric Roth, *The Good Shepherd*

**THRILLER MASTER AWARD:** James Patterson

## NED KELLY AWARDS
### (Crime Writers' Association of Australia)

**BEST NOVEL:** Garry Disher, *Chain of Evidence* (Text Publications)

**BEST FIRST NOVEL:** Adrian Hyland, *Diamond Dove* (Text Publications)

**BEST TRUE CRIME (TIE):** Liz Porter, *Written on the Skin* (Macmillan); and Debi Marshall, *Killing for Pleasure: The Definitive Story of the Snowtown Murders* (Random House Australia)

**LIFETIME ACHIEVEMENT:** Sandra Harvey and Lindsay Simpson

## DILYS AWARD
(Independent Mystery Booksellers Association)

Louise Penny, *Still Life* (St. Martin's Minotaur)

## LEFTY AWARD
(Left Coast Crime)
(best humorous mystery novel in the English language)

Donna Moore, *Go to Helena Handbasket* (Point Blank)

## HAMMETT PRIZE
(International Association of Crime Writers, North America Branch)

Dan Fesperman, *The Prisoner of Guantánamo* (Knopf)

## AWARDED IN 2006 FOR MATERIAL PUBLISHED IN 2005

## DAGGER AWARDS
(Crime Writers' Association, Great Britain)

**SHORT STORY AWARD:** Robert Barnard, "Sins of Scarlet" (*I.D.: Crimes of Identity*, Comma Press)

**ELLIS PETERS HISTORICAL CRIME AWARD:** Edward Wright, *Red Sky Lament* (Orion)

## ANTHONY AWARDS
(Bouchercon World Mystery Convention)

**BEST NOVEL:** William Kent Krueger, *Mercy Falls* (Atria)

**BEST FIRST NOVEL:** Chris Grabenstein, *Tilt-a-Whirl* (Carroll & Graf)

**BEST PAPERBACK ORIGINAL:** Reed Farrel Coleman, *The James Deans* (Plume)

**BEST SHORT STORY:** Barbara Seranella, "Misdirection" (*Greatest Hits*, Carroll & Graf)

**BEST CRITICAL/BIOGRAPHICAL:** Marvin Lachman, *Heirs of Anthony Boucher* (Poisoned Pen)

**BEST FAN PUBLICATION:** *Crimespree Magazine*, edited by Jon and Ruth Jordan

**SPECIAL SERVICE TO THE FIELD:** Janet Rudolph, for Mystery Readers International

**LIFETIME ACHIEVEMENT:** Robert B. Parker

## SHAMUS AWARDS
### (PRIVATE EYE WRITERS OF AMERICA)

**BEST NOVEL:** Michael Connelly, *The Lincoln Lawyer* (Little, Brown)

**BEST FIRST NOVEL:** Louise Ure, *Forcing Amaryllis* (Mysterious Press)

**BEST ORIGINAL PAPERBACK NOVEL:** Reed Farrel Coleman, *The James Deans* (Plume)

**BEST SHORT STORY:** Michael Wiecek, "A Death in Ueno" (*Alfred Hitchcock Mystery Magazine*, March)

**THE EYE (LIFE ACHIEVEMENT):** Max Allan Collins

## MACAVITY AWARDS
### (MYSTERY READERS INTERNATIONAL)

**BEST NOVEL:** Michael Connelly, *The Lincoln Lawyer* (Little, Brown)

**BEST FIRST NOVEL:** Brian Freeman, *Immoral* (St. Martin's)

**BEST NONFICTION:** Melanie Rehak, *Girl Sleuth: Nancy Drew and the Women Who Created Her* (Harcourt)

**BEST SHORT STORY:** Nancy Pickard, "There Is No Crime on Easter Island" (*Ellery Queen Mystery Magazine*, September–October)

**SUE FEDER HISTORICAL MYSTERY AWARD:** Jacqueline Winspear, *Pardonable Lies* (Holt)

## BARRY AWARDS
### (*DEADLY PLEASURES* MAGAZINE)

**BEST NOVEL:** Thomas H. Cook, *Red Leaves* (Harcourt)

**BEST FIRST NOVEL:** Stuart Macbride, *Cold Granite* (St. Martin's)

**BEST BRITISH NOVEL:** Denise Mina, *The Field of Blood* (Bantam)

**BEST PAPERBACK ORIGINAL:** Reed Farrel Coleman, *The James Deans* (Plume)

**BEST THRILLER:** Joseph Finder, *Company Man* (St. Martin's)

**BEST SHORT STORY:** Nancy Pickard, "There Is No Crime on Easter Island" (*Ellery Queen Mystery Magazine*, September/October)

**DON SANDSTROM MEMORIAL AWARD FOR LIFETIME ACHIEVEMENT IN MYSTERY FANDOM:** Janet A. Rudolph

## NERO WOLFE AWARD
### (WOLFE PACK)

Tess Gerritsen, *Vanished* (Ballantine)

## ELLEN NEHR AWARD
### (FOR EXCELLENCE IN MYSTERY REVIEWING)
### (THE AMERICAN CRIME WRITERS LEAGUE)

Dick Adler, *Chicago Tribune*

# OBITUARIES IN 2007

## Edward D. Hoch (1930–2008)

On the morning of January 17 I lost one of my closest friends in the mystery-writing community. Ed Hoch's death was the sort we wish for ourselves and those we care about, instant, without pain. He got up and went to take a shower and his wife heard a thump from the bathroom and he was already gone, apparently from a massive heart attack. He would have been seventy-eight in another five weeks. His ambition was to write a thousand short stories but he died something like fifty short of that goal.

I first met him in the late sixties, a year or two after he had left his advertising job to write full time. Over the decades we corresponded endlessly, appeared on panels together, did things for each other. I edited two collections of his short stories, recommended him for Guest of Honor at the Pulpcon the year after I had that slot (he should of course have been asked long before I was), gave him my extra copy of Fred Dannay's all but impossible to find autobiographical novel *The Golden Summer* (1953, as by Daniel Nathan). The day after each year's MWA dinner I'd have breakfast with Ed and Pat at the Essex House on Central Park South, where they habitually stayed on their frequent visits to the city, and we'd talk the morning away. All the things he did for me would fill a book even if one didn't mention the countless hours of reading pleasure he gave me.

He was such a kind man, so generously giving of himself to so many others, so modest and tolerant and thoughtful. It was typical of him that when an interviewer wanted to describe him as a devout Catholic, he said it would be presumptuous to apply that adjective to himself and that he preferred "observant," a word generally associated with the Jewish tradition. If there was anyone remotely like him in the genre, it was Anthony Boucher. Both men loved and were immensely knowledgeable about mystery fiction, both wrote far more short stories than they did novels, both edited superb anthologies of short fiction in their genre, both combined deep religious feeling with total openness of mind and heart and deep respect and appreciation for those of other faiths or none.

Ed was the polar opposite of a stereotypical Type A personality. He never seemed harried or rushed, never lost his temper, always had time for others' concerns and yet never fell behind schedule with his own work. His ability to devise mystery plots was astonishing. Where did they come from? Wide and constant reading—almost anything he came across in a novel or story or nonfiction book might become a springboard for him—coupled with a mind like no other. About twenty years ago we attended a cocktail party at a New York publisher's office whose roof garden offered a fine view of the then new Marriott Marquis hotel with its glass-walled elevator traveling nonstop up and down the side of the building from top floor to street and back again. "What if someone was seen entering that elevator," I asked Ed idly, "and wasn't there when it stopped at the other end?" Almost anyone could come up with a wild premise like that. Ed made it work, made one of his neatest impossible crime stories out of it, and thanked me by naming one of its minor characters Nevins.

He's gone now. The genre he loved and to which he contributed so much will never see anyone like him again. But maybe in a sense he's still with us. There's a Jewish saying that you haven't really died until the death of the last person with fond living memories of you. In that sense Ed Hoch will live for generations, as his finest stories will.

—Francis M. Nevins
Professor of Law, Emeritus
Saint Louis University School of Law

**RAY ALAN** (1921–2007). Pseudonym of J. L. Valls-Russell, author of two suspense novels, notably *The Beirut Pipeline* (1980).

**HOLLIS ALPERT** (1916–2007). Well-known author and entertainment critic who published a single intrigue novel, *A Disappearance* (1975), under the name of "Robert Carroll."

**JAMES ANDERSON** (1936–2007). British author of a dozen mystery novels, 1969–88, notably *The Affair of the Bloodstained Egg Cosy* (1975).

**ELLIOT BAKER** (1922–2007). Screenwriter and novelist who authored a single crime novel, *Pocock & Pitt* (1971).

**MARC BEHM** (1925–2007). Author of a well-regarded private eye novel, *The Eye of the Beholder* (1980), plus three other thrillers, some fantasy.

**EDWARD BEHR** (1926–2007), Former war correspondent who authored one suspense novel, *Getting Even* (1980).

**A. I. BEZZERIDES** (1908–2007). Hollywood screenwriter who published two crime novels, *Long Haul* (1938, filmed as *They Drive By Night*) and *Thieves Market* (1949, filmed as *Thieves Highway*). He also adapted Spillane's *Kiss Me Deadly* for the screen.

**MICHAEL BLODGETT** (1939–2007). Actor and screenwriter who authored three thrillers, 1980–86. Both *Hero and the Terror* and *White Raven* were filmed.

**A. J. CAROTHERS** (ca. 1931–2007). Screenwriter who published two suspense novels, one a novelizations of the film *Hero at Large* (1980).

**FRANCINE CARROLL** (1924–2007). Creator and writer of the TV detective series "Amy Prentiss," who might also have written youthful mysteries for Black Mask and other pulps under an undisclosed pseudonym.

**SEAN CERNACH** (1922–2007). Pseudonym of John F. W. McCaig, author of *The Howland Axe Murders* (self-published, 2000).

**NEIL F. COLEMAN** (1923–2007). Author of *Honeycomb* (1999).

**ALAN COREN** (1938–2007). Former editor of *Punch* who authored occasional Sherlockian and crime stories.

**PHILIP R. CRAIG** (1933–2007). Author of more than a dozen mystery novels starting in 1969, most with Martha's Vineyard settings. He also collaborated with William G. Tapply on three novels.

**COLIN CURZON** (ca. 1919–2007). Pseudonym of British author Peter Cooper, who wrote two detective novels, *The Case of the Eighteenth Ostrich* and *The Body in the Barrage Balloon*, both in the early 1940s.

**DON DARELIUS** (1918–2007). Apparent pseudonym of Donald Philip Carlson, author of *Summer Search* (1994).

**JOSE LUIS DE VILLALLONGA** (1920–2007). Spanish writer and actor, author of *Furia*, translated and published in Britain in 1976.

**MICHAEL DIBDIN** (1947–2007). British/American author of nearly twenty mystery novels, notably *Rat King* (1988), first of his eleven Aurelio Zen novels and winner of CWA's Gold Dagger. Husband of the mystery writer K. K. Beck.

**ARNOLD DRAKE** (1924–2007). Author of mystery and SF comic books who published a hardboiled paperback novel, *The Steel Noose* (1954).

**CHARLES EINSTEIN** (1926–2007). Sportswriter and screenwriter who published five suspense novels, notably *The Bloody Spur* (1953), filmed as *While the City Sleeps*, and *The Naked City* (1959), a collection of eight stories from the TV series. His stories also appeared in EQMM, AHMM, Manhunt, and elsewhere.

**CYPRIAN EKWENSI** (1921–2007). African author of one suspense novel, *Yaba Round the World* (1962).

**ROGER ELWOOD** (1943–2007). Prolific science fiction anthologist during the 1970s, he published four mystery novels, all in 1993, three with World War II backgrounds.

**ROBERT ENGLISH** (1936–2007). Australian author of two mysteries, including *More Deaths Than One*, published in America in 1995.

PAUL ERDMAN (1932–2007). Author of nine best-selling novels of financial intrigue, 1973–97, starting with *The Billion Dollar Sure Thing*, winner of the MWA Edgar for best first novel, and *The Silver Bears* (1974), an Edgar nominee for best novel.

KAY HARRIS EVANS (1906–2007). Co-author with her husband of five mysteries as by "Harris Evans" and one as by "Brandon Bird," all published 1950–60.

CLIVE EXTON (ca. 1930–2007). British screenwriter who scripted novels by Agatha Christie and Ruth Rendell, among others.

FLORENCE FAULKNER (1899–2007). Author of *Season of Deception* (1981) and other suspense novels, apparently the oldest member of the Mystery Writers of America. In 1951 she collaborated on "Theo Durrant's" novel *The Marble Forest*.

(JAMES) BRIAN FINCH (1936–2007). Author of several British TV mysteries.

HAL FISHMAN (1931–2007). Co-author of two thrillers, starting with *The Vatican Target* (1979).

DENNY MARTIN FLINN (1947–2007). Actor, screenwriter, and author of two mysteries, *San Francisco Kills* and *Killer Finish* (both 1991).

JOHN GARDNER (1926–2007). British author of more than fifty thrillers, including eight about Boysie Oakes, starting with *The Liquidator* (1964), and more than a dozen about James Bond, starting with *Licence Renewed* (1981).

GRIFFIN T. GARNETT (JR.) (1914–2007). Author of two mysteries, starting with *The Sandscrapers* (1995).

ROSEMARY GATENBY (1918–2007). Author of nine suspense novels, 1967–79, starting with *Evil Is As Evil Does*.

TUDOR GATES (1930–2007). Popular British playwright who authored a suspense novel, three TV novelizations, and three suspense plays, 1967–91.

**MODENA (F.) GELIEN** (1908–2007). Author of *Walking Shadows* (1978).

**JONATHAN GOODMAN** (1931–2007). British true-crime writer who also published four suspense novels, 1961–78, starting with *Instead of Murder*.

**PETER HAINING** (1940–2007). Well-known British author and anthology editor who produced some 150 books, mainly fantasy and mystery anthologies, notably *Supernatural Sleuths* (1986), *Murder on the Menu* (1991), *The Television Detectives' Omnibus* (1993), *Murder by the Glass*, *Tales from the Rogues' Gallery*, *The Television Crimebusters Omnibus* (all 1994), and *The Orion Book of Murder* (1996).

**DONALD HAMILTON** (1916–2006). Author of three dozen novels, twenty-seven in the popular Matt Helm series, notably the Edgar-nominated *The Retaliators* (1976). His notable nonseries novels included *The Steel Mirror* (1948).

**ELIZABETH HARDWICK** (1916–2007). Author, critic, and co-founder of *The New York Review of Books*, she published a single suspense novel, *The Simple Truth* (1955).

**W(ILLIAM) L(EDBETTER) HEATH** (1924–2007). Author of four suspense novels set in Alabama, notably *Violent Saturday* (1955).

**JOE L. HENSLEY** (1926–2007). Indiana attorney and judge who authored some twenty novels, starting with *The Color of Hate* (1960), and three collections of short stories, most recently *Deadly Hunger* (2001).

**SHARON HERBST** (?–2007). Food writer who began her career with short mysteries, including a story in the August 1976 issue of *Mike Shayne Mystery Magazine*.

**FRANK E. HEWENS** (1912–2007). Author of *The Murder of the Dainty-Footed Model* (1968).

**ARTHUR (ABEL) HOFFE** (1920–2007). Author of *Something Evil* (1968).

**CAROLYN HOGAN** (1943–2007). Author of three mystery novels under her own name and one as "Malcolm Bell." She also collaborated with her husband on six novels as "John F. Case," including *Ghost Dancer* (2006), a nominee for the Hammett Award.

**GENEVIEVE HOLDEN** (1919–2007). Pseudonym of Genevieve Long Pou, author of seven mystery novels, 1953–76, starting with *Killer Loose!*

**EDNA HONG** (1913–2007). Author of *Wild Blue Berries* (1987).

**JOHN (RYDER) HORTON** (1920–2007). After his retirement from the CIA he published three spy novels, 1987–91, all set in Mexico City.

**E. HOWARD HUNT** (1918–2007). Government figure during the Nixon years who authored nearly fifty suspense and espionage novels, under his own name and as by "Gordon Davis," "Robert Dietrich," "P. S. Donoghue" and "David St. John."

**ELIZABETH JOLLEY** (1923–2007). British/Australian mainstream writer whose novels and short stories sometimes ventured into crime and murder.

**BOB JONES (ROBERT DOUGLAS JONES)** (1919–2007). Canadian/American author of two Sherlockian pastiches and a collection of Holmes golfing mysteries.

**(WARREN) KEELING JORDAN** (1931–2007). Author of *The Miramar Seduction* (1980).

**LELIA KELLY** (1958–2007). Author of three legal thrillers starting with *Assumption of Guilt* (1998).

**WALTER KEMPOWSKI** (1929–2007). German author of a single suspense novel, *Dog Days* (1991).

**MICHAEL KENYON** (1931–2005). British author of nearly twenty novels, notably *May You Die in Ireland* (1965) and *The Whole Hog* (1967). Two of his novels were published in America as by "Daniel Forbes."

**BENEDICT KIELY** (1919–2007). Irish author of two suspense novels beginning with the suspense fantasy *The Cards of the Gambler* (1953).

**RACHEL KIMOR-PAINE** (1951–2007). Israeli/Canadian author who published her first mystery novel, *Death Under Glass*, in 2006.

HANS KONING (1921–2007). Pen name of Hans Koningsberger, mainstream author who published five crime-suspense novels, 1974–88, starting with *Death of a Schoolboy*.

ROSEMARY KUTAK (1905–1999). Briefly popular author of two novels, *Darkness of Slumber* (1944) and *I Am the Cat* (1948).

HORACE P. LANDRY (1920–2007). Author of *Death Under Tall Pines* (1998).

STERLING LANIER (1927–2007). Author of two short story collections about the oddly-named Brigadier Ffellowes, 1972–86, mainly fantasy but some crime.

E(VELYN) L. LARKIN (1922–2007). Author of at least five romantic suspense novels set in Seattle.

JAMES LEASOR (1923–2007). British author of more than twenty intrigue novels, several about Dr. Jason Love starting with *Passport to Oblivion* (1964). He also published a collection of short stories, *A Week of Love* (1969) and six novels as by "Andrew MacAllan."

MADELEINE L'ENGLE (1918–2007). Well-known fantasy writer who published two suspense novels, *The Arm of the Starfish* (1965) and *A Severed Wasp* (1982).

MARION JAMES LEVIEN (1917–2007). She was a novelist and screenwriter who published one mystery, *Odds on Murder* (1974).

IRA LEVIN (1929–2007). Famed author of ten suspense novels and plays, notably his Edgar-winning first novel *A Kiss Before Dying* (1953), *Rosemary's Baby* (1967), *The Stepford Wives* (1972), and the hit Edgar-winning play *Deathtrap* (1979). He was awarded the MWA Grand Master in 2003.

ELY LIEBOW (1924–2007). Active in Bouchercon fan organizations and author of a biography of Dr. Joseph Bell, Doyle's inspiration for Sherlock Holmes.

ALEX MADSEN (1930–2007), Author of *Borderlines* (1975).

**NORMAN MAILER** (1923–2007). Famed mainstream writer whose many books include four crime-suspense novels: *An American Dream* (1965), *The Executioner's Song* (Pulitzer Prize, 1979), *Tough Guys Don't Dance* (1984), and *Harlot's Ghost* (1991).

**ROOSEVELT MALLORY** (1940–2007). Author of four mysteries, 1973–76, starting with *Harlem Hit*.

**DAVID X. MANNERS** (1912–2007), Author of two mystery novels, 1946–47, starting with *Memory of a Scream*.

**DAVID RALPH MARTIN** (1935–2007). TV scriptwriter who published two detective novels, starting with *I'm Coming to Get You* (1995).

**EDWIN (STEWART) McDOWELL** (1935–2007). Author of *The Lost World* (1988).

**JILL McGOWAN** (1947–2007). Scottish author of 13 police procedurals starting with *A Perfect Match* (1983), plus nonseries mysteries as by "Elizabeth Chaplin."

**TED MEYER (THEODORE E. MEYER)** (1931–2007). Author of *Body Count* (1982).

**PATRICIA (ALICE) MUSE** (1923–2007). Author of three romantic suspense novels, 1971–76.

**MAGDALEN NABB** (1947–2007). British author of some fifteen novels, many about Florentine sleuth Marshal Guarnaccia, starting with *Death of an Englishman* (1981).

**THOMAS HAL PHILLIPS** (1922–2007). Author of *The Loved and the Unloved* (1955).

**RICHARD S. PRATHER** (1921–2007). Author of some three dozen paperback novels and collections, mainly about private eye Shell Scott, starting with *Case of the Vanishing Beauty* (1950). Recipient of a Lifetime Achievement Award from Private Eye Writers of America, he also published two TV novelizations as "David Knight" and a nonseries novel *The Peddler* (1952) as "Douglas Ring." In 1960 he edited an MWA anthology, *The Comfortable Coffin*.

**BARRIE ROBERTS** (1939–2007). British author of at least eight mystery novels, five about Sherlock Holmes, and short stories in *The Strand*.

**MARIANNE RUTH** (1931–2007). Hollywood journalist and author who published six romantic suspense novels, 1973–77.

**FRANCIS RYCK** (1920–2007). Pseudonym of Yves Deville, French author of more than fifty suspense novels, six of which were translated and published in Britain. Only one, *The Stern Charter* (1976), appeared in America.

**FRED SABERHAGEN** (1930–2007). Well-known fantasy writer whose work included five mystery-fantasy novels, notably *The Holmes-Dracula File* (1978).

**PETER GRAHAM SCOTT** (1923–2007). British TV writer-producer who authored two thrillers, *Dragonfire* (1982) and *A Feast of Vultures* (1983).

**BARBARA SERANELLA** (1956–2007). Author of several mysteries about Munch Manchini, starting with *No Human Involved* (1997). Winner of the 2006 Anthony Award for best short story.

**MELVILLE SHAVELSON** (1917–2007). Author of *The Eleventh Commandment* (1977).

**DAVID SHAW** (ca. 1917–2007). Author of *The Levy Caper* (1974) and co-author of the mystery musical *Redhead* (1959). Brother of the novelist Irwin Shaw.

**SIDNEY SHELDON** (1917–2007). Screenwriter and author of at least ten best-selling suspense novels, notably *The Other Side of Midnight* (1974) and *Bloodline* (1978).

**STEVE J. SPEARS** (1951–2007). Australian author of three crime novels, starting with *Murder at the Fortnight* (2003).

**DANIEL STERN** (1928–2007). Mainstream novelist and short story writer who authored *The Suicide Academy* (1968).

**MADELINE B. STERN** (1912–2007). Bookseller and author who discovered and edited several volumes of thrillers published anonymously by Louisa May Alcott.

**FRED MUSTARD STEWART** (1932–2007). Best-selling author whose work included three suspense novels, notably *The Mephisto Waltz* (1969).

**FRANCINE MORRIS SWIFT** (1938–2007). Active Sherlockian who authored a brief Holmes adventure, *The Hound's Tale* (1992).

**GEORGE TABORI** (1914–2007). Hungarian-born playwright and screenwriter who authored three suspense novels, starting with *Beneath the Stone* (1945) and co-authored the screenplay for Hitchcock's *I Confess* (1953).

**REAY TANNAHILL** (1929–2007). British author of food histories and historical fiction, she published two nineteenth-century mysteries (1978–81) as "Annabel Laine," and two more historical suspense novels (1992–98) under her own name.

**JACK VALENTI** (1921–2007). Political and motion picture figure who published *Protect and Defend* in 1992, ghost-written by Max Allan Collins.

**PETER VIERTEL** (1920–2007). Novelist and screenwriter who authored two suspense films, *We Were Strangers* (1949) and *Decision Before Dawn* (1951).

**KURT VONNEGUT** (1922–2007). Famed mainstream novelist who published a single suspense novel, *Mother Night* (1962).

**PAUL WALKER** (1942–2007). Science fiction writer who authored an SF suspense novel, *Who Killed Utopia?* (1980), and a mystery, *Altar* (1983).

**LESLIE WALLER** (1923–2007). Novelist and screenwriter who published some eighteen crime and intrigue novels, fourteen under his own name, one as "C. S. Cody" and three as "Patrick Mann," notably *Dog Day Afternoon* (1973).

**KEITH W. WANDER** (1941–2007). Author of two suspense novels, *Last Resort* (1990) and *Brother for Life* (1991).

RONALD C. WEYMAN (1915–2007). Author of three Sherlockian novels, 1989–94, about Holmes in Canada.

JEROME BERNARD WHELAN (1911–2007). As "R. N. Brien" he authored a single novel, *The Missing Solicitor* (1952).

CHARLES WHITING (1926–2007). Author of more than twenty-five thrillers starting in 1974, some as by "John Kerrigan" and "Leo Kessler."

ROBERT ANTON WILSON (1932–2007). Co-author of *The Illummatus Trilogy* (1975), three SF novels with strong criminous elements.

R(ODNEY) D. WINGFIELD (1928?–2007). Author of five novels about Inspector Jack Frost, popularized on British TV, starting with *Frost at Christmas* (1984). A final novel is due in 2008.

NICHOLAS (WILLIAM) WOLLASTON (1926–2007). Author of *Eclipse* (1974).

ANNE WORBOYS (?–2007). British novelist whose work includes twelve romantic suspense novels under her own name and five as by "Vicky Maxwell," most unpublished in the United States.

—Edward D. Hoch

# MULHOLLAND DIVE
*By Michael Connelly*

Michael Connelly is the author of eighteen novels and one collection of nonfiction crime stories. Among his novels are *The Black Echo*, *The Last Coyote*, *The Poet*, *Blood Work*, and *The Lincoln Lawyer*. He is a past president of the Mystery Writers of America. He lives with his family in Florida.

**B**urning flares and flashing red and blue lights ripped the night apart. Clewiston counted four black-and-whites pulled halfway off the roadway and as close to the upper embankment as was possible. In front of them was a firetruck and in front of that was a forensics van. There was a P-one standing in the middle of Mulholland Drive ready to hold up traffic or wave it into the one lane that they had open. With a fatality involved, they should have closed down both lanes of the road, but that would have meant closing Mulholland from Laurel Canyon on one side all the way to Coldwater Canyon on the other. That was too long a stretch. There would be consequences for that. The huge inconvenience of it would have brought complaints from the rich hillside homeowners trying to get home after another night of the good life. And nobody stuck on midnight shift wanted more complaints to deal with.

Clewiston had worked Mulholland fatals several times. He was the expert. He was the one they called in from home. He knew that whether the identity of the victim in this case demanded it or not, he'd have gotten the call. It was Mulholland, and the Mulholland calls all went to him.

But this one was special anyway. The victim was a name and the case was going five-by-five. That meant everything about it had to be squared away and done right. He had been thoroughly briefed over the phone by the watch commander about that.

He pulled in behind the last patrol car, put his flashers on, and got out of his unmarked car. On the way back to the trunk, he grabbed his badge from beneath his shirt and hung it out front. He was in civies, having been called in from off-duty, and it was prudent to make sure he announced he was a detective.

He used his key to open the trunk and began to gather the equipment he would need. The P-one left his post in the road and walked over.

"Where's the sergeant?" Clewiston asked.

"Up there. I think they're about to pull the car up. That's a hundred thousand dollars he went over the side with. Who are you?"

"Detective Clewiston. The reconstructionist. Sergeant Fairbanks is expecting me."

"Go on down and you'll find him by the— Whoa, what is that?"

Clewiston saw him looking at the face peering up from the trunk. The crash test dummy was partially hidden by all the equipment cluttering the trunk, but the face was clear and staring blankly up at them. His legs had been detached and were resting beneath the torso. It was the only way to fit the whole thing in the trunk.

"We call him Arty," Clewiston said. "He was made by a company called Accident Reconstruction Technologies."

"Looks sort of real at first," the patrol officer said. "Why's he in fatigues?"

Clewiston had to think about that to remember.

"Last time I used Arty, it was a crosswalk hit-and-run case. The vic was a marine up from El Toro. He was in his fatigues and there was a question about whether the hitter saw him." Clewiston slung the strap of his laptop bag over his shoulder. "He did. Thanks to Arty we made a case."

He took his clipboard out of the trunk and then a digital camera, his trusty measuring wheel, and an eight-battery Maglite. He closed the trunk and made sure it was locked.

"I'm going to head down and get this over with," he said. "I got called in from home."

"Yeah, I guess the faster you're done, the faster I can get back out on the road myself. Pretty boring just standing here."

"I know what you mean."

Clewiston headed down the westbound lane, which had been closed to traffic. There was a mist clinging in the dark to the tall brush that crowded the sides of the street. But he could still see the lights and glow of the city down to the south. The accident had occurred in one of the few spots along Mulholland where there were no homes. He knew that on the south side of the road the embankment dropped down to a public dog park. On the north side was Fryman Canyon and the embankment rose up to a point where one of the city's communication stations was located. There was a tower up there on the point that helped bounce communication signals over the mountains that cut the city in half.

Mulholland was literally the backbone of Los Angeles. It rode like a snake along the crest of the Santa Monica Mountains from one end of the city to the other. Clewiston knew of places where you could stand on the white stripe and look north across the vast San Fernando Valley and then turn around and look south and see across the west side and as far as the Pacific and Catalina Island. It all depended on whether the smog was cooperating or not. And if you knew the right spots to stop and look.

Mulholland had that top-of-the-world feel to it. It could make you feel like the prince of a city where the laws of nature and physics didn't apply. The foot came down heavy on the accelerator. That was the contradiction. Mulholland was built for speed but it couldn't handle it. Speed was a killer.

As he came around the bend, Clewiston saw another firetruck and a tow truck from the Van Nuys police garage. The tow truck was positioned sideways across the road. Its cable was down the embankment and stretched taut as it pulled the car up. For the moment, Mulholland was completely closed. Clewiston could hear the tow motor straining and the cracking and scraping as the unseen car was being pulled up through the brush. The tow truck shuddered as it labored.

Clewiston saw the man with sergeant's stripes on his uniform and moved next to him as he watched.

"Is he still in it?" he asked Fairbanks.

"No, he was transported to St. Joe's. But he was DOA. You're Clewiston, right? The reconstructionist."

"Yes."

"We've got to handle this thing right. Once the ID gets out, we'll have the media all over this."

"The captain told me."

"Yeah, well, I'm telling you too. In this department, the captains don't get blamed when things go sideways and off the road. It's always the sergeants and it ain't going to be me this time."

"I get it."

"You have any idea what this guy was worth? We're talking tens of millions, and on top of that he's supposedly in the middle of a divorce. So we go five by five by five on this thing. *Comprende*, reconstructionist?"

"It's Clewiston and I said I get it."

"Good. This is what we've got. Single-car fatality. No witnesses. It appears the victim was heading eastbound when his vehicle, a two-month-old Porsche Carrera, came around that last curve there and for whatever reason didn't straighten out. We've got treads on the road you can take a look at. Anyway, he went straight off the side and then down, baby. Major head and torso injuries. Chest crushed. He pretty much drowned in his own blood before the FD could get down to him. They stretchered him out with a chopper and transported him anyway. Guess they didn't want any blow-back either."

"They take blood at St. Joe's?"

Fairbanks, about forty and a lifer on patrol, nodded. "I am told it was clean."

There was a pause in the conversation at that point, suggesting that Clewiston could take whatever he wanted from the blood test. He could believe what Fairbanks was telling him or he could believe that the celebrity fix was already in.

The moonlight reflected off the dented silver skin of the Porsche as it was pulled up over the edge like a giant beautiful fish hauled into a boat. Clewiston walked over and Fairbanks followed. The first thing Clewiston saw was that it was a Carrera 4S. "Hmmmm," he mumbled.

"What?" Fairbanks said.

"It's one of the Porsches with four-wheel drive. Built for these sort of curves. Built for control."

"Well, not built good enough, obviously."

Clewiston put his equipment down on the hood of one of the patrol cars and took his Maglite over to the Porsche. He swept the beam over the front of the high-performance sports car. The car was heavily damaged in the crash and the front had taken the brunt of it. The molded body was badly distorted by repeated impacts as it had sledded down the steep embankment. He moved in close and squatted by the front cowling and the shattered passenger-side head-light assembly.

He could feel Fairbanks behind him, watching over his shoulder as he worked.

"If there were no witnesses, how did anybody know he'd gone over the side?" Clewiston asked.

"Somebody down below," Fairbanks answered. "There are houses down there. Lucky this guy didn't end up in somebody's living room. I've seen that before."

So had Clewiston. He stood up and walked to the edge and looked down. His light cut into the darkness of the brush. He saw the exposed pulp of the acacia trees and other foliage the car had torn through.

He returned to the car. The driver's door was sprung and Clewiston could see the pry marks left by the jaws used to extricate the driver. He pulled it open and leaned in with his light. There was a lot of blood on the wheel, dashboard, and center console. The driver's seat was wet with blood and urine.

The key was still in the ignition and turned to the on position. The dashboard lights were still on as well. Clewiston leaned further in and checked the mileage. The car had only 1,142 miles on the odometer.

Satisfied with his initial survey of the wreck, he went back to his equipment. He put the clipboard under his arm and picked up the measuring wheel. Fairbanks came over once again. "Anything?" he asked.

"Not yet, sergeant. I'm just starting."

He started sweeping the light over the roadway. He picked up the skid marks and used the wheel to measure the distance of each one. There were four distinct marks, left as all four tires of the Porsche tried unsuccessfully to grip the asphalt. When he worked his way back to the starting point, he found scuff marks in a classic slalom pattern. They had been left on the asphalt when the car had turned sharply one way and then the other before going into the braking skid.

He wrote the measurements down on the clipboard. He then pointed the light into the brush on either side of the roadway where the scuff marks began. He knew the event had begun here and he was looking for indications of cause. He noticed a small opening in the brush, a narrow pathway that continued on the other side of the road. It was a crossing. He stepped over and put the beam down on the brush and soil. After a few moments, he moved across the street and studied the path on the other side.

Satisfied with his site survey, he went back to the patrol car and opened his laptop. While it was booting up, Fairbanks came over once again.

"So, how'z it look?"

"I have to run the numbers."

"Those skids look pretty long to me. The guy must've been flying."

"You'd be surprised. Other things factor in. Brake efficiency, surface, and surface conditions—you see the mist moving in right now? Was it like this two hours ago when the guy went over the side?"

"Been like this since I got here. But the fire guys were here first. I'll get one up here."

Clewiston nodded. Fairbanks pulled his rover and told someone to send the first responders up to the crash site. He then looked back at Clewiston.

"On the way."

"Thanks. Does anybody know what this guy was doing up here?"

"Driving home, we assume. His house was in Coldwater and he was going home."

"From where?"

"That we don't know."

"Anybody make notification yet?"

"Not yet. We figure next of kin is the wife he's divorcing. But we're not sure where to find her. I sent a car to his house but there's no answer. We've got somebody at Parker Center trying to run her down—probably through her lawyer. There's also grown children from his first marriage. They're working on that too."

Two firefighters walked up and introduced themselves as Robards and Lopez. Clewiston questioned them on the weather and road conditions at the time they responded to the accident call. Both firefighters described the mist as heavy at the time. They were sure about this because the mist had hindered their ability to find the place where the vehicle had crashed through the brush and down the embankment.

"If we hadn't seen the skid marks, we would have driven right by," Lopez said.

Clewiston thanked them and turned back to his computer. He had everything he needed now. He opened the Accident Reconstruction Technologies program and went directly to the speed and distance calculator. He referred to his clipboard for the numbers he would need. He felt Fairbanks come up next to him.

"Computer, huh? That gives you all the answers?"

"Some of them."

"Whatever happened to experience and trusting hunches and gut instincts?"

It wasn't a question that was waiting for an answer. Clewiston added the lengths of the four skid marks he had measured and then divided by four, coming up with an average length of sixty-four feet. He entered the number into the calculator template.

"You said the vehicle is only two months old?" he asked Fairbanks.

"According to the registration. It's a lease he picked up in January. I guess he filed for divorce and went out and got the sports car to help him get back in the game."

Clewiston ignored the comment and typed *1.0* into a box marked *B.E.* on the template.

"What's that?" Fairbanks asked.

"Braking efficiency. One-oh is the highest efficiency. Things could change if somebody wants to take the brakes off the car and test them. But for now I am going with high efficiency because the vehicle is new and there's only twelve hundred miles on it."

"Sounds right to me."

Lastly, Clewiston typed *9.0* into the box marked *C.F.* This was the subjective part. He explained what he was doing to Fairbanks before the sergeant had to ask.

"This is coefficient of friction," he said. "It basically means surface conditions. Mulholland Drive is asphalt base, which is generally a high coefficient. And this stretch here was repaved about nine months ago—again, that leads to a high coefficient. But I'm knocking it down a point because of the moisture. That mist comes in and puts down a layer of moisture that mixes with the road oil and makes the asphalt slippery. The oil is heavier in new asphalt."

"I get it."

"Good. It's called trusting your gut instinct, sergeant."

Fairbanks nodded. He had been properly rebuked.

Clewiston clicked the enter button and the calculator came up with a projected speed based on the relationship between skid length, brake efficiency, and the surface conditions. It said the Porsche had been traveling at 41.569 miles per hour when it went into the skid.

"You're kidding me," Fairbanks said while looking at the screen. "The guy was barely speeding. How can that be?"

"Follow me, sergeant," Clewiston said.

Clewiston left the computer and the rest of his equipment, except for the flashlight. He led Fairbanks back to the point in the road where he had found the slalom scuffs and the originating point of the skid marks.

"Okay," he said. "The event started here. We have a single-car accident. No alcohol known to be involved. No real speed involved. A car built for this sort of road is involved. What went wrong?"

"Exactly."

Clewiston put the light down on the scuff marks.

"Okay, you've got alternating scuff marks here before he goes into the skid."

"Okay."

"You have the tire cords indicating he jerked the wheel right initially and then jerked it left trying to straighten it out. We call it a SAM—a slalom avoidance maneuver."

"A SAM. Okay."

"He turned to avoid an impact of some kind, then overcorrected. He then panicked and did what most people do. He hit the brakes."

"Got it."

"The wheels locked up and he went into a skid. There was nothing he could do at that point. He had no control because the instinct is to press harder on the brakes, to push that pedal through the floor."

"And the brakes were what were taking away control."

"Exactly. He went over the side. The question is why. Why did he jerk the wheel in the first place? What preceded the event?"

"Another car?"

Clewiston nodded. "Could be. But no one stopped. No one called it in."

"Maybe . . ." Fairbanks spread his hands. He was drawing a blank.

"Take a look here," Clewiston said.

He walked Fairbanks over to the side of the road. He put the light on the pathway into the brush, drawing the sergeant's eyes back across Mulholland to the pathway on the opposite side. Fairbanks looked at him and then back at the path.

"What are you thinking?" Fairbanks asked.

"This is a coyote path," Clewiston said. "They come up through Fryman Canyon and cross Mulholland here. It takes them to the dog park. They probably wait in heavy brush for the dogs that stray out of the park."

"So your thinking is that our guy came around the curve and there was a coyote crossing the road."

Clewiston nodded. "That's what I'm thinking. He jerks the wheel to avoid the animal, then overcompensates, loses control. You have a slalom followed by a braking skid. He goes over the side."

"An accident, plain and simple." Fairbanks shook his head disappointedly. "Why couldn't it have been a DUI, something clear-cut like that?" he asked. "Nobody's going to believe us on this one."

"That's not our problem. All the facts point to it being a driving mishap. An accident."

Fairbanks looked at the skid marks and nodded. "Then that's it, I guess."

"You'll get a second opinion from the insurance company anyway," Clewiston said. "They'll probably pull the brakes off the car and test them. An accident means double indemnity. But if they can shift the calculations and prove he was speeding or being reckless, it softens the impact. The payout becomes negotiable. But my guess is they'll see it the same way we do."

"I'll make sure forensics photographs everything. We'll document everything six ways from Sunday and the insurance people can take their best shot. When will I get a report from you?"

"I'll go down to Valley Traffic right now and write something up."

"Good. Get it to me. What else?"

Clewiston looked around to see if he was forgetting anything. He shook his head. "That's it. I need to take a few more measurements and some photos, then I'll head down to write it up. Then I'll get out of your way."

Clewiston left him and headed back up the road to get his camera. He had a small smile on his face that nobody noticed.


Clewiston headed west on Mulholland from the crash site. He planned to take Coldwater Canyon down into the Valley and over to the Traffic Division office. He waited until the flashing blue and red lights were small in his rearview mirror before flipping open his phone. He hoped he could get a signal on the cheap throwaway. Mulholland Drive wasn't always cooperative with cellular service.

He had a signal. He pulled to the side while he attached the digital recorder, then turned it on and made the call. She answered after one ring, as he was pulling back onto the road and up to speed.

"Where are you?" he asked.

"The apartment."

"They're looking for you. You're sure his attorney knows where you are?"

"He knows. Why? What's going on?"

"They want to tell you he's dead."

He heard her voice catch. He took the phone away from his ear so he could hold the wheel with two hands on one of the deep curves. He then brought it back.

"You there?" he asked.

"Yes, I'm here. I just can't believe it, that's all. I'm speechless. I didn't think it would really happen."

*You may be speechless, but you're talking*, Clewiston thought. *Keep it up.*

"You wanted it to happen, so it happened," he said. "I told you I would take care of it."

"What happened?"

"He went off the road on Mulholland. It's an accident and you're a rich lady now."

She said nothing.

"What else do you want to know?" he asked.

"I'm not sure. Maybe I shouldn't know anything. It will be better when they come here."

"You're an actress. You can handle it."

"Okay."

He waited for her to say more, glancing down at the recorder on the center console to see the red light still glowing. He was good.

"Was he in pain?" she asked.

"Hard to say. He was probably dead when they pried him out. From what I hear, it will be a closed casket. Why do you care?"

"I guess I don't. It's just sort of surreal that this is happening. Sometimes I wish you never came to me with the whole idea."

"You rather go back to being trailer park trash while he lives up on the hill?"

"No, it wouldn't be like that. My attorney says the pre-nup has holes in it."

Clewiston shook his head. Second guessers. They hire his services and then can't live with the consequences.

"What's done is done," he said. "This will be the last time we talk. When you get the chance, throw the phone you're talking on away like I told you."

"There won't be any records?"

"It's a throwaway. Like all the drug dealers use. Open it up, smash the chip, and throw it all away next time you go to McDonald's."

"I don't go to McDonald's."

"Then throw it away at The Ivy. I don't give a shit. Just not at your house. Let things run their course. Soon you'll have all his money. And you double dip on the insurance because of the accident. You can thank me for that."

He was coming up to the hairpin turn that offered the best view of the Valley.

"How do we know that they think it was an accident?"

"Because I made them think that. I told you, I have Mulholland wired. That's what you paid for. Nobody is going to second guess a goddamn thing. His insurance company will come in and sniff around, but they won't be able to change things. Just sit tight and stay cool. Say nothing. Offer nothing. Just like I told you."

The lights of the Valley spread out in front of him before the turn. He saw a car pulled over at the unofficial overlook. On any other night he'd stop and roust them—probably teenagers getting it on in the backseat. But not tonight. He had to get down to the traffic office and write up his report.

"This is the last time we talk," he said to her.

He looked down at the recorder. He knew it would be the last time they talked—until he needed more money from her.

"How did you get him to go off the road?" she asked.

He smiled. They always ask that. "My friend Arty did it."

"You brought a third party into this. Don't you see that—"

"Relax. Arty doesn't talk."

He started into the turn. He realized the phone had gone dead.

"Hello?" he said. "Hello?"

He looked at the screen. No signal. These cheap throwaways were about as reliable as the weather.

He felt his tires catch the edge of the roadway and looked up in time to pull the car back onto the road. As he came out of the turn, he checked the phone's screen one more time for the signal. He needed to call her back, let her know how it was going to be.

There was still no signal.

"Goddamnit!"

He slapped the phone closed on his thigh, then peered back at the road and froze as his eyes caught and held on two glowing eyes in the headlights. In a moment he broke free and jerked the wheel right to avoid the coyote. He corrected, but the wheels caught on the deep edge of the asphalt. He jerked harder and the front wheel broke free and back up on the road. But the back wheel slipped out and the car went into a slide.

Clewiston had an almost clinical knowledge of what was happening. It was as if he was watching one of the accident recreations he had prepared a hundred times for court hearings and prosecutions.

The car went into a sideways slide toward the precipice. He knew he would hit the wooden fence—chosen by the city for aesthetic reasons over function and safety—and that he would crash through. He knew at that moment that he was probably a dead man.

The car turned 180 degrees before blowing backwards through the safety fence. It then went airborne and arced down, trunk first. Clewiston gripped the steering wheel as if it was still the instrument of his control and destiny. But he knew there was nothing that could help him now. There was no control.

Looking through the windshield, he saw the beams of his headlights pointing into the night sky. Out loud, he said, "I'm dead."

The car plunged through a stand of trees, branches shearing off with a noise as loud as firecrackers. Clewiston closed his eyes for the final impact. There was a sharp roaring sound and a jarring crash. The airbag exploded from the steering wheel and snapped his neck back against his seat.

Clewiston opened his eyes and felt liquid surrounding him and rising up his chest. He thought he had momentarily blacked out or was hallucinating. But then the water reached his neck and it was cold and real. He could see only darkness. He was in black water and it was filling the car.

He reached down to the door and pulled on a handle but he couldn't get the door to open. He guessed the power locks had shorted out. He tried to bring his legs up so he could kick out one of the shattered windows but his seat belt held him in place. The water was up to his chin now and rising. He quickly unsnapped his belt and tried to move again but realized it hadn't been the impediment. His legs—both of them—were somehow pinned beneath the steering column, which had dropped down during the impact. He tried to raise it but couldn't get it to move an inch. He tried to squeeze out from beneath the weight but he was thoroughly pinned.

The water was over his mouth now. By leaning his head back and raising his chin up, he gained an inch, but that was rapidly erased by the rising tide. In less than thirty seconds the water was over him and he was holding his last breath.

He thought about the coyote that had sent him over the side. It didn't seem possible that what had happened had happened. A reverse cascade of bubbles leaked from his mouth and traveled upward as he cursed.

Suddenly everything was illuminated. A bright light glowed in front of him. He leaned forward and looked out through the windshield. He saw a robed figure above the light, arms at his side.

Clewiston knew that it was over. His lungs burned for release. It was his time. He let out all of his breath and took the water in. He journeyed toward the light.

James Crossley finished tying his robe and looked down into his backyard pool. It was as if the car had literally dropped from the heavens. The brick wall surrounding the pool was undisturbed. The car had to have come in over it and then landed perfectly in the middle of the pool. About a third of the water had slopped over the side with the impact. But the car was fully submerged except for the edge of the trunk lid, which had come open during the landing. Floating on the surface was a lifelike mannequin dressed in old jeans and a green military jacket. The scene was bizarre.

Crossley looked up toward the crestline to where he knew Mulholland Drive edged the hillside. He wondered if someone had pushed the car off the road, if this was some sort of prank.

He then looked back down into the pool. The surface was calming and he could see the car more clearly in the beam of the pool's light. And it was then that he thought he saw someone sitting unmoving behind the steering wheel.

Crossley ripped his robe off and dove naked into the pool.

# EVERYBODY LOVES SOMEBODY

*By Sandra Scoppettone*

Sandra Scoppettone has written numerous novels, including three under the pseudonym Jack Early. Under her own name she produced the five-book series of mystery novels featuring New York private eye Lauren Laurano. Most recently she created two books about Faye Quick, a private eye in 1940s New York City. This is her third published story. Visit her Web site at www.sandrascoppettone.com.

A ll my life I ran away from everything. When I was fifteen I made tracks outta Clinton, PA to the Big Apple fast as I could. I left my Mama, Daddy, brother Tom and my little sister, Beth Ann. I wrote a note tellin them not to look for me, I'd be okay. It wasn't that stuff was bad in my house, no drunks or my Daddy comin into my room late at night, or Tom haulin off on me. It was cause it was boring in Clinton and I didn't like boring.

I also left a guy. Wayne Preston. He was cool. But not cool enough. Good lookin. People was always sayin, "Look at the two of them, him with the blonde hair like Brad Pitt and her with that red hair like the gal on CSI" and "Wayne and Deb make such a cute couple." Guess we did. But I knew if I stayed Wayne and me would get married when he was eighteen and I was sixteen and I'd have a kid right away. We'd live in some fallin down house and Wayne would get a crummy job and then any fun we'd been havin would all go away. I'd seen it happen to more than one.

I left a note for Wayne, too, tellin him not to look for me. I told him Fran Karanewski had a big crush on him and he should take her out. They'd be good together. I figured it'd take Wayne about a week before he gave her a call.

When I got off the bus in the New York City terminal, I blew off the pimps who tried recruiting me and made my way to a subway. I had everything planned out so I knew where I could find a cheap room.

I found one all right. It was a dark place. The paint was comin off the walls and it smelled like old people. I hated it. But I couldn't afford nothin else.

I got a job same day in a coffee shop waitin on tables. That was the only job I knew how to do. The place was in the West Forties. It was your usual, with menus offering the world. The food stunk. A guy named Nick ran the joint. He didn't ask me to show any proof when I said I was eighteen. I looked it, but I think he knew and didn't give a rat's ass. The ass he cared about was mine.

The short-order cook, Buzz, found a way to rub up against my tits almost every time I passed him. I had the graveyard shift and was the only soup jockey there. So when there weren't any customers Buzz and Nick made my life hell.

It didn't take me too long to run away from that job. But every gig I got it was the same story so I ran away from one job after another. Until I met Edward.

"You live alone, Deborah?"

He wouldn't call me Deb.

"Yeah, I do."

"You like that?"

"It's okay."

"You like the place where you live?"

By then I'd moved to another room but it was just as gloomy as the first.

"Not a whole lot," I said.

"I think you should go out with me. I like your green eyes." He blew a perfect smoke ring.

I turned him down a lotta times until I got tired of the routine and I said I'd go. We went to a real fancy restaurant and he ate snails. It made me sick to watch him. He ordered for me and when the steak came it was runnin blood and looked like it was just cut from the cow. I could hardly get it down. Edward knew and I think he thought it was funny.

Afterwards, we went back to his place which was like somethin outta a magazine. I can't say I didn't know what was gonna happen cause I did. Me and Wayne been doin it for a couple a years so I wasn't no innocent.

What I didn't know was Edward had plans for me.

He moved me into his place three days after that first time and treated me like a queen. Four weeks after that he started bringing home the men. I couldn't say no. I liked livin there and I liked not havin to sling hash for a livin.

"You do whatever they ask," he said.

"Okay."

"You understand this, Deborah?"

" 'Course I understand. You think I'm a moron?" I lit a Marlboro Light.

"I think you're a beautiful girl and we can make a lot of money."

I laughed to myself. I knew I'd never see a penny and I didn't.

I had my own room with a 32-inch Plasma TV and could order anything I wanted to eat, and Edward bought my clothes, but as for cash, nada.

After six months I took the cash I found underneath Edwards briefs in the top drawer of his dresser, some from his coat pocket and ran away. The money came to seven hundred and two dollars.

Funny thing about New York was it wasn't that easy to hide. I knew Edward would be lookin for me so I got on a bus and went to New Jersey. Waitress jobs were easy to get in Kearny. So were rooms.

My life went on like that, me runnin away from men and jobs and rooms and states even. By the time I was twenty I was livin in New London, Connecticut. That's where I met Julius all dolled up in his sailor suit. He was fine lookin, like a movie star.

"I got this garage, hon. An auto place. Me and my dad. We make good money there. And you wouldn't have to work no more."

"You'd take care of me?"

"You bet. I wouldn't want my wife to work."

"Wife?"

"Yeah, what did ya think?"

"I dunno. You proposin, Jule?"

"You want I should get down on one knee or somethin?"

"I just didn't know."

"Okay. How about you and me send our laundry out in one bag?"

Soon as he was outta the Navy we got married at City Hall and that afternoon we got a bus to Gary, Indiana, where he was from. I woulda gone anywhere with Julius.

His folks were okay. They drank a little more than I liked. And Jules, who'd hardly drank before, was knockin them back, too. I tried to keep up but I'd just get sick. We lived in an apartment over his folks garage. Cindy, his mother, said I could decorate any way I wanted so that kept me busy for the first month. After that I didn't know what the hell to do with myself.

Then came the beatings. Jules would get drunk after work and come home late. That's when he found everything wrong with me and the place I thought I'd made so nice. He didn't like the slipcover on the couch, the curtains, the placemats, you name it. Especially, he didn't like me. He hated my freckles, my nose was too big, and my tits were too small.

He called me a bitch, a whore, a slut, a cunt, a liar and a thief. Always a thief. I never did find out what I was supposed to have boosted 'cause I didn't stay around after the twelfth time. I didn't know why I'd stayed that long, but I vowed I'd never do it again. So I ran away and I ended up in Detroit, Michigan.

It took me a bunch of rides and a bus to get there. Not sure I woulda stayed if I'd known I'd be cold all the time. Except summer. I was only good at one thing so I got a job at a luncheonette run by a dude named Randolph who everybody called Randy. And he was. Didn't take me long to find that out.

He wasn't a looker like Jules, but I told myself maybe the lookers were the worst ones. Randy kept his grayin hair in a pony tail and always wore a leather vest with silver studs over a black t-shirt, jeans and black boots he never cleaned. He kept a Harley out back and he spent most of his time workin on that hunk a metal. Least when he was romancin that thing he was leavin me alone. But when he wasn't foolin with the bike he was tryin to fool with me. And when he wasn't doin that he was dealin coke.

Finally it came down to the job or Randy. I figured I could get another job somewhere, but I knew there'd be another Randy. There'd always be another Randy. Besides, if it got too bad I could take off.

He had an apartment over the luncheonette and I moved in with him from a dingy room I had ten minutes away.

I figured this was what my life was gonna be. One waitress job, one lousy room, one dickhead after another.

His place was a mess so I cleaned it up, made it nice. After two days I saw the safe. It was in the wall of the bedroom closet behind his clothes.

That night I was lyin on the bed paintin my finger and toenails silver. Anything in the red line clashed with my hair. "Burglars come in here, Randy, that safe isn't gonna be hard to find."

"What fuckin safe?"

"The one in the closet. You got more than one?"

"You spyin on me?" Randy drank from his bottle of Bud.

"I was cleanin the closet." He hadn't said word one about how nice everything looked. "Anyways, it wouldn't be hard to find in there."

"Yeah, but burglars would have to know the combination."

"I thought safe crackers didn't need combinations. Don't they just listen to the clicks?" I lit a cig.

"You watch too much TV."

"But it's true. Safe crackers can get into any safe."

"Shut your trap."

I didn't let on I knew about his dealin and I figured he had a lot of cash in that safe.

"Whatcha got in there, Randy?"

"Wouldn't you love to know?"

"Yeah, that's why I'm askin." I blew some smoke outta my nostrils like the movie stars in them old black-and-white flicks.

He walked right up to the end of the bed where I was lyin. His face was red like a cherry. And if I hadn't known better I would've sworn steam was comin out of his ears like in a cartoon.

He pointed a finger at me and twirled it like it was on a ball bearing. "You listen to me, bitch. I don't wantcha askin about that safe or goin near it. You understand?"

"Sure. I was just kiddin around. No need to get so crazy about it."

Then he yelled. "I'm not gettin crazy. Don't ever say that again."

"Okay, okay. Everything's cool."

"It better be."

My life with Randy was mostly boring. On my days off I went to the movies. And when it wasn't busy in the luncheonette I read my mystery novels.

"Whaddaya read that junk for?" Randy asked, scratchin his balls.

"It's not junk. They're good stories."

"Lemme see."

I handed it over.

"*Elmore* Leonard?"

"What about him?"

"Sounds like a fag. Least you could do is read some of them guys like Spillane, or that other one."

"What other one?"

"You know."

"I don't."

"You know. What's his name?"

"Randy, I don't know who you're talkin about."

"McBain. Yeah. Ed McBain."

"I like what I'm readin."

"Faggot." He handed the book back. "Waste of time readin. Let's go for a ride."

I hated ridin on the back of that Harley. Scared me. But I knew if I said no he'd make my life miserable. Randy never hit me (I wouldn't put up with that again), but he'd sulk. Sulkin was the worst. I hated sulkers. Randy made the whole apartment black and soon I was depressed and ready to jump off a bridge.

So I put my blue and gold helmet on and hopped on the back of the goddamn Harley. I remember this day cause when we got back Bobby Mazard was waitin on Randy for the short-order cook job he'd advertised. Bobby was real good-lookin. Black eyes that matched black hair. A smile that brought out dimples and a nice full mouth. The body wasn't bad either.

Randy gave Mazard a hard time so I went upstairs. When I came back down I saw that Bobby had the job.

Bobby and me got to be friends right away. I never liked anybody so much so quick. Then one night when Randy was out dealin, and we were closin up, Bobby kissed me.

I was shocked. For two reasons: that Bobby would do that, kiss me just like that, and because I'd never felt that way before when I was kissed. I remember thinkin 'so this is what it's supposed to be like.'

I looked back at all the guys who'd kissed me and there wasn't a one made me feel like that. I knew I was in trouble. Big trouble. We started makin out and before I knew it we were on the floor of the kitchen and our clothes were flung every which way. And when I came it was like an explosion, like nothin I could've ever imagined.

We knew we had to be careful so we got dressed right away. Bobby kissed me goodbye and said real sweet, "Tomorrow, Princess."

That night when Randy came home I was wide awake in our bed, but I pretended to be asleep cause the thought of him puttin a finger on me made me want to throw up.

The next mornin I couldn't wait for Bobby to come to work.

Randy said, "Why're you actin so fidgety?"

"I don't know whatcha mean. You give Bobby a key?"

"No. Ya think I'm crazy givin out a key after one day's work?"

"I'm goin down to open up." I went downstairs and saw that Bobby was waitin outside the door. I unlocked. Those black eyes made me melt. We pretended like nothin happened and I got the coffee goin while Bobby got the grill ready.

Weeks went by and whenever me and Bobby could be together we was. Sex got better and better. I couldn't believe what I'd been missin all those years.

I don't know why but one day I said to Bobby, "Randy's got a safe in the bedroom closet."

"What's in it?"

"He's a dealer."

"Yeah, I know. Weed?"

"Coke."

"You ever try it?" Bobby asked.

"No. You?" '

"Tried it once. Made me sick. I'm not into it. I smoke a little weed now and then."

"Yeah, sure. Who doesn't?" Truth was *I* didn't. I didn't like it.

"So you think Randy's got product in that safe?"

"Maybe. But mostly money from dealin."

"How much?"

"Don't know, but I think it's a lot."

"Like what?"

I shrugged.

"Over ten thou?"

"Gotta be," I said.

"Sweet. How can we find out?"

I stroked Bobby's cheek. "Gotta get the combination."

"How?"

"That's the problem. Randy won't tell me. He won't even talk about the safe with me. Once when I asked him what was in there he went nuts."

"So there's gotta be mucho money in it."

"Yeah."

We talked about a lot of ways to get that safe open, but nothin we came up with was really gonna do it. Bobby said once we got the money we'd split this town and go somewhere warm. Like Mexico. Sounded good to me.

The more days went by the more impatient we got and the more Bobby hated me sleepin in a bed with Randy. I couldn't stand it when he tried to touch me. I kept makin excuses but I didn't know how long that would work. Least Randy wasn't the warm and fuzzy type, always huggin and kissin. But Bobby was, whenever there was a chance.

It was Thursday nights Randy opened that damn safe and put whatever he had inside. Bobby said that was when Randy made his deliveries and pickups. We figured we'd have to knock Randy out once he'd opened the safe. It was the only way.

Bobby was no safe cracker and me neither. And whatever the

combination was it was in Randy's head and no place else, 'cause I knew that's how he was.

"You won't hurt him too bad, will you, Bobby?"

"Just a knock on the head that'll keep him out long enough for us to get the cash and beat it outta here."

We were gonna jump in the car, cross the border to Canada, drive across it and down to the West Coast where we'd buy a new car, then go all the way to Mexico. The good thing was Randy couldn't report anything to the cops.

When Thursday night came and we closed up, Bobby and me went upstairs. We made love and it was as good as ever. I especially liked doing it on Randy's bed. I had my suitcase packed and in Bobby's car.

About half an hour before Randy usually came home we took our places. I was in bed reading my mystery book and Bobby was hidin with a hammer at the far end of the closet behind my clothes I wasn't takin. The safe was in the middle.

It was nerve wrackin waitin for Randy and I kept readin the same sentence over and over. Then I heard his bike, him parkin it, his feet crunchin the gravel. The luncheonette door opened and the little bell rang. I hated that fuckin bell.

I heard him walk to the apartment door then come up the steps. He crossed the livin room to the bedroom where I was waitin for him.

"Hey, Randy."

He grunted.

He was carryin his beat up briefcase, faded brown with a metal lock that didn't work. He went to the closet right away, opened the door, put the briefcase on the floor. His back blocked me from seein him turn the combination. That was the way he always did it.

I saw the safe door open and coughed twice. Bobby's cue. Randy looked to the side, surprised. Bobby hit him on the head with the hammer and Randy went down.

I jumped out of bed. Bobby kept hittin Randy. That wasn't in the plan.

"Hey," I said.

Blood was flyin all over the place, gettin on Bobby's shirt and face. And the back of Randy's head was so red with blood it didn't even look like a head.

"That's enough, Bobby. You'll kill him."

Bobby paid no attention to me and kept on hittin Randy.

Finally I screamed, "Stop it, stop, stop."

Bobby heard me then and stepped back from Randy's ruined head and limp body. I didn't want to get any closer to Randy, but I had to know.

Bobby was breathin like a horse. It was hard to look at the mess that was Randy's head so I kept my eyes on his arm and wrist. I leaned down and felt for a pulse even though I knew.

"You killed him, Bobby."

"It's better this way."

"Why? He couldn't of turned us in."

"Yeah, I know. But he could've tried to find us, sent somebody after us. We'd, never be sure, lookin over our shoulders all the time."

"But now the cops will get in on this."

"They'll think it was a drug hit."

"Even if we're gone?"

"Don't worry about it."

I let it go.

"Look in the safe," I said.

"Jesus, Deb there's a lot in here."

"I told you," I said, as if that made all the difference. As if Bobby hadn't just done a murder.

We took the money from the safe and the briefcase, careful not to leave prints on those things. Our prints would be all over the place but that didn't matter.

I got Randy's old suitcase out of the closet and we both dumped the money inside. Then Bobby took a shower, changed clothes and I got dressed.

We turned off the lights and went downstairs. The creaking of the linoleum floor spooked me. When we got to the door Bobby turned and said, "Don't worry about nothin. I'll take care of you now." And then she kissed me.

Outside, we went around the corner where Bobby had parked her car. She opened the door for me like she always did and said, "We're on our way, babe."

And in another minute we were.

# MAKING AMENDS
*By Jeffery Deaver*

The author of twenty-two novels and two collections of short stories, Jeffery Deaver has been nominated for six Edgar Awards from the Mystery Writers of America, an Anthony award, a Gumshoe Award, and is a three-time recipient of the Ellery Queen Reader's Award for Best Short Story of the Year. In 2001, he won the W. H. Smith Thumping Good Read Award for his Lincoln Rhyme novel *The Empty Chair*. In 2004, he was awarded the Crime Writers' Association of Great Britain's Ian Fleming Steel Dagger Award for *Garden of Beasts* and the Short Story Dagger for "The Weekender." Translated into twenty-five languages, his novels have appeared on a number of best-seller lists around the world, including the *New York Times*, *The Times* of London, and the *Los Angeles Times*. *The Bone Collector* was a feature release from Universal Pictures, starring Denzel Washington as Lincoln Rhyme. *A Maiden's Grave* was made into an HBO film retitled *Dead Silence*, starring James Garner and Marlee Matlin.

J amie Feldon woke up one cool Monday morning in April and I decided to change his life.

The night before, he'd fallen asleep on the couch, thinking about a sitcom he'd just watched. It was great, really kick-ass. Most TV comedies were just plain stupid: twenty-five-year-olds tossing out one-liners, then mugging for the camera while the Laugh sign goosed the audience to make noise.

No, this show was different. The hero was a guy who'd had an Oh-Jesus moment or something and was making amends for everything bad that he'd done in his life. Each episode, he'd track down some-body he'd screwed over or hurt and apologize and make it up to them.

Pretty damn sharp.

Jamie'd lain on the couch, mesmerized by the show, laughing and once or twice even crying, which was something he never did.

You can believe it, real tears.

He'd thought about that show for hours until, still dressed, he'd fallen asleep.

Now, at seven-thirty A.M., the forty-two-year-old rolled over and rubbed his face, feeling the creases left by the corduroy slipcover. He squinted hard and studied what sat beside him on the coffee table: half a bottle of Wild Turkey bourbon, an overflowing ashtray, and a bag of popcorn with a bunch of unpopped old maids inside; the microwave was on its way out.

Swinging his feet to the floor, Jamie pulled the remote control out from under him, the smell of sweat and unwashed clothes wafting around him. He wrinkled his nose, then wiped it on the sleeve of his pale-blue dress shirt. The TV set was still on but quiet; he'd hit the mute button in his sleep. On the screen, an early morning talk-show host was silently moving his lips. He seemed real sincere. A picture flashed on—two Asian kids holding bowls of rice. They were happy. Back to the host. He now looked happy too.

Jamie shut the set off. It crackled as the screen went black.

He stretched and felt his belly pressing his waistband. He figured the Big-Macs-for-lunch, pizza-for-dinner diet he'd been on lately was finally catching up. His head throbbed with the drumbeat of a marching band.

He happened to glance at the mail, dumped on the floor the other day. He hadn't looked at it then. He now saw that the letter on top was from the family court. What now? he wondered sourly. He'd had a problem—wasn't his fault—and had missed picking up his son last month. The ex'd made a big stink about it. Maybe she was trying to modify visitation. What a bitch. Or maybe it was something else. Was he late with the maintenance or the child-support check? He couldn't remember. He didn't know what the hell she had to complain about, though, even if he was a little late. Christ, she got fifty-six percent of his salary. (Though that wasn't exactly a gold mine; as a claims agent for a small insurance agency, Jamie made squat.)

He eased forward and cradled his aching head, crowned with an unruly fringe of thinning red hair, lost in his depression, the relentless troubles. The words that popped into his mind were "the bottom."

*That's where I am. I've hit bottom. . . .*

And just like the night before, watching that TV sitcom, tears welled in his eyes.

Sitting here, in his shabby two-bedroom apartment, the graying walls decorated with stains and scuff marks, some of them dating back to when he moved in four years ago, Jamie couldn't get that show out of his thoughts: the guy making amends for all the bad things in his past.

Then he began considering the offenses in his own life: fellow workers, his brother, ex-bosses, girlfriends, students at his community college, his ex-wife, his mother, even kids in his grade school.

Pettiness, cheating, insults, and—just like the hero of the TV show—even a few crimes.

His initial reaction was to offer excuses.

*It wasn't so bad, it was an accident, everybody acts that way, everybody cheats from time to time. . . .*

But then he stopped cold.

Furious with himself. Excuses, excuses, excuses.

No more!

Instinctively he reached for the whisky.

Then, as if he was watching himself from a distance—viewing himself on a TV screen—he saw his arm slow.

Then it stopped.

*No, my friend, that's not the way it's going to be this time.*

He was going to change. Just like that guy on TV, he'd look back over his life, he'd make a list of all the bad things. And he'd set them right.

Making amends . . .

Jamie rose unsteadily, picked up the liquor, and poured it down the kitchen sink. He returned to the living room and eyed his cigarettes. Well, he knew he couldn't give *them* up, not completely. But he was going to limit himself to ten a day. . . . Wait, no, five. And he'd never smoke before noon. That was reasonable. That was *mature*.

He staggered into the bathroom and took a fiercely hot shower, then a freezing one. He toweled off and walked into his kitchenette, had half a bagel with no butter, and coffee without cream.

It was a very different Jamie Feldon who stepped from his apartment into the bright New England morning twenty minutes later, virtually sauntering to the parking lot. He dropped into the seat of his battered Toyota, started the engine, and headed for Route 128, which would take him to his office, twenty miles north of Boston. Normally the congestion drove him crazy. But today, he hardly noticed it. He was thinking about the possibility of a future real different from the disaster his life had been. He could actually foresee being content, being happy.

*Making amends . . .*


And yet, Jamie realized sitting at his desk later that day, it might be easy to work up the determination to stick to your moral convictions, but there were practical issues to consider, logistical problems.

In the TV show, for instance, the hero had spent a half-hour or so coming up with a list of people he'd offended or hurt.

But that was fiction. In real life, coming up with a list of offenses would take a lot of work. So at quitting time, he went to his boss and asked for the rest of the week off.

The chunky, disheveled manager swung back and forth slowly in his old office chair. He clearly wasn't happy with the idea. But Jamie was determined to stick to his plan, so he added, "I'm talking without pay, Mr. Logan."

"Without . . ." The boss was working to get his head around this idea.

"Unpaid leave."

The words were sinking in, but Logan still seemed uncertain, maybe wondering if Jamie was scheming—hoping the boss would say, *Naw, it's okay, I'll pay you anyway.*

Jamie said sincerely, "I mean it, Mr. Logan, really. Something personal's come up and I really need the time."

"You sick?"

"No. But there're a few people need my help."

"Yeah, you doing good deeds?" Logan laughed.

"Something like that."

"Well, you find somebody to cover for you, yeah, then I guess it's all right."

"Thanks, Mr. Logan. I appreciate it. I really do."

As he left he glanced back and noticed his boss studying him with a perplexed smile—as if he was looking at a brand-new Jamie Feldon.

Returning home that night, Jamie called around until he found a temp worker who was familiar with the company. He arranged for the man to start the next morning as a replacement.

On Tuesday, Jamie woke early, showered, dressed, and ate a bowl of cereal with low-fat milk. Then he cleaned his kitchen table off and went to work. A pad of yellow paper in front of him, he began the list. It wasn't easy, compiling all the bad things in your life. Some were hard to deal with—he felt so much shame about them. Some, he wasn't sure if they'd actually occurred. Were they figments of his imagination, dreams, a result of the booze?

He also realized that he had to decide which offenses to include. Some were serious, some seemed laughably minor. He told himself at first not to worry about the small things.

But something stiffened within him when he thought that.

No, he thought angrily. Either you do this right or you don't do it at all. He'd include the smallest infractions, as well as the most serious. He worked for two days straight and finally came up with a list of forty-three incidents. Then he spent another day identifying the people involved and finding out their most recent addresses. Some he knew, others required detective work. Using the phone book, directory assistance, and his computer, as well as actually pounding the pavement, he managed to get at least a lead to nearly everybody.

By Thursday night, Jamie was finished with the list and he celebrated with a tall glass of Arizona iced tea, mint-flavored, and a cigarette. Before he headed off to bed, though, he considered another question: Should he start with the older offenses, or the newest?

Jamie debated this for some time and decided that he'd start with the most recent. He was worried that he'd get bogged down finding people from decades ago, and he was eager to get his new life under way.

So, the most recent.

Who was first?

A glance at the list. The name on the top was *Charles Vaughn, Lincoln*.

The man awoke on Friday morning with the Memory.

This had happened nearly every day since the incident a month and a half ago.

The Memory was there when he awoke, and it was there when he fell asleep. And it popped up all by itself a couple of times during the day, too.

It was one of those things you try to forget, but the harder you try the more you relive it.

Then your gut twists, your palms grow clammy, and a chill pall of dread fills you. Anger too.

You hope that time will take care of it. And probably that'll happen eventually, but like when you're wracked with the flu, you just can't imagine you'll ever feel better.

Charles Vaughn had a good life. He was a senior sales manager for a large Internet software company. He'd gotten his MBA at New York University and had played with the big boys in the Wall Street finance world for a long time, then moved to Bean Town to join a startup. A year ago he jumped to his present company. He was tough, he played hardball (but never screwing around with the heavy-hitters, the IRS or the SEC), and he did well. Now, at forty-nine, he knew what the real world was about: doing a good job, being invaluable to your customers—and, just as important, if not more, to your boss— and paying attention to details. Looking over your shoulder, too— making millions and making enemies go hand in hand.

He'd moved up through the ranks of the company fast and had a shot at being president in the next few years.

The businessman had a beautiful home in Lincoln, a wife who was a successful realtor, and two kids headed for good colleges in the next couple of years. He had his health.

Everything about his life seemed perfect.

And it would have been, except for the goddamn Memory. It just wouldn't leave him alone.

What happened was this: Vaughn and his wife and daughter made the mistake of spending St. Patrick's Day at that tourist trap of stores and restaurants in Boston, Faneuil Hall, along with, of course, about a billion other people. Just as they were about to head home, his daughter remembered she needed to get a birthday present for her friend.

"We're out of time on the meter," Vaughn pointed out.

"Dad, it's, like, what? A quarter?"

They'd been shopping for two hours, and only now she remembered the present? Vaughn sighed. "I'll be in the car."

"We'll just be a minute." His daughter and wife disappeared back inside. Vaughn pumped another quarter into the meter and climbed into the car. He started the engine and cranked up the heater to cut through the infamous Boston spring chill.

Of course, it wasn't "a minute" at all. In fact, twenty of them rolled by without the two ladies surfacing. Vaughn sat back and was thinking about a man at work, a rival salesman who was making a move on some accounts that were up for grabs and that Vaughn really wanted. The rival wasn't as good a salesman, but he knew the tech side of the product better than any other employee, except the programmers themselves. Vaughn'd have to come up with some plan to stop him. He was considering what he could do when he heard a honk. He glanced into the street and saw a driver in a car pausing next to him. The man had a pudgy face and was about Vaughn's age, maybe a little younger.

He said something.

Vaughn shook his head and opened his passenger window. "What's that?"

"You leaving?" Gesturing at the parking space.

"Not just yet," Vaughn replied with a smile. "Waiting for the wife."

Which any man would understand was humorous shorthand for: It could be five minutes, could be an hour.

But the guy in the battered car didn't smile. "Just pull out and wait for her up there. Double-park."

Vaughn blinked at the man's bluntness. "Rather not. She and my daughter are expecting me here."

"I'm not saying drive to the Cape. Just pull up a car or two. You're leaving anyway."

"I'm not sure how long they'll be."

"It can't be that long. Your engine's running, isn't it?"

Vaughn's face grew red; he was angry and uneasy. "Think I'd rather wait here." He shut the engine off.

"Oh, that was cute," the man snapped. He seemed drunk.

St. Patrick's Day . . . piss-poor excuse for a holiday.

Vaughn turned away and rolled up the window. He glanced at the shops, hoping he'd see his wife and daughter.

The other driver shouted something else, which Vaughn couldn't hear. He stared at the control panel of his Acura, thinking that if he ignored the guy he'd go away.

*Come on*, he thought to his family, growing angry at them for putting him in this position.

It was then that he glanced toward his right, into the street, and saw that the door on the battered car was open. Where—

A rush of motion from the sidewalk. Vaughn's car door was jerked open before he could reach the door-lock button.

The driver was leaning down, directly in Vaughn's face. With a steam of drunken, smoky breath between them, the man said, "Listen up, asshole. I don't need anybody to dis me like that. The hell you think you are?"

Vaughn fixed his eyes on the scruffy man. Not in great shape, but big. Both scared and angry, Vaughn said, "I'm not leaving until my family's here. Live with it."

"Live with it? I'll give *you* something to live with." He flicked away a cigarette and ran his key along the side of the Acura, scraping off a line of paint.

"That's it!" Vaughn pulled his cell phone from his pocket, hit 9-1-1.

A police dispatcher came on immediately. "This is nine-one-one. What's the nature of your emergency?"

"I'm being attacked. Please send somebody—"

"You prick," the assailant muttered and reached for him, but Vaughn leaned back into the car.

"Your name, sir?" the dispatcher asked. "What's your address?"

"Charles Vaughn . . . I live in Lincoln but I'm in my car at Faneuil Hall, near Williams-Sonoma. He's drunk, he's attacking me. I—"

The big man lunged forward, snatched the phone away, and flung it to the sidewalk, where it shattered. Bystanders jumped back, though most stayed close—to watch whatever was going to happen next. A couple of drunk teenagers laughed and started chanting, "Fight, fight, fight."

The man gripped Vaughn's jacket and tried to pull him out of the car.

"Get off me!" Vaughn gripped the wheel and the men played tug of war until a siren sounded nearby, getting closer.

Thank God . . .

The assailant, his face red with rage, let go and stood frozen for a moment, as if he was wondering what else he could do to Vaughn. He settled for repeating, "You prick," and ran back to his car. He spun the wheels in reverse, disappearing around the corner. Vaughn strained his neck looking back but he couldn't see the license plate.

Hands shaking, breath ticking with the fright, Vaughn felt weak with fear and dread.

The police arrived and took a statement, made a note of the incident and the damage to the car. Vaughn was giving them what information he could remember when another thought occurred to him. His voice faded.

"What, sir?" an officer asked, noticing the businessman's troubled face.

"He heard me give nine-one-one my name. And where I lived. The town, I mean. Do you think he'll try to find me to get even?"

The police didn't seem concerned. "Road rage, or parking rage, whatever, it never lasts very long. I don't think you're in any danger."

"Besides," one officer added, nodding at the damage to the paint, "looks like he already did get even."

The police talked to passersby—with less enthusiasm than Vaughn would have liked—but nobody had gotten the man's tag number—or was willing to admit it if they had. Then another call came in on their radio—another fight in progress.

"St. Paddy's Day," one of the officers spat out, shaking his head. They hurried off.

"You okay?" one of the bystanders asked.

"Yeah, thanks," Vaughn said, not feeling the least bit okay. He ran his hand across the long scratch in the paint. He kept replaying the incident. Had it been his fault? Should he have given the guy the space? Of course not. But how had he sounded? Was he abrupt, insulting? He hadn't thought so, certainly hadn't meant to be.

Finally his wife and daughter returned from the hall, toting several small bags. They noticed the damage to the car and the pieces of Vaughn's cell phone sitting in the backseat.

"What happened, honey?"

He explained to them.

"Oh, Dad, no! Are you all right?"

"Fine. Just get in."

He locked the doors and drove away fast. On the turnpike Vaughn checked the rearview mirror every few seconds. But he saw no sign of the attacker's car. His wife and daughter chatted away as if nothing had happened. Vaughn was quiet, upset about the incident. And the anger—at them and at himself—wasn't going away.

When they were a few miles from home Judy asked, "Something wrong, honey? You're not still bothered by that crazy man, are you?"

"No," he said. "I'm just a little tired."

"Don't worry," she said. "It's just paint. They can fix it up like new."

Sometimes women just didn't get it at all.

"Oh, Dad," his daughter said urgently, "can we stop at Beth's? I want to give her the necklace."

"No."

"But it's right up there."

"I said no."

"But—"

"No," he snapped. "You'll see her at school tomorrow."

The girl wasn't happy—the friend's house was, after all, on the way home—but Vaughn wouldn't change his mind.

When they arrived at home he pulled his wife aside and told her his big concern—that the man had heard Vaughn mention his name and the town they lived in.

"Oh." Now Judy seemed miffed. His impression was that she was upset he'd gotten into the fight in the first place and hadn't just given the guy the parking space, then double-parked to wait for them. As if it was male ego that'd caused the problem.

He came a millisecond away from reminding her that their last-minute shopping spree was the ultimate cause of the whole thing, but self-preservation kicked in and he managed to restrain himself. He said, "The police don't think it's anything to worry about. But just keep an eye out." He described the man.

"Keep an eye out," she muttered, and walked off silently to make dinner.

Vaughn didn't eat much that night (his excuse was that his stomach was upset from the fast food they'd had for lunch, which his wife had ordered—a fact he managed to work into his explanation, with some petty satisfaction).

After his family went to bed that night, Vaughn climbed the stairs to the study above the garage and stayed awake for a long time, keeping a vigil, staring out at the street, looking for any sign of the assailant.

At three A.M. or so he fell asleep with the Memory prominently sitting in his thoughts.

And the next morning he awoke with it.

Vaughn forced himself to relax and, even though he was groggy from lack of sleep, he made breakfast for the family, spent a cheerful half-hour with them, and then headed off to work.

But the good mood didn't last. The Memory kept coming back. He replayed the incident a hundred times that day. He regretted not fighting back, not grabbing the man and wrestling him to the ground, pinning him there until the cops arrived. He felt he was a coward, a failure.

He was so distracted he missed the lunch he'd set up to woo the big client that his rival was after.

Over the next six weeks things grew worse. Several times on the way to work he spotted cars that might have been the assailant's, and skidded off the highway, desperate to escape. Two weeks ago he'd nearly slammed into a woman's SUV in a grocery store parking lot while staring at a car behind him. And another time, leaving a local bar, he'd seen a man in sunglasses across the street; Vaughn believed he looked like the assailant. Panicked, the businessman leapt back inside the bar, knocking into several people and spilling drinks. He nearly tripped down the back stairs of the bar as he fled.

All of these incidents turned out to be false alarms—the men he'd seen were not the attacker—but he couldn't shake the fear that consumed him.

Finally, he couldn't take it anymore. One morning Vaughn canceled a meeting at work and drove to a building outside of town, a place he'd found in the Yellow Pages, a gun shop and shooting range. There he bought a 9mm semiautomatic Glock pistol and enrolled in the course that would give him a Class A firearm permit, allowing him to carry a concealed weapon.

Today, at lunch, he was going to complete the course and get the license. From now on he could carry the gun wherever he wanted to.

Jamie Feldon woke up at nine on Friday, well rested and ready to get started on his new life.

Unlike the typical evening from his past, last night he'd slept in his bed, under clean sheets, wearing clean pajamas, and, even though he'd had a beer with dinner, he'd gone to sleep sober. He'd also stuck to his rule of only two cigarettes for the entire evening. He brushed his teeth for a full minute.

Now, eating a modest breakfast, he looked over the notes he'd taken about Charles Vaughn. The businessman lived in Lincoln. But Jamie wanted to see him without his family around, so he'd Googled the name and found him mentioned on some computer industry websites. He learned where the man worked, an Internet company about ten miles away.

Jamie decided to take something along with him, and after some thinking he had a brainstorm: Champagne. Vaughn, he recalled, was a man who dressed well and would probably have good taste.

After washing his breakfast dishes, Jamie jumped in his car and headed off to the nearest wine store, figuring he'd spend some serious money on the bottle. You can't scrimp when you're working on a new life.

"Good shooting," the man said.

He was a well-toned fifty-year-old with cropped gray hair. Tendons and muscles were prominent in his arms and neck. His name was Larry Bolling, and he was the senior instructor at Patriot Guns and Shooting Range, where Charles Vaughn had been taking his lessons.

Vaughn pulled his ear protectors off. "What?"

"Good shooting, I said."

"Thanks." Vaughn put the black semiautomatic pistol down on the bench in front of him as the instructor reeled the target back in. The eight shots were grouped tight in the silhouette's chest.

The shooting wasn't competition-level but he was satisfied.

The idea that Charles Vaughn would be spending any time at all thinking about grain weight of bullets and the advantages of a SIG-Sauer safety (a thumb lever) versus a Glock (a second trigger) was hilarious. Here was a man who made his living with credit reports and product-spec sheets, and yet he was spending his lunch hour shooting at images of Bin Laden and John Q. Thug.

But even more ironic was that Charles Vaughn had turned into a pretty damn good shot.

At first he'd held the gun stiffly, in a way that seemed to mimic what he'd seen actors do in the movies.

"Now, sir," Larry Bolling had explained at the first lesson, "you might not want to do that."

"What's that?"

"Hold your weapon that way."

"Okay. Sure. Why not?"

"Because when you pull the trigger, the slide—See that part there—is gonna fly back at, oh, about a thousand miles an hour, and it'll take a portion of your thumb with it. What you do is just rest one hand on the other. Sorta like this."

"This?"

"That's right. Now let's go put some holes in a target."

Well, at first he hadn't put a lot of holes in anything but the bullet trap at the back of the range. But today he'd been rewarded for his skill.

*Good shooting . . .*

After the lunch-hour lesson today, Vaughn dismantled the gun, then cleaned, reassembled, and reloaded it.

He found Bolling in the front office, hunched over some papers. He motioned Vaughn to take a chair.

"So, I get my ticket?" the businessman asked.

"Not quite yet, sir."

Vaughn frowned. He'd passed all the tests with perfect scores. He'd also passed the background checks. He'd attended all of the video and live-instruction sessions, had done all his homework.

"I thought that was it."

"Nope," Bolling explained. "There's one more thing that I include in my classes."

"Okay, what's that?"

"You need to answer a question."

"Go ahead."

"Why do you want a carry permit? You never told me."

"I'm a wealthy businessman. I'm concerned about my family. There's a lot of crime in Boston."

"That's all true—at least I can attest to the last one of those, and the other two are no doubt right, as well. But why don't you tell me the real reason?"

Vaughn could only laugh. He shook his head and explained about the attack on St. Patrick's Day.

"Okay, sir, I understand that was upsetting. But that's not a good reason to carry a weapon."

"But he was dangerous."

"Let me ask: That was six weeks ago, give or take; you seen hide or hair of that man since then?"

"I don't think so," Vaughn said defensively.

A nod toward the pistol on the businessman's hip. "You've done good in the course. You know safety and you've got every legal right to carry that. My advice to you is to take it home, put it in a lockbox, and leave it there until the next time you come here to have some fun. Then take it home again and put it back in the box. You get my drift?"

"But—"

"Listen to me."

Vaughn looked up into the man's steely eyes. He nodded.

"Most people, in their entire lives, there's a one in a million chance that there'd be a good reason to draw their weapon on the street, and even less of a chance they ought to use it. The absolute best possible thing you can do in a confrontation is turn and run like a rabbit, calling for help at the top of your lungs. I'll tell you from my heart that that's exactly what I'd do."

"Run."

"As fast as your feet can carry you. And if you're with your grand-mother, or your child, you sling 'em over your shoulder and carry 'em with you. . . . A gun's for that one time in your life when you're trapped, there's no help around, and your assailant intends to kill you. That situation in Boston, naturally it upset you, and no doubt that man was a solid-gold son of a bitch. And you're thinking you were a coward. But I'm telling you, it's braver to live with a feeling like that than to go looking for trouble."

"Well, duly noted," Vaughn said. "I appreciate your comments."

"There, I've said my piece." Bolling produced a temporary permit. "Good luck to you, sir."

Leaving the gun shop and range, returning to his car, Charles Vaughn was thinking about Bolling's words. But they didn't stay with him long. He was aware of a curious feeling. It was as if something fundamental in his life had changed. He thought back to the incident in Boston and found, to his surprise, his gut didn't twist, his heart didn't pound quite so fast. The anger—at the attacker, and at himself for his cowardice—was almost gone.

Charles Vaughn walked to his car and headed back to work, buoyed by a confidence that he hadn't felt for months. Maybe even years.

At five P.M. that evening Jamie Feldon sat in the front seat of his Toyota, listening to the radio and watching people leave the office of NES Computer Products.

He didn't know if Charles Vaughn was a workaholic—a lot of times those Internet guys really put in the hours—but Jamie would stay as long as he needed to in order to see the guy. Beside him was a grilled chicken sandwich from McDonald's, an iced tea, and a bottle of Champagne whose name he couldn't pronounce, which meant that it had to be good.

He ate his dinner, listened to the radio, and thought about the other people on his list.

Then, at seven P.M., Jamie saw Charles Vaughn leave by the front door, look around, and then head toward the parking garage.

Jamie took a deep breath.

Making amends.

A new life.

He grabbed the Champagne, stepped out of the car, and started up the sidewalk to the garage.

Approaching his car, Charles Vaughn examined the paint job. The body shop had completely erased the damage from when the psycho had keyed his car outside Faneuil Hall.

Just like the gun on his hip had erased the psychic scarring.

He no longer felt defenseless, no longer felt scared. In fact, despite the gun instructor's advice (which Vaughn thought was a bit hypocritical, considering his job), he was hoping the man *would* make his move.

*I'm ready for you.*

It was then that he heard a snap—or some sound—not far away. He froze and looked around. The garage was deserted here; after his lesson at the gun shop he'd returned to find parking only on the fifth floor. His was the only car here now. He shifted his briefcase to his left hand. His pistol was only a few inches away from his right. But, he told himself, how would the punk know where he worked? He might've been staking out Lincoln, but here? Impossible.

Though if the guy was really determined, it wouldn't be impossible to find out his company. Vaughn squinted, scanning the floor behind him. Was that the shadow of someone on the far stairwell? He couldn't tell.

His heart beating quickly, he remembered the man's face, remembered the anger in his eyes, the smell of liquor, the uncontrolled hands as they gripped Vaughn's lapels.

A chill tickled his spine. But it wasn't fear; it was exhilaration.

Keeping his right hand free, Vaughn set his briefcase down and fished for his car keys, while he scanned the garage in the direction he believed the sound had come from.

The sound again.

He hit the unlock button on the key. But still didn't get inside. He tapped the gun with his right palm.

Vaughn tensed as the sound of tires squealing filled his ears. He laughed to himself, watching the pickup truck squeal down the exit ramp from the top floor, where maintenance workers and contractors were supposed to park. That was the noise he'd heard, the men loading up the truck.

It was then that a man's voice behind him said, "Excuse me, Mr. Vaughn? You probably don't remember me . . ."

Vaughn gasped, dropping the car keys. He stared at the figure approaching him, carrying something large in his right hand. It looked like a club, a bowling pin.

*Jesus, it's him, it's the attacker!*

Instinctively, Vaughn dropped into a combat shooting pose, drew his gun, and aimed directly at the man's chest. He started to pull the trigger.

Jamie Feldon gasped, holding up a hand as if it could ward off the bullet that was about to end his life. "No! Please!"

Neither Jamie nor Vaughn moved.

Time was frozen.

Jamie heard nothing, he felt nothing.

It was so quiet. . . . Had the gun actually gone off? Maybe it had and he was dead.

But then he felt wind on his cheek and heard a truck shifting gears nearby. A horn honked in the distance. His heart, too . . . he could actually hear it.

"Please," he whispered. "Please don't. . . ."

Vaughn was squinting at Jamie. "Could you . . . I'm sorry, could you step into the light there?"

Jamie did.

Vaughn studied his face, then the Champagne. He slumped. "My God, my God, my God . . ." The gun lowered and the businessman leaned against his car. "I thought . . . I'm sorry, I thought you were somebody else."

Feeling his hands quiver madly, Jamie gave a breathless laugh. "Who?"

Vaughn said, "This guy I had a run-in with in Boston. On St. Patrick's Day . . . I'm so sorry. I couldn't see you clearly." His shoulders slumped. "Or maybe I was just so paranoid." He glanced down at the gun with wide eyes and quickly put it in the holster on his hip. "Are you . . . are you all right?"

Jamie laughed. "Well, I've gotta say I'm a lot better now that you put that thing away. Thought I'd pee my pants for a minute there."

"Who are you?"

"My name's Jamie Feldon."

Vaughn shook his head. "Do I know you?"

"Not really, but we've met."

"What can I do for you?"

Jamie said brightly, "I've come to see you about making amends." He nodded at the Champagne.

"Amends?" Vaughn asked, frowning. "What did you do to me?"

"Oh," Jamie said, "it's not what I did to *you*. It's what you did to *me*."

"To you? What—?" Vaughn asked. But before he could continue, Jamie lunged forward and swung the bottle into the side of the businessman's head.

The businessman went down like a rock.

Five minutes later Charles Vaughn came to.

Jamie was standing over him, aiming the man's pistol at his chest, the grip of the gun wrapped in a napkin he'd found in a nearby trash bin.

"What," Vaughn gasped, "what's this all about?" He squinted.

"Amends," he said. "Like I said."

"But I don't even know you . . . What'd I do?"

"You really don't remember, do you?"

"No. I swear."

"Well, take a good look."

"I'm sorry. Really. Please put down the gun. We can talk about it."

"Think back," Jamie said in a smooth voice. "Think back to late March. You were in the Lincoln Brew Pub."

"I go there all the time."

"I know. But this particular day you should remember. You started to walk out the door, but all of a sudden you jumped back, like you saw a goddamn ghost. You spilled my Bloody Mary all over me. And then you just run out the back door." Jamie gave a cold laugh. "Do you say you're sorry? Do you offer to pay for the dry cleaning? No."

"Wait . . ." Vaughn was shaking his head. "I remember that. But . . . Wait, how did you find me?"

"Just asked the bartender at the Lincoln Pub what your name was. Then I Googled you and found where you lived and worked. Had to see you alone, of course. Didn't want your family around."

"You have to understand—at the bar back then in March? That guy I was telling you about, the attacker? I thought he was outside. I was afraid."

Jamie shrugged. "I was supposed to pick up my kid for visitation but I had that drink all over me. Couldn't pick him up looking like that, could I? I had to go home and change. I was late and his mother'd taken him someplace with her by the time I got there. Made a big deal about it with the court, too."

"I'm sorry, but—"

"Sorry, but," Jamie mocked. "See, I've been putting up with crap like that all my life. People've insulted me, cheated me, made fun of me, *bumped into* me ever since I was a kid. And I've never had the guts to fight back. I just swallowed it all. . . . I get walked over and I never have the balls to do anything. But a week ago I decided I'm not going to put up with it anymore. People're going to make amends to me for what they've done. And you're the first on my list."

"Make amends?" Vaughn gasped. "But I just spilled something on you. What do you want? You want money?"

"No, I want you to die," Jamie said matter-of-factly and shoved the gun against Vaughn's head, then pulled the trigger.

After he cleaned the blood off his own face and hands Jamie wrapped the dead man's fingers around the gun and quickly left the garage. He looked around. Nobody seemed to have heard the shot. He walked slowly down the stairs and out to the lot where he was parked, carrying the Champagne. Jamie'd taken the bottle to use as a weapon; it was something that nobody would be suspicious of. He'd planned to either beat Vaughn to death with it, or, if it broke, use the jagged neck to slash the man's carotid artery.

But Vaughn had actually been carrying a gun! If the businessman was really so jittery about whatever'd happened on St. Patrick's Day, the cops might get the idea he'd gone over the edge and killed himself. Or maybe they'd think that guy who'd attacked him had finally tracked him down.

Jamie climbed in his car and drove slowly out of the parking lot. He kept hearing Vaughn's words in his mind.

*At the bar back then in March? That guy I was telling you about, the attacker? I thought he was outside. I was afraid.*

Excuses, Jamie reflected in disgust. There were always excuses.

And he wasn't going to accept them anymore.

Jamie was going to be true to his resolution. The TV show he'd seen had changed him forever. People had to make amends for their transgressions, and he was going to be the angel of justice to make sure they did.

Who next? He glanced down at the list and noticed his wife's name, but she was at the bottom. He'd have to handle that one carefully since he'd be a prime suspect in her death.

But there were plenty of scores to settle before her.

He saw the name below Vaughn's.

Carole, in Scituate. She was a thirty-five-year-old bank manager he'd taken out on a date in February. They'd gone to the Red Lobster, All You Can Eat . . . and she sure had.

But afterwards, a double insult: She'd refused to sleep with him and then she'd never called, like she'd promised.

It was seven-thirty. Did he have time to take care of Carole tonight?

Sure he did, Jamie decided. Tomorrow was Saturday; he could sleep in. Besides, there were a lot of names on his list; it'd feel good to mark another one off.

He lit a cigarette, only his fourth of the day, and headed for the turnpike.

# A VISION IN WHITE

## By Lawrence Block

Lawrence Block's novels range from the urban noir of Matthew Scudder (*All the Flowers are Dying*) to the urbane effervescence of Bernie Rhodenbarr (*The Burglar on the Prowl*), while other characters include the globe-trotting insomniac Evan Tanner (*Tanner on Ice*) and the introspective assassin Keller (*Hit Parade*). He has published articles and short fiction in *American Heritage*, *Redbook*, *Playboy*, *Cosmopolitan*, *GQ*, and the *New York Times*, and eighty-four of his short stories have been collected in *Enough Rope*. In 2004, he became executive story editor for the TV series *Tilt*. Larry is a Grand Master of Mystery Writers of America, and a past president of both MWA and the Private Eye Writers of America. He has won the Edgar and Shamus awards four times each and the Japanese Maltese Falcon award twice, as well as the Nero Wolfe and Philip Marlowe awards, a Lifetime Achievement Award from the Private Eye Writers of America, and, most recently, the Cartier Diamond Dagger for Life Achievement from the Crime Writers' Association (UK). In France, he has been proclaimed a Grand Maître du Roman Noir and has twice been awarded the Société 813 trophy. He has been a guest of honor at Bouchercon and at book fairs and mystery festivals in France, Germany, Australia, Italy, New Zealand, and Spain, and, as if that were not enough, was presented with the key to the city of Muncie, Indiana. Larry and his wife, Lynne, are enthusiastic New Yorkers and relentless world travelers.

T he game changed over time. Technology made change inevitable: Racquets were larger and lighter and stronger, and even shoes got a little better every few years. And human technology had much the same effect; each generation of tennis players was taller and rangier than the one before it, and players improved on genetics by getting stronger through weight training and more durable through nutrition. So of course the game changed. It had to change.

But the players still—with rare exception—wore the traditional white clothing, and that was one thing he hoped would never change. Oh, some of them sported logos, and maybe that was inevitable, too, with all the money the corporations were throwing around. And you saw colored stripes on some of the white shirts and shorts, and periodically the self-appointed Brat of the Year would turn up in plaid shorts and a scarlet top, but by and large white prevailed.

And he liked it that way. For the women, especially. He didn't really care what the men wore, and, truth to tell, found it difficult to work up much enthusiasm for the men's game. Service played too great a role, and the top players scored too many aces. It was the long drawn-out points that most engaged him, with both players drawing on unsuspected reserves of strength and tenacity to reach impossible balls and make impossible returns. That was tennis, not a handful of 120-mile-an-hour serves and a round of applause.

And there was something about a girl dressed entirely in white, shifting her weight nervously as she waited for her opponent to serve, bouncing the ball before her own serve. Something pure and innocent and remarkably courageous, something that touched your heart as you watched, and wasn't that what spectator sports were about? Yes, you admired the technique, you applauded the skill, but it was an emotional response of the viewer to some quality in the participant that made the game genuinely engaging, and even important.

Interesting how some of them engaged you and others did not.

The one who grunted, for example. Grunted like a little pig every time she hit the ball. Maybe she couldn't help it, maybe it was some Eastern breathing technique that added energy to her stroke. He didn't care. All he knew was that it put him right off Miss Piglet. Whenever he watched her play, he rooted for her opponent.

With others it was something subtler. The stance, the walk, the attitude. One responded or one didn't.

And, of course, the game the woman played was paramount. Not just the raw ability but the heart, the soul, the inner strength that enabled one player to reach and return shots that drew no more than a futile wave from another.

He sat in his chair, drew on his cigarette, watched the television set.

This one, this Miranda DiStefano. Sixteen years old, her blond hair hanging in a ponytail, her face a perfect oval, her nose the slightest bit retroussé. She had a slight overbite, and one close-up revealed braces on her teeth.

How charming . . .

He'd seen her before, and now he watched her play a match she was not likely to win, a quarterfinal that pitted her against one of the sisters who seemed to win everything these days. He liked both sisters well enough, respected them as the dominant players of their generation, but they didn't engage him the way Miranda did. She didn't have to win, he just wanted to watch her play, and do the best she could.

A vision in white. Perfectly delightful and charming. He wished only the best for her.

There were sports you could see better on television. Boxing, certainly. Even if you sat at ringside, you didn't get nearly as good a view of the action as the TV camera provided. Football was a tossup; at home you had the benefit of good close-up camera work and instant replay, while from a good stadium seat you could watch a play develop and see the whole of a pass pattern. Basketball was better in person, and hockey (if you could endure it at all) was only worth watching in person; on TV, you could never find the bloody puck.

TV covered tennis reasonably well, but it was much better in person. The court was small enough so that, from a halfway decent seat, you were assured a good view of the whole of it. And, of course, watching in person had other benefits that it shared with other sports. There were no commercials, no team of announcers droning on and on, and, most important, it was exciting in a way that televised sport could never be. You were there, you were watching, it was happening right before your eyes, and your excitement was magnified by the presence of hundreds or thousands of other similarly excited fans.

He'd been here for the entire tournament, and was glad he'd come. He'd managed to see some superb tennis (as well as some that was a good deal less than superb) and he'd made a point of watching all of Miranda DiStefano's matches. The blond girl won her first two matches in straight sets, and he'd sat there beaming as she dispatched both opponents quite handily. In the third round, his heart sank when she double-faulted to lose the first set tiebreaker, then had her serve broken midway through the second set. But she rallied, she summoned up strength from within, and broke back, and went on to win that set. The final set was no contest; Miranda, buoyed by her second-set comeback, played brilliantly, and you could see the will to win drain out of her opponent, a black-haired Croatian girl who was five inches taller than Miranda, with muscles in her arms and shoulders that hinted at either steroids or a natural abundance of testosterone.

And Miranda crushed her. How his spirit soared to see it!

Now she was playing in the quarterfinals, and it looked as though she was going to beat the bigger, taller girl on the opposite side of the net. A strong player, he thought, but lacking finesse. All power and speed, but no subtlety.

A lesbian, from the look of her. He hadn't heard or read anything to that effect, but you could tell. Not that he had anything against them. They were as ubiquitous in women's sports as were their male counterparts in ballet and the design trades. If they played good tennis, he could certainly admire their game.

But he wouldn't leave his house to watch a lesbian, let alone travel a few hundred miles.

He watched, his heart singing in his chest, as Miranda worked the ball back and forth, chasing her opponent from one side of the court to the other, running the legs off the bigger girl. Running her ragged, crushing her, beating her.

He was there two days later, cheering her on in the semifinals. Her opponent was one of the sisters, and Miranda gave her a good fight, but the outcome was never in doubt. He applauded enthusiastically every time she won a point, cheered a couple of difficult returns she managed, and took her eventual loss in good grace—as did Miranda, skipping up to the net to congratulate the girl who beat her.

A good sport, too. The girl was one in a million.

He knew better than to write to her.

Oh, the impulse was there, no question about it. Sometimes he found himself composing letters in his head, but that was all right. You could write anything to anybody in the privacy of your own mind. It was when you put your thoughts on paper and entrusted them to the mails that things could go wrong.

Because there were a lot of lunatics out there. An attractive young woman could find herself an unwitting magnet for the aberrant and the delusional, and a letter from a devoted fan could seem as fraught with potential danger as one threatening the life of the President. There was a difference, you wouldn't get in trouble writing a fan letter, but the effect on its recipient might be even greater. The President of the United States would never see your letter, a secretary would open it and hand it over to the FBI, but a young tennis player, especially a relative novice who probably didn't get all that much fan mail, might well open it and read it herself.

And might take it the wrong way. Whatever you said, however you phrased it, she might read something unintended into it. Might begin to wonder if perhaps this enthusiastic fan might be a little too enthusiastic, and if this admiration for her athletic ability might cloak a disturbing obsession.

And what, really, was the point in a fan letter? To reward the recipient for the pleasure her performance had brought him? Hardly, if such a letter were more likely to provoke anxiety than to hearten. What kind of a reward was that?

No, it was the writer's own ego that a fan letter supported. It was an attempt to create a relationship with a stranger, and the only fit relationship for two such people was distant and anonymous. She played tennis, and sparkled on the court. He watched, rapt with enjoyment, and she didn't even know he existed. Which was as it should be.

In the letters he wrote in the privacy of his own mind, sometimes he was a wee bit suggestive, a trifle risqué. Sometimes he thought of things that would bring a blush to that pretty face.

But he never wrote them down, not a sentence, not a word. So where was the harm in that?

Her game was off.

Last month she'd played in the French Open, and the television coverage had been frustrating; he'd only been able to see one of her matches, and highlights of others. She didn't make the quarterfinals this time, went out in the third round, beaten in a third-set tiebreaker by an unseeded player she should have swept in straight sets.

Something was missing. Some spark, some inner fire.

And now she was back in the States, playing in the women-only Virago tournament in Indianapolis, and he'd driven almost a thousand miles to watch her play, and she wasn't playing well. At game point in the opening set, the girl double-faulted. You just didn't do that. When the serve had to be in or you lost the set, you made sure you got that serve in. You just did it.

He watched, heartsick, as his Miranda lost point after point to a girl who wasn't fit to carry her racquet. Watched her run after balls she should have gotten to, watched her make unforced errors, watched her beat herself. Well, she had to, didn't she? Her opponent couldn't beat her. She could only beat herself.

And she did.

Toward the end, he tried to inspire her through sheer force of will. He narrowed his gaze, stared hard at her, willed her to look at him, to meet his eyes. And she just wouldn't do it. She looked everywhere but at him, and a fat lot of good it did her.

Then she did look over at him, and her eyes met his and drew away. She was ashamed, he realized, ashamed of her performance, ashamed of herself. She couldn't meet his eyes.

Nor could she turn the tide. The other girl beat her, and she was out of the tournament. He'd driven a thousand miles, and for what?

He wrote her a letter.

*I don't know what you think you're doing,* he wrote, *but the net result— no pun intended—is to sabotage not merely a career but a life.*

He went on to the end, read the thing over, and decided he didn't like the parenthetical *no pun intended* bit. He copied the letter over, dropping it and changing *net* to *overall.* Then he signed it: *A Man Who Cares.*

He left it on his desk, and the next day he rewrote it, and added some personal advice. *Stay away from the lesbians*, he counseled her. *They're only after one thing. The same goes for boys. You could never be happy with someone your own age.* He read it over, copied it with a word changed here and there, and signed it: *The Man Who Loves You.*

The following night he read the letter, went to bed, and got up, unable to sleep. He went to his desk and redrafted the letter one more time, adding some material that he supposed some might regard as overly frank, even pornographic. *The Man For Whom You Were Destined.* The phrase struck him as stilted, but he let it stand, and below it, with a flourish, he signed his name. He destroyed all the other drafts and went to bed.

In the morning he read the letter, sighed, shook his head, and burned it in the fireplace. The words, he thought, would go up the chimney and up into the sky, and, in the form of pure energy, would find their way to the intended recipient.

Her next tournament was in a city less than a hundred miles from his residence.

He thought about going, decided against it because he didn't want the disappointment. He'd developed a feeling for her, he'd invested emotionally in the girl, and she wasn't worth it. Better to stay home and cut his losses.

Better to avoid her on television as well. He wouldn't tune in to the coverage until she was eliminated. Which, given the massive deterioration of her game, would probably come in the first or second round. Then, once she was out of it, he could sit back and watch the sport he loved.

But, perversely, she sailed through the opening rounds. He read the sports pages every morning, and noted the results of her matches. One reporter commented on the renewed determination she was showing, and the inner reserves upon which she seemed able to draw. *There's a sparkle in her eye, too*, he added, *that hints at an off-court relationship.*

He was not surprised.

She won in the quarterfinals, won again in the semis. He didn't watch, although the pull toward the television set was almost irre-sistible. If she reached the finals, he promised himself, then he would watch.

She got there, and didn't have to contend with either of the for-midable sisters; one had skipped the tournament with a sore heel tendon, while the other lost in the semis to Ana Dravic, the Croatian lesbian he'd watched Miranda lose to in a quarterfinal match when she was still his Miranda, pure and innocent, glowing with promise. Now Miranda would play Dravic again, for the tournament, and could she win? Would she win?

She lost the first set 4-6, won the second in a fierce tiebreaker. She was on serve in the first game of the third and final set, won that, and then broke Dravic's serve to lead two games to none.

And then her game fell apart.

She double-faulted, made unforced errors. She never won another game, and, when she trotted up to the net to congratulate the hulking Croatian, the TV commentators we're at a loss to explain what had happened to her game.

But he knew. He looked at her hand as she clasped Dravic's larger hand, caught the expression on her face. And then, when she turned and looked into the camera, looked straight at *him*, he knew that she knew, too.


Her next tournament was in California. It took him four days to drive there.

He went to one early-round match, watched her win handily. Her tennis was purposeful, efficient, but now it left him cold. There was no heart and soul in it. It had changed, even as she had changed.

At one point, she turned and looked him right in the eye. Her thoughts were as clear as if she'd spoken them aloud, as if she'd shouted them into his ear. *There! What are you going to do about it?*

He didn't go to any more of the matches, hers or anyone else's. He stayed in his cheap motel, smoked cigarettes, watched the television set.

When he smoked, he removed the white cotton glove from the hand that held the cigarette. Otherwise, he kept the gloves on while he was alone in his room.

And periodically he emptied his ashtray into the toilet and flushed the cigarette butts.

He was ready. He knew where she was staying, had driven there twice and scouted the place. He had a gun, if he needed it. It was untraceable, he'd bought it for cash at a gun show from a man with a beard and a beer belly and a lot to say on the subject of government regulation. He had a knife, equally impossible to trace. He had his hands, and flexed them now, imagining them encircling her throat.

And there was nothing to connect him to her. He'd never sent a letter, never met her face to face, never given another human being the slightest hint of the way he and she were bonded. He'd always driven to the tournaments he'd attended, always paid cash at the motels where he stayed, always registered under a different false name. Never made a phone call from his room, never left a fingerprint, not even so much as a DNA-bearing cigarette butt.

He would stalk her, and he would get to her when she was alone, and he would do what he'd come to do, what he had to do. And the world would never know why she'd died, or who had killed her.

He was confident of that. And why shouldn't he be? After all, they'd never found out about any of the others.

# PONY GIRL
## *By Laura Lippman*

Laura Lippman has published twelve novels—nine in the award-winning Tess Monaghan series and three stand-alones, including the *New York Times* best-seller *What the Dead Know*. An anthology of her short stories is planned for fall 2008. She lives in Baltimore.

## TREMÉ

She was looking for trouble and she was definitely going to find it. What was the girl thinking when she got dressed this morning? When she decided—days, weeks, maybe even months ago—that this was how she wanted to go out on Mardi Gras day? And not just out, but all the way up to Claiborne Avenue and Ernie K. Doe's, where this kind of costume didn't *play*. There were skeletons and Mardi Gras Indians and baby dolls, but it wasn't a place where you saw a lot of people going for sexy or clever. That kind of thing was for back in the Quarter, maybe outside Café Brasil. It's hard to find a line to cross on Mardi Gras day, much less cross it, but this girl had gone and done it. In all my years—I was nineteen then, but a hard nineteen—I'd only seen one Mardi Gras sight more disturbing, and that was a white boy who took a magic marker, a thick one, and stuck it through a piercing in his earlobe. Nothing more to his costume than that, a magic marker through his ear, street clothes, and a wild gaze. Even in the middle of a crowd, people granted him some distance, let me tell you.

The Mardi Gras I'm talking about now, this was three years ago, the year that people were saying that customs *mattered*, that we had to hold tight to our traditions. Big Chief Tootie Montana was still alive then, and he had called for the skeletons and the baby dolls to make a showing, and there was a pretty good turnout. But it wasn't true old school, with the skeletons going to people's houses and waking up children in their beds, telling them to do their homework and listen to their mamas. Once upon a time, the skeletons were fierce, coming in with old bones from the butcher's shop, shaking the bloody hanks at sleeping children. Man, you do that to one of these kids today, he's likely to come up with a gun, blow the skeleton back into the grave. Legends lose their steam, like everything else. What scared people once won't scare them now.

Back to the girl. Everybody's eyes kept going back to that girl. She was long and slinky, in a champagne-colored body stocking. And if it had been just the body stocking, if she had decided to be Eve to some boy's Adam, glued a few leaves to the right parts, she wouldn't have been so . . . disrupting. Funny how that goes, how pretending to be naked can be less inflaming than dressing up like something that's not supposed to be sexy at all. No, this one, she had a pair of pointy ears high in her blond hair, which was pulled back in a pony-tail. She had pale white-and-beige cowboy boots, the daintiest things you ever seen, and—this was what made me fear for her—a real tail of horse-hair pinned to the end of her spine, swishing back and forth as she danced. *Swish. Swish. Swish.* And although she was skinny by my standards, she managed the trick of being skinny with curves, so that tail jutted out just so. *Swish. Swish. Swish.* I watched her, and I watched all the other men watching her, and I did not see how anyone could keep her safe if she stayed there, dancing into the night.

Back in school, when they lectured us on the straight-and-narrow, they told us that rape is a crime of violence. They told us that a woman isn't looking for something just because she goes out in high heels and a bustier and a skirt that barely covers her. Or in a champagne-colored body stocking with a tail affixed. They told us that rape has nothing to do with sex. But sitting in Ernie K. Doe's, drinking a Heineken, I couldn't help but wonder if rape *started* as sex and then moved to violence when sex was denied. *Look at me, look at me, look at me*, the tail seemed to sing as it twitched back and forth.

Yet Pony Girl's downcast eyes, refusing to make eye contact even with her dancing partner, a plump cowgirl in a big red hat, sent a different message. *Don't touch me, don't touch me, don't touch me.* You do that to a dog with a steak, he bites you, and nobody says it's the dog's fault.

Yeah, I wanted her as much as anyone there. But I feared for her even more than I wanted her, saw where the night was going and wished I could protect her. Where she was from, she was probably used to getting away with such behavior. Maybe she would get away with it here, too, if only because she was such an obvious outsider. Not a capital-T tourist, not some college girl from Tallahassee or Birmingham who had gotten tired of showing her titties on Bourbon Street and needed a new thrill. But a tourist of sorts, the kind of girl who was so full of herself that she thought she always controlled things. She was counting on folks to be rational, which was a pretty big count on Mardi Gras day. People do odd things, especially when they's masked.

I saw a man I knew only as Big Roy cross the threshold. Like most of us, he hadn't bothered with a costume, but he could have come as a frog without much trouble. He had the face for it—pop eyes, broad, flat mouth. Big Roy was almost as wide as he was tall, but he wasn't fat. I saw him looking at Pony Girl long and hard, and I decided I had to make my move. At worst, I was out for myself, trying to get close to her. But I was being a gentleman, too, looking out for her. You can be both. I know what was in my heart that day and, while it wasn't all over pure, it was something better than most men would have offered her.

"Who you s'posed to be?" I asked after dancing awhile with her and her friend. I made a point of making it a threesome, of joining them, as opposed to trying to separate them from one another. That put them at ease, made them like me.

"A horse," she said. "Duh."

"Just any horse? Or a certain one?"

She smiled. "In fact, I *am* a particular horse. I'm Misty of Chincoteague."

"Misty of where?"

"It's an island off Virginia." She was shouting in my ear, her breath warm and moist. "There are wild ponies, and every summer the volunteer firemen herd them together and cross them over to the mainland, where they're auctioned off."

"That where you from?"

"Chincoteague?"

"Virginia."

"My family is from the Eastern Shore of Maryland. But I'm from here. I go to Tulane."

The reference to college should have made me feel a little out of my league, or was supposed to, but somehow it made me feel bolder. "Going to college don't you make you from somewhere, any more than a cat born in an oven can call itself a biscuit."

"I love it here," she said, throwing open her arms. Her breasts were small, but they were there, round little handfuls. "I'm never going to leave."

"Ernie K. Doe's?" I asked, as if I didn't know what she meant.

"Yes," she said, playing along. "I'm going to live here forever. I'm going to dance until I drop dead, like the girl in the red shoes."

"Red shoes? You wearing cowboy boots."

She and her friend laughed, and I knew it was at my expense, but it wasn't a mean laughter. Not yet. They danced and they danced, and I began to think that she had been telling a literal truth, that she planned to dance until she expired. I offered her cool drinks, beers and sodas, but she shook her head; I asked if she wanted to go for a walk, but she just twirled away from me. To be truthful, she was wearing me out. But I was scared to leave her side because whenever I glanced in the corner, there was Big Roy, his pop eyes fixed on her, almost yellow in the dying light. I may have been a skinny nineteen-year-old in blue jeans and a Sean John T-shirt—this was back when Sean John was at its height—but I was her self-appointed knight. And even though she acted as if she didn't need me, I knew she did.

Eventually she started to tire, fanning her face with her hands, overheated from the dancing and, I think, all those eyes trained on her. That Mardi Gras was cool and overcast, and even with the crush of bodies in Ernie K. Doe's, it wasn't particularly warm. But her cheeks were bright red, rosy, and there were patches of sweat forming on her leotard—two little stripes beneath her barely-there breasts, a dot below her tail and who knows where else.

Was she stupid and innocent, or stupid and knowing? That is, did she realize the effect she was having and think she could control it, or did she honestly not know? In my heart of hearts, I knew she was not an innocent girl, but I wanted to see her that way because that can be excused.

Seeing her steps slow, anticipating that she would need a drink now, Big Roy pressed up, dancing in a way that only a feared man could get away with, a sad little hopping affair. Not all black men can dance, but the ones who can't usually know better than to try. Yet no one in this crowd would dare make fun of Big Roy, no matter how silly he looked.

Except her. She spun away, made a face at her cowgirl, pressing her lips together as if it was all she could do to keep from laughing. Big Roy's face was stormy. He moved again, placing himself in her path, and she laughed out loud this time. Grabbing her cowgirl's hand, she trotted to the bar and bought her own Heineken.

"Dyke," Big Roy said, his eyes fixed on her tail.

"Yeah," I said, hoping that agreement would calm him, that he would shake off the encounter. Myself, I didn't get that vibe from her at all. She and Cowgirl were tight, but they weren't like *that*, I didn't think.

When Pony Girl and Cowgirl exited the bar, doing a little skipping step, Big Roy wasn't too far behind. So I left, followed Big Roy as he followed those girls, wandering under the freeway, as if the whole thing were just a party put on for them. These girls were so full of themselves that they didn't even stop and pay respect to the Big Chiefs they passed, just breezed by as if they saw such men every day. The farther they walked, the more I worried. Big Roy was all but stalking them, but they never looked back, never seemed to have noticed. And Big Roy was so fixed on them that I didn't have to worry about him turning around and spotting me. Even so, I darted from strut to strut, keeping them in my sights. Night was falling.

They reached a car, a pale blue sedan—theirs, I guess—and it was only when I watched them trying to get into it that I began to think that the beers they had drunk had hit them awfully hard and fast. They weren't big girls, after all, and they hadn't eaten anything that I had seen. They giggled and stumbled, Cowgirl dropping her keys—Pony Girl didn't have no place to keep keys—their movements wavy and slow. The pavement around the car was filthy with litter, but that didn't stop Pony Girl from going down on her knees to look for the keys, sticking her tail high in the air. Even at that moment, I thought she had to know how enticing that tail was, how it called attention to itself.

It was then that Big Roy jumped on her. I don't know what he was thinking. Maybe he assumed Cowgirl would run off, screaming for help—and wouldn't find none for a while, because it took some time for screams to register on Mardi Gras day, to tell the difference between pleasure and fear. Maybe he thought rape could turn to sex, that if he just got started with Pony Girl, she'd like it. Maybe he meant to hurt them both, so it's hard to be sorry for what happened to him. I guess the best answer is that he wasn't thinking. This girl had made him angry, disrespected him, and he wanted some satisfaction for that.

But whatever Big Roy intended, I'm sure it played different in his head from what happened. Cowgirl jumped on his back, riding him, screaming and pulling at his hair. Pony Girl rolled away, bringing up those tiny boots and thrusting them at just the spot, so he was left gasping on all fours. They tell women to go for the eyes if they's fighting, not to count on hitting that sweet spot, but if you can get it, nothing's better. The girls had all the advantage they needed, all they had to do was find those keys and get out of there.

Instead, the girls attacked him again, rushing him, crazy bitches. They didn't know the man they were dealing with, the things he'd done just because he could. Yet Big Roy went down like one of those inflatable clowns you box with, except he never popped back up. He went down and . . . I've never quite figured out what I saw just then, other than blood. Was there a knife? I tell you, I like to think so. If there wasn't a knife, I don't want to contemplate how they did what they did to Big Roy. Truth be told, I turned my face away after seeing that first spurt of blood geyser into the air, the way they pressed their faces and mouths toward it like greedy children, as if it were a fire hydrant being opened on a hot day. I crouched down and prayed that they wouldn't see me, but I could still hear them. They laughed the whole time, a happy squealing sound. Again I thought of little kids playing, only this time at a party, whacking at one of those papier-mâché things. A piñata, that's what you call it. They took Big Roy apart as if he were a piñata.

Their laughter and the other sounds died away, and I dared to look again. Chests heaving, they were standing over what looked like a bloody mound of clothes. They seemed quite pleased with them-selves. To my amazement, Pony Girl peeled her leotard off then and there, so she was wearing nothing but the tights and the boots. She appeared to be starting on them as well, when she yelled out, in my direction: "What are you looking at?"

Behind the highway's strut, praying I couldn't be seen, I didn't say anything.

"Is this what you wanted to see?" She opened her arms a little, did a shimmying dance so her breasts bounced, and Cowgirl laughed. I stayed in my crouch, calculating how hard it would be to get back to where the crowds were, where I would be safe. I could outrun them easy. But if they got in the car and came after me, I wouldn't have much advantage.

The girls waited, as if they expected someone to come out and congratulate them. When I didn't emerge, they went through Big Roy's pockets, took the cash from his wallet. Once the body—if you could call it that—was picked clean of what little it had, Pony Girl popped the trunk of the car. She stripped the rest of the way, so she was briefly naked, a ghostly glow in the twilight. She stuffed her clothes, even her ears and her tail, in a garbage bag, then slipped on jeans, a T-shirt, and a pair of running shoes. Cowgirl didn't get all the way naked, but she put her red hat in the garbage bag, swapped her full skirt for a pair of shorts. They drove off, but not at all in a hurry. They drove with great deliberation, right over Big Roy's body—and right past me, waving as they went.

I suppose they's smart. I suppose they watch those television shows, know they need to get rid of every little scrap of clothing, that there's no saving anything, not even those pretty boots, if they don't want the crime to be traced back to them. I suppose they've done this before, or at least had planned it careful-like, given how prepared they were. I think they've done it since then, at least once or twice. At least, I've noticed the little stories in the *Times-Picayune* this year and last—a black man found dead on Mardi Gras day, pockets turned out. But the newspaper is scanty with the details of how the man got dead. Not shot, they say. A suspicious death, they say. But they don't say whether it was a beating or a cutting or a hot shot or what. Makes me think they don't know how to describe what's happened to these men. Don't know how, or don't feel it would be proper, given that people might be eating while they's reading.

Just like that, it's become another legend, a story that people tell to scare the little ones, like the skeletons showing up at the foot of your bed and saying you have to do your homework and mind your parents. There are these girls, white devils, go dancing on Mardi Gras, looking for black men to rob and kill. The way most people tell the story, the girls go out dressed as demons or witches, but if you think about it, that wouldn't play, would it? A man's not going to follow a demon or a witch into the night. But he might be lured into a dark place by a fairy princess, or a cat—or a Cowgirl and her slinky Pony Girl, with a swatch of horsehair pinned to the tailbone.

# PRAYERS FOR THE DYING

## A JOHN CUDDY STORY

*By Jeremiah Healy*

Jeremiah Healy, a graduate of Rutgers College and Harvard Law School, is the creator of the John Francis Cuddy private-investigator series and (under the pseudonym "Terry Devane") and the Mairead O'Clare legal-thriller series, both set primarily in Boston. Jerry has written eighteen novels and over sixty short stories, sixteen of which works have won or been nominated for the Shamus Award. He served a four-year term as the president of the International Association of Crime Writers (IACW), and he was the American Guest of Honour at the 35th World Mystery Convention (or "Bouchercon"—phonetically: "BOUGH-shur-con") in Toronto during October 2004. Currently he serves on the National Board of Directors for the Mystery Writers of America.

## ONE

"Mr. Cuddy, do you know what the expression 'intercessory prayer' means?"

I sat in a visitor's chair across the desk from Charles M. Shilas, M.D. Or, at least that was the name on the little oaken plaque screwed to his office door, like "John Francis Cuddy, Confidential Investigations," was stencilled onto the pebbled glass in my door a mile away toward downtown Boston. For all the credentials framed on the wall to his left, though, I thought my view of the Park Street subway station at the northeast corner of the Commons beat his pie-wedge one of the Charles River.

I said, " 'Intercessory' as in somehow intervening by prayer?"

"Exactly." Shilas leaned back in his chair. He was about six-one and big-boned, a grizzly bear my age plus-or-minus a couple of years. But the receding hairline made him seem older, and the craggy brow made him look sinister, though he'd as yet given me no reason to believe his character tended in that direction. "I'm directing a study in this hospital on whether people praying for cancer patients can actually affect the latter's ultimate outcomes."

It had been a while since I'd lost my wife, Beth, to a brain tumor, so, while I cringed, I hoped that by now the reaction stayed entirely internal. "I understand your words, Doctor, but I'm not sure I follow them."

"Fair enough." Shilas came forward in his chair. "A couple of years ago, there was an experiment that supposedly validated the following premise: If people in three countries prayed for women in a fourth country undergoing in-vitro fertilization, the females being prayed for were virtually *twice* as likely to become pregnant as otherwise similar women in the fourth country who were *not* prayed for."

The word I focused on was "supposedly."

"But the experiment really didn't prove the theory?"

"No. Worse, two of the study's authors were con men who used various aliases over their 'careers.' The fudging in the experiment also had grave consequences for a leading fertility specialist who involved himself in the research."

"Doctor, are you telling me there's a problem with your cancer/prayer experiment?"

Shilas leaned back again. Maybe, given his hulk, it was the only variation on "presence" he could use without being intimidating. "That's what I want you to find out."

Now Beth's last days started slipping from history into memory. "Since I don't have any background in science, much less medicine, I might not be your best candidate."

"On the contrary." Shilas opened a manila folder on his desk. "As it happens, we grew up within blocks of each other in South Boston."

Southie has gentrified now, but back then, it was a blue-collar to no-collar neighborhood, with a predominantly Irish-American demographic except for a section of Lithuanian-Americans. "And therefore?"

"And therefore, I know about your wife having died of cancer."

I forced courtesy to trump anger. "I don't enjoy being played like a hooked fish, Doctor."

"And that's the last thing I want to do as well." Shilas hooded his eyes, the effect—given the craggy brow—like watching two eyes inside the entrance to a cave. "But when I realized I needed an outside investigator, I wanted one whose bias on the issue was already established. So I knew what and whom I was dealing with."

I considered it. "You think your problem goes beyond just—what, sloppy record keeping?"

Shilas sighed, a truly resonant sound. "Our study is still very preliminary. But, so far it seems that prayer helps at approximately the rate of that fertility experiment."

I suppressed a whistle. "Twice as many patients have lived if they were being . . . prayed for?"

"Precisely. But I have my doubts."

No kidding. "What are they?"

"My assistant, Catherine O'Brien, is a fully licensed nurse, could make double her salary in that field. But her husband died of cancer, and she's committed—no, devoted—to our research."

"I don't hear that 'problem' so far."

"Our hospital director is virulently opposed to this study. We also have a Korean-American chaplain who is as actively supportive of intercessory prayer. And then there's Ruth Lantner."

"And she'd be . . . ?"

"A patient of mine—brain cancer—who, with her husband, Henry, raised the possibility of my launching this research in the first place."

"Forgive me, Doctor, but aside from internal debate among your colleagues, I still don't see the problem."

Shilas tilted back in his chair again. "I lost my father and his brother to cancer. Also my mother and two of her sisters. And one of my cousins has just been diagnosed."

An old proverb seemed to apply: I cried because I had no shoes until I met a man who had no feet.

"Mr. Cuddy, you can't swim away from your gene pool. If there is *any* chance that prayer, even by strangers, can help with cancer, I owe it to my own children to pursue the theory."

If I were a hooked fish, Shilas had just landed me. "Does something about your research data look wrong?"

"No. In fact, it looks almost too good."

"Then I'm lost again."

"A factor of one-hundred-percent differential between the survival rates of those cancer patients prayed for versus those not would be earth-shaking."

The light finally dawned on Marblehead. "Only you don't want to end up like the fertility-study authors."

"Exactly."

"So, you'd like me to . . . ?"

"Speak with the people I've mentioned, using an objective, non-medical approach." Dr. Charles M. Shilas came forward, twisting his huge hands in a way that made me glad mine weren't between them. "Tell me whether I'm looking at a Nobel Prize, or an expose in *People* magazine."

## TWO

"So, Mr. Cuddy, how can I be helping you?"

Shilas had introduced me to Catherine O'Brien in her cubicle down the hall from his own, enclosed office. After she rolled over another chair from an adjacent, empty cubicle, we both sat down, less than four feet apart. O'Brien was about thirty-five, angular rather than slim, with dusty red hair, a smile you could read by, and a brogue you could hug.

I said, "Dr. Shilas tells me you're administering the intercessory-prayer study involving his cancer patients."

"Yes, but they don't all belong to Chuck."

Chuck: Informality reigns. "Whose are they, then?"

"Well, even a busy, cutting-edge oncologist might not have enough patients in his own practice for a large study. So, the ones in ours come from a slew of different doctors."

"Can you explain how the study works?"

"Easily enough, I think." O'Brien's hands flapped open. "Picture if you will two groups of patients, identical as possible in their representing a cross-section of the community."

"The community of cancer patients?"

"Ah, no. No, I mean more a parallel demographic. In each group, we have men and women, old and young, advanced and incipient. To know whether the prayer could work, you see, we need two groups as internally diverse as possible, but as externally identical to each other as possible, too."

I got my mind around that. "So, the two parallel groups, receiving the same medical care, one group is 'prayed' for, and the other—"

"—the control group—

"—isn't?"

O'Brien's dazzling smile somehow grew even brighter. "Bang on. Technically, we call it a 'prospective, double-blind, randomized clinical trial.' Layman's language: Neither the patients in the two groups, nor their doctors, know who the outsiders are praying for. Chuck and I have been at it for just five months so far, but the results are nothing short of amazing."

"Dr. Shilas also told me some colleagues here at the hospital are decidedly in one of two camps, either supporting the research or opposing it."

"Chuck's on the mark there, too. As he is about most things."

"You have any suggestions on who I should talk to next?"

O'Brien paused, and you could see a bit of the devil in her, as an Irish aunt of mine used to say. "I'd start at the top, at least as far as *he's* concerned."

I asked Catherine O'Brien if she could compile a list of the staffers on duty during the times when each of the 'control group' patients died.

"Give me an hour, then, and meanwhile, good day to you, sir."

"Doctor Mongrinni, Mr. Cuddy."

The hospital's director rose from his chair, acknowledging his receptionist with barely a flick of his hand. Short and dapper, Louis Mongrinni struck me more as a lawyer than a doctor, a well-dressed peregrine falcon with short, curly hair moussed an inch down his forehead. Then I glanced up at his wall of frames, and, lo and behold, there was a law degree from Boston University next to his medical diplomas and above a shelf of golfing trophies.

"Mr. Cuddy," said Mongrinni, sitting back down after his departing receptionist had closed the door, "you look old enough to remember Andy Warhol."

Somehow, Mongrinni didn't. "Yes."

"And therefore his prediction that, in the future, each person would have his or her 'fifteen minutes of fame'?"

"I remember that, too."

"Well, my view differs. Call it 'Mongrinni's Corollary.' "

No ego in this boy. "Which is?"

"Everybody I'm *not* interested in whatsoever gets no more than *ten* minutes of access time with me."

"Meaning, I'm down to nine already."

"And fading fast."

Best cut to the car chase, then. "You're aware of Dr. Shilas and his 'intercessory prayer' study."

"Aware? I've demanded weekly updates from the horse's mouth."

"And?"

"Mr. Cuddy, Chuck cleared his hiring of you with me. I think he's doing the right thing. Not by that hair-brained research, but by his being skeptical of its preliminary results."

Just "Chuck" again. "Those results sounded pretty impressive."

Mongrinni shook his head, but the Julius Caesar hairdo didn't budge. "Mr. Cuddy, cancer is a disease, not an . . . attitude. Patients can't just toss off a tumor off like," he waved at his golf trophies, "a bad day on the back nine."

"Even when other people are praying for them?"

Mongrinni tented his fingers on the desktop. "*If* the patient knew folk were on bended knee every night invoking their version of the Almighty, then maybe—*maybe*—there'd be more of a spirit in him or her to fight, to persevere. But that's the very *point* of Chuck's thesis: The patients can*not* know they're in the 'blessed' half, or his experiment, however questionable to start with, would become irrevocably tainted."

"Dr. Shilas gave me the impression you don't support his work."

"Mr. Cuddy, I support *any* project, however crackpot, that brings research grants to this institution." A pause. "Did Chuck tell you about his . . . family tree."

"He did."

"Well, then, where I differ with him is his pursuit of whacko ideas as a hopeful advocate rather than a skeptical scientist. And especially theories whose own course of research isn't yet completed."

"You're an atheist, then?"

"More an agnostic. And a rather tolerant one. But I will not let Chuck release his 'findings'—even to the popular media—in a way that will make this hospital a laughing stock."

"Basically, you don't buy his 'intercession by prayer' concept, period."

"Basically, I think it's nonsense. But, stop and think: If I *were* going to submarine Chuck's study, wouldn't I be killing the patients who *were* prayed for, instead of the ones who were not?"

Try as I might, I couldn't recall bringing up the possibility of homicidal intervention with the good Dr. Louis Mongrinni.

"And you must be Chuck's private eye."

As I shook hands with Lee Chan Park, I decided everybody in the hospital called Shilas by his nickname. Park was about thirty, no more than five-seven and spare, with a cowlick of unruly black hair that didn't look as though axle grease could tame it. The color of his glass frames matched the slanted eyes behind the lenses, but there were flashes of fire in his pupils.

We began to create a logjam in the busy corridor. I said, "There some place we can talk?"

"My office. Just off the chapel."

When he reached the chapel, though, it was empty, and Park said, "Do you mind if we sit in here?"

"No."

We took the same pew, leaving the equivalent of a seat between us.

Park looked around the small enclosure. "I like to spend as much time in this chapel as I can. It gives me the sense of what the patients' families might be going through. Kind of a last room they've occupied as opposed to a last meal they've eaten?"

"You sound like a C.S.I. techie."

A laugh, but good-natured, even jubilant. "Actually, my major in college was to be Criminal Justice, but fortunately my university had a Divinity School, too, and I transferred over to it."

"And you enjoy your work here at the hospital?"

" 'Enjoy?' " Park seemed to mull that. "Well, I find it fulfilling. In the extreme. But my days and nights are often difficult. So many of our doctors call them 'patients,' naturally, but I think of them more as children." A hand came up in a stop sign. "I know that's kind of patronizing, because I'm less than half the age of most. Only that's how I really *do* feel: As though they are sick children that I can help spiritually, if not physically."

"Physically, meaning . . . medically?"

"Meaning, I'm not sure." Park gave the impression of recalibrating. "I think there really *are* positives to approaching an illness beyond surgery and drugs."

"The power of prayer, for example?"

"Now you've returned to being Chuck's private eye, right?" Park shrugged. "I really do hope he's right, you know? If prayer could be proved to work . . . well, 'miracles,' I—and every other cleric I know—would feel pretty validated."

"Now you sound unsure of Dr. Shilas's study?"

"No, just that I can't ethically become involved in it."

"I don't follow you."

Park took a deep breath, let it out slowly. "I can't just pray for one group, and then *not* for Chuck's control group."

"So, you don't pray for either?"

"No, Mr. Cuddy," said Chan Lee Park, leveling as steady a gaze at me as I've ever experienced. "I pray for both, even if—theoretically—that could wreck the experiment itself."

## THREE

Clients, like Dr. Charles M. Shilas, come and go. As do, at least in Boston, restaurants and night clubs. But some places remain depressingly permanent.

Cemeteries, for example.

I moved down the row of stones to hers, engraved "ELIZABETH MARY DEVLIN CUDDY," the letters fading a bit due to weathering, but the birth and death dates never, ever changing.

*John? You seem troubled.*

I nodded, then explained the matter I'd been asked to investigate.

*Well, it is cancer, but it's not MY cancer.*

I nodded again. "Except my next stop, at least so far as I can see, is a woman suffering from a brain tumor."

*I'm truly sorry. Can you somehow "duck" the interview?*

"Not and do my job."

*I didn't think so, and I wouldn't wish so.*

"No offense, Beth, but easy for you to say."

It was leagues worse than I imagined.

When my wife was dying, the methods of prolonging life were more . . . primitive, maybe? A few tubes and machines, the latter seeming to perform only one task each. Kind of a medical-science string quartet.

Ruth Lantner, on the other hand, was hooked up to a symphony orchestra.

Hard to guess the age of someone so far into the illness, but if she looked seventy, her husband, who introduced himself as "Henry," appeared a decade older. That's the problem with cancer, though, for the patient or the spouse: It's less the years and more the mileage that devastates both.

"Mr. Cuddy," said Ruth, tapping an index finger against the sheet covering her.

"Mrs. Lantner, I'm trying to help Dr. Shilas with his study findings."

"I'm sure that if Chuck hired you . . . I can trust you."

The nickname barely registered this time, it was so obviously difficult for her to speak.

Belatedly, I thought, Henry Lantner said, "I trust you, too, Mr. Cuddy. What do you want to know?"

"Mrs.—"

"Ruth, please. It's . . . faster. And I'll call you 'John.' "

Beth'd said something so similar to one of her doctors that I had to swallow once before continuing. "Other people have implied that you were the inspiration for the 'intercessory prayer' experiment."

"Only because I . . . thought of it first."

"How?"

Henry stepped in. "Ruth and I have belonged to the same congregation for thirty-eight years. Our rabbi asked other members to pray for those in jeopardy, but the gist of his message was only—what's the word, Sweetie?"

"Haphazardly."

"Right, right. 'Haphazardly.' " Henry turned to me. "Ruth was an English teacher, forty years, ever since we got married." Henry cleared his throat. "She thought, maybe there was a way to prove somehow that prayer helped. And not just Jewish prayers for Jewish patients, but more—like, in general?"

I said, "And Dr. Shilas was willing to give that possiblity a try."

"Yes," from Ruth, more a wheeze than a word. "And Chuck told me that . . . so far, it's working."

Henry hung his head. "But not . . . I mean, not in every case."

I wasn't sure I could bear to be with them too much longer, extending their anguish with questions that bothered me nearly as much as the Lantners. "Any reason you can think of why the experiment might be going awry?"

"Awry?" said Henry, obviously stunned.

"John," Ruth using her fingers to squinch the top sheet toward her, "that's not something . . . Henry and I . . . dwell on."

Feeling my own heart tearing in the middle, I thanked them for their time, and wished them the best of luck.


Catherine O'Brien, Shilas's assistant, had compiled the shift-work details on everyone involved with the study. I went through the Human Resources print-outs once quickly, then again more slowly, comparing them to the fatality records of the two groups of patients. By my count, the preliminary findings of a two-to-one ratio of deaths was born out: If you were prayed for, you had twice the chance of survival of someone in the control group.

But then I began to correlate for who had been working on the nights that control group patients died. And there were some anomalies.

I'm sure a computer itself could have done the scut work faster, but I came to a pretty unshakeable conclusion. One I'd have to check out, though, with the person evidently—and, perhaps, ultimately—responsible.

## FOUR

"Dr. Shilas? A moment of your time?"

The physician's quick glance at a wrist watch that wouldn't allow him any leisure. "I really have to be—"

"Actually, not a moment, but more like ten minutes. And I think it will be worth your while."

Another—now defeated—glance at that watch before, "Very well."

"I understand you prefer to go by '*Doctor* Park.' "

A sheepish grin and shrug. "Doctor of divinity, not medicine. But sometimes it's easier on the patients."

Or helps to deceive them. "Could we have another word? Privately?"

"Let's try the chapel again, see if—"

"No, I think this time your office would be a better choice."

A frown, but if you weren't staring at him, you might not have noticed, so quickly did he replace it with another grin.

Once inside his office, we sat simultaneously. "So," Park rolling his head on his neck, "how can I help you now?"

"I've checked some of the records. It seems that every time a patient in Dr. Shilas's study dies, you're there."

"Of course I am."

" 'Of course?' "

That jubilant laugh again. "Mr. Cuddy, I'm the chaplain. I tend to my—I already told you I think of them as 'children,' correct?"

Deadpan, I said, "Correct."

"So, it's my duty—and calling—to be at the bedside when a given patient is failing."

"And how do you know *to* be there?"

Another shrug. "How do you think?"


"Mr. Cuddy. Will you be needing any more print-outs?"

"No, Ms. O'Brien. But maybe some more answers."

Catherine O'Brien closed her eyes briefly, then bade me to roll over that chair from the adjacent, empty cubicle.

Sitting, I said, "The staff records show that Dr. Park attended every death, in both groups of Dr. Shilas's patients."

A tick-tocking of the head. "That's possible, I suppose. But I don't see how that means much, as I would be there, too."

"Yes," I said. "Yes, you would. And were."

She unclipped a little device from the belt of her skirt. "We all do carry pagers, Mr. Cuddy."

"And if I were to check the pager records, would I find you were always paged for the 'prayer' group, but never for the 'control' one."

O'Brien closed her eyes again. "You don't know what it's like to lose a spouse to cancer."

"As it happens, I do."

The eyes came open like old-fashioned window shades, snapping onto their spindles. "I . . . I didn't . . . know."

"You prayed long and hard for your husband's recovery."

"Absolutely."

"Me, too. For my wife's. It didn't help either of them, did it?"

"If you mean, provide a 'cure,' then no."

"But it did 'help' them?"

"My husband, yes. He was a devout Catholic, Mr. Cuddy. He believed that what I was doing *could* help him. Not with the pain, no. But with the hope, the spirit to keep holding on, maybe until there *was* a cure."

"And the people in the . . . 'control group?' "

"They weren't being prayed for."

"By definition."

A violent shaking of her head. "Not what I mean. Without someone praying for them, what hope did they have? For God's sake, why not end their suffering when there was no chance a cure by prayer would alleviate their condition."

"And, as a nurse, you had access to 'alleviating' drugs."

"Yes. Don't you see?" O'Brien locked onto my eyes. "I gave the poor souls in the control group enough pain-killers to ease their passing. Now then, that's hardly a crime, is it?"

"I'm afraid the authorities believe otherwise."

"Well," Catherine O'Brien straightening in her chair like a defiant schoolgirl before an authoritarian priest, "It shouldn't be now, should it?"

# DEVIL DOG
*By Dick Lochte*

Dick Lochte's popular crime novels include his most recent, *Croaked!*; *Sleeping Dog*, which won the Nero Wolfe Award, was nominated for the Edgar, the Shamus, and the Anthony, and was named one of the 100 Favorite Mysteries of the Century by the Independent Booksellers Association. His column, Mysteries, appeared bimonthly for nearly a decade in the *Los Angeles Times*, earning him the 2003 Ellen Nehr Award for Excellence in Mystery Reviewing. Lochte, who lives in Southern California with his wife and son, is also an award-winning drama critic and has written screenplays for such actors as Jodie Foster, Martin Sheen, and Roger Moore.

T hat Tuesday morning, I was parked along a quiet oak-lined residential street in West L.A., sipping a tall cup of good but over-priced black coffee, the earbuds of a tiny MP3 player firmly in place, listening to Dinah Shore singing the Johnny Mercer classic "Blues in the Night," a rendition so heartfelt it never fails to send a chill down my spine. Not coincidentally, I was also keeping a half-lidded eye on a Spanish-style bungalow a few lots away.

It was a comfortable-looking house, nestled in shrubbery and separated from the tree-buckled sidewalk by a well-tended lawn. It had been painted recently: ivory-colored stucco with a red front door and shutters that sort of matched the faded red-tile roof. I was appreciating the music and speculating on how much paint my place would take when Joe Addis finally decided to greet the day and get mobile.

The guy was built like a speed swimmer, tall, thin-waisted with broad shoulders and a small head that he shaved to the scalp. Where the swimmer look fell apart was a black mustache-and-beard combo bushy enough to slow Aquaman down to a crawl. The beard surrounded a face with close-set eyes separated by a nose long enough to get in the soup. He was wearing what passed for business garb in L.A.: Ray-Bans, baggy denims, and a dark full-cut jacket over a black T-shirt.

Before he could shut his front door, a fierce-looking cocoa brown mastiff tried to leave with him. The mutt was weirdly silent while Addis used his right leg to push him into the bungalow and slam the front door on him. You can bet I made mental note of the dog.

My name is Leo Bloodworth, sole proprietor of the Bloodworth Detective Agency, in business in scenic downtown Los Angeles continuously since 1982. I was on Addis at the behest of the television personality Pierre Reynaldo. I assume you're familiar with Pierre since he's all over cable news day and night, hobnobbing with actors, politicians, and other sociopaths, and hosting specials of a spectacular if not always genuine nature. Wavy black hair. Swarthy but clean-shaven. Wears bow ties and bright suits and a smug expression that any right-thinking viewer would want to personally slap into sadness.

In recent years there's been a fine line separating television news from bullshit. Pierre has more or less erased that line—and grown rich doing it. He lost some of his loot in a libel suit a few years back, and since then, he's thrown a few bucks my way to check out information coming from less than reliable sources.

He was hoping to use most of the current questionable material in a special on Satanism in Southern California (tentatively titled "The Devil in Paradise"). So far, I'd spent the better part of a week doing follow-ups, with less than positive results. The surfer dude who'd claimed to have seen Beelzebub and a dozen of his minions hanging ten at Rincon wasn't sure if the vision had occurred just before or just after he'd chased a fifth of Jack Black with a crack cooler. The pharmacist in Redondo Beach who'd been arrested, according to one news report, for engaging in Satanic practices, turned out to be nothing more than a twisted horndog who'd been supplying his female customers with birth control, diet, and pain pills in return for them letting him kiss and lick their feet. The Prince of Darkness aspect had been his insistence on bathing those feet in something he called Lucifer Lotion, a combination of vanilla extract and codeine cough syrup.

Such was the state of devil worship in our corner of paradise.

This was not the sort of reality Pierre wanted. He took that report in, scowled, threw an air punch that was about as sincere as one of his editorials, and said, "That leaves us with the Addis asshole."

According to one of his cop sources, a neighbor of Joe Addis had called in a complaint that she had observed him and others prowling around his place wearing black robes and hoods, mumbojumboing. It was not something the police rushed to investigate, the practice of one's religion in one's home not being a crime just yet. And the woman, who called herself J. Roberts, was a frequent complainer—usually about loud parties past curfew and other "sinful" acts. Still, a uniform had been sent out. He'd reported back that though Addis had a "thick accent of some kind," had seemed "a little flaky," and had "one big mother of a dog," he saw no evidence in or around the premises of "devil worshipry."

That satisfied the law, but not our Pierre, who was growing more and more desperate for evidence that Satan was still alive and well. "Okay, Leo," he said, "it's up to you, amigo. Make this very special show happen. Bring me something I can use. Money is no object."

Those magic words I don't hear every day. I told him I would do my best.

My first move had been a visit to J. Roberts, who lived next door to Addis in a bungalow evidently designed by the same architectural hand as his. But she wasn't quite as house-proud. While his lawn looked nice and neat, hers was sprinkled with patches of uncut grass that resembled an alopecia victim's scalp. The bungalow needed a few coats of paint and some serious rescreening.

The woman who answered the door could have used a little upkeep, too. She was tall and lanky, with watery brown eyes and dull brown hair combed with fingers if at all. She was wearing rumpled faded-blue bib overalls over an aqua-green T-shirt that, as far as I could read around the bib, invited all to "Feel the Rapture." She wore no lipstick, no makeup of any kind. But there was enough red paint left on the toenails of her sandaled feet to suggest there had been a time when she might have cared about such things.

"Miz Roberts?"

"Yes?" Something fat and furry scooted across the hardwood floor and wound itself around her ankles. A yellow and white tabby, much better kempt than its owner, who was too engaged in giving me the fish-eye to respond to its arrival.

I told her my name and that I'd like to talk with her about Joseph Addis's suspicious behavior. I did not identify myself as a member of the LAPD, but I did nothing to discourage her from that assumption.

"I got the impression you cops figured I was fantasizin' about him calling up the Devil," she said, more weary than angry. "Like there's no evidence of his Satanic presence over there in Iraq, either."

She noticed the furry critter, scooped up the cat in one bony arm and stood with it licking her chin. "She's my widdle girl, Sheba is," J. Roberts said, rubbing her cheek against the cat's. "Just won't leave her mommy alone."

Her large brown eyes shifted to me, suddenly suspicious. "Something happen to change your mind about Addis?"

"My mind is like Ralph's supermarket," I said, "always open. I read your statement and I was hoping I could ask you a little more about what you saw."

"Why not?" She moved aside to let me enter a small, surprisingly neat living room. The walls were bare except for a large framed portrait of Jesus Christ hanging over the mantle.

"C'mon back to the kitchen," she said. "Lemme sign off."

The kitchen smelled of coffee and toast. It seemed to be the hub of the house. Its pale green linoleum was worn in spots near the entryway and beside the sink where a dishwasher thrummed. A wooden table occupied the center of the room, places set for two diners. There were three wooden chairs.

The fourth was supporting J. Roberts, who sat at a small table against one wall, still holding the cat in one arm while using her free hand to peck at the keyboard of a computer. She was signing off from a website that identified itself as The Truth-Seeker Network.

"With you in a minute," she said. "Coffee's on the stove, if any's left. Cups in the cabinet."

The electric range was from the '50, squat, square, with burners on either side of a cooktop. It triggered a faint, pleasant, youthful memory that I didn't bother to pursue. A ceramic coffeepot rested on one cold burner.

I found a cup, poured a couple of inches of thick black tepid coffee and took it to a place at the table that had not been set for dinner.

A gauzy white curtain with three green stripes at the bottom was doing its best to minimize glare near the computer. Its mates were all open, brightening the room and giving me a clear view of Joe Addis's bungalow and rear yard. No activity visible.

In a few seconds, J. Roberts joined me, dragging her chair over. The cat was on its own, lapping at something gooey in a white plastic bowl on the linoleum floor near the sink. I made a big thing of removing the MP3 player from my pocket and pressing its side, as if I had a clue how to record what she was about to tell me. The fact was, it took the kid who gave me the gizmo for my birthday nearly an hour to show me how to plug it into the office computer and transfer my songs onto it. Neither she nor I had been all that anxious to explore its other uses, like recording conversations.

"Fancy," J. Roberts said, squinting at the tiny silver device.

"I'm a big believer in using the latest technology," I said. "Why don't you tell me what you saw that night over at Addis's?"

She wrinkled her nose. "Man's unholy. Him and his devil dog."

"I'm sorry. What?"

"That giant dog of his. I'm sure he uses it in his black arts. Never barks. Never makes a sound. Unnatural." She shivered. "A few weeks ago, the devil dog was in our back yard, digging up my vegetables. Don't know how he got past the fence. Barry went and told the freak to take care of his animal or he'd shoot it. Barry would, too. Barry's like me. We're cat people. Got no feeling for dogs, whatsoever."

"Barry's your husband?"

"Baby brother," she said. "I never married. Took care of my sainted father till he passed away, must be nine years. Take care of Barry now."

"Can you tell me exactly what you witnessed Joseph Addis doing the night you mentioned in your complaint?"

"I'll do better than that." She got up and went to the smaller table where she punched a few computer keys. Eventually, the printer beside the computer spit out a sheet of paper.

"I keep a diary," she said, handing me the sheet.

The excerpt was from a Saturday, three weeks before. At approximately 10 P.M., Roberts and her brother, Barry, had observed Addis and two other men, all dressed in black robes, moving through the bungalow next door. Eventually, the lights had been turned off in the bungalow, replaced by the glow of candles.

"That seemed curious behavior to me and Barry," she wrote. "So we went outside and stood by the fence out there where we could hear better. Addis and his unholy brethren were speaking in the profane language of Satan. This is too much for good Christians to abide."

The diary entry ended there.

"I'm not sure I understand what you mean by 'language of Satan'," I said. "What were they saying, exactly?"

"It would take one of Satan's followers to decipher it," she said. "And Addis had this shiny thing he was waving around, some kind of weapon. The other two sinners were on their knees, babbling like crazy men in that devil language."

"Then what happened?" I asked.

"They just kept on doing that."

"Umm," I said. "No blood, chickens with their heads chopped off?"

"There was nothing like that. You mocking me?"

"No, ma'am," I said. I was a bit let down, getting a mental image of Pierre Reynaldo's wallet being folded and put back into his pocket.

"I do have something I didn't have when I went to the station," she said. "From last week. I took them with a new little camera they gave Barry at the studio. He builds sets and they needed something done in a rush, so he spent his own time last weekend and they gave him a camera."

She played with the keyboard some more and the printer spun out another sheet. This one contained six color snapshots of Addis wandering in his rear yard with his dog. He was wearing a long black robe and a scowl and seemed more than ready to summon up dark deeds.

"Well? Does that look like a son of Satan, or what?"

"Could I keep this?" I asked, thinking that it would definitely be something Pierre would want to see.

Before she could reply, we heard the front door open and a male voice say, "Yo, Jules, I'm home early. McGuire's back got hurting him, so they closed down for the day and sent every—who the heck is this?"

He was a guy about my size, six-two or -three, maybe a pound or two lighter and twenty-five years younger. Same dull brown hair as his sister. A couple of days' growth of beard. Wearing a khaki cap, bill backwards, a paint-stained brown workshirt, denims that were powdered with sawdust, a utility belt weighed down on the right by a ball-peen hammer, and pale brown boots that were made for stompin'.

"This is Detective Bloodworth, Barry," his sister said. "It's about the Unholy."

"Detective, huh?" He scowled at me. "He show you a badge?"

"No, he didn't."

"I don't carry a badge," I said, folding the print-outs and shoving them and my MP3 player into a pocket. "I'm a private investigator."

Barry Roberts took a threatening step toward me. "Why you bothering my sister, Jack?" he asked, right hand resting on the hammer hanging from his belt. "You pay him any money, Jules?"

"N-no."

"And you're not gonna," he said. "Get moving, Jack. I see you around here again, you're gonna feel my boot up your be-hind."

Pierre Reynaldo was encouraged by the photos of Addis in basic black. "I smell success, Leo," he said. "Get me more."

And that's why I was in my car, waiting, when the bearded and bald Mr. Addis slid into a battered white Yugo and took off in a plume of exhaust thick enough to send the clean-air arrow into the red zone.

I quickly finished the pricey coffee, and when the Yugo was halfway down the block brought the Chevy to life. I exchanged the car radio for the MP3 player, since the batteries don't last forever and I hate to get stuck on a stake-out with only my thoughts to occupy my time.

The Yugo took me on a journey from West Los Angeles through the morning traffic along Wilshire to Fairfax, then over to Holly-wood Boulevard, finally coming to rest in an empty metered space along Vine.

I drove past, then pulled to the curb and watched the subject in the rearview. When he entered the Good Life, a flash bar a few doors down from Hollywood Boulevard, I turned off the engine and bought a temporary piece of the street, too.

Then I tucked the earbuds into place and fired up the MP3 player.

The temperature was still in the low eighties and it was pleasant sitting there, listening to Frank Sinatra singing the bejeezus out of the Mercer tune "Midnight Sun," self-amused to be doing so in the shadow of the Capitol Records building, which the composer had built and the singer's albums had helped to finance.

After another three or four Mercer tunes, I got a little curious about what Addis was up to. I locked the headset and player in the glove compartment and headed for the Good Life.

It was cool and dark inside. A sound system was turned down so low the music was more like white noise. When my eyes adjusted to the change from daylight, I was looking at a barroom of moderate size, all black and chrome, black-and-white photos on the walls of performers like Elvis and the Rolling Stones. The small tables and chairs looked sad and empty. To my right was an onyx bar with the silver outline of a martini glass visible through the stools. Behind the bar was a long mirror and above the mirror a sign spelling out in cursive blue neon: "It's Martooni Teem."

At the far end of the room was another blue neon sign over an arched portal. This one read: "Club Caviar." It was accompanied by a blue neon arrow pointing up.

There were three men in the room, none of them Addis. They looked like brothers. Big beefy boys in their late twenties to early thirties, curly black hair, ugly as gargoyles, skin the color and texture of partially mashed potatoes. Dressed alike in white shirts and black trousers.

The oldest was behind the bar. He headed my way with a pasted-on smile. "Yes, sir. What you have? Apple martini?" He had a Slavic accent.

Trying not to think too much about how awful an apple martini might taste, I asked, "You the manager?"

"Sure, I'm manager," he said, prompting a snicker from one of the others. "So?"

"Douglas Furshaddle," I said, offering my hand.

"So?" he repeated, ignoring my hand.

"I represent the CNCV," I said.

"The what?"

"The Council of Northern California Vintners. I've been visiting some of the better clubs in the Hollywood area, telling them about our champagne and—"

"Not interested," he said.

"But if you have just a minute or two . . ." I continued to scan the room, trying to figure out where Addis had gone and what might have drawn him there. Probably not apple martinis.

"You don't hear so good." The bartender reached for something under the bar. It looked like a kid's baseball bat.

"Whoa, at ease, Vlad," the youngest of the three said without a trace of an accent. "As you can probably tell, my brother isn't who you want to talk to. Our father deals with salesmen."

"Great," I said. "Is he here?"

The young man glanced back at the arched doorway. "He's busy," he said. "Come back later."

"Will do," I said and turned to go.

"Hold on a minute," the third man said. "You say California champagne?"

I nodded.

"Don't bother to come back," he said without any emotion. "Our customers don't go for domestic."

"They would be if they tried our champagne," I said.

"Good-bye, Mr. Furshaddle. Peddle your pisswater elsewhere."

Addis lived The Good Life for another twenty minutes. When he exited, he was followed by a stocky, gray-haired man who was patting him on the back and grinning like a monkey.

Addis returned the smile, said something, and the two men hugged.

The old man went back inside the club. Addis watched him go, then headed for the parked Yugo. He was no longer smiling. In fact, he looked troubled.

I kept some distance between us as I trailed him back to his bungalow. He went inside. I waited for a few minutes to make sure he was settled before daring to drive to the nearest gas station washroom to get rid of the aftereffects of the coffee I'd been drinking all morning.

I'd returned the washroom key to the cashier and was heading for the Chevy when a pretty, very dark-skinned woman in a business suit fell in beside me. "Hi," she said.

"Hi," I replied. "Nice day, huh?"

"Could go either way," she said.

We arrived at the Chevy. She seemed to have something on her mind.

"Can I help you?" I asked.

"Maybe," she said. She opened the rear door and slid in.

"Hey," I said. "What's going on?"

I realized then that another woman was already in the car, on the passenger seat. This one was white and not so pretty. She was holding a .45 in her left hand, pointing it at my chest. "Get in, Mr. Bloodworth."

With a sigh, I slid behind the wheel and closed the door. "What now, ladies?"

"Place both hands on the steering wheel, Mr. Bloodworth," the woman with the gun said.

The black woman leaned forward and reached over my shoulders to prod my chest for a weapon that wasn't there. I could have headbutted her, but her white sister would have shot me dead and then where would I be.

"No weapon," I said.

The white woman slid closer, jammed the gun in my ribs and felt around my waist, then down my legs. "Clean," she said. She rested the gun hand on her lap, the barrel pointed away. I took that to be a gesture of trust, so I relaxed a little.

"What are you up to, Mr. Bloodworth?" the black woman asked.

Locking eyes with her in the rearview mirror, I said, "You first."

"Fair enough," she said. "We work for the government."

"Oh, please don't tell me Homeland Security," I said.

The white woman chuckled. "No need to get offensive," she said. Her free hand slipped inside her jacket and withdrew a leather folder.

She flipped it open, exposing a colorful shield on which a goose took flight against a bright rising sun and a whale leapt from the sea.

"You ladies are with Fish and Wildlife Service?" I asked, not quite believing it.

"F & WS, Division of Law Enforcement," the black woman said. "I'm Agent Andrews from Division One in Portland. Agent Calabrese is from the local office in Torrance. Joseph Addis is assisting us in an investigation. So, why are you following him?"

"Since you know who I am—from my license plate, I'm guessing—you probably know how I earn a living."

"Are you working for the Sogorskys?" Agent Calabrese asked.

"Never heard of 'em," I said.

"Wrong answer," Agent Calabrese said, covering me again with her weapon.

"Are they part of the men-in-black crew?" I asked.

"The men in black?" Agent Calabrese said. "You mean from the church?"

"Is that what they call it? A church?"

"What else?" Agent Andrews asked.

"I don't know," I said. "Do Satan worshipers have churches?"

The two agents exchanged glances. Then Calabrese started making a sound like a kid imitating a machine gun. Her version of laughter.

Andrews kept her amusement down to a crooked smile. "You think Joseph Addis is a Satanist?" she asked.

"That's what I'm trying to find out," I said. "He and some other guys have been seen running around his house wearing these black outfits, mumbling incantations."

Calabrese was shaking her head. She had tears in her eyes. "He can't be making it up," she said.

"You've been following the man because you think he's got this black mass thing going?" Andrews asked. "You interested in selling your soul or something?"

I wondered if that's what I was doing, working for Pierre Reynaldo. I said, "No. I'm gathering material on devil worship in Southern California. So I'm following up a tip I got on Addis."

"This guy is priceless," Calabrese said between ack-ack-acks.

Andrews was no longer even slightly amused. "An hour ago, we saw you go into the Good Life. What were you doing in there?"

"Addis was inside there awhile. I got curious about what was going on."

"What *was* going on?" Andrews asked.

I told her about the three guys in the bar who looked like brothers; that Addis was probably upstairs in a room they call the Caviar Club, talking with the owner; that a few minutes after I left the club, Addis showed up on the sidewalk with an old guy that I assumed was the club owner.

"I'm guessing they're the Sogorskys?" I said. I was hoping for a confirmation or a denial, but I got neither.

"We've wasted enough time here," Andrews said to her partner. "For the record, Mr. Bloodworth, Joseph Addis is not a devil worshiper. Quite the contrary. So strike him from your list of things to do. If I see you anywhere near him again, I guarantee you will wind up in a small steel-and-cement room for a long, long time. Am I clear?"

"Like crystal," I said.

I watched the two agents march to a black Infiniti and take their leave with a squeal of tires.

Then I started my engine and, driving a bit slower than they, headed to Pierre with the bad news.

His reaction surprised me. Instead of shouting or throwing a fit, as he'd done in similar situations, he just sat behind his massive black oak desk, lost in thought.

A couple of minutes of that and he shouted for his assistant, Luna, a handsome Latina with a steel-trap mind I would put up there with Stephen Hawking's. "See what you can find on the name 'Sogorsky' and the Good Life bar on Vine Street," he told her.

He watched Luna depart, then said, "She hates me, you know."

"Doesn't everybody?" I said.

He laughed.

"I didn't think you'd be so cheery about losing another devil worshiper," I said.

"I'm getting a feeling this might be just as good. I sense something . . . unique. Fish and Wildlife. What's their franchise, anyway?"

"I think they go after bear hunters," I said. "Fish poachers."

"What do you suppose they're doing with our Addis?" he asked.

In just a few minutes, Luna brought us the answer in the form of hard copies of Internet info. One set for Pierre, one for me.

"You get the picture, Leo?" Pierre asked when we'd finished perusing the pages.

I told him I did.

Luna made it clear enough. First, there were copies of a "sogorsky.com" website announcing to the world that they, Russian nationals all, in addition to having "one of the nation's most popular nightclubs, located at the historic crossroads of Hollywood and Vine," were "among the Pacific Southwest's leading importers of smoked salmon, foie gras, and truffles."

There were newspaper accounts concerning the threat of sturgeon extinction leading to a recent worldwide ban on wild-caviar production. And, clever lady that she is, Luna added a news item about the president of an import company in Miami being convicted of smuggling the salty eggs into this country. The investigation had been conducted by the U.S. Fish and Wildlife Services Law Enforcement Division in conjunction with U.S. Customs and the Food and Drug Administration.

Pierre wiggled his eyebrows, his indication of extreme interest. "The Sogorskys are smuggling caviar," he said. "And this Addis jamoke is somehow involved."

"I think you'll find the answer to that on page four," I said.

He flipped to the page. "Russian Orthodox Church . . . problems with funding." He scanned the article. "I didn't bother reading . . . oh, I dig, the caviar thing again."

The news item started out by explaining that perestroika had put a lot of Russian Orthodox churches back into operation without providing the funding to keep them going. So some church officials eventually felt the need to get in bed with questionable "donors."

The article took its own sweet time getting to the current news: thirty-two Russian priests were accusing the very powerful bishop of a diocese along the Ural of an assortment of moral and legal failings stemming from way back at the start of perestroika. Among them was his cooperation with a gang of caviar poachers whom he'd given a free pass to cast their nets into the diocesan waters.

"And I should be interested in this because . . . ?" Pierre asked.

"Agent Andrews told me that Addis was helping them. She also said he was the opposite of a Satan worshipper. He speaks with a thick accent, sports a big furry beard, and wears black robes. What does that tell you?"

"So he's a Russian Orthodox priest," Pierre said. "Big whoop."

"Let's say he was this bad old bishop's contact man on the West Coast. Like his fellow priests back home, he gets religion and decides God isn't smiling on this smuggling thing. So he blows the whistle on this end of the operation, which happens to be run by the Sogorskys."

"It's not Devil worship," Pierre said, begrudgingly, "but it's something. Presented properly, this Addis might just turn out to be a major heroic figure." He raised his hands as if positioning letters on a marquee. "Father Joe Addis, Environmental Champion."

He shouted for Luna.

"Get me Joseph Addis on the phone. You got a number for him, Leo?"

I gave Luna the phone number.

She was back in a minute. "Not there," she said. "I left a message to call us."

"Go to his place, Leo. When he shows, bring him here."

"The guy's in the middle of a federal criminal investigation," I said.

"So? How's talking with me gonna interfere with that?"

"I was thinking more of *me*," I said. "Agent Andrews promised that if I showed up in his vicinity, she'd toss me in the clink."

"That's why I hire lawyers," he said.

"I'm not that fond of jails."

"Not even for a grand each day you spend inside?"

What with pulling a few twenties out of a nearby ATM and washing down a beef stromboli with a Moretti at Bruno's, it was nearly three o'clock before I arrived at Addis's bungalow.

There was no sign of the black Infiniti sedan that agents Andrews and Calabrese has been using earlier. No sign of anybody watching Addis's house. That made some sense, if Addis was elsewhere.

But his battered Yugo was parked in front of the bungalow.

I eased the Chevy toward the curb. With the engine idling, I dialed the bungalow's number. And got his answering machine. So he was out somewhere being chauffeured. He had to return home sometime.

I killed the engine and prepared to wait. I wondered if Andrews had just been blowing smoke with that threat of arrest. I wasn't breaking any laws I knew of. But if she did arrest me, Pierre's legal scoundrels would work their magic.

And if they dragged their feet, I'd be collecting a grand a—

An unpleasant sound interrupted my dream of short-term wealth. I lowered the window to get a better fix on it.

It was the whimper of an animal in pain. Coming from Addis's bungalow.

As I got out of the Chevy I heard another whimper. It wasn't coming from inside the house. I headed toward a gate that led to a rear yard along a shoulder-high thick bush that separated Addis's property from the Roberts'.

I paused at the gate, studying the area before opening it. Back in the yard, Addis's brown mastiff lay on its side, its heavy breathing causing its massive rib cage to rise and lower.

The animal whimpered again.

I was still a little nervous about sharing a yard with him. "Hey," I yelled.

The mastiff tried to raise its huge head, but hadn't the strength.

I opened the gate and moved toward the wounded dog.

I could hear its ragged breathing now, along with the whimpering.

It was in seriously bad shape. The back of its head was pulpy. There was blood on his muzzle and on his front paws. I wondered if it was his or if he'd gotten a piece of the bastard who'd walloped him.

I didn't think there was much that could be done for the poor critter, other than putting it out of its misery. I took out my cellular with the idea of letting the West L.A. ASPCA make that decision. I was waiting for Directory Assistance to provide me with that number when I happened to look in the direction of the bungalow.

The back door was wide open and just a few feet from it, Joseph Addis was sprawled on a brick walkway, looking pretty damned still. I stared at that open door, wishing I'd been one of those guys who loves the feel of a gun on his hip.

There were enough windows to give me a pretty good view inside the bungalow. Nothing seemed to be stirring.

I moved to Addis's body. His skull had not been as sturdy as the dog's. The walkway bricks beneath his ruined head were coated with thickened blood. Just on the odd chance he might still be alive, I pressed fingers against his neck searching for a pulse.

Finding none, I backed away, eyeing the open door, half expecting some crazy yahoo to rush through it waving a bloody lead pipe.

The dog's whimper had grown so faint I could barely hear it as I double-timed it through the gate. In front of the bungalow, feeling a little less vulnerable, I dialed 911. A female took down the information without batting a verbal eye. She said the officers who'd be arriving shortly would decide what to do about the wounded dog.

She also suggested that, should the perpetrator still be in the vicinity, I was to take no action that might place me in jeopardy.

Like I had to be told.

The blue-and-white arrived with sirens blaring, as though the officers were hoping to chase off the killer rather than confront him. Through the Chevy's rear window, I saw J. Roberts at her window, gawking at the uniformed cops as they exited their vehicle. This was better than TV.

The pale, freckled officer looked to be in his early twenties. His dark-skinned partner had about ten years' seniority on him and was calling the shots. He asked me a few quick questions about the situation in the backyard, ending with, "You didn't see nobody moving around in the house?"

I told him I didn't.

"Okay, Mr. Bloodworth. You say you wore the blue, so you know the drill. Detectives are gonna wanna talk to you. Just sit tight. We'll take it from here."

I watched them move to the open gate, arming themselves, then heading toward the rear. They'd know what to do about the dead man. But the dog might pose a problem.

Not mine, any more.


Before too long more uniformed cops arrived. And plain clothes detectives. And technicians. The media would get there eventually, but Agent Andrews beat them to the scene.

She arrived in a Crown Vic, with a guy in a smartly tailored suit and tinted glasses. His face was the shape and color of a bruised tomato. It looked like he and Andrews were arguing. When she saw me, she started toward my car. He wasn't finished whatever he was saying. He called to her. When she didn't respond, he shook his head and moved off to where the action was.

"Where's Vlad Sogorsky, Bloodworth?" she asked, getting into the car beside me.

"Which one is he, again? The bartender, right?"

"The bartender who broke Agent Calabrese's wrist with his little baseball bat."

"Aw, Jeeze. How's she doing?"

"Better than Father Addis," she said. "Here's what I want, Bloodworth. I want you to have been lying to me earlier today. I want you to be working for the Sogorskys. Because then I could offer you some kind of deal, maybe a slightly reduced sentence, if you put me in Vlad's direction."

"Look, lady, the only thing I'm guilty of is letting that poor animal in the yard continue to suffer."

"An LAPD tech just put the sad old thing to sleep," she said. She sighed in frustration. "What the hell are you doing here, Bloodworth?"

"Waiting to give the detectives a statement. I discovered the body and called it in."

"So I hear," she said. "What I want to know is why you're still here. If you had been involved with the Sogorskys you'd have run, right?"

"Definitely," I said.

"Damn, I've got nothing," she said. "This has been a total screw-up."

"What happened to the surveillance on Addis?"

She gave me an angry look. "That's your doing," she said.

"Mine?"

"Our plan had been to hang tight and wait for the Sogorskys to get their next shipment. Then we'd net them, the shippers, and the smugglers, and reel them all in. But you spooked us. Calabrese and I believed your Devil worship story, but the man in charge of the operation, Agent Hidalgo of Customs—that's him over there," she pointed to the bruised tomato face, who was shouting at one of the LAPD cops, "he called us amateurs for cutting you loose.

"He said we couldn't take the chance you wouldn't tip the Sogorskys. So we had to move on them immediately before they could clean house."

"And that left Addis out here all by his lonesome," I said.

"We didn't know Vlad would slip out of the net and come here and do this."

"Why did he come here?" I asked. "Especially if he was on the run?"

"Either he thought Father Addis betrayed the family and was looking for vengeance," she said, "or he was looking for help from his priest. Either way, something set him off and he used his baseball bat again."

She was looking so miserable, I said, "Would a witness to the murder help?"

"Don't kid around."

I pointed in the direction of J. Roberts who was still at her window. "She doesn't miss much. You might want to suggest to Agent Hidalgo that he talk to her."

"Hell with Hidalgo," she said, opening the car door. "Come on. You can introduce me to the lady."

As we walked to the Roberts house, I overheard Hidalgo calling one of the LAPD detectives a jackass. "They've shot people for less," I told Andrews.

"You make my mouth water," she said.

J. Roberts took her time answering the bell. She opened the door just a few inches and asked, "Yes?"

"Hello, Miz Roberts," I said. "Leo Bloodworth, remember? With me is Special Agent Andrews. She'd like to talk to you about the trouble next door."

"W-what about it?"

"Can't we come in?" Agent Andrews said.

"Might as well let 'em in." The voice was clearly her brother's.

He was standing in the living room, looking a little less like a workman and more like a slacker without his utility belt. He'd also exchanged his paint-stained T-shirt and Levi's for a pair of rumpled khaki slacks and a gray warm-up sweater with the Warner Bros. logo covering most of the front.

He gestured toward me with his stubbled chin. "I know Blood-worth isn't official," he said to Agent Andrews. "You got some real tin you can show me, brown sugar?"

Scowling, agent Andrews held out her badge.

"The beaver patrol, huh?"

"I'm a federal investigator, Mr. Roberts," she said. "With full arrest power. You may want to keep that in mind."

"Okay, lady, what do you wanna know? But make it fast. I got things to do."

Agent Andrews turned to the sister. "Have you been home all day, Ms. Roberts?"

Before J. Roberts could reply, her brother Barry said, "We went over to the Westside Pavilion around noon. Ribs at Roma's. Caught the new Mel Gibson on a three-dollar matinee. Weird flick, all those dudes wearing white powder. Nothing like 'Passion of the Christ.' Anyway, we just got back maybe an hour, hour and a half ago. Right, Jule?"

His sister nodded obediently.

"Then I guess you didn't see anything unusual next door?"

"Heck, there was always something unusual over there. The dude was a nutcase, queer for Satan."

"He was a Russian Orthodox priest," Agent Andrews said.

Barry Roberts blinked, clearly surprised. "Get serious," he said. "What about that black robe? And the goofy-looking hat?"

"It's what they wear," Andrews said, "when they pray to what I suppose is the same God you pray to."

"Oh, Barry," J. Roberts said. "A priest."

Barry Roberts looked almost as shaken as his sister. "I thought he was some kind of . . . well, never mind what I thought. It don't matter anyway."

"Well, thank you both for your cooperation," Agent Andrews said. "I'm sure the homicide detectives will want to talk with you, too."

"We'll tell them same's we told you. We weren't here when the dude . . . when it went down."

"Where's your cat, Miz Roberts?" I asked.

She blinked and shifted her eyes to her brother.

"Sheba's outside somewhere," he said.

"They have this nice big cat," I said to Agent Andrews. "Sweet old tabby."

J. Roberts's eyes were moistening.

Barry moved quickly to her side, put his arm around her. "You're upsettin' Jule," he said. "You better leave now."

"I'm surprised to hear Sheba's outside," I said. "Especially since Jule told me that the cat never left her alone."

She was weeping now. She pulled away from Barry and leaned against a wall, her body shaking. Agent Andrews approached her, placed a hand on her arm. "What's the matter, ma'am?"

"You two are the matter," Barry Roberts said, moving between the agent and his sister. "All this stuff going on. The cops. You coming here with all your gosh-darned questions."

"I bet Sheba's in the back yard," I said, ignoring him. "Now that the big dog next door is dead and can't get through the fence, I guess it's safe for her to be out there."

Agent Andrews turned to me, a puzzled look on her face. "Blood-worth, what in the world are you—"

Barry Roberts had moved behind her and used his left arm to place her in a choke hold. Pulling her back against him, he yanked her weapon from its holster. Then he tossed her aside.

"You nosy son of a buck," he said, aiming the gun at me. "Just won't let it alone."

"The cops will figure it out anyway," I said, talking fast, hoping to distract him from pulling the trigger. "They'll discover it's cat blood on the dog's muzzle. They'll find the hole in the fence. Once they're here, it's just a matter of checking out that ball-peen hammer of yours and the clothes you were wearing earlier."

"That devil dog killed Sheba," he said, holding steady on the gun. "Tore the sweet baby apart. In our own back yard. Right in front of our gosh-darned eyes." He was crying now, too. "Even after I cracked the darned dog's skull, it still crawled back through the fence."

"The dog's dead now," I said, hoping to calm him a little. "You did what had to be done."

"You got that right," he said. He inhaled deeply and noisily through his nose and blinked away a tear. "That . . . foreigner. I don't care if he was a priest. He brought his devil dog into our neighborhood. Killed our little Sheba.

"Still, I didn't mean to do him any harm. If only the dog had died in our yard, I'd never have gone onto another man's property. And if he hadn't come out of his house to try and stop me from killing that hellhound . . .

"I been a good, God-fearing Christian all my life. Now I'm a murderer. Standin' here with a gun in my hand."

He held the weapon out. "Here, take this thing."

I didn't wait for him to change his mind.

"I haven't heard any 'thank-you-Pierre's for putting your mug on our newscasts last night," the TV entrepreneur was saying at brunch the next morning. We were at his "special" table at Farmer's Market on Fairfax, within shouting distance of a group of usually rowdy and frequently funny screenwriters who seemed to enjoy sending insults his way.

"I'm not sure publicity is a good thing in my game," I said, polishing off the remnants of what had once been eggs-over-easy with corned beef hash.

"Maybe not the Tony Pellicano type of publicity," Pierre said. "But you're a hero. Even the black girl—what's her name?"

"She's a woman. Evelyn Andrews."

"Whatever. Even she says you broke the case. Not the LAPD dicks or the Customs guy, Hidalgo, which is how the *Times* played the story."

"Speaking of the *Times*," I said, "I read they caught Vladimir Sogorsky on the 405, heading for Mexico."

"He's agreed to cooperate with Customs, so they're pulling in the whole smuggling operation," Pierre said. "A twenty-million-dollar business, can you believe it? Fish eggs. Anyway, it's a happy ending for everybody but Addis and his dog."

"And Barry Roberts," I said.

"He'll walk," Pierre said. "They can't get a murder case to stick out here. And there's sure to be one cat lover on his jury. Know why his sister calls herself 'J. Roberts'? Her first name is Julia. Julia Roberts. Can you imagine what that musta been like for her, walking around with that name, with a mug like hers?"

"Pierre, there's stuff I should be doing," I said. "If there's a reason you're buying me brunch, maybe we ought to get to it."

He gave me a half smile. "I was thinking you might wanna come up with some pages for me."

"I'm sorry, what?"

"The CW network's looking for a crime-adventure show with broads. Something different. This Fish and Wildlife Service is a whole new franchise. You've done some writing. Put together a series synopsis for me. Shouldn't take you that long."

"I don't know, Pierre," I said. "I've written fiction, but TV . . . I don't know."

"Use the Sogorsky story, punch it up with some gunplay and car chases, only make sure you copy far enough away we don't get sued. Dawn will love the fighting-for-the-environment angle, and I know Les is always looking for something a little different."

In Hollywood, hope is the thing with residuals, not feathers. I looked at the screenwriter's table. The guys there seemed relaxed and happy. And wealthy. I recognized one of them—a mystery novelist who at one time had been called the next Raymond Chandler but who'd given it up for movie gold.

"Would it be okay if I wrote it like a short story?" I asked.

"Geeze, Leo, how long you been livin' out here in La-La? Haven't you learned by now that in TV it's not the writing that matters, it's the selling. Write it any way you want. Just give me some paper with words on it. I'll take it from there."

# A PRISONER OF MEMORY

*By Robert S. Levinson*

Robert S. Levinson is the best-selling author of *In the Key of Death, Where the Lies Begin, Ask a Dead Man, Hot Paint,* and *The James Dean Affair.* His short stories appear in *Alfred Hitchcock Mystery Magazine* and *Ellery Queen Mystery Magazine,* whose readers cited him in the annual EQMM Award poll three consecutive years. Bob wrote and produced two Mystery Writers of America Edgar Awards shows, followed by the International Thriller Writers Thriller Awards shows of '06 and '07, while his first play, *Transcript,* premiered last year at RiverPark Center in Owensboro, Kentucky. His work has been praised by Joseph Wambaugh, T. Jefferson Parker, Nelson DeMille, Clive Cussler, Heather Graham, David Morrell, Heather Graham, Joe R. Lansdale, and James Rollins. More at www.robertslevinson.com.

H ey, handsome! Need your help."

She was a presence out of my past, but I knew at once it was Laura Dane. There was no mistaking the growl exploding in my ear with that trained stage actor's ability to send a whisper up to the back of the second balcony, every precisely enunciated word blasting its way out of a throat sandpapered by years of chain-smoking.

I made sure anyway, verifying the source like the good newspaperman I am: "Laura?"

"I should be insulted that you'd have to ask," she said. Coughed out a web of phlegm. "I didn't have to wonder if it was you on the phone, Neil, did I?"

"You called me, Laura."

"Still smart as a whip, you are, the same way you were so snappy smart in untangling the truth about Elvis and Marilyn in the long ago." She was talking about a rumored love affair, which led to a series of murders I had a hand in solving. "Got something for you not nearly as glamorous, but dangerous. Down the line it'll make front page headlines and some damn fine fodder for that *Daily* column of yours."

"Dangerous how?"

"Like I could be dead any minute, murdered, before you have a chance to mount your white charger and ride to my rescue, the way Errol Flynn—bless his dear, drunken soul—did in Fort Worth."

"I remember Flynn in *San Antonio* and *Virginia City, Santa Fe Trail*, but *Fort Worth*? I don't know that movie. Is it out on DVD?"

"Not a movie. We were in Fort Worth on a war bond tour, Errol and me and a bunch of other Warner Brothers contract players. That crazy galoot saved me from having to go to bed all by my lonesome." She laid in a lusty groan. "Think he'd also saved all the other dames on the tour before the Superchief got us back to L.A." Another cough from lungs that sounded in trouble. "So, what do you say, Neil? Come give an old broad a helping hand?"

"As dangerous as you say, aren't you better off calling the cops?"

"You hear why straight from the filly's mouth, you'll understand why not. At Burbank Studios. On the *Melancholy Baby* set the rest of the day. I'll leave your name on the pass list at the Barham gate."

She was off the line faster than I could raise another question.

A couple hours later, I tagged a "-30-" to tomorrow's column, an emotional screed decrying the destruction of another landmark, the Ambassador Hotel and its fabled Cocoanut Grove, where the stars came out to play when Hollywood was Hollywood and Laura Dane was a name-above-the-title movie star who specialized in playing "the other woman," much as she had done in real life most of her life, wreaking havoc on Kay Francis, Miriam Hopkins, Claire Cavanaugh, Bette Davis, Barbara Stanwyck, Joan Crawford, and others of her peers.

I e-mailed the piece downtown and took off for a landmark that had withstood the ravages of progress, the Warner Bros. Studio, renamed the Burbank Studios after a shotgun marriage of economic convenience with Columbia Pictures. It was a typical Los Angeles afternoon, the slate blue sky lush with cumulus clouds, the Hollywood Freeway flush with bumper-to-bumper traffic, impatient drivers answering one another with honking horns and expressive middle fingers.

After forty minutes, I pulled up to the Barham Boulevard entrance. A gatekeeper hiding behind reflective shades checked my name against the list on his computer screen and overacted giving me a once-over twice over, logged in my aged Jag's license number, and directed me to the outdoor set where *Melancholy Baby* was shooting.

The company had broken for lunch.

Nobody seemed to know who I was talking about when I asked for Laura Dane, except a prune-faced actor in his late seventies or early eighties, costumed in Sunday best, an extravagant handlebar mustache, and a halo of thick white hair, who stepped over at the mention of her name and said, "Check Marnie Nichols's trailer. Back there, the biggest one of all. Can't miss it."

Marnie Nichols.

The name gave me a smile and a jolt of memory as electric as my first dose of morning coffee.

When I met her, she was this fresh-faced kid from Columbus, studying acting with her Great Aunt Laura, driven by the usual wide-eyed dreams of fame and fortune that's oversold in bulk on television and magazine racks. She'd become one of the few who could cash in her bus ticket back home, as attested to now by the glitter-speckled gold star adhered to the door of her trailer. I rang the bell and when that got me nowhere hammered with my fist and called her name.

After a few more failures, I turned to leave, till I heard the door creak open a crack. A voice full of challenge demanded to know: "That you, Neil Gulliver?"

"In living Technicolor," I said, swinging around again to confirm it was Laura.

"Get the hell hurry-up inside," she said, pushing the door wide enough for me to see the Colt .45 caliber automatic she had aimed at my chest, struggling with criminal intensity to keep her two-handed grip steady.

"That's a prop gun, right?"

She ignored the question. "C'mon, handsome, give it the gas," she said. "Inside before the son of a bitch spots me."

There was more luxury to Marnie Nichols's motor home than to my Westwood condo, all the accoutrements of the stardom earning her twelve million dollars a movie and a modest chunk of the gross, more than your most basic math told me I'd make over my lifetime, however long or abbreviated.

And nobody would ever mistake Marnie for trailer trash, especially not looking the way she looked now, in repose like Ingres' *Grande Odalisque*, the risqué Mademoiselle Airière, on a plush chaise lounge covered in crimson velvet about halfway back, twenty-five feet or so, across carpeting a foot deep from an entertainment center out of Mission Control.

Her smile was warm and inviting, her almond-shaped cerulean blue eyes ablaze with the suggestion of more than homespun hospitality—unlike Laura, who alternated looks of dread and fear. Laura's thread-thin lips ticked recklessly into her hollow cheeks, her gray eyes dulled by time, shifting left and right while she used the .45 to direct me to the driver's seat. The equipment that had earned Marnie the deserved sobriquet "Body Bountiful" was on full display under a pink silk camisole, and I made a mess of averting my gape, drawing a tinkling giggle of appreciation from her.

Laura said, "You notice anything strange going on?"

"Outside or in here?"

"Not a laughing matter, handsome. Tell him, Marnie, how it's not a laughing matter."

Marnie threw an arm across her breasts, putting an end to my peep show. "It's truly not, Mr. Gulliver. Somebody has been stalking my auntie, threatening to kill her."

I returned Laura's anxious stare with one of my own, briefly bagging her head to toe with disbelieving eyes. Long gone was the sex kitten who could get a gent's pulse skipping beats with a simple wink, replaced by a woman somewhere in her mid eighties, with the sallow complexion and wasted body of someone ill beyond repair.

Laura had turned into half the woman I'd dealt with before, when the astonishing key-ring waist and conical breasts of her stardom had given way to an elephantine body she routinely hid inside tent dresses. The hair she had let go naturally white then and wore like a tight snow bonnet had become a hodgepodge of cotton tufts and random strands.

She coughed into her fist again and asked, "You heard her. More than having to take my word for it."

I slipped Marnie a glance.

She answered with a wink and a furtive nod that seemed to say, Play along with her.

I said, "When did the stalking begin, Laura?"

Laura closed her eyes and nodded to a silent count that ended with her deciding, "Forty years ago, maybe more."

At once, I had visions of a stalker using a walker. "A pretty determined fellow. And the threats on your life? Also forty years ago?"

"Starting ten days, maybe two weeks ago. Calling me up again and again, and how he got the unlisted numbers, I don't know. Every time telling me he's close as my shadow, and one day soon, he'll show himself, punch my ticket for good."

Laura parked the .45 on the copilot's seat, studied my reaction while scoring a cigarillo from the flip-top box on the dashboard. She slotted it in a corner of her mouth, tossed me the Zippo lighter on the dash, and crooned, "Put your hot one to my cold one and make my cold one hot, baby." Like I was Cagney in a scene burnt into my memory from the movie where he torched a cigarette for her, then used the smoldering butt to brand her on the neck.

She said, "You're doubting me, aren't you, handsome? I see it written on your kisser as clear as a Catalina sunrise." She shot a jet stream of smoke at me. "Marnie, handsome here doubts me. Tell him what else, go ahead."

Marnie eased into a sitting position with her legs crossed yoga style, picked up a throw pillow, and hugged it to her chest. "Auntie Laura's been staying with me since her operation, my place at the Oaks. I'd come home from the studio and find her in a state of panic over the phone calls. Two nights ago, there was a break-in attempt.

We both were awakened by sounds coming from downstairs, like someone trying to crack open one of the French windows. Armed security got there inside of ten minutes the silent alarm going off. Also police responding to my 911."

"And?"

"Whoever it was got away. Security said it was probably this band of gypsies that's been working Griffith Park, down over at the Estates and across the boulevard in Laughlin Park."

"We know better, don't we, sweetheart?"

"We do, Auntie Laura," Marnie said, heaping on a patronizing smile.

"Did you tell the cops about the calls?"

Marnie said, "Yes. They even checked, but it was a dead end. They said it probably was a disposable cell phone he used."

Laura added, "All they could do for now, they said, which is how I came to remember you, handsome. What a peach of a guy you were when it mattered."

"I don't know that I can be of any more help than the police, Laura."

"You're here, so already you're doing more than them, and—" She drew a puzzle on her face. "—just how did you know where to find me? I'd been on the lookout for you before the lunch break, but nobody at all knew I was even here."

I told her about the actor who had directed me to Marnie's trailer.

"And he was decked out in a bib and tucker?"

"Resplendent. And a handlebar mustache begging for a barbershop quartet."

She swung her face to Marnie. "You hearing what Neil just said, sweetheart? That's him, finally, the SOB who's out to get me. My stalker's here on the lot."

⸻

I searched Marnie's for confirmation, saw it as her expression slowly dissolved into mild alarm.

She said, "We were originally scheduled to do the ballroom scene today, but construction had a problem with the grand staircase collapsing, so word came down that we'd move instead to the standing outdoor setup. No fancy dress called for. Strictly street wear, me in one of the great Orry-Kelly outfits Bette Davis originally wore in *Now, Voyager.*"

"And the guy who steered me here—"

"He wouldn't have known about the change unless he was on the cast list and got the late call from the A.D., same as everybody else—"

"Not if he were working off a shooting schedule he somehow got his hands on. He would finagle his way onto the lot today dressed for the ballroom."

"Exactly," Marnie said.

"But that doesn't explain how he'd know you'd be bringing Laura with you."

"Stalkers stalk, that's how," Laura said, her head unable to settle on a direction. "He saw us leave. It didn't take a crystal ball to figure out where we were heading in the studio limo." She looked around for someplace to extinguish what was left of her cigarillo.

The beanbag ashtray on the dash was a mountain of butts. Grumbling, she maneuvered to the door, pushed it open, tossed away the butt, and quickly pulled the door shut. "He's out there," Laura said, struggling for breath. "I saw him right now, across the drive, not twenty feet away, and he saw me too. He waved at me. The SOB waved at me."

It took a few seconds for the news to sink in.

I grabbed the .45 and charged out the door after Laura's stalker, checking in all directions for a tuxedo among the dozens of extras returning from the meal break, all of them costumed for an afternoon stroll along a section of street dressed like a quaint New England village.

Mustache Man had shown terrific speed for his age.

No sight of him.

Back inside the trailer, Laura was more distraught than ever, clutching Marnie like a life preserver, wailing about her stalker's ability to sneak onto the lot, get this close to her. Insisting through crocodile tears that she'd be dead sooner rather than later if he had his way. Begging an answer from anywhere to questions that were on my mind as well: Why me, dear Lord? Why now, after forty years? Who is this creature?

Before I could ask them, an A.D. was knocking on the door, calling out that Marnie was needed in wardrobe in ten to double-check a fitting. Laura made a sound like she'd just been pricked with a needle, and her eyes exploded with dread. She pushed away from Marnie and threw herself against the door. Her words a soulful moan, she begged, "You can't leave me now, not now, sweetheart, not with knowing he's right outside there somewhere."

"Auntie Laura, of course not. You'll come along."

"No, no, no." Laura was adamant. "No. Outside, not safe, not safe at all." She looked to me for confirmation. "Not safe at all."

"I'll stick around and wait with you here," I said. "It'll be you, me, and—" putting the .45 on display "—our friend Mr. Colt."

The answer didn't satisfy her. "Not safe at all, not anywhere here," she said, wailing the words like they were lyrics out of a Billie Holiday songbook. "Anywhere but here. Anywhere. Here, not safe at all." The declaration set off a spate of uncontrollable coughing. She looked at her hand despairingly, rubbed it dry on the floral-patterned muumuu that fit her like a practical joke.

Marnie said, "Would you feel safer at the house, Auntie Laura? I'm sure Mr. Gulliver would be happy to take you and would keep you company until I get home." She gave me a hopeful smile.

Her place took five or six minutes to reach once I turned off Los Feliz and onto Fern Dell Drive, gliding over the creek bridge, past the lush vegetation, the quaint waterfalls, and the cedar, pine, and leafy fern trees bringing modest relief from a summer heat now in the high eighties that had drawn an unusual number of midweek picnickers unconcerned about the shopping cart bums who'd made this part of Griffith Park their home and the gay extroverts sunbathing on the grassy slopes, to Star Bright Lane.

A series of ascending turns led to Star Bright Circle, one of the many hillside cul-de-sacs with flat lots and a magical overview of Los Angeles that extended past the downtown high-rises, long a favorite of celebrities who could afford a fancy pricetag that lately had reached seven and eight figures, going back to the heyday of Ramon Navarro, Cary Grant, and Randolph Scott, and more recently Diane Keaton, Nicolas Cage, Brad Pitt, and briefly my ex, Stevie Marriner, the one-time "Sex Queen of the Soaps."

Marnie's two-acre estate was situated behind a shoulder-high wall of natural stone topped by coiled barbed wire. The gate slid open to the numerical code fed me by Laura, and I drove into a rustic court-yard where, were this France, D'Artagnan might have met up with Porthos, Aramis, and Athos. The open-faced garage had space for six cars; adjacent to it was an empty stable.

"Pretty hoity-toity, huh?" Laura said, indicating the house. "When she went shopping for a place, this here reminded her of a house she stayed in the south of France, Provence, when she was there filming *Adieu Times Two* a couple of years back. Piece of junk, you ask me, but it got my sweet girl an Oscar nomination, so what the hell. That place was in the hills above Luberon National Park and here was Griffith Park, so Marnie didn't even quibble about the price. Wrote out a check on the spot."

The house was typically village provincial, unpretentious in design and construction. A comfortably sized living room was furnished simply around a hand-built fireplace of eccentric stone that stretched from the natural wood floor to the wood-beamed ceiling. The kitchen was twice as large and outfitted with top-of-the-line profes-sional appliances, a well-stocked walk-in freezer and larder, and a carved wood dining table large enough to seat a dozen or two without crowding. A wrought-iron staircase took me upstairs to three bed-rooms feeding off a mezzanine lounge, whose stucco walls featured framed posters of the movies that had starred either Marnie or Laura, the only signs of star ego anywhere.

I hung out there for a few minutes, enjoying the view of the Grif-fith Park Observatory before heading back to my Jag to fetch Laura, who'd insisted on locking herself inside until I checked out the house for a stalker in residence.

Halfway down the stairs, I heard noises that suggested her fear might be well placed.

They were coming from Marnie's master bedroom, a room I'd

given cursory inspection, barely a glance, anxious not to invade her privacy.

I pulled Laura's .45 from inside my belt, got a good two-handed grip on it, and used my foot to ease open the bedroom door. Jumped inside and did a lot of that robotic twisting around the police do for real as well as on *Law & Order*, ready to squeeze the trigger if it came to that. Instead, it came to a couple of pigeons that had flown in through the patio window that overlooked the courtyard. They were psycho in a major way, banging into walls and knocking over doodads trying to find their way back out.

I windmilled my arms and shouted instructions that finally got them soaring in the right direction, but not before they'd rewarded my good intentions with a series of pigeon bombs that caught me on the head and shoulders.

I stepped onto the patio to curse them farewell.

Looking down, I saw the front passenger door of the Jag was open. Laura wasn't in the car or anywhere visible.

After ten or twelve minutes of exploring the grounds, I found her cowering at the rear of a stall in the stable, knees drawn to wattles and anchored by a trembling grip. The place smelled of equestrian history and fresh dung I assigned to squirrels, rats, skunks, coyotes, and other park animals scavenging for food or seeking shelter from bad weather. I kicked aside a stale pile and, settling along side her, said as gently as I could: "Laura, you okay?"

At first, she looked at me like I was a stranger, but recognition set in and she ripped me full of guilt with her icicle stare, challenging, "Where were you when I needed you? The stalker, he came after me, handsome. I saw him first, though, and I got away. Got away. Got away. Where's the gun? Go after him. Go get him. Okay, handsome? Now. You'll do that?"

I eased out of my jacket and used it to blanket her. "What did he look like, Laura?"

"What do you think? Like you said. Big handlebar he had, and gussied up for a ball or something. An old fart, moving like the dickens, but I spotted him before he saw me and got in here in the nick of time.

Go now. Find him for me and kill the SOB." She pressed a bony hand against my cheek. "For me, handsome, and I'll owe you big time," she said, like she was offering me a free pass to her bedroom.

It was the same tone she'd used on the drive here from the Burbank Studios, a failed try at recreating the insinuatingly passionate voice of her stardom years, while resurrecting one memory after another, like they were a cure for her cough and the cobwebs of time.

Some of Laura's stories I remembered from our brief history together, others from her uproarious, outlandish visits with Johnny Carson on *The Tonight Show*. They flowed out of her like she was reading from a well-rehearsed script, leaving no doubt they were imprisoned in her memory as well as the autobiography that rode the bestseller lists for half a year, *Dane, Down & Dirty*.

"I was once a hooker, you know that?" she had said early in the drive, anxiously, needing to hold center stage. I played along. "Yeah, top of the batting order in Hollywood's blue-ribbon pussy palace, a favorite with all the important chippy chasers at all the talent agencies and studios. How I met the gent who engineered the breaks that landed me my contract with Warner Brothers and in bed with every star and costar you care to mention—no names, please—and even a leading lady or two."

When Laura tired of those anecdotes, she opened a new chapter. "I suppose you know I was roommates with Marilyn? She was always Norma Jean to me and I was always Dubinsky to her. My real name, did you know? Jack Warner, Steve Trilling, they heard that and said, No way, which is how I got to be Laura Dane. From the Fox movie *Laura*, with Gene Tierney and Dana Andrews, because Colonel Warner said I resembled a blond Gene, and Dane rang his bell better'n Dana did. The moguls at Fox decided on Marilyn after she picked Monroe in honor of her granny, but that's old news already." Laura rattled off a telephone directory of names rich and famous from the Fifties and into the Sixties, challenging me to guess who of them had been bedded first by her, then by Marilyn. Abruptly changing her mind with a flick of the hand. "Let's us just call it a tie, okay, baby? Although I hate to admit I never made it into the White House any more than the White House ever made it into me."

Abruptly, she changed the subject. "You know I was AA?"

"Heard something about it somewhere."

"The career turns sour, the need turns more and more to sour mash, so to speak. Can't get a call through or a callback from anybody who could throw me a life preserver. Won't even try to describe what it looks like below the bottom, but I was there, baby, riding the merry-go-round to nowhere, until I woke up one day knowing I wouldn't wake up some day if life kept leading me on this way. So, I quit. Cold turkey after one last fling with Wild Turkey, you dig? I dragged myself into AA, said hello to familiar faces, and signed autographs for the others, and stuck with it, still, one day at a time. Anytime I felt like abandoning the wagon, which was often, I helped myself to a smoke. The habit climbed up to two, sometimes three packs a day, but it kept me off the sauce, and I'm still here, so that's that."

Now, when Laura paused for a dry mouth cough in the middle of telling me how she'd come to work for Hollywood's most notorious madam in a mansion above Sunset Plaza Drive available almost exclusively to the elite of show business, I said, "You think it could be a guy from those days who's finally acting on a grudge he's been holding for forty years?"

"Baby, when I loved 'em, they stayed loved. And loving."

"How about when you and Marilyn were roomies, or maybe somebody at Warner Brothers who—"

"No and no, and . . ."

It was as if she'd stumbled onto an idea that made sense.

She snapped her face to me and broke out a half smile edged in hope. "There was this gawky-looking kid, a gofer trying to make his mark, sucking up to Hal Wallis, Johnny Huston, Jerry Wald, even Mike Curtiz, who was busy turning the English language into a jigsaw puzzle when he wasn't taking Bogie or Flynn through their paces. Crawford was playing him for a pet until she wangled that Oscar, and after, that's when he became my uninvited shadow. Finally, I had to say something to Trilling about the pest not leaving me alone. Before the day was over, the kid was on his way to the unemployment line." She played with the notion. "Elrod was his name. Elrod Stump. You know what any studio would do with that moniker he ever got signed on as an actor. Stumpy, everyone called him. He bothered me a while longer before the murder put him out of commission."

"The murder?"

"Stumpy caught on at Monogram, or maybe it was Republic, and got involved in a love triangle with some B actress and the exec who booked the studio's casting couch. Next anybody knew, the exec was dead and a judge was sending Stumpy to San Quentin to learn how to make license plates."

"That might account for the forty-year hiatus."

"What?"

"This Stumpy holds a grudge against you for getting him fired, which led to the murder and the conviction. His need for revenge festers for forty years before he's finished serving out his sentence or gets paroled. And your stalker is back, only now with your murder on his mind as well. How's that sound, Laura? Make sense?"

"What?"

"What I was suggesting about Stumpy?"

"Who?"

"Elrod Stump. Your stalker."

A deep crevice developed between her brows. Then, her eyes brightened with enough wattage to light a premiere at Grauman's Chinese. "That's him, the bad apple! You nabbed him, handsome. Bless you." She pushed herself off the dirt floor and onto her feet with a suddenness that brought on a sonic change in her pulse and caused her to falter. She reached for the wall as dizziness buckled her legs and swooned.

I caught Laura before she hit the ground, cradled her in my arms, and stepped from the stable into the courtyard, anxious to get her into the house. Even in a fading daylight, backlit by the exotic blend of orange, lavender, and scarlet painted across the skyline, I recognized the man moving in on me by his elaborate handlebar mustache.

Marnie skipped out of the limo idling across the courtyard, calling, "It's okay, he's with me," and raced toward me shouting her aunt's name, asking, "What is it? What's wrong? What's happened to her? Is she all right?" She tripped over a moss-covered rock jutting from the ground and vaulted forward, belly-flopping on the dirt.

Mustache Man wheeled around and helped her up, stepping back while she shook the surprise from her face and dusted herself off. Once again he had moved with a speed belying his age. "I'm fine, Mr. Hatcher," she said. She tugged her sweater and a pair of jeans that fit her like body paint into place, covered the rest of the distance between us, and waited for me to tell her about Laura.

"A fainting spell that doesn't look to be serious," I said. She let out enough breath to stir a windmill. I asked, "She do that a lot?"

Marnie's modest overbite disappeared behind pursed lips while she weaved her head left and right in slow motion. "Not as often as we have to change her sheets," she said.

"What's his story?" I said, inclining my head toward the Mustache Man.

"Let's get Aunt Laura to her room first, okay? Clifton, give Mr. Gulliver a helping hand, won't you?"

We settled in armchairs across from one another on the mezzanine landing, separated by a glass-topped table decorated with fashion magazines and outdated issues of *Daily Variety* and *The Hollywood Reporter*, silently waiting for Marnie to finish with Laura and join us. Mustache Man avoided me by leafing through the trades, while I subtlety examined him over the top of a *W Magazine* whose cover offered one of those sexily posed someones mostly famous for being famous.

On close inspection, there was something tricky about his face. It didn't match the body that had traded in the fancy dress for casual wear, tailored slacks, and a camel's hair jacket, high collar dress, shirt open at the neck, showing off a gaudy sterling silver cross nesting on a bed of reddish brown hair.

He looked up from his *Reporter*, caught me staring. "Clifton," he said. "Clifton Hatcher." His voice stronger, far more vibrant than it had sounded at the studio. "Miss Nichols told me all about you on the ride over. I read your column once in a while, Mr. Gulliver. It's not so bad."

*Once in a while.*

*Not so bad.*

Mustache Man knew how to win friends.

I said, "What don't I know about you?"

"Enough to fill one of your columns," he said, suddenly my greatest fan, his overripe smile exposing an abundance of capped teeth. "I'm an actor. You probably figured that out by now."

"The face isn't familiar."

"Not even under this ton of makeup, but someday," he said. "It's for a Brynie Foy movie shooting next door to Miss Nichols's film on a third of the budget. My friend the casting director got me the gig knowing I needed a credit to keep from losing my SAG medical. Only a bit, one line, delivered by an old geezer." He rose and took a few tottering steps away, touched his brow with the back of a hand like he was measuring a fever, tilted up his chin, and recited in a British accent: *Yes, so teddibly hot for this time of year.* His makeup was better than his accent.

"And you made a wrong turn on your way over and wound up on the set of *Melancholy Baby.*"

"Knew from the trades it was Miss Nichols's flick. I'm a big fan, so when I heard the shoot was so close to ours, I took a chance and headed there instead of for the lunch wagon. Arrived in time to see her entering her trailer. Guessed that might be Laura Dane with her. Her aunt, and an actress my pappy admired in his day. Time ran out and I had to split before I could catch them to say so much as hello."

Marnie had rejoined us in time to hear his gushing adoration and picked up the thread. "I asked around after you and Auntie Laura left and learned the shoot on Stage Eight was pirating a standing set from the Dennis Morgan and Jack Carson shoot, *Two Guys from Surrey.* Natty, my flack from the publicity department, went looking for me and located the man with the mustache, Mr. Hatcher here. Since seeing is believing, I invited him to come home with me, so she could meet him and confirm for herself it was no stalker closing in on her today."

He pressed a palm to his heart. "A beaucoup thrill," he said, enthusiastically, pronouncing it *bow-coop.* "And you won't forget about the autographed photo, will you?"

"I have a better idea," I told Marnie. "One that can put an end to this stalker business once and for all."

Marnie motioned us into Laura's room after about twenty minutes.

Laura was propped up in a reclining position in her canopy-covered bed, under a pair of lace-trimmed pillows.

Her eyes struggled for focus as I pushed Clifton Hatcher forward; hands locked behind his back, urging, "No tricks, nothing stupid, if you know what's good for you," loud enough for her to hear. At her bedside, I announced: "Look at the gift I brought you, Laura. This him? This the stalker you spotted at the studio today?" She reared back against the pillows. "Not to worry. He's cuffed."

She raised her head and squinted against the dull light, signaled me to bring the Mustache Man nearer. I applied pressure to Hatcher's shoulder blades, moving his face to within inches of hers. She studied him through eyes that quickly grew wide with alarm. "Him, yes!" she said.

"I also want you to hear him speak, confirm it's the voice you heard on the phone," I said, then pulled Hatcher upright and ordered, "Recite the words I told you, mister."

Hatcher said, "I am as close as your shadow, Laura, and will be coming after you soon," in what I imagined he imagined was a nifty impression of Pacino as Scarface. How this guy got any acting jobs was beyond me.

Laura made a frightful noise. "Yes! Yes! Him, the SOB! Get the police!" she said and managed to pull the covers over her head.

Marnie eased Hatcher aside and, comforting Laura with her voice while she worked back the covers enough to level a kiss on her aunt's forehead, said, "The police are here already, dear, waiting outside to take him away once you've provided positive identification."

"Positive, positive, positive!"

A half hour later, the limo was whisking Hatcher and his autographed photo of Marnie back to the studio, and she and I were relaxing against my Jag, alone except for park creatures noisily scavenging in the hillside brush, exploring the truth of what had occurred today.

"The trick with Mr. Hatcher, I can't thank you enough for that,

Mr. Gulliver. I think it's enough to satisfy Auntie Laura she doesn't have a stalker to worry about anymore."

"There is no stalker, is there?" I said.

"Yes, there is—in Auntie Laura's mind. Back to haunt her forty years later. Before that, she was getting daily calls from her agent, Meyer Mishkin, about a costarring role he said she was perfect for, with Randolph Scott and Lee Marvin in a Budd Boetticher film coming up at Universal."

"All of them long dead and gone."

"Not to Auntie Laura . . . The stalker made his first call soon after Meyer Mishkin called saying Gail Russell had been cast in the role and she sank into a deep depression, spent days in bed, bemoaning that Gail Russell has a bigger drinking problem than she ever had, so what was that all about?"

"It must be tough on you, Marnie."

"The half of it."

"The cough, her weight loss—the other half?"

Marnie stared into the darkness. "She's my auntie, Mr. Gulliver. I'd still be Marnie Who? not Marnie Nichols, if not for Laura Dane." She twisted around and pressed herself against me in a hug to end all hugs. Plastered my lips with a kiss that set my mouth on fire and was over far too soon. She whispered, "Thank you for recognizing her condition early on and playing along anyway," then hurried back inside the house.

I heard from Marnie again three days later, shortly before six in the morning.

She called to tell me Laura was dead.

Murdered.

Smothered to death with one of her bed pillows.

Her voice drained of emotion, Marnie described how she was awakened around four A.M. by strange noises coming from Laura's room and charged over. It was too late to help her auntie, but she saw the killer's face when he tossed the pillow away, shoved her aside, and fled.

"It was Clifton Hatcher," she said. "Clifton Hatcher in that stupid makeup, the handlebar mustache and all the rest. Almost like he wanted me to know it was him."

"Did you report this to the police?"

"They're here now. Yes. Detectives are on their way over to the studio, the *Two Guys from Surrey* set, but they figure it's unlikely he'll show up, seeing as how I recognized him and all."

"In makeup again. We never got a look at his real puss."

"No, but the detectives said they'd know soon enough, if they had to, through the casting director or his agent. That there has to be his photo around somewhere."

There wasn't.

By midafternoon, the detectives had determined that everything about Clifton Hatcher was fake, not only the mustache. He wasn't in the Brynie Foy movie. He'd used it to angle his way onto the lot. The Screen Actors Guild had no member named "Clifton Hatcher." AFTRA records came up with a member who used that name professionally and gave an address and a phone number in Studio City for a private mailbox service that went out of business four years ago.

His real name was Elrod Stump, Jr.

⌐══════⌐

He's still out there somewhere, Elrod Stump, Jr., under some name, some face I wouldn't recognize. Were I to stumble across him, Elrod Stump, Jr., would doubtless be surprised by what I'd have to say to him, words he'd probably least expect to hear out of my mouth: *Thank you.*

Before he murdered Laura Dane, she was another of those half forgotten stars who retreat into the past, a prisoner of memory until their minds fail them, then their bodies. They get a final, brief review on the obituary page, sometimes accompanied by a photograph of the star that was, not the relic they became.

By killing Laura, Elrod Stump, Jr., restored her to stardom. He gave her the leading role in a murder mystery that remains unsolved to this day. He put her name and her photograph on page one of newspapers throughout the world. He turned her into another of the enduring icons in an exclusive club, the Stars of Scandal, whose members live in perpetuity in books, magazine articles, and films.

He took Laura Dane's life and gave her legend.

Who could ever ask for more than that?

Certainly not Laura, who lived to be remembered.

# A SAVING GRACE

## By Patricia Abbott

Patricia Abbott has published crime fiction in publications such as *Hardluck Stories, Thrilling Detective, ThugLit, Pulp Pusher, SHOTS, Murdaland, Demolition, Spinetingler, MystericalE, Shred of Evidence,* and the forthcoming *ThugLit* anthology *Sex, Thugs, and Rock & Roll.* Her recent literary fiction has appeared in journals such as *Portland Review, Potomac Review, Baltimore Review, Inkwell, Fourteen Hills, Bayou Review,* and *Storyglossia.* She lives and works in Detroit, Michigan. Please visit her at pattinase@blogspot.com, where you will find links to many of her online stories.

H e could get to work fairly quickly by taking the Interstate. Five turns of the wheel and he was pulling up at the shop. The blacktop was smooth; the state had resurfaced it only last summer and the traffic was light at 7:00 a.m., mostly eighteen-wheelers moving steadily to the west.

But he hated driving the Interstate, miles of jockeying with traffic that passed through the area as quickly as possible; every Mom and Pop cafe that had catered to the truckers for half a century had failed in the last few years and even the distraction of billboards had disappeared. He had driven that road into the city for years when he did detective work and had to travel it. Every time he gave in to the Interstate's promise of a swifter trip now, he was transported back to that time and its gut-wrenching tension.

So instead he usually drove a circuitous route that took twice the time, much of it passing through farm country. He liked to watch the lights coming on and then blinking off in the farmhouses, the smoke drifting out of the chimneys, the distant figures moving toward outbuildings or into the fields, the children waiting on jiggling legs for the school bus to take them into town, the occasional braying of animals, the smell of dung, bacon, cheap fuel.

She was standing on the road for the fourth Tuesday in a row. He had debated offering her a ride the second, then third time he saw her, but she looked away as if sensing his intention and declining. The fourth week, he held her glance and stopped. He said the usual things; she laughed the way his mother's friends always had, with a hand covering her mouth. A true farm woman's gesture. It made him feel protective. She climbed into his truck, hugged the door for the twenty-minute ride, and thanked him profusely before scuttling into the library.

He still lived outside Shelterville though his ex-brother-in-law told him he could make triple his salary if he moved to Chicago, Kansas City or maybe even Des Moines. He lost track of Cindy, his ex-wife, a million years ago, but her brother, Buddy, his best friend before and after his brief marriage, still called him on the occasional Sunday when the rates went down.

"Don't you ever crave a Thai dinner?" Buddy asked him only last week. "Don't you ever want to bang a girl you didn't know in grade school? Or, better yet, her daughter."

"Sure," Jim agreed. "But I can drive into the city once or twice a month for that stuff. How often do you really want Thai when you got good burgers and pizza here at half the price?"

"She's pregnant again," Buddy said softly.

"Third one?" Jim guessed.

"Fourth. Craig's still chasing after a son."

Cindy was made for motherhood, but he hadn't been ready for anything like that ten—no, fifteen years ago. Wasn't sure he was now. If men were rated on the simplicity of their needs, he'd be at the top of the list. In descending degree of urgency, he looked for: beer, books, basketball, broads. He didn't need many friends—hadn't really made a new one since high school. Hell, he had hardly met anyone new in the twenty years since he graduated.

He wasn't attracted to the woman on the roadside, or at least he told himself that. A small degree of revulsion actually flitted through his stomach: a warning perhaps? Each time he saw her she was standing just to the right of the mailbox, perilously close to the edge of the drainage ditch like this precise spot had been agreed on. Her legs were pressed together as if standing in an open-legged stance was improper. Or maybe it was just habit or a family thing. Maybe her whole family stood like that, much the way his folks walked on their heels and had earlobes attached to the skull.

Even from the distance in the flat terrain, he could pick out her lavender raincoat and her black patent leather purse, hanging limply from her right arm. She never wore another coat in all the months he knew her and never once went without it. It hit 90 degrees more than once that summer and she must have been sweating heavily beneath the polyester. Even on the warmest days, she wore stockings that made her knees gleam as they pressed together on the seat beside him. Her knees were large for such a slight woman, nearly the size of his. Once, but only once, he mistakenly put his hand on a knee when reaching for the gearshift. She jumped as if he had struck her, and his hand heated up like an electric stove burner in the moment or two it rested there. A second passed and then she laughed, a muffled, choking sound he was both drawn to and repelled by.

After his daily tour of the countryside, he arrived at the body shop at 7:30 A.M., leaving each day by 4. He was good at the work. He had looked for work like this—something clean, simple, uncomplicated—after leaving the force. Eventually, he'd realized it wasn't just the administrative crap, not just the series of sadistic superiors and guffawing peers who couldn't make the force in any other town on earth. It was the nature of police work itself that ground him down to a shivering nub of the man he'd been.

He'd set up on his own, briefly, as a P.I., but that stint was neither financially rewarding nor psychologically appealing, and had only underlined that it was the work itself he couldn't take. He was simply not suited for tangling with people in the midst of domestic strife: the bread and butter of the private investigator. He was not made for scrutinizing the detritus of humanity on a daily basis: women cheating on their husbands, employees with their hands in the till or scurrying back to their workplace after hours to siphon some gas out a tank, some paper out of a backroom, some spare parts out of the garage. And, most especially as in his last case, men chasing down teenage boys or girls through the Internet. That one had chewed him up more effectively than the bout of cancer he had dealt with last year.

So here he was—a grease monkey at almost forty.

But he had his routine down pat now and felt sane. His trailer required about minute's maintenance a day and he only turned on his TV to watch sports and the occasional old movie. Most nights, he made himself a quick meal and headed for Taffy's, the nearest bar that didn't make him worry about fights and food poisoning. He took his usual stool, where the bar made a turn, and ordered two beers over the next ninety minutes, listening more than he talked, breathing in more smoke than was good for him, sitting too long without exercise.

Everybody liked him well enough, but he wasn't sought out—not by either sex. Maybe no one quite trusted him with even the most ordinary stories or gossip—he still was a cop to them. Maybe they thought he'd been privately hired to tell their wife about their Friday night destination, or to report to their boss that they carried an awful lot of change in their pockets. All the actual paraphernalia of his years as a dick sat in a storage unit out on the highway, but apparently the essence of it still clung to him like yesterday's sweat. "You've got those crazy eyes," one of his scantily dressed escorts had told him once. "It always feels like you're watching me." She shivered a little and he understood what she meant even though he couldn't change it.

Maybe he just didn't understand how to be one of the guys. He never played pool at the table in the back and never sank quarters into the juke box. He never picked up a woman at Taffy's, not wanting to piss where he lived. For that urge, he frequented a second place farther out of town, but only two or three times a month. The only other thing he did was read but he was a champion at that, reading four or more books a week. That habit, one his mother had insisted on in childhood despite his father's derision, had stuck.

Louise—that was the woman's name—was talkative despite her mousy exterior. Her high-pitched voice prattled on about the price of

gas, a soccer game her son had played in—yes, she had children, two
of them—or the surprising success of the lantana in her garden. He
didn't listen closely to much of what she said, at least the parts about
recipes for watermelon pickles and fundraising drives. Instead he
watched the pulse beat in her wrist, the throb of it. Steady at times
and jumpy at others, it nearly hypnotized him. And he breathed in her
scent, a sort of loamy, yeasty smell that had all but disappeared from
other country women.

"Do you bake your own bread?" he asked once and she nodded.

"Perry likes fresh bread every morning. I get up before five to have
it on the table." She didn't say this proudly but with a kind of resig-
nation. Perry and Louise owned a small farm, but both of them
worked in town to make ends meet. On Tuesdays, Perry went to
Lynchburg and beyond on deliveries so Louise was without transportation. "He picks me up on the way back when he can," she told
Jim, looking out the truck window. "Oh my, the Ryan farm is up for
sale." He leaned past her to look and they sighed simultaneously.

Louise never said what kind of deliveries Perry made and Jim
didn't ask, but her emphasis on the word—deliveries—made him
uneasy. Was that idiot selling drugs? He tried to picture this husband
of hers—this Perry—but failed. He could check to see if there was a
police file on him, but that would send him back into the fray. Asking
about Perry would make it seem like he was setting out on his own
again. Was he? Was that it?

Likewise, Louise's son and daughter seemed like characters in fiction until one day when she pulled out their school pictures. Both
were slightly stout, square-headed farmer's children wearing clothing
as well-worn as hers. Perhaps it was her clothing, saved from her
childhood in the seventies in some attic trunk.

For her contribution to the family income, Louise worked the
checkout desk at the library, coming in early to dust, mop and clean
the unisex restroom.

"I get the first pick at new books," she said with a giggle. "Trouble
is, I don't read much." When she saw what was probably a look of
disapproval on his face, she amended it. "Well, if I do get a chance to
read, I like romances. I buy used paperbacks at the bookshop."

He nodded, knowingly. The back table at Fred's Books was a veritable landfill of love stories. He preferred crime fiction, biographies and stories set in Africa or Asia—some place exotic—although he'd traveled so little most places could qualify as that. After he'd been driving Louise to town for a few months, he picked up a romance out of curiosity but couldn't get beyond the first few pages. The writing was stiff, the characters stock. But mostly he was embarrassed by such sentiment and lust.

It was always on Tuesday then: Louise chattering away and Jim mostly looking at the road ahead. When he had the temerity to look at her face, he sometimes saw the bloom of purple and blue on her chin, her cheek, her eye. She was shockingly inept at covering it up. He would have thought it deliberate except for the badly-applied lipstick, the run in her stocking, the hem coming loose. He could smell the soap on her hands, but the nails needed filing.

On occasion, a small scarf around her neck slid up or down to reveal what looked like fingerprints or small cuts. Once she wore a sling for two weeks, and another time, she couldn't climb into his truck because of the pain in her hip. He jumped out and gave her a hand, feeling that strange heat again when he touched her.

"You're the clumsy sort, I guess," he said, thinking maybe she would confide in him, but hoping even more that she wouldn't. What would he do with such information? Take her home with him? Challenge her husband to a shoot-out? Was he still trying to put a case together?

"That's what Perry always says," she said hurriedly, wincing. "I hope the kids don't inherit it," she said, looking at him hard. Later, he would wonder if she meant him to do something about it that day. But Perry was rarely mentioned after that except in terms of having needs and desires she had to meet, "Perry needs me to go to the bank. Could you drop me there?" Or, "Perry has a prescription needs filling at the drugstore."

Talk of her children though brought light into her eyes. She talked about Brownies, dentist appointments, soccer, piano lessons and PTA meetings till he knew their schedule as well as she did. "My parents never let me do any activities," she explained, emphasizing the word.

"So I make sure my kids join all of them." When he looked at her quizzically, she said, "My mother was always sick and my dad needed me to do her chores after school." He wondered if her mother had been beaten too. He knew such patterns existed. Wife-beaters looked for women used to such treatment. Women who didn't talk—who expected it. That was the profile he saw again and again in his years as a detective. Dully the same.

Despite his revulsion at her treatment and their growing, if odd, friendship, there was something about her that made his fists clench. She wore her wounds like a soldier might, like they'd been earned or were signs of some personal valor. Why couldn't she cover them better? Or why didn't she put an end to it all and leave her brute of a husband? If she was so sensitive to the needs of her children, why did she continue to expose them to his savage treatment? He thought about mailing her a brochure on wife-battering he had seen circulating at the police department years ago, but feared her husband—Perry—might find it first. There was nothing to do but go on, continue driving her into town each Tuesday and hoping for the best. Trying not to investigate every aspect of her life as his old training suggested he do.

She brought the little girl with her in October. "This is Sierra," Louise said, lifting the little girl onto the seat and climbing in after her. "The school boiler broke down so she has the day off. Perry took Dylan along with him."

"Hi, Sierra," he said, helping the child to slide to middle of the bench. He couldn't think of anything to say after that and Sierra seemed similarly at a loss.

"Sierra's gonna help me put the books away today," Louise explained, smoothing the little girl's skirt down and adjusting her coat.

He wondered if this was true. Sierra looked too young to know the Dewey Decimal System, too short to restock shelves. It was then he noticed a yellowish bruise on Sierra's upper arm and felt the coffee and oatmeal he had eaten an hour earlier rise in his throat. The child couldn't be more than six or seven. He jerked the wheel without thinking and all three of them lurched toward his door, Sierra nearly falling on the floor.

"Be careful, Jim," Louise ordered. "We don't want any more accidents just now." She looked pointedly at the child's arm. "Sierra's inherited my clumsiness, I guess."

Jim nodded. "Looks like it's a family problem." He realized at once the double meaning of his remark but Louise looked placidly out the window, patting Sierra's knee every now and then. He had never seen a sadder little girl. When they got out of the truck in front of the library, he realized Sierra had never said a word. Was she afraid of men because of her father?

Two Tuesdays later, Louise wasn't there. As he approached the spot from the distance, he thought perhaps she had finally put on a new outfit—something less noticeable than lavender—and that was why he didn't see her. But when he pulled up to the mailbox, she wasn't there. He stopped the truck, got out, walked around, waited for nearly fifteen minutes and finally drove off.

On the way home from Taffy's that night, he drove by her house. It was dark by then but no lights were on inside. He drove by the next morning too and the next night and still saw no lights, no movement. Louise had told him more than once that they had cows, chickens, and a few other farm animals so someone must be feeding them—a neighbor, a relative. He drove as close to the house as he dared but saw nothing.

Why did he feel that he couldn't drive right up to the house and knock on the door? Why couldn't he at least pick up the phone and call? She must have told Perry she had a ride from him on Tuesdays. He had been giving her a ride for six or seven months. But for some reason, he felt he should keep a distance. Was he afraid of a face-to-face meeting with this mythical Perry who beat his wife and child and probably sold drugs? Was this part of the real reason he had left the force and detective work? Was he a coward? Was that at the heart of it? Or was he afraid of himself, of his own reaction to this monster?

The next Tuesday, she was back at the spot, her lavender raincoat looking freshly pressed, the buttons stitched on tight for once. "What happened last week?" he asked as soon as she climbed in the truck. He didn't let on he had been out to her house a dozen times in the interim. "I almost called you to see if things were okay."

Her eyes fluttered. "Good thing you didn't do that, Jim. Better not to call me at home. Perry's kind of funny. . . ."

"Were you visiting family?" he pressed.

She shook her head. "We had to go into the City for a few days. Sierra fell down the cellar steps and broke her arm and a rib or two. Her doctor in Shelterville wanted an orthopedist in the City to set it right."

She looked at him. "Oh, it wasn't so bad. We stayed at the Red Roof Inn, ate out every night. Sierra got treated like a queen. Afterwards, he's always so ni. . . ." She stopped suddenly and looked out the window. "He just gets so mad sometimes." Her mouth clamped shut. Then, "Anyway, we're home now."

"Is Perry the one who gets them off to school on Tuesdays?" Jim asked after a few minutes. He could almost picture Perry lolling in bed while the kids put on their old worn clothing and ate cold cereal in total silence so as not to wake the sleeping bear.

"No, I see them off before I leave the house. The school bus comes early—at 7:00 A.M." She looked at him quizzically. "Perry doesn't leave till nine or so. Says it doesn't pay to show up at his delivery stops too early," she explained. "He likes having the one day to sleep in a quiet house." She sighed, shaking her head a little.

Jim nodded and dropped the subject. In a few minutes, Louise was prattling on about an upcoming bake sale and whether her lemon squares could measure up to Lila Mueller's. He rarely listened to her conversation; he realized that again.

It was a week or two before he went out to her house. He didn't act hastily, giving himself plenty of time to consider his moves, even thinking a good scare might be all it took to put things right. Although Jim's father had never beat his wife or sons, he was a similar sort of man. A bully. Jim's mother had never once missed having dinner on the table when he came in the door at six. Never once served him a dish he didn't like or failed to have his shirts pressed, his shoes shined. And there were a million other things she had done to avoid his wrath, his insults, his jibes. All for naught, of course. His father got too much pleasure out of humiliating her to not find a reason.

Jim knew many such men. The town was filled with them: men who took their failures out on their wives; men jealous of their sons' youth, berating them at every turn; men fearful of their daughters' beauty, who demeaned their intelligence; men in bars looking for a fight if their opponent looked smaller or weaker; men who used the war or the government or religion as an excuse to yell, to pick up a rock or a gun.

He knew these men, but he wasn't one of them and would never be; he had made sure of that when he left the force, had reiterated it when he gave up the lease on the private office and threw the plaque in that ill-fitting desk drawer. A friend or two had expressed surprise at his decision. "But you're a natural at this work," one or two had said. And he did have the nose, the patience and even the intelligence or instinct for it. What he didn't have was the gut for it, nor the ability to step away. He was inside of every case looking out. His reclamation had begun all those years ago when he asked Cindy for a divorce the morning after he had grabbed her hard enough to make her face go white with fear.

And here he was literally inside. The house was still when he entered it. He had dropped Louise off, convinced she had no idea of his plan despite his jittery feet, his sweaty palms, and returned via the Interstate, parking his truck in some brush down the road and walking quickly across the field. He still remembered how to be invisible, how to slip into a situation without being detected. Those skills would always be part of him but better left alone.

Most people still left their doors unlocked in the daytime around here and Louise's house was no exception. He stepped inside, easing the door closed behind him. The kitchen still smelled of cooked cereal, of eggs, of coffee. Perry's place was set, the other spots cleared away. It was a neat kitchen but in ill repair. Plaster leaked from a spot on the ceiling, handles were missing from several cabinets, the windows rattled loosely in their frames. It was certainly Louise's house. It even smelled like her. A dull burning filled his stomach—like when he'd drunk too much coffee before eating breakfast.

He climbed the stairs. Although the farmhouse probably dated from the late 1800s, the steps were thickly carpeted in some garish runner. Perhaps Perry didn't relish bouncing his family members off the wooden steps so had this carpeting installed. As Jim neared the top, he heard the shower running. It didn't make much difference where he confronted Perry: in the shower, in the bedroom, at breakfast, he would be equally surprised by a pistol in his face at eight o'clock in the morning. He edged nearer the bathroom door and pushed it further open with his foot. He could see the water running in an empty stall. No one at the sink either. He had begun to turn when he felt something at his back.

"Did you really think there'd be anything worth taking in this old place. Or do you have other business here?"

Before Jim could respond, the voice continued. "Now turn around real slow with your hands where I can see 'em so my rifle don't get any funny ideas and go off." Jim turned and saw his quarry at a barrel distance. Perry was a funhouse mirror image of his children: stout, square-headed and red in the face but of gargantuan proportions. He certainly weighed in at 275 lbs or more and was probably crowding 6'4". His hair was so white he appeared to be bald at first. His skin was only a shade darker. Jim was face-to-face with a giant.

Jim's situation was so ludicrous that he felt no surprise when inspiration suddenly seized him. "I'm no burglar, Perry. Louise asked me to come out here for her. She left her key to the library on her bureau—or some such place." He plastered a smile on his face and looked up, up, up at his prey. The holes in this explanation were even larger than Louise's husband.

But after a strained second, the expression on Perry's face changed and the gun was lowered. "Hey, you must be Jim. That guy who runs her into town Tuesdays." Perry smiled. "I bet she left her key on the kitchen table. That girl has no memory. I have to run after her 'bout half the time with her keys or her purse." Surprisingly, Perry sounded fond of Louise. Jim's father had never managed to sound fond of his mother. His voice had a curl to it whenever he said her name. He could remember it still—Ruth—the one syllable dragging out to three in his father's mouth.

This was a new idea; that a wife-beater could still love his wife. He realized Perry was still talking, thanking him for the weekly rides, offering him coffee and leftover eggs. "I usually make breakfast myself," Perry said. "That Louise can't cook for beans." He laughed. "Hey, for beans. Get it?"

Jim nodded, smiling nervously. What was going on here? This guy didn't seem capable of hurting anyone, wasn't nearly angry enough, didn't fit the profile. He wasn't like Jim's father or any of the men who broke into fights at the drop of a hat. Not like any of the men Jim had come across over the years. His mind tried to wrestle with this even as he stood there in Louise's kitchen.

Though there was the rifle, Jim reminded himself. But what man living in the country didn't have firearms, he thought fingering the pistol in his pocket. "Sure," he said finally. "I got time for a cup." Instantly, he regretted it. The smart thing to do would have been to get out of here before circumstances changed. What if Louise called?

"Sure, Louise probably hooked up with the librarian by now and is inside cleaning her johns. Sit down." Perry poured him a cup of coffee and looked in the oven for the promised eggs. He slid them out of the iron skillet and onto a plate, pushed the ketchup across the table and sat down.

"Say, Sierra's wounds are healing real good," Perry said, after a minute, rounding up some loose sugar on the table with his finger. "Did Louise tell you that?"

"No, but that's good news," Jim said, barely able to hide his surprise. Did men like Perry discuss their bad deeds with strangers?

"She should of told you that. Hey, fellow, it's not your fault, you know," Perry told him, licking his sugary finger and dipping it into the pile of sugar again. "I hope Louise didn't let you think we blamed you for Sierra taking a tumble when you opened the truck door. Easy to forget how high trucks are these days." He paused. "And what does a bachelor know about kids? Especially Sierra who's as clumsy as her brother. That bone doctor says she'll be good as new in a couple weeks."

"And her mother too," Jim said, trying to keep up with the direction Perry was headed in. "She's clumsy too, I mean."

"Louise ain't clumsy," Perry explained. "She just gets mad easy and flies into things." He laughed but without much mirth. "Walls, the kids. But especially me. She's taken that iron pan to my head more than once." He nodded to the skillet, sitting in the sink with water in it. He paused. "Matter of fact, when I heard you in the kitchen I thought maybe she'd finally hired herself someone. A hit man maybe." Jim laughed lightly to break the tension, but Perry didn't seem to hear him. "Anyway, just wanted you to know we don't blame you for Sierra's injuries. Hell, you're the guy who gives Louise a ride." He stood up. "Can't imagine where her key could be." He started to look around.

"Like you said, she's probably inside the library by now. Well, I'd better get to work." Jim rose and headed for the door. Perry followed him.

"Listen, I wonder if you could tell Louise I won't be able to give her rides anymore," Jim asked, putting his hand on the knob. "I've been putting off telling her 'cause I know she counts on me, but I'm changing jobs next week. I'll be taking the Interstate."

"Well, sure," Perry said. "I'll tell her. She can just take the bus in like she used to. Or she'll find someone else to drive her in. Louise's real resourceful that way." He smiled. "And thanks again. She'll probably want to thank you herself . . ."

"No need for that," Jim said quickly. "Your thank you is more than enough." He stepped outside and the door closed behind him. He headed for the truck, taking the Interstate back to town.

# CADAVER DOG

*By Bryon Quertermous*

Bryon Quertermous's first play was a shameless rip-off of *The Maltese Falcon* and was produced when he was nineteen. His short stories have appeared in several print and online magazines and in the anthology *ThugLit Presents Hardcore Hardboiled* (Kensington Books). He is the editor and publisher of *Demolition* magazine in a debt of literary karma. More information is available at www.bryonquertermous.com.

B lues progression in D, slowly.

We work at night because it's easier on the dogs. It doesn't do anything for the stench of the place though. Tonight we're searching a landfill on the northern edge of the county, about 15 miles away from the closest town. My steel rake feels like it's melting into my hands and my back is ready to snap in half. The dog, Ranger, has boots on his feet and he's sniffing for corpses while I shovel trash. I'm not sure which of us is worse off.

The whole place has an eerie glow from the spotlights sweeping the landfill. It's like we're in some sort of horrible post-snuff film. It's approaching 2 A.M. and a gentle quiet is in the air, the sounds of bull-dozers and helicopters from the day crews long faded.

There are about 20 of us and ten dogs. Three German shepherds, several golden retrievers, two Rottweilers, and my dog, a Belgian Malinois. The woman we're looking for was a jogger and she disappeared a week and a half ago.

Ranger's getting excited so I start moving the trash faster to give him a deeper area to work in. The more I shovel, the faster his tail moves, until I finally have to push him away to get to the area he's interested in.

I feel bad for the dogs. If they don't find anything they get discouraged, if they do find anything it's usually just pieces of a person and the dogs know they found something bad. Ranger started as a search and rescue dog and was accustomed to the excitement of finding a live person before I had him retrained.

When my wife died I stopped looking for survivors.

Five years ago we were happy. I'd always wanted to be a cop and I'd always wanted a dog. Amy worried about me and the dogs. I never worried about her. She was an accountant. We had a house and two cars and friends on the church bowling league. My life was set up perfectly to be ripped out from underneath me.

Ranger's got his paw into something but he can't move the trash around enough to get at it. Normal dogs claw their way through things but cadaver dogs are trained to move their paws relaxed so they don't disturb crime scenes. It makes being a dog damn near impossible.

I get excited too when I see a clump of hair and toss my rake aside. Like a garbage bin archeologist, I use small tools and careful maneuvering to claim my treasure intact and keep the surrounding area unmolested.

Ranger senses my excitement and circles behind me waiting for his treat. There won't be a treat for him though, the hair is not attached to anything and no remains seem to be nearby. I feel responsible for getting the dog riled up though so I dig a little further hoping to find something worth while. Eventually I do.

We were married in the summer out in the middle of nowhere in a chapel with no air conditioning. The dog came with us on our honeymoon because I was still in the training program and he had to go everywhere with me. He watched us make love for the first time from across the room.

I tried to put him in the bathroom long enough for Amy and I to have some romance, but the dog kept squealing and finally the desk clerk called and told us to shut him up so I let him watch. He was shot in the head a month later during a drug bust and I never had another dog that squealed after that. I started playing the electric guitar later because I missed his squealing.

The hair we find is in several clumps mostly contained in a small plastic baggie. I finger through it wondering if Ranger knows what it is if it doesn't smell like decomposing flesh. He takes a couple swipes at it with his nose and starts to growl. The old guy next to me figures it's probably from a barber shop and says he's been nailed with the same thing a few times since he's been doing this.

"Kinda creepy when you find yourself wishing the hair in your hand was attached to a dead man's head," he says.

I nod and Ranger continues growling.

The first song I ever wrote was about a woman's hair. She was blonde and had just been promoted to detective. We met at a crime scene and she had her hair rolled up in a bun but it was bursting against the pins and clips she had holding it together and my imagination ran away with me and wondered what happened to her hair at night. I sang the song for my wife and she didn't talk to me for a week after that.

It's not the hair that piques my interest. I stuff as much of them as I can into the nearby plastic bag and hand it off to the old guy next to me. He's got a name, but hell if I can remember what it is. Everybody calls him Old Man.

"Gonna make me a wig outta all this one of these days," he says, taking the baggie. "Can't look any dumber than the flat cats they try and sell me now."

The front piece of a locket is clinging to the lip of an empty creamed corn can. I pick it up and run my fingers over the surface. It's not an antique or particularly interesting for any reason other than the fact that I know the woman who used to own it.

I bought my wife a watch for our first anniversary. It was one of those tacky bangle watches that were in fashion at the time. She claimed to get claustrophobic when she wore watches that were tight to her wrist so I bought it as a joke. It backfired and she wore the damn watch every day until she died. She wore it in the shower, and in bed.

She was wearing the watch the first time I hit her. If she hadn't been so shocked I think she would have clocked me across the face with that watch, taking my eye or a chunk of my nose with it.

The old guy knows I've found something. So does Ranger. I know it's not important to this case, it didn't belong to the woman we're looking for so I pocket it and try to play off the find. Eventually the old guy's boredom gets the best of him and he leaves to take the hair to our leader. Ranger's not as easily fooled.

He nuzzles up between my legs as I'm digging around in the area looking for something else to claim as treasure. It starts as a friendly and competitive thing with him, thinking I'm going after his treat. I give up trying to cover it up when he starts biting.

I can't hit Ranger. I've tried. He scares the hell out me. His eyes get to me. They aren't pathetic or pleading or even friendly. They're knowing.

Amy always wanted a locket, one that meant something. One year, for her birthday, I talked my mom into letting me give her one of my grandmother's broaches. So much for it being the thought that counts. I smacked her after dinner and she gave me a lousy blowjob.

She never knew there was a locket in the family. I only found out myself shortly after our five year anniversary. My grandmother died and she left me some of her things. The locket was holding her place in the last book she read. Some inspirational romance about virtuous pioneer women. I'd already started my affair with Lacey by then and thought she might like it.

Ranger and I are reassigned to a 15-square-foot section near the front gate of the landfill that's already been covered twice. It's a bullshit move and I know they're wondering about what I found. I finger the locket as I walk Ranger over to the new site. He's still not friendly with me, but he's a professional and he knows what he needs to do and he knows he needs me to do it.

The empathy of an animal is one of nature's great miracles. It's a beautiful thing to see an animal internalize the pain of someone he loves unless you own the animal and it's your wife he's siding with.

There were plenty of songs about Lacey. She had beautiful skin and fiery eyes and ignited the primal needs inside of me. I was playing a lot of nights at a blues club in the city mostly to get out of the house. Those days I was mostly using a beat up old acoustic instead of my electric guitar. The scream reminded me of my first dog and that reminded me of Amy. So I switched to the old acoustic and started playing the blues.

> *Fire eyes and love's gone crazy*
> *Liquor me up and be my lady.*

Key change, harder strumming

The rest of the guys probably assume I'm talking to myself. Lyrics are starting to come together and I'm trying to hum out the skeleton of a melody. I'm not great at it, but I'm serviceable and it makes me feel good. A good song's just as honest emotionally as a dog but doesn't guilt me up the same way.

We don't last long in our new location. Ranger's angry, I'm distracted, and the heat's getting the best of all of us. The crew leader comes around 3 A.M. and tells us to go home. I wander around the site a few minutes trying to gather my thoughts before I take Ranger to my track and get the hell out of there.

I put the locket on the sunken space in the dashboard between my steering wheel and the instrument panel so I can view it and ponder it on my way home. Ranger's too valuable to let him ride in the back of the truck so he gets the front seat and a specially made animal seatbelt. The window is down halfway in child lock mode so he doesn't fall, or jump, out of the truck. When I drive through at McDonald's Ranger makes nice with the attendant and gets us a couple of packages of McDonaldland cookies. The cookies are hell on Ranger's digestive system so I make sure he doesn't get a hold of them.

Back at my house I give Ranger one of the treats from the cookie jar Amy bought specifically for him and put the cookies in the cupboard for my nephew if he comes back for a visit. The guitar is still on the couch where I left it to go to work.

A small pile of yellow notebook pages records my futile attempts to work out Amy's death through song. Ranger watches me sit down and pluck at the guitar. Some blues players name their guitars and I wondered if that might help me play better, but a male name seems weird and if I name it after a woman I'd probably snap its neck.

Love never really had anything to do with it. Amy and I certainly connected on several levels, emotionally, physically, and sexually of course. And I suppose, if pressed to answer, I did love her in my own way, but there was always something missing. I don't know if it would have been better if we never married or if we'd married later, but I doubt it. I never felt trapped or anything, I just eventually didn't like being around her.

I'm not going to pretend it was her fault I hit her, or even try to justify it. I'm also not going to apologize. We've all got our demons. I don't drink or smoke or do illegal drugs and I don't lose any sleep at night over it.

Ranger falls asleep as I pluck away on the guitar. I've given up on the song about Amy; perhaps it's just my curse to deal with it instead of being able to work through it. I know, at some level, Ranger knows what happened and it makes me wonder why he still acts the way he does. He only gets upset when I do something to directly offend him, there's no overarching sense of him being wronged by me. Maybe that's what he's trying to do.

When I was younger my dad only hit me a couple of times. That's all it took. After the first time he almost knocked me out, just the threat of him dealing with me was enough to keep me straight. One other time after that, my mom caught me smoking with the girl down the road and she told me that my dad would take care of me. She didn't mention when.

For three weeks after that I was in constant fear of my dad and what he would do to me. When it eventually came, the pain was almost a relief compared to the sense of dread I'd been carrying.

I don't have air conditioning, never have. Something about the humidity is comforting like a gooey wet blanket wrapped around me, but it's starting to get stuffy in the house so I move with my unnamed guitar out to the back porch and grab two cans of Labatt on the way out. I'm on the porch about five minutes when Ranger joins me.

He doesn't look at me, just circles in front of my feet and drops into a ball next to me. My playing eventually gets Ranger so he leaves me on the porch and wanders around the backyard. He's got the whole yard, but he stays around the middle near a bed of roses I planted after Amy died.

> Cadaver dog comin' for you
> Cadaver dog knows what you do.

Roses said "I'm sorry" and candy said "I love you," according to Amy. I bought her roses the day she died. Subconsciously I must have known what I was going to do, though I don't want to think I could be premeditated about something like that.

It's always the little things that get the nastiest arguments started. Amy and I could argue about money and religion and politics civilly and never raise our voices, but damn if I didn't incite her wrath when I popped the tab off of her pop cans.

Our last argument flared up when I made her a grilled cheese sandwich with white bread instead of wheat bread. To me, white bread is the only way to make grilled cheese or peanut butter and jelly. She said it tasted like wax and refused to eat it. I yelled. She yelled. And one of us may, or may not, have thrown a hot frying pan.

I fall asleep on the porch with my guitar across my lap and the humidity in my system. When I wake up again, the sun is coming across the horizon and the neighbor boys are helping Ranger dig around in the rose beds. The other neighbor kids see how much fun they're having so they join in and the digging goes into full gear.

The roses themselves aren't in good shape so I don't mind seeing them go, but what's buried a little deeper might cause me some trouble. I know what's coming and I'm just waiting for it to be done. Like with my dad and the impending whooping.

Amy was buried back in Arizona next to her brother and grandfather. I wasn't able to make it to the funeral because I couldn't fly with Ranger and he gets too sick in the car on long trips. Part of me was happy he couldn't be there for her because I know the bond he had with Amy was stronger than the one he has for me. I want to hate him. I want to shoot him right between his knowing eyes but I can't. He hasn't done anything to me. Not yet at least.

Ranger finds a finger first, and for a minute nobody really knows what it is. It's only when the older neighbor boy pulls out an arm that it starts to fall into place what they're digging up. I'm still strumming on my guitar when the neighbor boys' father comes over to see why his kids are screaming. And a melody is finally starting to come to me when the first police car arrives.

I was with Lacey the day they buried my wife. She was wearing the locket while we made love and that pissed me off. It seemed disrespectful considering how much Amy had wanted it. But Lacey wouldn't budge. We were in the middle of sex when I had enough and pushed her off of me. I went to the garage and got an ax and cut her head off.

Most of the body parts along with her head went into separate garbage bags that I disposed of in dumpsters all over the county. But I kept her arms and hands and buried them when I planted the roses in honor of Amy.

Ranger is watching me as the officers handcuff me and lead me away. His eyes don't scare me anymore because he doesn't have anything to hold over me. He led them to my secret and that's what I wanted. Now I have a reason to kill him.

> *Cadaver dog, poor four legged fool*
> *Cadaver dog, they'll never find you.*

# ANNIVERSARY
## By Hilary Davidson

Hilary Davidson is certain that she is the only writer in the world who has published work in both *Martha Stewart Weddings* and *ThugLit*. Since interning at *Harper's Magazine* in 1995 she has written fifteen travel guides, including *Frommer's New York City Day by Day* and *Frommer's Toronto*. Her work has also appeared in *Discover, American Archaeology*, and *Reader's Digest*. A Toronto native, she has lived in New York since October 2001. Visit her website at www.hilarydavidson.com.

He had spent all afternoon shopping and now he was late. He'd envisioned having dinner ready for Helen at seven, the two of them toasting with a twenty-four-year-old Bordeaux. The wine was from the year Helen was born, a fact he knew she would appreciate. Only now, with the clock ticking and the water on the stove refusing to boil, he realized he'd never make it. The thought made the santoko knife quiver and slide right out of his hand as he tried to dice an onion. It clattered against the granite counter and dropped, the seven-inch blade embedding itself in the floorboards not an inch from his foot. He crouched to pry it free by the handle, leaving a thin scar on the varnished wood. He set the santoko on a dishtowel and got another Japanese knife out of a drawer. *Steady hands*, he reminded himself. This just wasn't like him. He didn't trust anything but cautious, painstaking planning. The devil was always in the details, like his father said. Lack of preparation only invited disaster.

He knew that and still the devil had tripped him up that afternoon. He'd started out with a shopping list culled from his mother's recipe for Lobster Thermidor, and he'd mapped out the route he planned to follow. But somewhere between picking up fresh tarragon for the béchamel sauce and choosing fresh lobsters, he realized that he hadn't actually bought an anniversary gift for Helen. True, the wine was specially selected for her, and he had already given her that goddess-like long blue dress that would make her look like Rita Hayworth in *Down to Earth* at dinner that night. But he didn't have a bow-topped box for her to unwrap with barely concealed greed.

He knew Helen had a frivolous side; he had watched her while she shopped at the holiday market in Grand Central Terminal, trying on sparkly necklaces and rings that made her lips part and eyes widen with desire. But it was January now and the market was gone and he wasn't sure where to go. He'd stood in the Essex Street Market, sweat trickling down his back even though it was a cold day. Then it hit him, the place that Holly Golightly went to shed the mean reds. What was the movie called? *Breakfast at Tiffany's.* He'd already come into Manhattan to shop, he reasoned, so why not make the trek to Midtown? He was angry at himself for not thinking of it earlier, when he would have had the luxury of shopping online. Instead, grocery bags in hand, he took the subway up to Fifty-ninth Street and spent the longest twenty-two minutes of his life peering into locked glass cases and feeling despair as voices in a dozen tongues crowded his thoughts right out of his head. It embarrassed him that the salesmen were better dressed than he was, that they were able to turn a polished *Can I help you, sir?* into an insult. But their smirks had given way to slack jaws when he had pointed to a white-gold bracelet and paid for it with cash.

The money didn't matter, but the cost in time made him frantic. With the trip up and then back to the market for the lobsters, he'd lost more than an hour, and the train home to Brooklyn stopped twice without explanation. He had raced home from the station, slipping twice on glare ice. Only after he got to his house and locked the front door behind him did he feel some of the pressure lift off his chest. Before he'd even taken off his coat, he'd ducked into the old-fashioned parlor, poured two fingers of scotch from the sideboard and belted it down. He poured two more and carried the tumbler into the kitchen. *Company while I'm cooking*, he told himself. He didn't want Helen to see him drunk. That could get messy.

He'd shrugged off his coat and tossed it on a chair, ignoring the blinking light of the message machine on the countertop. Its red eye meant one thing to him: tenants with complaints, none of which he wanted to deal with now. He was a veterinarian by training and inclination—he'd always preferred animals to people—but when his parents died, they had left their only child their Brooklyn home and the three brownstones they owned. Upkeep and maintenance was a full-time job, he'd found. Four years back, when the responsibility for the buildings landed on his shoulders, he'd tried to hire out the work. He quickly learned that people didn't give a damn about doing things properly. Maybe they never had, but watching old movies had left him with the impression that times really were better when Jimmy Stewart was young. Everything had gone downhill since then, including the quality of Manhattan tenants. Just yesterday he'd had to waste an afternoon snaking a series of sinks because one overpaid Wall Street nitwit had installed a garbage disposal unit and dumped what looked like a dozen Chinese takeout containers into it. The backlog had shot back through the pipes and into two neighbors' kitchen sinks. It was this kind of thing that drove a man to drink.

But not tonight. He took a sip of scotch and forced himself to put the tumbler down. This was his night, his and Helen's, their two-week anniversary. He knew people might laugh at him for being such a cornball about it, but he couldn't help himself. He had been in love with her for so many quiet, hopeless months. She was fifteen years younger than him, graceful and beautiful and kind. He hadn't even believed it the first time she'd smiled at him. That had been last summer and, even though it was a happy memory, it made his heart constrict. He wasn't a man for whom lovely women often spared smiles. Helen had been dating one of his tenants then, a soulless bond trader who had the neighbors complaining about his loud music and late-night parties. That was one face that wasn't missed around the building, he was sure.

He checked the water and vinegar in the stockpot and decided that it could pass for a rolling boil. He had always loved cooking for the discipline and precision it demanded, but tonight he was too unsettled to take pleasure from it. He threw the two lobsters into the pot, put the lid on, and immediately felt guilty. When he cooked a lobster he normally took the time to hypnotize it first, a trick he'd learned from his father. *They like the hot water*, his father had told him. He was old enough to know that wasn't actually true, but he held on to the custom of rubbing the space between their antennae to lull them into accepting their fate. There was no sense in being unnecessarily cruel, not to an animal, anyway, he thought. Still, it was too late to do anything about it now.

At least the béchamel sauce was doing alright. The flour had finally melded with the scalded milk, and a *bouquet garni* was simmering next to the diced vegetables. If he was quick about it he could take a moment to make himself presentable. There was so much to do—candles to light, a table to set, lights to be turned down low and music turned on—but he didn't want Helen seeing him looking a mess. He raced upstairs just as the phone started to ring, which reminded him that he needed to unplug it. *So much to do*, he thought as he pulled off his sweater and pants in the doorway of his bedroom. He took a white shirt out of the closet, buttoned up the front and reached for a gray suit. It was a double-breasted number that Cary Grant might have worn. He had a wardrobe full of fine clothes and few occasions to wear them. Still, it paid to be prepared. He'd had the suit freshly pressed a couple of days before, and had already selected a paisley tie and knotted cufflinks to go with it, so there was no moment of indecision now. He grabbed the accessories and a well-polished pair of wingtips and headed back to the kitchen.

The tricky thing with Lobster Thermidor, he knew from experience, was timing. He took a large pair of tongs out of a drawer and pulled the lobsters out of the pot, one after the other. He grabbed the first claw and twisted it right around. It came away with the knuckles attached as it was supposed to, but the water that squirted out scalded his hand. He twisted the other claws off and put them back in the pot. He ran his hands under cold water and swore softly. *Battle wounds*, he would tell Helen over dinner. *Battle wounds, earned for you.* He knew it sounded hokey but it might make her laugh, and he loved to hear her laugh.

He gulped down more scotch, then got a mixing bowl and whisked together the egg yolks and cream. He wondered if Helen was as nervous as he was. He'd had crushes before but had never been in love. For a long time he'd wondered whether there might be something wrong with him. Then Helen had come along and shown him that he was capable of love—deep, abiding love, the kind they made movies about. Even when that love was unrequited, as it had been at one time with Helen, he was steadfast and loyal. He finished his drink and got another bottle of scotch out of the cupboard. He opened it up and made a generous pour before letting it be. It would wait till he finished cooking.

By the time he had deveined the lobster, cracked the claws, and set the meat into a baking dish with the béchamel, it was close to eight. He sprinkled some grated Parmesan over the dish and put it into the oven to cook. He sat down for the first time since coming home, put on his shoes and fastened the cufflinks. There was a mirror in the hallway just outside the kitchen. He took his tie and his glass, which he set on the table while he fussed with getting the knot right. He looked at himself and smiled shyly. He knew he was no Cary Grant, but he wasn't half bad. A little on the short side, maybe, but he'd lifted weights for two decades and had a powerful body, corded with muscle. His face was pleasant looking, his mother had always said; from certain angles you didn't even notice his lazy eye. He ran a hand through his dark, wavy hair and tilted his head to the side. Then he remembered the phone. He unplugged it and put it in a drawer, then went back to the mirror, and belted down the scotch. He picked up the Tiffany's bag, unlocked the door to the basement and went downstairs.

"Is that you?" Helen called out in a tentative voice. She was sitting on the heart-shaped pink bed in the center of the room, wearing the blue dress that left one shoulder bare and cascaded over the other with its fine, shimmery fabric. Her resemblance to Rita Hayworth never failed to take his breath away. Auburn hair, creamy skin and blue eyes. A slender dancer's body that was delicate and lithe.

"Y-y-y-yes," he stammered. Then he remembered to smile. Helen smiled back at him as he moved closer. She closed her book and put it on the bedside table. "F-f-f-for y-y-you," he said, handing her the

Tiffany's bag. It wasn't as grand as what he'd meant to say but he didn't mind that when he saw Helen's megawatt smile.

"You're wonderful," she said. "You're the most thoughtful man in the world. Thank you, darling." She set the bag down without opening it. She looked at him and her smile retreated. "I think . . . I think I'm bleeding again. Would you please take a look?" She held out her bare legs and he noticed that the bandages on her ankles were freshly red. The cuts should have been healed up by now; it occurred to him that Helen might be poking and prodding at the tendons to make them look worse than they really were. "I'm so worried about it," she said. "I think I really need to see a doctor. It might be infected."

He stroked her feet and nodded absently. There was a doctor he knew, a tenant who'd had some problems with self-prescribed pharmaceuticals. Perhaps he'd call him later; perhaps it wouldn't be necessary.

"Would you take me to the hospital?" said Helen in a soft voice. "Please, darling."

He kissed the instep of her left foot and then her right. "*T-t-t*-time *f-f*-for *d-d-d*-dinner," he said. He reached down and picked Helen up. She was so light and so fragile. He held her in his arms for a moment before he kissed her on the lips. He noticed a tear running down her cheek when he pulled his head back slightly to look at her. "*I-I-I*-I love *y-y*-you." It amazed him that he never stuttered when he said *love*. It was the one word that never tripped him up.

"I love you, too," said Helen, closing her eyes.

He picked up the Tiffany's bag—she could open it later—and let it dangle from one arm as he carried Helen up the stairs. It wasn't true that a person couldn't walk after her Achilles tendon was cut; one lost the ability to propel oneself forward, but slow, mincing steps were possible. Stairs were another matter: Helen would have had to crawl to get up the steps by herself. But she would never have to do that because he'd always be there to carry her. It was the sort of detail another man might overlook, but that had never been his style.

# SOMETHING OUT OF THE ORDINARY
*By Kerry Ashwin*

Kerry Ashwin is a freelance writer covering many genres. Her main field is writing for boating magazines, which comes naturally, as she and her family live on a 44-foot yacht in Townsville, Australia. Kerry has also been published in travel and lifestyle magazines, and her short stories, poetry, and radio plays have been broadcast on radio around Australia. She has an interest in the Web, and has two blog sites besides contributing to e-magazines. Her keen interest in writing extends to competitions, and she has been shortlisted several times in Australia and England, but as yet, first place eludes her. She hopes, on a personal level, to circumnavigate the globe in early retirement with her family and write about the adventure.

N orman Stickleback, that's me. I'm not what you would call a go-getter, I don't excel at anything. In fact at school the other kids used to call me Nothing Special N.S. or Normal Norman.

I had no great aspirations at school. No one expected me to have any and so I didn't disappoint them. It became easy to conform to mediocrity. I can say though I only did that with an average C. As a small boy my mother would say to the shopkeeper that I was of average size for my age. My shoes were average and my hair cut was of the times, no fuss easy to manage and perfectly satisfactory as my father said.

I didn't sail through my school years nor did I fall behind. The most the headmaster could say was that I attended punctually; and that was about the sum of it. The teachers regarded me as a fixture in the classroom, third row in the middle. The rowdy lot sat at the back, the swots in the front, and I filled the gap in between. That suited me because I hardly ever was called upon for anything. Sports weren't my thing, but I did run when required, coming the middle of the pack. Even when there were only three in the race I came second.

My parents were never ones to make a fuss and so we lived our lives in quiet anonymity. My father was a butcher and I followed in his path. He was kept busy but never overworked. My mother was a homebody, who went about her daily business with quiet contemplation. The Sticklebacks just got on with the daily grind of living.

So no one was expecting it when I murdered my wife.

The papers didn't rate her disappearance and it wasn't mentioned. After all, people go missing all the time. Some said she was hounded by mediocrity and couldn't take any more. But after a day or two no one inquired and I didn't volunteer and so she slipped into the past tense like she never existed.

We used to like one another, before she got ideas above her station. She wanted me to be one of those go get 'em ideas man. I tried to impress upon her that I was just your ordinary Joe, nothing special. Still she tried to drag me up to the rarified air of the elite. I told her I would get vertigo. Then one day she bought me a new apron for work. A blue and white number with the shop name on the front. She said it had class. I didn't see it that way. Just drawing attention to yourself. Showing off. I refused to wear it. She wasn't hurt more like raving mad. She followed me into the cold room and I walked out and shut the door. Just habit I guess, but she stayed there, for about 4 days. I couldn't say when she gave up. But after the bank holiday and the long weekend she stopped trying to make me something I wasn't.

I kept working, catching the same bus, taking the same short walk to the butchers shop, eating the same ham sandwiches like I always did. Nothing much changed for me.

Oh I had to dispose of the body, but it was a small matter to cut her up at work. I kept her in the cold room. Then one morning before I opened the shop, I portioned her up, much like a pig. I had a mincing machine, so I did all the entrails with the belly fat and made sausages. Not that I intended to eat them but more of a private joke. She used to whinge that sausages were for the lower classes. Never mind I used to say that mine had prime beef or pork in them. And now she was a sausage. Justice in there somewhere, I think. By the time I had finished I was only left with the head. I popped it in the brine barrel and got ready to open up.

She once said she would like a pet. I gave her a dog from the pound. She wanted one of those fancy type dogs and the poor mutt I bought didn't cut the mustard. We gave it away in the end and her little yap dog (as I called it) only lived a year or two. Overpriced and overbred I thought. Well the animal shelter was glad of her sausages, they thanked me for my generosity. She would have seen the sense in feeding the hungry animals. Doing good works I think she called it.

Some portions I froze and then every now and again I would take her fishing. I never caught much but she made good bait. I remarked to myself on more than one occasion that she turned out good for something in the end. She always said I was good for nothing. Even though I gave her everything I think she saw me as only a butcher and she didn't want to be known as the butcher's wife.

I still had the head and it was pickled, so I decided to try my hand at crabbing. I never really enjoyed crustaceans but I reckon I could get used to them when I snapped up six beauties with my bait. It wasn't long before I just had a bone left. I wasn't quite sure how to get rid of it, until I saw a programme on the television about a place that was an old volcanic crater. It was reputed to be bottomless and so I thought I would toss her in after all she thought I was a bottomless pit of money.

I closed up shop for a few days which was a first for me, because I'd never had a holiday. I drove to Mt. Gambia and the Blue Lake. I stayed in the caravan park, and decided to enjoy myself with the tourist trail. I did the heritage walk and the short bush walk then I took her to the Blue Lake for a boat ride. I had her in a paper bag and I took the tour of the lake's centre. It was very informative telling us about the colour, depth, age and recent explorations. She said I was a workaholic and never took her anywhere. But here she was at this tourist spot getting a bird's eye view. When everyone went to one side of the boat to look at the sunset, I gently let go of the bag on the other side. I had taken the precaution of weighing her down with her gold jewelry. She said she never had anywhere to wear her jewels. The bag went straight into the depths. And then I rejoined the others to enjoy the view.

Six months later I had to chuckle about a news item on the television. Apparently a skull was found draped in gold chain, thought to be a significant find in the Blue Lake. Sacrificial some said. No, I remarked no sacrifice on my part.

They put her in a museum claiming to have found ancient human remains. She wasn't ancient, 40 more like. I liked Mt. Gambia and made it an annual holiday destination. Of course I visited the display. She looked pretty good after six years. Hadn't aged a bit, and now she got her wish to be consorting with people of standing, people with letters after their name.

Every year for two weeks I booked in at the Blue Lake Caravan Park, and visited the wife. I used to bring my ham sandwiches to the museum, and I'd have a bit of a chat to her.

We seemed to strike up quite a friendship. She'd mellowed over the years and we started to like one another. Funny how time can alter a person's outlook. I began to see she wasn't such a bad ol' stick after all. Then one day the attendant said he noticed me and we got to talking. He said they were hunting for the lower jaw.

"Oh I've got that," I said.

He didn't believe me at first, but when I produced it he believed me. They matched up of course. I don't know why they thought they wouldn't, although with her fillings, she didn't look ancient any more. She said she was glad we had made it up after all these years.

And Doctor, you know, she said, I was something out of the ordinary. Her first kinds words for years.

# DEAD AS A DOG
## By Doug Allyn

The award-winning author Doug Allyn is a Michigan writer with an international following. He has written seven novels and nearly a hundred short stories, his first short story won the Robert L. Fish Award for Best First from the Mystery Writers of America and subsequent critical response has been equally remarkable. He has won the coveted Edgar Allan Poe Award (plus six nominations), the International Crime Readers' Award, three Derringer Awards for novellas, and the Ellery Queen Readers' Award an unprecedented eight times. Published internationally in English, German, French, and Japanese, more than two dozen of his tales have been optioned for development as feature films and for television.

A girl asked me about killing Hitler today," I said.
Janie gave me a taut smile but it was all she could manage. The hospice aide who was massaging Janie's calves glanced up at me with arched eyebrows.

"I teach Political Science at Hancock State," I explained. "We're covering assassinations this week. Martin Luther King, JFK, Sadat. How destructive to society their deaths were. But if a student asks me about killing Hitler or Stalin, I know it's going to be a good class."

"So you teach 'em what? That whacking out some folks ain't such a bad idea?" the aide asked dryly. She was an older black woman with a soft Afro, liquid eyes, strong hands. Her name tag read Norma. I wondered how she could work every day in a place where most patients were dying. Like Janie. My wife. My life.

"I try to impart a given number of facts," I said. "And beyond that, I hope they learn to think for themselves."

"Wish I'd had your class," Norma smiled. "If I'd thought a little harder, would've skipped nursing school, found me a rich man to marry instead."

"And miss all this excitement?" Janie murmured.

And we laughed. Partly because it was funny, mostly because it's amazing that a woman in her condition can joke at all.

My wife is dying. A glioblastoma, a cancerous tumor, is wrapped around her spinal cord. Inoperable. Terminal. And very aggressive. It's early October now. They tell me she won't see Christmas.

So I laughed, though it wasn't much of a joke. There aren't many smiles in my life these days.

After my morning hospice visit, I headed home for lunch. I wasn't hungry but Sparky would be.

Our suburban house is larger than we need. We'd planned to fill it with more children so it sits on a large, five-acre lot, bordering a forest. When we first looked the place over, I think the land was more important than the house to Janie.

She loved the outdoors, a four-season girl. Skier, cross-country runner, backpacker. Anything to be out in the wind. I do those things too, but only to be with her. The flame of Janie's vitality could melt a snowman's heart. But it's burning low now. And I'm not sure I can go on without her. Or want to.

But I don't have a choice. We have twins, Seth and Josh, seven and a half years old. Fraternal twins, not identical. Seth is more like me, dark and slender. Josh, more like his mother, blond, square-faced, a blocky little body, bursting with energy.

The boys are staying with my in-laws for the duration. A blessing, though I miss them terribly. With Janie's illness and the teaching schedule that maintains our health insurance, I have all I can handle.

Silence greeted me as I walked in the foyer. Usually Sparky, Janie's bull terrier, charges the door when I come home, barking, a barrel-chested black and white pirate of a pup. The noisy greeting lasts until he sees I'm alone. Then he gives me a dutiful tail-wag and goes on about his business.

Not today. Tossing my jacket on an easy chair, I walked through the house. "Sparky?"

Nothing. Probably outside. He has his own dog-door exit into our fenced backyard. I walked through to the den and scanned the yard through the picture window. Still no Sparky. The yard was empty . . . Damn! The back gate was open.

Double damn. I'd noticed him jumping at it the other day, meant to tie it shut . . . Grabbing my binoculars off the window ledge, I quickly scanned the field beyond the fence. And felt a flood of relief as I spotted the little terrier lounging in the grass just outside the gate.

I opened the back door. "Sparky! Lunch!"

He raised his head, then lay back down. "Sparky! Come on!" This time he didn't move at all.

Odd. Concerned now, I started across the lawn toward the gate. But halfway there I broke into a run. Even at that distance I could see the blood.

"Arnie?"

I glanced up. Dr. Dave Westbrook, our veterinarian, rested a hand on my shoulder. And I could read the bad news in his face. "How is he?"

"I'm sorry, Arnie. He's gone. Too much blood loss."

"What happened to him?"

"I was hoping you could tell me," he said, glancing around his busy waiting room. "Could you step back here, please?"

I followed him into the sterile operating room. Sparky was laid out on a stainless steel table. The wound in his guts had been cleaned up a bit, but it was still a vile, savage hole.

"My God, David, what would cause something like that?" I whispered.

"A hunting arrow, I think. Where did you find him?"

"In the field behind our house. He got loose, may have been running in the woods—"

"And deer season opened three days ago," Dave finished for me.

"It's not open season on family dogs and we own that land. You think a hunter shot him?"

"I'm not sure. I've seen arrow wounds before, but never one quite like this. Some high-tech broadheads pop open like switchblades when they strike. This one apparently blew clean through, more like a rifle."

"Then why do you think it was an arrow?"

"See these blue smudges around the wound? It's chalk dust from a tracking string."

"Chalk dust? I don't understand."

"Some bow-hunters attach a string to their arrows, dusted with chalk. When the arrow strikes and the animal bolts, the string drags on the ground, leaving a trail they can follow. But I've never seen blue dust before. Most hunters use Day-Glo orange chalk, easier to spot."

"My God. Day-Glo dust? Switchblade arrows? I thought hunting was supposed to get you back to nature."

"I know, it seems cruel. But the truth is, once the animal's been hit, anything that kills them quicker is more humane in the end. Not that there's anything humane about the sonofabitch who did this. We have a crematorium here. If you like, I can take care of the remains for you."

I just stared at him.

"The remains," he repeated, not unkindly. "If you—never mind. I know a thing like this is a helluva shock, Arnie. Go home, take a break. You can call me if you decide to—"

"Thanks, David, but I'll take him home with me."

"Are you sure?"

"No. Right now I'm not sure about anything." But as I drove back to town, I had a small parcel in the trunk of my car. The final remains of our beloved dog. Which left me with two impossible questions.

One. How could anyone do a thing like that? Kill a harmless pet?

And two, what on earth was I going to tell Janie?

The second problem had an easier answer than the first. I lied, flat-out. Perhaps the first time I've ever lied to my wife about anything serious.

A risky thing to do. Ordinarily, Janie can read me like a neon bill-board. And her first question is always "How are the boys? And Sparky?"

"He misses you," I said. And she missed the fib. Perhaps because her eyes were closed. She was in a lot of pain. Some days it takes all of her concentration to keep it at bay.

I didn't stay long. When the pain gets this intense, they have to sedate her to prevent seizures. The intervals between attacks keeps getting shorter.

But God help me, just this once, I was almost grateful for it.

Driving through the village on my way home, I passed the Algoma Sporting Goods. On impulse, I parked in front and went inside. A big store, family owned, in an older building, barn-board walls with a high, embossed metal ceiling.

The front of the store was mostly filled with school gear, baseball gloves, cleats, basketball jerseys. I bought a Nerf football for my boys here once. But halfway back, the games change, from high school sports to woodland slaughter.

No Nerf gear back here. The clothing is heavy canvas, color camouflaged to resemble the northern Michigan forest. The entire back wall is a gigantic display of firearms, rifles and shotguns, three tiers of them, floor to ceiling. Every caliber from a Boy Scout beginner's twenty-two popgun to a monster 458 Winchester magnum, capable of killing an Alaskan grizzly at three hundred yards. Even if the bear's hiding behind a tree.

But it was the display beside it that caught my eye. Modern hunting bows of enormous complexity, equipped with offset pulleys and wheels and counterweights and telescopic sights, arrows of aluminum, titanium and fiberglass composites. Robin Hood wouldn't have recognized a damned thing on that wall.

"Can I help you?" A redneck salesman materialized at my left shoulder. Paunchy with a scruffy beard, wearing a faded flannel shirt. This definitely wasn't The Gap.

"Do you carry chalk dust for tracking strings?"

"Sure, right over here," he said, moving behind the counter. "What's your poison, pal, Day-Glo orange or neon yellow?"

"How about blue?"

"Blue? Sorry, we don't carry it. I expect you can get blue dust down the street at the hardware store, though."

"Do you know anyone who uses blue chalk?"

He blinked, confused by the question. And glanced over my shoulder, as if the answer might be behind me. "Blue? Naw, not off-hand. You ain't a bow-hunter, are ya, mister?"

"No."

"Didn't think so. 'Scuse me, I got other customers." He beat a hasty retreat, jumpy as a kid with a crib sheet up his sleeve. I turned to see what he'd looked at . . . and froze. The wall behind me held a stunning display as surreal as a Star Wars set.

Crossbows. But not the ancient arbalests of the middle-ages. More like weird weapons from Middle Earth. Ultra-modern killing machines. Hollow plastic stocks, geared cranking mechanisms, bipods and rifle scopes. Names like Revolution XS, Quad-400 and Talon Super Max.

They didn't fire standard arrows, they shot bolts of steel, with replaceable broad-head tips, some with serrated bleeder blades sharp enough to transfix an elk.

Or gut a small dog.

At home, I actually paused in the doorway a moment, waiting for Sparky's welcoming racket. Which was crazy. He was in the box under my arm. And he'd never welcome anyone again. But as bad as I felt about it, I couldn't let my guard down now.

With Jane in the hospice and the boys staying with our in-laws, we didn't need the added stress of a slaughtered dog. Better to tell everyone Sparky just . . . ran away. It was thin but I could probably sell it. But to make it work, I had to conceal the evidence.

Grabbing a spade from the garden shed, I carried Sparky out of our back yard into the grassy field beyond our fence. The greenbelt stretches the full width of the subdivision, nearly a quarter mile, room for the kids from a dozen families to play together. The homes are all similar, faux New England saltboxes with vinyl siding, set on two-acre lots that end at the edge of the field. Our lot is a bit larger, a full five acres that extend well into the deep woods beyond.

Halfway across the field, some juniper bushes shielded me from view. It would have to do. Gently setting the box down, I began to dig. In the soft, moist earth, it didn't take long. The hole, two feet square, four feet deep, seemed much too small to contain the spirit of our rambunctious little dog. For a moment I could see Janie running across this very field with Sparky in hot pursuit . . .

I slammed the slide projector of my memory shut. Hard. I can't afford to think too much about Janie. If I start to cry, I'm not sure I'll be able to stop. Janie's always been the strong one, irrepressible. But it's my turn to carry the weight now. She needs my strength, and so do the boys. Somehow I have to manage this. So mostly, I try to shut myself down. To keep from feeling anything at all.

But burying Sparky in that empty field, alone, was one of the hardest things I've ever done.

Placing him gently in his little grave, I recited the Lord's Prayer. Couldn't think of anything else. Then I carefully covered him over.

The turned earth looked too raw, too visible. I was gathering scraps of underbrush to camouflage it, when I noticed the blood.

Glistening crimson dewdrops, darkening to maroon now as they congealed in the autumn air. Sparky must have dragged himself past this spot earlier. Bleeding. And dying. In agony. Trying to get home.

In the late afternoon sun, the blood trail gleamed like a beacon in the grass. Showing where he'd passed. And where he'd come from.

I don't recall consciously making the decision. But when I'd finished concealing Sparky's grave, I turned and marched slowly into the forest, tracking the blood spoor, clutching my spade like a spear.

It was like stepping back in time. At first, the trees were scattered, mostly aspens at the edge of the wood, new growth that had sprung up after the land had been leveled for the subdivision. But a few yards beyond them, I was already deep in the primeval woodlands, poplars and pines towering overhead, their swaying limbs splintering the sunlight, dappling the forest floor, making the blood trail damned difficult to follow.

But I managed. As I took each careful step, totally focused on the sparse red spatters on the matted leaves, I felt myself slipping into an ancient rhythm. A mind-set left over from an earlier age, when men had stalked this land for survival, when losing a blood trail might mean slow death from starvation . . .

It faded out. The distance between blood dots had been gradually lengthening, until I had to stop at each small spatter and scan the ground ahead for the next one. Twice, I lost the trail and had to circle the last dot until I crossed the next. But not this time. The blood had vanished altogether.

And as I straightened up and took stock, I realized why. This was the place. I was standing in the killing zone.

Off to my left, the forest floor was roughed up in the center of a small clearing, leaves scattered, the soil gouged, torn by the paws of a small dog thrashing about in agony. I was certain of the spot. Some of the displaced leaves were smudged with blue chalk marks. And smeared blood.

I did a slow pirouette, scanning the forest around me. Most hunters favor the dawn hours and late afternoon. Perhaps the man I wanted to meet was watching me even now . . .

Then I spotted it. Thirty yards off. A small hut, a shooting blind, hand built of dun-colored canvas and dead branches. Artfully camouflaged. If I hadn't been looking, I would never have noticed it.

I approached it warily, gripping my spade fiercely with both hands. But there was no need. The blind was empty. As I peered inside, I realized I was trembling with tension, taut as a bowstring. Or a cocked crossbow. I'd really wanted the bastard to be here.

But he wasn't. So instead of splitting his skull with my shovel, I took my rage out on his handiwork, ripping his hut apart with my bare hands, hurling the pieces as far into the forest as I could. In two furious minutes I reduced his hunting blind to a few bits of scattered wreckage. A stick here, a shred of canvas there. Nuked. Utterly destroyed.

Like my world.

Half an hour later, I was in the school gym, helping with my sons' Pee Wee basketball practice. It was a hoot, short-legged little grubbers charging about like puppies in a pen, lofting impossible shots, blundering out of bounds, fouling one another with glee, having a grand time as suburban dads like myself try to teach them a few basics along the way.

I've never missed a practice or a game, struggling to keep things as normal as humanly possible for the twins as their mother fades out of our lives. But today I was especially eager to be here. The assistant coaches are all part-timers. And one of them, Jerry Landry, is an Algoma County deputy sheriff.

He was at a corner basket, teaching the rudiments of rebounding to a half-dozen half pints, tossing a ball against the backboard so they could scramble for it on the way down, grinning as they knocked each other sprawling.

"Can I talk to you a second, Jerry?"

"Sure. What's up, doc? Or should I call you professor?" He lobbed up another ball, letting it drop into the scrum. A tall, raw-boned man, thinning reddish-blond hair, western sideburns, a torn Algoma High sweatshirt, striped uniform slacks and soiled sneakers. A single dad, divorced. A club I'll be joining soon enough.

"What are the penalties for killing a dog?"

"Depends. On where the dog was and what it was doing. And who did the killing."

"The dog was on my property—"

"Let me guess, you live in that new Birchcrest subdivision?"

"That's right. So?"

"So don't feel like the Lone Ranger, Professor. We've had beaucoup complaints about dogs and cats being killed in that neighborhood."

"What are you doing about it?"

"Not a lot. We're the Sheriff's Department, not the pet patrol— hey! Settle down out there! This is basketball, not Saturday Night Smackdown!"

"You're telling me some loony's killing pets and you're not even trying to find him?"

"No need to," Landry said evenly. "We know who he is, or think we do. That's the problem."

"I don't understand."

"That's because you're not from here. You moved up here to teach at the college, bought a nice house, probably joke about the local rednecks in the teachers' lounge, right? But now your dog's dead. Well, welcome to my world, pal."

"What are you saying?"

"Probably more than I should. Can we go off the record a minute? Not a citizen beefing to a cop, just two guys talking in a gym?"

"Of course."

"Okay, here's the deal. We're fairly sure the guy killing the animals is Chandler Sinclair. That name mean anything to you?"

"You mean—?"

"Right. Sinclair Paper Mill, Sinclair Timber, the Sinclair Library at the U. The folks who employ about four hundred people in this town. That Sinclair family."

"And? Because they've got bucks they're above the law?"

"Nope, not for a second. If Chan runs a stoplight or shoots the mayor, I'll bust him like any other perp. But since his fat campaign contributions helped get my boss elected, our little force has better things to do than worry about pets disappearing in Chan's neighborhood."

"It's not his neighborhood, it's mine."

"It used to be his. All of it. At one time, his family owned most of this town."

"So what am I supposed to do?"

"Anything you want, Professor. Just don't expect us to do it for you. Truth is, Chan Sinclair's not wrapped too tight. All he gives a rip about is taking game with high-tech weapons that probably cost more than my car. When his dad was alive he could control him, more or less, but the old man died last year and now Chan's off the leash. He's only got a sister left and treats her like hired help. You can file a complaint and I'll have a talk with Sinclair. But even if you could prove he killed your dog, Chan would only pay a fine and it might bring retaliation from Chan or his lawyers. The law's a little different up here for strangers like you and a local guy like Chan. He may be a crazy sumbitch, but he's our crazy sumbitch."

"And his plants employ a lot of local men, I understand that. But that doesn't give him the right to kill people's pets."

"Nobody said it did. I'm not telling you to let this go, Professor. If he'd killed my dog, I'd damn sure do something about it. Don't know a man who wouldn't. I'm just saying you'd best keep it off the books, if you get my drift. Hey, Jake! Don't hold the ball like that, they'll tie you up every time. Swing your elbows, boy, clear yourself some room!"

"That's a little rough, isn't it? For grade school?"

"We ain't just teaching basketball, Prof, we teach life here. And it's good advice. If you mess with Chan Sinclair, you'd best come down swingin' your elbows. High and wide."

Interesting advice. Especially from a cop. After basketball practice, I took the boys out for greaseburgers at McDonald's. Chose it deliberately, because it has a playroom. The twins had a great time scrambling through the tunnels. And I had time to think.

And what I thought was: this was no time to swing my elbows at Chandler Sinclair or anyone else.

With Janie ill, I had to stay focused and keep things together. I don't have tenure at Hancock State, my contract runs year to year. The administration has been very understanding about Janie's illness, but the fact is, our income has been cut in half. I need my job to keep food on the table and to maintain our health insurance. And the Hancock administration is ever so proud of its new Sinclair Library wing.

So I decided to do the prudent thing. The adult thing. I would let it pass. And I did.

Until the next day. When all hell broke loose.

After morning classes, I stopped by the hospice to sit with Janie awhile. She was getting her rubdown, listening without comment while I rattled on about school. I was afraid her silence might indicate pain. And it did. But not the way I thought.

Halfway through the rubdown Janie gave Norma a look, and the woman excused herself. Janie sat up slowly, and turned to face me, squinting against the pain the effort caused her. I reached out to help but she shook her head.

"I had a visitor earlier," she said coldly. "Yvonne Westbrook, the veterinarian's wife? She brought me flowers. Thought I might be depressed because of Sparky."

Damn. "She had no right to tell you."

"It's not her fault, Arnie. It probably never occurred to her you'd lie to me about something so serious. I'm not gone yet, you know. I'm still a part of this family. And I'm entitled to the damned truth! From what Yvonne said, I gather someone deliberately killed our dog. Is that true?"

I hesitated, then caved. "Yes."

"What happened?"

"Sparky got out the back gate and went exploring in the woods behind the subdivision. He was apparently shot by a hunter."

"Where was he?"

"Maybe . . . forty or fifty yards into the woods. A bow hunter had a shooting blind there."

"But . . . we own that land, don't we?"

"I think so, yes."

"A bow and arrow," she said flatly. "My god. Do you think the children might be in danger?"

"No, of course not. I know it's difficult to accept, but Sparky was only a dog."

"And you're positive that a psycho who could shoot a helpless animal and leave it to die might not do the same to a child? You're willing to bet the lives of my sons on his sterling character and judgment?" She closed her eyes, fighting against a wave of nausea. Then took a shallow, ragged breath.

"Did you report it to the police?"

"Of course. Well, sort of. I talked to Jerry Landry at the gym, he's a deputy sheriff. He said that even if we could prove it, the man would only get a fine. And he might retaliate against us."

"How? By killing our dog? Or will—?" She broke off in a spasm of coughing. Then lay carefully back on her pillows, utterly ashen. The aide hurried in a moment later. Janie would need absolute quiet now to avoid a seizure. I had to leave.

Outside the door, I lingered in the hallway, wanting desperately to go back in, to somehow change the look in her eyes. Erase the contempt. In nine years together, she'd been angry with me many times. But never like this. We needed to talk this out. But we couldn't.

I swallowed, hard, only a notch away from crying. Started walking, so no one would see. And realized I was right on the edge of losing it. My love was dying, I'd be raising our sons alone, my job was shaky, and now . . .

Enough! I just couldn't take any more. Couldn't deal with one more goddamned thing.

But at the same time, I realized that any chance of letting Sparky's killing pass was gone now. I'd have to do something about it.

The Sinclair house wasn't hard to find. Algoma's a small town and Chandler Sinclair was listed in the phone book with everyone else. Nor was his home particularly plush. The yard was broad enough for football but the house was a rambling red brick ranch-style, set on a hill that looked down on the wood behind our subdivision.

We were practically neighbors.

I rang the doorbell, a woman answered. Wearing designer slacks and a red silk blouse. Mid-twenties, pudgy, dark hair, dark circles under her eyes.

"Can I help you?"

"I'm Professor Dylan, from Hancock State College. Is Mr. Sinclair in?"

"He's in, but he doesn't see many people. What's it about?"

"I'm sorry, you are . . . ?"

"Dana Sinclair."

"Ah, the sister, of course. I really do need to talk to Mr. Sinclair. It's about hunting."

"You don't look much like a hunter, but maybe he'll see you. It's all he really cares about." She hit an intercom button, set in the wall beside the door. "Chan? Some guy to see you, says it's about hunting. You in?"

The croaked reply through the small speaker sounded like a frog's command. I couldn't understand it but Dana apparently could. Long practice, no doubt.

"He's in the den. Through the living room, that door over there."

"Thank you." Odd décor for a living room. Hardwood floors, no carpeting. Furniture widely spaced. More like a rough country cottage than a wealthy home. The den door was intricately hand-carved, though. A hunting scene. I knocked, and went in.

And stopped. It wasn't a den, it was a trophy room. The upper walls were lined with mounted heads, dozens of deer, bear, coyotes. Below them, a rack of weapons that could have equipped a small army. Rifles, pistols, and at least a dozen different crossbows, ancient and modern.

The man coming toward me was equally shocking. Bloated, misshapen, he was dressed in full military camouflage, olive drab, but he didn't look like any soldier I've ever seen. More like an egg with broomstick arms. And withered legs. His thighs were thin as sticks thrust into boy-sized boots. He was in a power wheelchair with four oversized wheels. Built like a tank. Or an ORV. Its cleated treads were powered by an electric motor that hummed like a dynamo.

"What?" he asked, stopping in front of me. "Oh. They didn't tell you about my chair."

"No," I managed. "I didn't know—"

"That I was handicapped?" he finished. "I'm not. They are." He gestured at the trophies with a withered talon of a hand. "They're dead. I'm still here. Dana said something about hunting?"

"Actually, it's about killing. I believe you killed my dog, Mr. Sinclair."

"No kidding? So what's the problem? Was it an expensive dog?"

"That's not the point."

"Then what is? We've got a leash law in this county, mister. A licensed hunter can shoot any dog guilty of chasing deer. Which makes any dog loose in the woods fair game."

"He was on private property."

"What property?"

"The five-acre plot at the end of the Birchcrest subdivision."

"It was you!" he said, his bug eyes bulging. "You're the sonofabitch who tore up my blind!"

"I destroyed a blind. It was on my land."

"Your land? My family owned and hunted that section for a hundred years. Trophy bucks don't give a damn about property lines, they range five to ten miles a day—"

"I don't care what bucks do or what your parents used to own. We own it now, and you're not welcome. You had no right to kill our dog."

"I didn't kill your damned dog! Every time somebody whacks out a mutt around here they blame it on me. Usually because they want a payoff. If they ask nicely, sometimes I pay. But not this time. Where do you get off wrecking that blind? Do you have any idea how hard it was for me to build it, with these hands? Even with Dana helping, it took me days."

"You should have built it somewhere else."

"There isn't anywhere else! Not for me. Not that I can get to in a chair."

"You should have thought of that before you killed my dog."

"I already said I didn't kill it."

"Unfortunately, I don't believe you." I moved to the display of crossbows on the wall. Steel bolts with savage broad-heads were on the shelf below them. Along with a cardboard vial of chalk dust. Blue. "Why do you use blue chalk dust, Mr. Sinclair? I'm told most hunters use orange."

"That's why I don't. It's a bit difficult for me to track game with my . . . situation. If another hunter spots an orange mark, he knows it's a wounded buck. He might find it first, claim it for his own. Make off with it."

"Maybe you should take up a gentler sport. Like chess."

"Screw you, Dylan. You don't hunt, do you?"

"No."

"Didn't think so. You should try it. Men are natural predators, you know. All men. It's in our genes. Even snobs like you."

"You know nothing about me."

"Wrong, I know a million self-righteous wimps like you! You think eating tofu makes you morally superior to people who kill their own food. I've got news for you, pal, taking game is a reality check for life. From the eagles in the air to the worms that get us when we die, every natural creature on this earth spends most of its time hunting. God must love hunters, he sure made enough of them. Including us. Especially us. You ought to give it a shot, Dylan. Hunting's how the world really works. Puts you in touch with your inner predator."

"Be careful what you wish for, Mr. Sinclair. And from now on, stay the hell off my land."

Sinclair stared down at his clawed hands for a moment, as if wishing for the strength to strike me. Just once. When he looked up, his eyes were as blank and hard as a lizard's. Crippled or not, he was a very formidable man.

"Maybe I will, maybe not. If you want trouble, you came to the right place, sport. When you wrecked my little hut in the forest, you messed with my life. Maybe I'll return the favor."

"I'd stick to dogs, if I were you. They can't shoot back."

I stalked out of the den, slamming the door behind me. Dana Sinclair overtook me in the foyer at the front door.

"I couldn't help overhearing. I'm very sorry about what happened, Professor Dylan, but . . . well, you see how he is. Was your dog black and white? A little guy?"

"You saw him? You were there?"

"I'm always there. I have to walk Chandler out to his blind in case his chair gets stuck. He did kill your dog. And others too."

"Would you talk to the police about it?"

"No! And forgodsake don't tell anyone I told you. Things are hard enough for me as it is."

"Then why do you stay?"

"He's my brother," she said simply. "When I was a girl, we lived in a lovely home on State Street. Three stories with winding spiral staircases. But after Chan was born, the stairs were too difficult for a wheelchair, so we moved here. One level, easier for him to get around. No one asked me whether I wanted to move. It was all for Chan. And when my father died, he left everything to Chan because he knew damned well if I had two nickels of my own I'd be gone. This is my home as much as his, but I'm just a housekeeper here."

"Sis!" the intercom crackled to life. "Come here, please. My colostomy bag's almost full."

"I have to go. But you'd better watch yourself, Professor. Chan's mean. When he warned you about your house, he wasn't kidding. He'll get even somehow."

As I backed out of Sinclair's driveway, I noticed a patrol car parked in the turnout at the end of the block. Couldn't see who was behind the wheel, maybe Jerry Landry, maybe someone else. But it wasn't just sitting there, it was idling.

As I drove off, the prowl car pulled out, tailed me half a block, then made a U-turn and drove back to the Sinclairs. And stopped.

It could have been a coincidence, but I didn't think so. It felt more like a message. That in this town, the Sinclairs had their own private police force. Bought and paid for.

"We're flunking the Hitler test," Janie murmured. "The law failed us when they left that psycho running loose. We'll have to deal with him ourselves." I was sitting by her bedside at the hospice. It was noon, but the shades were drawn and the lights dimmed to avoid any strain on her eyes. Her equilibrium was very fragile now. Teetering on the edge of the abyss.

"How do you mean that?" I asked.

"You're the political scientist, how do governments manage a problem like this?"

"Well, if a nation is attacked or its citizens are injured, it can counter with a measured, equivalent response sufficient to deter future aggression. The police actions in Korea and Desert Storm I, for example. Or it can retaliate on a massive scale to remove the threat. As in World War II and Desert Storm II. I think we can skip the nuclear option."

"Do any of those apply?" Janie asked. "I can't think."

"I don't think so, honey. Even if we found a way to strike back, would retaliation help the situation or make it worse? I'm not sure the man's playing with a full deck. And he's wealthy enough to cause serious trouble for us."

"More than I have now, do you think? Too bad it didn't happen a few months ago, when I could still hobble around. If I could move, I'd do something about this maniac. God knows I've got little enough to lose."

I caught the savage edge in her tone, and realized her anger was a stimulant, pumping her adrenaline, keeping her mind off the pain. But her judgment was as shaky as her condition.

"Janie, we can't respond with anything illegal. If I get caught, the kids will have no one. The law isn't perfect but it's all we have. We should leave it to them."

She didn't speak for a very long while. I thought she might have fallen asleep.

"Arnie, please don't take this the wrong way, but . . . you're a teacher. You love to discuss things, talk them out. So leaving Sinclair to the law is a . . . convenient option for you. Because it means you don't have to do anything at all. But it's also very dangerous. Because if that lunatic harms one of our children, it'll be too late for talk. And if that happens, I don't think you could forgive yourself. Nor could I. I'm sorry, I can't think clearly enough to help you, so you'll have to decide. But if we're truly dealing with a Hitler situation here, you have to do the right thing, Arnie. Whether it's legal or not. You have to."

"I will, my love," I said softly. "Trust me." But I don't think she heard. Her breathing had gone shallow as the sedation took hold, carrying her far away.

A giant splotch of red greeted me when I pulled into our driveway. At first I thought someone had struck a deer in the road, then I realized the whole house had been splattered with red explosions. Paintballs, the bloody mess drooling off the roof, streaks of crimson down the siding like blood, as though our home had been butchered.

Skidding my Toyota to a halt in front of Algoma Sheriff's Department, I stalked inside, slamming the door open so hard that the officer behind the counter jumped, startled. Deputy Jerry Landry. One look at my face was enough.

"What happened?" he asked.

"I don't want to put you in the middle of this, Jerry, I need to see your boss."

He started to argue, thought better of it. "Come on, I'll walk you back."

I trailed him down the narrow corridor to an office at the end. He rapped once, showed me in.

If anything, the office was more Spartan than the squad room. Institutional green concrete, tiled floors, a metal desk. A heavyset cop behind it, squared off and gray as a concrete block. His name tag read Wolinski.

"Sorry to bother you, Stan," Landry said. "This is Professor Dylan, teaches at the college. He has a problem."

"That's why we're here, " Wolinski said. "What seems to be the trouble, Professor?"

I told him, about Sparky's death, my run-in with Chandler Sinclair, and the vandalism at my home. When I finished, Wolinski arched an eyebrow at Landry, and Jerry confirmed that I'd reported it.

"Did you write it up, Landry?" he asked.

"Yes sir. And the Prof here isn't the only one. We've had a number of reports about pets being killed in that area."

"Reports?" Wolinski echoed. "Has anyone actually filed a complaint against Chan?"

"No sir, no official complaints."

"Can't say I blame 'em," Wolinski sighed. "Can I ask you something, Professor? If you don't hunt, why should you care what Chan Sinclair does in those woods?"

"Maybe I wouldn't if he hadn't killed my dog."

"I understand that, and killing a dog is serious business. It's also a dangerous charge to make without proof. Do you have any evidence that Chan did it? Did you see him, or did he admit to it?"

"I was told that he killed the dog by someone who would know."

"Does that someone have a name?"

"I'd promised not to involve them. My dog was killed with a crossbow bolt. Does anyone else in the area hunt with a crossbow?"

"Not that I'm aware of, but the fact that the man owns a crossbow is hardly conclusive. Mr. Sinclair owns a lot of things."

"He also dusts his tracking string with blue chalk, which I understand is quite unusual. There were blue chalk marks around my dog's wound."

"Several of the other reports mentioned blue chalk too," Landry offered.

"Even so, with all due respect, Professor, from where I sit, this comes down to a disagreement between neighbors. This part of the state, we're a little more casual about property lines than folks are down in Detroit, or wherever it is you come from. Up here, a fella hunts another fella's land, no one thinks much of it. If a dispute arises, grown men should be able to work it out."

"This is a lot more than a dispute!"

"So I gather. And I want you to know we take your concerns seriously. I'll have Deputy Landry here talk to Chan about the paint balls, but if he denies it, and I expect he will, our hands are tied. Every kid in town owns a paintball gun these days. And I'd advise you against taking any further action against Mr. Sinclair on your own, Professor. Don't tear down anymore blinds. There are laws against hunter harassment in this state."

Landry walked me out. In the corridor, he glanced around to be sure he wouldn't be overheard.

"Sorry about that," he said, "but I warned you. The sheriff's probably on the phone to Chan right now, telling him you were here. And as whack as he is, it might push him over the edge. You'd better look to your family, Professor. Especially your boys."

"How? What am I supposed to do?"

Again, Landry glanced around. "Look, I could lose my job for telling you this, but you won't get any help from this department. Sinclair owns it. The sheriff has to run for election and Sinclair's his biggest contributor. But that doesn't mean he owns all of us. Between you and me, I think Sinclair's dangerous. And if he were threatening my family . . . well. During hunting season he never misses a day in those woods. Hunting accidents happen all the time and they're damned hard to solve. We've been carrying a few on the books for years."

"What are you saying?"

"Nothing, Professor. We never had this conversation. If I can help, let me know how and I'll try. But keep in mind that I'm a police officer and I have to do my duty. And my duty is whatever that man in there says it is. You can see how things are here."

"Yes, I'm afraid I can."

"Then you do what you have to and good luck to you. See you at basketball practice next week. And remember, keep your elbows up."

That night, the unthinkable finally happened. Sometime in the early hours, Janie Doyle Dylan, my wife and my soul, slipped into a final coma. Her death was inevitable now. And irreversible. She might linger a few days or a few weeks, but would not regain consciousness.

Nor would there be any extraordinary efforts to hold her here. She had always been a bold spirit. And as her sturdy little body failed her and her time in this world became shorter and less endurable, she'd grown impatient. Ready for her Next Great Adventure. Eager for it, I think.

And now she was almost on her way. Already on board, waiting for takeoff. And I was left in the terminal, unable to do anything but watch her go. And so help me God, if not for the boys, I would have gone with her.

But I did not have that option. After calling my sister-in-law to update her on Janie's condition, I headed home to pack a few things. I'd already made arrangements to share Janie's room at the hospice for this final time.

But as soon as I stepped in our front door, I knew something was wrong. The furnace was roaring and I could feel a chilly draft from the rear of the house. I hurried through to the den. And found it open to the weather. The picture window had been smashed, glittering glass splinters were scattered all over the room. Stunned, I looked around for a rock or . . .

A crossbow bolt was stuck in the den wall. Titanium. Its broadhead buried just above a smiling photograph of Janie and the boys. Along the way it had knocked down the easel holding a watercolor painting of the back yard Janie had been working on. Her last painting. Unfinished. And now it always would be.

I knelt to retrieve the painting, but didn't rise. Stayed there awhile, just holding it. It wasn't very good. Janie daubed away with more enthusiasm than skill. But she loved doing it.

The arrow had slashed the picture, slitting it open as it ripped through. I flipped the painting over. On the back, on the pristine canvas, the faint smudges were obvious. Blue chalk.

I rose slowly, carefully replacing the watercolor on its easel. Considered calling the police. But I could almost hear Wolinski. 'Just because a man owns a crossbow doesn't make him guilty. Mr. Sinclair owns a lot of things.'

Including the local police.

Janie was right, this was a true Hitler test. Letting it pass wouldn't mollify Sinclair, it would only make him bolder. Like leaving a rabid dog running loose in a neighborhood full of children. My children. My neighbors' children.

If evil is staring you in the face and you turn away and fail to act, then Dachau or Darfur or whatever follows is on your head. I knew I was moving into dangerous territory. I desperately needed to talk it through with Janie but I couldn't. She'd been my rock, my love and my life for nine short years. Long enough to know I could never be sure what she might do in a given situation. Especially not one as treacherous as this.

But I knew one thing for certain. She'd wouldn't let this pass. And neither could I.

Enough.

Trotting upstairs to the attic, I rummaged around for a particular cardboard box. And found it. It held my father's old Remington shotgun. A Kmart special, Model 870, common as dirt. I hadn't fired it since I was a boy. My mom shipped it to me after the old man's funeral, years ago. But with little kids in the house, I'd simply stored it away.

No one in Algoma knew I even owned a gun and I'd watched enough CSI to know shotgun pellets are impossible to trace.

And like the man said, hunting accidents happen all the time.

Keeping the gun mostly concealed beneath my coat, I trotted across the field behind my house, following the faint remains of Sparky's blood trail. Once I reached the bushes on the far side, I didn't bother to hide the weapon anymore. Amid the falling leaves of an October autumn, a man with a gun is unremarkable. Grouse season, deer season, rabbit season. All that's required is a taste for wild game and a hunting license.

And maybe there was something to what Sinclair said about men being natural predators. Moving through the woods, carrying my father's old gun, other afternoons came back to me. Half-forgotten memories of walking with my dad on golden afternoons like this one, in the sweet silence of the forest. The old man patiently explaining the art of the hunt. How the depth and span of a deer's hoofprint reveal its size and weight. How the texture of the soil can tell you whether a track is fresh or not, and how many hours since the animal passed through. How to use the wind to mask your movements and your scent.

In a way it was like slipping on a comfortable suit of old clothes I hadn't worn for a long time. But I didn't kid myself. Remembering a few boyhood ploys didn't make me an expert. I was in Sinclair's territory now and the murderous cripple was a proficient, highly skilled killer, much better at this game than I ever would be. I'd have to move very carefully. And keep my elbows up.

Checked my watch. Nearly three. Most deer hunters favor first and last light, early morning, late afternoon. Sinclair could be along anytime now. If he wasn't here already.

With his shooting blind destroyed he'd need a new spot. And it would have to be close by, somewhere near the deer trail. Starting from the old blind site, I began circling, looking for wheelchair tracks. And a likely spot for an ambush.

It wasn't hard to find. The power wheelchair limited his choices to high, firm ground. His new lair was in a low clump of young cedars with a few boughs cut and rearranged into a crude shooting box. Not as cozy as his earlier blind, but not half bad.

Crouched in his chair, Sinclair would be nearly invisible in there. The cedars would mask his scent and movements, and a long stretch of the deer trail would be well within the lethal range of his crossbow. A perfect spot for a killing. One way or another.

Backing away from the cluster of cedars, I began scouting for a nest of my own, cover that would conceal me but still give me a shot at Sinclair's lair. Couldn't find one immediately, and as the trees began to thin, I realized I was approaching the edge of the forest again.

Through the thinning stands of aspens I glimpsed my house. And the shattered window. The bastard must have fired from here. . . . No. He couldn't have. The angle was all wrong. The bolt would have stuck in the opposite wall.

Curious now, I began circling the edge of woods, looking for a second blind, or at least a spot that would line up with the smashed window and the bolt in our den wall.

And I found it. Perhaps forty yards along, I came upon a narrow access road, wide enough for a car or a pickup truck. Or a wheelchair. Probably used by the groundskeepers to bring their lawnmowers to the field.

This was the spot. I was now facing our den window straightaway. Fired from this angle, the crossbow bolt would shatter the den window and lodge . . .

No, not here either. The house was too far off now, two hundred yards or more. A crossbow could shoot that far, but Sinclair would have to tilt his weapon upward to compensate for the distance. If it had been fired from anywhere near here, the bolt would have been dropping sharply when it crashed through the window. Lodging in the floor, not the wall.

Sinclair must have gotten closer somehow. No problem. There were enough bushes to offer concealment for a cautious stalker, especially one crouched in a chair.

But he obviously hadn't have come this way. The earth was moist and spongy. Much too soft to support the weight of Sinclair's wheelchair without leaving deep gouges. I knelt, scanning the ground closely for wheel tracks. No sign of any. But I did find tracks.

Footprints. Moving carefully, I traced the faint impressions to a small clump of underbrush at the edge of the field bordering the subdivision. The perfect spot. Easing down onto the moist earth, my elbows came to rest in two nearly invisible depressions. Steadying my weapon, I aimed it across the field. Directly at the shattered window of my own home.

I lay there for a time, thinking. Rethinking actually. Applying a different template over the same set of facts. And realized I wasn't dealing with a Hitler problem at all. More like a class struggle. Between the haves and the have-nots.

Any of a half dozen Shakespearean plots dealt with this situation. Macbeth, for one. But there was nothing academic about this problem. The trap was very real, artfully laid. And I had blundered right into to the middle of the killing zone. Like a lamb to the slaughter.

He could already have me centered in his sights, his finger poised on the crossbow's hair trigger. Ready to touch off that high-tech replica of medieval murder and slam a fletched shaft into me. The same way he killed Sparky.

No! I still didn't have it right. I didn't have to die for the plan to work. But my being out here made everything all too easy. And it would happen very quickly now.

Scrambling to my feet, I sprinted back into the forest, running flat out. Modern crossbows are lighter than the originals and their sights are deadly accurate, but they're still too bulky to swing quickly. My only chance was to keep moving. Fast.

Forty yards into the forest, I flattened myself against an aspen, panting, expecting a crossbow bolt to punch into my guts at any second. But it didn't. And as the moments passed, I gradually slowed my breathing, willing myself to calm down.

Listening.

Somewhere nearby I could hear the faint hum of Sinclair's power wheelchair, and I knew I only had a few moments left.

Glimpsing him coming through the trees, I edged toward the sound of the chair, keeping low. But not low enough, not for a born hunter. The chair stopped.

"Come out of there," Sinclair barked.

I stepped onto the path. His crossbow was mounted on a swivel attached to the chair. Centered on my heart, as near as I could tell. His sister was with him, both of them dressed in woodland military camouflage, ready for war.

"What are you doing out here?"

"Looking for you," I said.

"He's got a gun, Chan," Dana said, moving up behind the chair.

"I see that," Sinclair said. "Hunting, Professor?"

"Listen to me, Sinclair, this may sound crazy—"

"Kill him!" Dana hissed.

"What?" Chan said, stunned. "Are you off your rocker? He's—"

"He's here to kill us, you moron!" Grabbing the crossbow, she wrestled it out of her brother's hands. Easily. Despite his bearish appearance, Chan obviously had very little manual strength. As she struggled to bring it to bear, I raised my shotgun—

"Hold it," Jerry Landry shouted, his pistol at the ready. "Drop that gun, Dylan. Everybody just calm down half a second."

"He knows," Dana said, nodding at me.

"Knows what?" Chan Sinclair said, baffled. "What's going on here?"

"They're lovers, Sinclair. They mean to kill you. With you gone, Dana will inherit—"

"Shut your mouth!" Landry roared, raising his pistol to cover me. I started inching backward.

"Don't even think about it," Landry warned.

"You're the one who needs to think, Jerry," I said, swallowing. "Your story only works if I'm killed with a crossbow."

True or not, the thought froze him for a second. And I was off, sprinting into the trees as Dana sent a crossbow shaft whistling through the spot I'd been standing a moment before. Landry's shot followed a split-second later. Plan or no plan, they had to kill me now.

"Grab his shotgun," Landry roared at her as he charged into the brush after me. "Do your brother!"

I kept moving, dodging from tree to tree as Landry came on, firing at me wildly, gaining ground as I ducked this way and that, trying to keep trees between us. Knowing I wasn't going to make it. I was running out of cover. The trees were thinning out as we neared the edge of the wood and I'd have no chance at all in the open—someone screamed behind us! A woman, I think, but couldn't be certain. It barely sounded human.

"Dana!" Landry shouted, freezing in his tracks, scanning the woods, trying to spot me. I stayed put, a poplar at my back. The last tree big enough to use for cover.

"Dana!" No answer. Only a bubbling moan.

"My god!" Landry wheeled, sprinting back to the clearing. I turned too, running parallel, trying to keep him in sight. If I could get deeper into the forest—Landry stopped suddenly, raising his weapon! I froze too, but it was too late! He had me dead to rights, caught in the open, flat-footed. My only chance was to—but suddenly Landry lowered his pistol.

He turned toward me, a look of utter amazement on his face. And even at that distance I could see the feathered butt of a crossbow bolt protruding from his chest below the armpit. And the crimson circle widening around it as he dropped slowly to his knees. For a moment he desperately tried to pull the shaft out with this free hand, then pitched forward, sprawling face down in the golden leaves.

Dead? Couldn't tell from here. Had no idea where the arrow came from or who shot it. From that angle, it could have been meant for me.

Keeping low, I circled warily around to Landry's crumpled form, coming up behind him. Ready to bolt at the slightest move. But he wasn't moving. Wasn't breathing either. I reached carefully around for the service revolver still in his fist.

"Leave it," Sinclair said, humming his wheelchair into the clearing. His crossbow was back in its mount, loaded, and centered on my chest. Beyond him I could see the crumpled form of his sister, cowering against a tree, clutching her arm.

"What happened?" I asked, rising slowly.

"Dana tried to pick up the shotgun. I ran her down with the chair. I think her arm is broken. And you've got some explaining to do. Why did you come out here? With that gun?"

I thought about lying to him, something in his eyes told me not to.

"I came to have it out with you. To kill you, if it came down to it."

"Over your dog?" he said, disbelieving. "I told you I didn't shoot it."

"It was more than that. Landry and your sister were planning to get rid of you and lay the blame on me. To make it work, they vandalized my home, and one of them, probably Landry, fired a crossbow bolt through my den window. It could have killed somebody. And it was dusted with blue chalk."

"Dana, most likely. I taught her to shoot a few years ago. Thought hunting might make her more self sufficient. It didn't, though. Some people don't have what it takes to cut it in this world."

I couldn't tell if the irony was intended or not. "What happens now?"

"A hunting accident," Chan said coolly. "Poor Jerry stumbled into my line of fire, got himself killed. His family will collect a nice settlement, the department will avoid a scandal, and my sister will stay out of jail."

"She meant to kill you."

"She's still my sister. My responsibility."

"What about me?"

"Nothing about you, Dylan. You were never here. Any problem with that?"

"No. I've got troubles of my own."

"So I understand. I made a few calls about you after your visit the other day. I'm sorry about your wife."

"So am I. I have to get back. Do you . . . need anything from me?"

"Take your gun with you, it'll save me some explaining. Do you have a cell phone with you?"

"No."

"Neither do I. I hate the damned things, especially in the forest. Ruins the atmosphere. When you get home, would you call 911 for me? Just tell them where I am. I'll take it from there."

"You can't really believe you'll get away with this."

"Sure I will. I can handle Stan Wolinski and as for the rest, well, I'm used to coping. Been doing it all my life. No choice. When I tell people I'm not really handicapped, I'm dead serious."

"Yes," I said. "I can see that now."

Retrieving my gun, I headed out, half expecting a crossbow bolt in the back with every step. But it didn't happen.

When I glanced back, Sinclair was where I left him. A half-man with withered legs and barely functional arms, sitting in his chair ten yards from the corpse of a man he'd killed. Talking quietly to his sister, enjoying the afternoon sun.

He was right. Despite the chair, he really wasn't handicapped. He could cope.

And if he could do it, maybe I could too.

I was losing my wife. But not forever. I believe in a hereafter. I will see her again.

Meanwhile, I have our sons to raise. And maybe some growing up to do myself.

As I left the woods, I noticed an eagle circling high in the autumn sky. Free and magnificent. A pure predator. Like Chan Sinclair. Or like most of us when you rough away the veneer of civility.

Which isn't necessarily a bad thing. As I scanned the trail ahead, my vision seemed sharper, my senses more alert. For danger. Or prey.

Perhaps it will fade after a few weeks back in the classroom. If I let it. But I don't think I will.

Someday soon, I'm going to bring my sons out here, to show them the countryside their mother loved so much.

And I'll teach them to hunt. With a camera or a weapon, their choice. I'll teach them to move silently, and listen. And track. And show them whitetail bucks battling over turf. And foxes stalking rabbits, and soaring hawks scanning the fields for mice.

I'll show them how the world really works.

So that later on, if they happen to meet Hitler? They'll know exactly what to do.

# DIES IRAE
*By Dorothy Salisbury Davis*

Dorothy Salisbury Davis was born in Chicago in 1916. She was married to the actor Harry Davis for forty-six years until his death in 1993. She is the author of twenty novels, thirty-some short stories, and was named Grand Master by the Mystery Writers of America in 1985. She received the Lifetime Achievement Award at Bouchercon in 1989 and was the Guest of Honor at Malice Domestic in 1994.

B RUTAL MURDER! She could still, at ninety, remember the bold headline in the Hope Valley News, and she could remember listening from the top of the stairs to her mother and father arguing in the kitchen about whether or not they would go to the funeral.

"Margaret, you don't even know if they'll hold a wake for him."

"Wake or no, they have to bury the man, don't they? You'll go alone if you're going, Tom. I knew he was trouble from the night I first laid eyes on him—a mouth like a soft prune and eyes you'd think were going to roll out of his head . . ."

Yes, she could remember the very words, for they were her mother's and therefore her own.

All three of them, her mother and father and the girl she was then, went to the funeral.

There were people there she didn't even know, and she had thought she knew everyone in Hopetown. She was her father's daughter in that; you couldn't get him away, talking to everyone he met on the street. Her mother would always wait in the car. Her mother's two cousins, first cousins—she called them Aunt Mary and Aunt Norah—stood next to each other beside the grave but with room enough between them for another grown person. Maybe there was, she had thought, and tried to imagine what Denny would have looked like with half his head blown off.

Father Conway always prayed as though he had a train to catch. Ed McNair, the sheriff, was there, and several deputies. Her father wasn't wearing his deputy sheriff badge. Donel Rossa was there.

When the gravediggers loosened the straps to lower the coffin, what flashed through her mind was the story her mother once had told her of the man who brought his wife, coffin and all, home to Ireland and buried her on land he claimed was stolen from him. She'd never found out if it was a true story or one of many her mother made up. In time she had asked her aunt Mary if it was true, for the sisters had come from the same village as her mother on the coast of the Irish Sea.

"She could as well as not have made it up," an answer the very ambiguity of which she had somehow found satisfying. She had discovered you could tell the truth with a lie. That may have been the moment when she first knew she was going to be a writer.

The sisters could barely have been more different from one another. Norah, the older, was thirty-four, tending to fatten as she grew older. She smiled a lot, but it never seemed to mean much, on and off. Mary said if she ever laughed it was under her breath. Mary, having met with a lifetime's share of troubles, tended at thirty-two to make fun of both her sister's and her own foibles. Rheumatism was already hacking away at her joints; she was more bone than flesh anyway, and her very blue eyes were sometimes shot red with pain. The devil trying to work his way in, as she put it. Norah was convinced he had already made it.

It was late on a morning of early August heat when Mary saw him come out from the shade of the last elms that arched Main Street. He stopped at the mailbox by Norah's walk and seemed to study the names. Norah's was first, Mary's scratched beneath it as though it was an afterthought, which, in a way, it was. After deciding, perhaps, which of the women it was he saw in the field between house and barn, he came directly to her. He stepped with care to avoid the potatoes she had forked from the ground. He was unshaven, and younger than she had thought at a distance, and for an instant she felt she had seen him before. He was young-old or, better, old-young. His clothes weren't shabby, but they'd not been in a wash-tub for a while. Nor had he. But his kind was not uncommon on the road, men without work, some wanting it, some not. The grain harvest, then silo-filling, were soon ahead.

"You're Mary O'Hearn, are you, ma'am?"

She looked hard at him—something familiar again—and he moistened his lips before saying more.

"You're welcome to a cup of water there at the pump," Mary said.

The pump with the well beneath it stood a few feet from the faded red building she had converted from the barn to the house she lived in. Beyond the pump, and shrouded in rosebushes, was the outhouse she still used. Norah had indoor plumbing.

His eyes shifted from the pump to the outhouse, then back to her. "Would it trouble you if I asked to use the wee house?"

It would, but she nodded, and dug the fork into the ground to lean on while she waited for him to go and come back. Cow's eyes, she thought, dark and murky. If he was Irish, and she felt he was, a Spaniard had got in there somewhere. Black Irish, they called them with his looks at home.

When he came back he asked, "Don't you remember the skinny runt of a kid that sang at your wedding? That's what they used to call me, Skinny-runt."

Mary grunted, remembering not the child, but the man beside her with tears in his eyes when she suddenly looked up at him. She could still hear the high, sweet trill of song, but what she had always seen, remembering, was the tears. "What was it you sang?"

"The 'Ave Maria.' That's what I always sang, the 'Ave Maria.' "

"And your name?"

"Denny. Dennis O'Hearn, the same as yours. It was my father's brother Michael you were married to, may he rest in peace."

There was almost mockery in the sound from her throat. Neither peace nor prayer came easy to her. "Your voice has dropped a notch or two since then."

"I was afraid it wouldn't ever," he said.

She gave a snort of amusement.

She brought him a cup of tea with bread and jam where he sat on the bench by the door. By then, she was sure, Norah would have a crick in her neck, trying to see what was going on.

"Bring your cup." She led the way into the house through the kitchen and into the room she called her parlor. The house was cool and dark, more walls than windows. She lit the one electric lamp and moved it to where it cast light on the portrait above the couch.

"That's him," Denny said, looking up at the tinted photograph, life-size, head and breast of a young policeman in his high-buttoned uniform. His mustaches bristled and his eyes had spark. "I wouldn't think I'd remember him so well, but I do."

Mary turned off the light and they went outdoors again without speaking. He knew when to keep his mouth shut, Mary thought. Within months of her marriage to Michael O'Hearn, he was killed in the line of duty. She squinted in the sudden sun to have a longer look at Dennis. "I don't see any resemblance at all."

"My mother's name was Castillo."

So she'd been right about the Spanish strain.

By midafternoon he had picked all the potatoes she'd harvested in two days' digging. It was easier for her to dig them up than to pick them and she'd have paid a boy from the town a nickel a bushel. She put off deciding whether to offer him the sixty-five cents. She watched him wash his hands and face at the pump and shake himself dry. She thought of the dog she no longer had. He wiped the dust from his shoes, one leg against the other. City shoes, she decided, even though they were high-laced, broken in a hundred miles south on the streets of Chicago.

"Have you no baggage?" she asked.

"I left a carryall with the stationmaster. I've to pick it up before dark."

"The mean bastard," she said. "It would kill him to turn on a light if there wasn't a train coming in."

He went back into the town before suppertime. And about time, Norah thought. She had watched, off and on, the whole afternoon and almost ruined a pattern trying to watch and use the scissors at the same time. As soon as he passed her house—a queer-looking dark fellow, half Indian, she thought, with the reservation a few miles north—she went across to where Mary was washing the smallest potatoes.

"Have you lost your senses, taking a stray like that into the house? And letting him use your convenience."

"Convenience!" Mary mocked.

"You could catch something from the likes of him."

"I could, and wouldn't that surprise you?" Mary gave her a bark of a laugh.

"Not in the least," Norah said, fairly sure she was being made fun of.

"I'm thinking I'll fix a cot for him in the back kitchen."

"So he's coming back, is he? And why not? The hospitality of the house. And never a word to me, Mary."

"Amn't I telling you now?"

"When you've already made up your mind. There was a piece in the paper last week if you ever read it, a man's watch stolen right from the table where he was asleep in his bed."

"My old clock wouldn't bring much," Mary said. Then she told her sister, "You can't call him a stray, Norah. He's Michael's nephew, his own brother's son."

Norah sucked in her breath, needing all of it. Michael, more than ten years dead, ought to have been out of their lives, but he never would be—a man she had never met, never wanted to meet, married to a sister she was sure she had saved from the streets after he died. Many times since she wished she hadn't and near as many times said so to Mary when goaded by her. Out of this roiling memory, she cried, "Did you invite him to come? Did you know he was coming?"

"What a crooked mind you have," Mary said. "I didn't know who he was till he told me. He sang at my wedding. A wisp of a boy then, he sang like an angel. Even Michael cried. His name is Dennis—Dennis O'Hearn." Mary lifted her chin saying it.

As though he was a child of her own, Norah thought with another surge of anger. She was as barren herself as Mary. More so, an old maid.

The two Lavery sisters had been brought over from Ireland, one after the other before either was twenty, by the childless couple from whom Norah inherited the farm, lock, stock, and barrel. It was not written into the bequest, but confided to the priest as well as to Norah, that it was hoped she would take care of her sister if ever she returned in need. Mary had run away within a year of her arrival. She was not greatly missed. Except by the farmer who had grown too fond of her.

Norah could see the change come over Mary. It was always like that with her after she had been mean. Mary touched her toe to the mound of potatoes the size of marbles. "Will you take a handful of these for your supper?"

"I will. They're sweeter by far than the big ones."

"Aye. Why shouldn't they be, coming to you for nothing?" She knocked the soap from the dish by the pump and filled it. "Bring the dish back the next time you come." When Norah was halfway along the path, Mary called, "Listen for the telephone in case I ring you later."

Mary was never without a drop of whiskey in the house. She kept a small flask of it under her pillow to ease the pain at night. Everyone knew but nobody told in the town where she got it. It would be a sad day for her when Prohibition ended, and the end was in sight. They'd be shipping the real thing in from Canada, and it wouldn't be half as good as what she got from Donel Rossa.

Rossa belonged to the first generation American Irish who farmed the rich soil of southern Wisconsin. His principal crop was corn, which he sold to a variety of consumers, some, no doubt, to members of his family said to have connections with the Chicago underworld.

Something Mary kept hidden in her heart was that soon after Michael was killed she began to receive, like clockwork and wherever she was, a pint every month marked "holy water." Since her coming back from Chicago, it was delivered by Donel himself, and if ever she mentioned paying him for it, he'd say, "Ah, Mary, Michael O'Hearn was a fine man. It comes to you with his pension." God and Mary knew the pension could take a supplement, but whenever question of where it was coming from bothered her, a tweak of pain put her conscience if not her bones at ease.

Donel was older than the sisters, closer in years to the old couple who had brought them over. Mary hadn't become close friends with him until she moved out of Norah's house, saying she'd rather live in the barn. The barn was an empty shell by then. Norah had auctioned off livestock, equipment, everything but the barn doors. And since Donel had had a hand, along with Father Conway, in bringing Mary back to where she wasn't wanted, he'd undertaken to help make the barn livable.

He was the first one Mary phoned to come round that night after supper. "I've someone here I want you to meet. Come and bring the missus."

"And I'll bring a smile," he promised.

A smile: his word for a bottle. As though she hadn't expected it.

Norah, as usual, put off going over for as long as she could stand not to go. She wanted them to wonder what was keeping her and at the same time suspected they wouldn't miss her if she didn't show up at all. They never tired of singing the old songs over and over, and she could hear the thump of Mary's stick on the floor as she beat time. When there was a quiet minute she imagined them passing the bottle to all there except Margaret and Tom's lump of a girl pretending to be asleep on the couch. Norah got her shawl from the hall stand, went out the front door and locked it behind her. You never could tell at night.

She moved with caution along the path, guided only by her memory of it in daylight. Rossa's voice was the loudest. It always was. She didn't like him. He treated Mary better than he did his wife, for one thing, but closer to the truth of it, Norah was sure he did not like her. She could never forget the look he had given her when she clapped her hands at news of Mary's marriage. The smile on his face had seemed to say, *So now it's all yours, all yours.* He'd been right, of course. And he was the one who came to tell her Mary's husband was dead, so soon. She would swear it was his cold eye that kept pity from coming over her. Now as she neared the barn, she tried to listen for a new voice among the familiar. The Angel Gabriel couldn't be heard over Rossa and the thump of Mary's stick.

Dennis O'Hearn wasn't bad-looking when you saw him up close, she decided, but she would never have taken him for an Irishman. There was a hangdog look to him, big sad eyes that reminded her of the dog Mary wanted to bring into the house when they lived together. Now he picked up on a tune Margaret hummed for him and put the words to it. Norah had not heard it before, a nursery song, nor had she heard a voice like his, deep and dark and soft as velvet. Her love for music was the truest thing in Norah's life. It drew her to High Mass on Sundays, and prompted her to buy a piano as soon as she had money. It stood mute in her living room save for the few chords she had taught herself to play so that she might know there was music in it.

It was strange the way Dennis O'Hearn's and her gaze met and locked as though their eyes had got accidentally tangled. He wiped his mouth with the back of his hand to hide a smile, she felt. And she sensed her color rising to the roots of her hair. She caught at the foot of the girl stretched on the couch. She'd had to push it aside to make room for herself. The young one pulled her foot away so fast Norah almost lost her balance. She flashed her a smile when she'd rather have pinched her. The upstart mimicked her smile back at her.

The room was stuffy and smelled of the men, sweat and tobacco smoke and the cow barn, and a whiff of Mary's liniment. Mary called this one big room her parlor. Norah always thought it resembled a gypsy's nest. To be sure, she'd never seen one. But, for example, instead of a door to the kitchen, the frame was hung with a curtain of beads Mary had bought off a peddler's wagon. The beads rattled if a wind came up or when someone passed from room to room. Mary's nook of a bedroom was to one side, chopped out of the kitchen. If Dennis O'Hearn roamed through the house at night, it occurred to Norah, Mary would hear him part the curtain. Would she call him in to the side of her bed and ask him to rub liniment into her knees? Surely not. But Mary was that way. She was as easy with men as she was with women.

The songs they sang came, most of them, out of *The Golden Book of Songs*. Norah had a pristine copy of it on her piano at home. Mary's copy looked like an old prayer book that had lost its covers. She tried to picture how this lot would fit in her parlor, where the piano took so much of the room. Mary, when first she'd seen it, let out a whoop. "Holy Mother of God! It looks just like Reverend Mother!" They wouldn't fit at all, Norah decided. They just didn't belong there.

"Can you sing 'Mother Machree,' Dennis?" Rossa asked. "I don't think it's in the book. 'There's a place in my heart which no colleen can own,' he started, not waiting for Dennis to answer. Suppose Dennis could play the piano, she thought. There were people who played by ear and he might. He picked up on "Mother Machree" and he knew the words by heart. Before he could finish, Rossa demanded "That Old Irish Mother of Mine."

"Give me a minute," Dennis said.

"Let the man wet his whistle," Mary said. "Isn't there a drop left in the bottle?"

Rossa sent his wife out to the car for the spare he kept hidden there.

"Norah." The girl's mother leaned toward her. She'd seen what happened between her and the upstart, but that wasn't on her mind at all. "Do you remember the queer woman at home who'd come out on the castle grounds just before dark? She'd sing 'The Last Rose of Summer.' Don't you remember? A veil round her head so you couldn't see her face. But every night she'd be there . . ."

"You know better than ask Norah about something back home," Mary said. "She'd turn to salt if she said the word 'Ireland.' "

That was Mary.

"I remember—I remember the roses on the castle grounds," Norah said. "And the wreath they sent of them for our mother's funeral."

"Oh, for the love of God!" Mary said, out of patience.

Dennis sang "The Last Rose of Summer."

There was no beat Mary could thump to liven "The Last Rose of Summer" and she felt the party turning into slop. She pulled herself up from her chair and announced she was going to fire up the kitchen stove and make tea. She swiped at the curtain with her stick and set it jingling.

"I think I'll go home now," Norah said. "It's been such a grand evening."

Dennis was on his feet before she was. "I'll walk you home, Miss Lavery," he said.

"Then you don't need to come back," Mary snapped, quick as a dart.

You could hear the chirp of the crickets.

"Oh dear, dear me," Rossa said then.

Tom Dixon added treacle. "Stay a while longer, Norah, and we'll all go out together."

Mary would have as soon seen them all go out then. A man as fond of the military as Tom was known to be, you wouldn't have thought such an appeaser.

But it was Dennis O'Hearn who set things right again. "Please come back and sit down, Aunt Mary. I know how to fire up the stove, and I'll put on the kettle for you."

"Denny, will you put the kettle on?" took on a familiar ring in the next few days, and finding that it pleased her, he brought her a cup of tea every morning as soon as he heard the creak of her bedstead. It was what he had done for his own mother till the day she died.

"She never wanted more than a half cup. She'd send me to spill it out if there was more, and it had to be hot as blazes. Then she'd let it cool off before she drank it."

"She wanted you more than she did the tea," Mary told him.

Denny shrugged. If it was so he didn't understand it.

Mary did not lie long abed on these harvest days—or many others, for that matter—but with morning tea and afternoon tea and the cup she would say she was perishing for in the evening, she learned enough about Denny to know why he had come to her. The last of four boys and by ten years the youngest, he could remember his father saying he should have drowned him the day he was born, the runt of the litter. Until he discovered, when Denny started to school with the sisters, that he had a voice the nuns called sacred. "He'd hire me out for weddings or funerals for a dollar or two. He'd give me a nickel and spend the rest before my mother got her hand out."

It was not the first time Mary had heard a story like it.

"Would you like to hear me sing the 'Dies Irae'?" he offered.

"I would not."

Most of Mary's necessities were obtained through barter, and while she was frugal she was not miserly. But Denny wasn't long with her before she began to calculate the toll it took of her preserves and garden produce to bring home a pound of bacon. The first time Donel Rossa stopped by after the night of Dennis's arrival, she broached the possibility of finding a job for Denny in the valley.

"So you've decided to keep him," Rossa said. "You're a soft touch, Mary."

Mary caught something in his tone too intimate for her taste. "Did you have something to do with him coming, Donel?"

"Whatever makes you ask a question like that?"

"It struck me he might be something else that came with my pension."

Rossa found a place clear of their feet to spit. "You're sharp as a tack this morning, Mary."

"I should be. I've sat on a few."

Rossa laughed. He toed the spittle into the ground. "You know, Mary, the holy water is going to run dry. I'm not saying the state'll go dry. God forbid. The Dutchmen have a powerful thirst for their beer, and they've a throttle on the legislature."

Mary pulled him over to the bench and hung on to his arm. "Sit down here and tell me what you're saying." She was never long on patience.

"It's time I'm thinking about, time and change. I have a horse that climbs the fence whenever I start up the truck. He goes wild. But any day now I'll go out and see him nuzzling the radiator and the next thing you know, he'll be willing to go tandem with it. It's what the wear of time does to man and beast."

"You're an old fart, Donel." Only Mary could say it with affection. She pointed to where Denny was crawling from one currant bush to another, at the bottom of the field. "He'll be coming up from there any minute. I sent him back to strip them clean. Now he'll be counting every currant he puts in the basket."

"Have you sent him around the town to make inquiries?"

"He'll need more starch in him for that," Mary said.

"Well, there isn't a hell of a lot of that in the family . . . Ah, now, Mary, I've offended you," Rossa said, for her chin shot out. "Michael had the heart of a lion. What about Norah? Isn't there work she could put him to?"

"She'd eat him alive!"

Rossa changed the subject in a hurry. "The nuns brought him up pretty well, didn't they?"

"He can do his sums," Mary said. "He's not a child, you know, and he's strong as a bull. He was digging ditches for the city of Chicago till they ran out of money."

"I hate to tell you what that qualifies him for on the farm, Mary."

She grunted. "And isn't the world full of it?"

Denny came up as Rossa was about to leave. His face was as red as the currants. "Do you want to do a day's work for me on the farm now and then?" Rossa asked him. "A dollar a day and your grub."

"On the farm," Dennis said, as though to be sure.

"Didn't I say on the farm? Would I be sending you to Australia? And you'll have to walk the five miles or hitch a ride on the road."

"I could pay Aunt Mary for my keep," Denny reasoned aloud but in no hurry to take up the offer.

Why? Mary wondered, when half the country was out of work. And why the "Aunt" Mary, which had been dropped after the first day?

"That's the idea, lad," Rossa said as though to a child.

It wasn't starch Denny needed. It was yeast. But Mary was pleased, too, at the prospect of getting him out from under her feet now and then, as long as it wasn't to Norah.

Norah had no great opinion of herself, though most people thought the opposite. Trying to get Denny out of her mind, she kept at the sewing machine until her eyes were bleary and her foot going numb on the treadle. She excused her back-and-forth trips to the window as the need to relieve cramps in her leg. She said the Hail Mary every time but she knew very well that her true intention was to catch sight of Denny going about his chores. She even numbered his trips to the outhouse, and noted when he carried Mary's pot with him, though it turned her stomach to think of it. Not often, but often enough to give her a surge of pleasure, and only when Mary was not in sight, he'd send a little salute her way—the tip of his fingers to his forehead to her. Sometimes she left the window open and sang while she worked, harking back to songs of her childhood even as Margaret had to "The Last Rose of Summer." It wasn't true that she despised Ireland. That was Mary belittling her. It was Ireland that let her go. Mary was the one with a passion for America.

But this was Norah's busiest season. The hand-me-downs were patched and freshened at home, but in most Hopetown families the oldest child got a new outfit at the start of the school year, and as often as not Norah was chosen over Sears, Roebuck to provide the girls' dresses. No one, at least to Norah's knowledge, ever remarked on the similarity between Norah's new dresses and last year's fashion in the Sears catalogue.

The morning Rossa came by and talked with Mary and then with Denny, Norah guessed rightly what it was about. She intercepted Denny on his way into town for Mary that afternoon. "Will you be going to work for Donel?" she asked outright, to be sure of a yes or no before Mary interfered. "He's a hard man, Dennis."

"I was thinking that myself and I'll have to walk five miles before starting the day's work."

"Doing what, do you know, Denny?"

"It's on the farm. I made sure of that."

Where else? Norah wondered, but before she could ask, Mary was at the barn door shouting to him.

"Amn't I waiting for the sugar? Get on with you, man."

Dennis went on and Norah sought out Mary in her kitchen. "I've sugar enough to let you have five pounds, Mary."

"He'll be back in time." She was picking over a great basin of currants, her hands stained bloodred. "Thank you, anyway," an afterthought.

Norah settled on a kitchen chair she almost overflowed. It creaked with her weight.

"You're fading away to a ton," Mary said with pleasure.

Where the inspiration came from Norah would never know. The thought just came up and out. "I've decided it's time to get rid of all those things of theirs in the cellar."

"They" or "theirs" always referred to the couple who had brought her over from Ireland. "There's some I kept for you, if you remember, when you first wanted a place of your own. You might want to take a look at them now."

A little twitch of Mary's nose betrayed her interest and Norah pressed on. "The wash boiler—pure copper—I ought to have sold it," she began, "and the mirror. It wouldn't hurt you to take a look at yourself now and then."

As soon as the jelly was sealed in jars, Mary took Dennis with her to Norah's. They went first to the cellar door, but Norah waved them around. It was his first time in her house, and she didn't even ask him to wipe his feet.

Dennis's great dark eyes took in everything Mary gave him time to see. She nudged him on with the knob of her cane. He wasn't a dumb animal, Norah thought, but she smiled and bit her tongue. Above all she wanted him to see the piano. Mary shoved him past the parlor door.

Norah had to lift the door to the storage room where it sagged on the hinges and scraped the floor.

"Maybe I could fix that," Denny said.

"Some rainy day when Mary has nothing for you to do."

"That'll be the day," Mary said, but by then her curiosity was picking up and she was the first into the room, where there was only a whisper of light from the ground-level window. Norah pulled the electric switch. Mary let out a squeak of pleasure at things she thought on sight she had a use for. Then she settled down to a careful selection. One glance at her own reflection eliminated the mirror. Nor did she want Norah's junk. Denny figured the most in her calculation, of course. The clothes wringer, for example, would have to be fastened to the sink board in the kitchen, where the only running water in her place came in. She'd not have needed it for her bits and pieces, but laundering a man's wear could put a terrible strain on her knotty hands. Denny carted the wringer to the cellar door. Norah, her arms folded, watched. With an eagle's eye, Mary thought. "Couldn't you go and sit down somewhere?"

"I'd be willing to help," Norah said.

"Isn't that what I'm talking about?"

On Denny's next trip between the storeroom and the cellar door, he brought back an old kitchen chair he'd seen near the furnace. He even dusted it with his bare hand. Norah sat.

"God save the queen!" Mary cried.

Norah's eyes and Denny's met, even as at the party, but not this time by accident. What she felt was like an electric shock. She was sure they had struck a bond.

Mary thumped her stick against a humpbacked trunk that stood beneath the window.

Norah snapped out of her reverie. "Leave that!"

Mary all but clapped her hands. "Is it the bones of a lover?" She'd read the story long ago. "Watch out for yourself, Denny!"

She was enjoying herself, Norah thought, making fun of her. That was Mary. Her own thoughts turned to what she could do or say that might engage Dennis. There wasn't much left in the room—the big wardrobe, the mirror, some picture frames she'd thought she'd use, but hadn't, the trunk, full enough, but not of bones, and the rusted garden tools even Mary wouldn't want. And here among them, half shrouded by an old umbrella, where she herself had hidden it one winter's night, was the old man's shotgun.

Mary hobbled to the outside door with a yardstick to measure whether they could get the wardrobe out that way. She had begun to think of making a room of his own for Denny. There was room enough in the barn, sure.

Norah got up and took the chair back herself to where it had come from. When she returned she saw that Denny had discovered the gun. He was bent over, trying to see it better, but not daring to touch. "Aunt Norah?" He looked round, his eyes jumping out of his head.

"Not now," she said, and chanced a wink.

He winked back.

There was no way Denny could transport the big cupboard from house to barn without help. Mary cursed the rheumatism and Norah refused to make a fool of herself trying. It was decided between the sisters that the wardrobe could wait till Donel Rossa's next visit. Mary and Denny left by the cellar door. Norah locked it, turned off the light, and went upstairs. She wasn't sure what had happened to her, but whatever it was had never happened to her before.

Mary put up her first crop of tomatoes by the end of the week. Dennis kept the kitchen range at top heat under the copper boiler, and though Mary denied her need for the clock, just to be sure she set the alarm for each step. The sweat ran down both their faces, and when a great drop fell from the tip of Mary's nose into a bowl of tomatoes she cackled, "Sure, they needed more salt."

In the evening they sat at the kitchen table where Mary marked labels "Mary's Best" for the jars she would seal with a final turn before bedtime. Hope Valley Market would take all she could provide. Through the open window they could hear an occasional car go by and the singsong chatter of katydids, and closer overhead, the frantic buzz of an insect caught on the sticky tape that dangled from the light. Sometimes music wafted their way from Norah's radio.

Dennis tilted back in his chair though she'd asked him not to do it. He sat upright suddenly and, pinching his nose, began to sing, " 'I'm just a vagabond lover . . .' "

"My God," Mary said, "where did you learn that?"

"From the radio. Didn't you ever hear Rudy Vallee?"

"I'd just as soon not," Mary said. "Try it without the clothespin."

He grinned, cleared his throat, and sang it in his own voice. The voice of the child she remembered was gone, but there was a deep, sad music in what she heard.

"Do you miss the city, Denny?"

"No."

"Neither do I," she said. It seemed many yesterdays since she'd come out from Chicago on the train with Donel Rossa to Norah's chilly welcome.

Both sisters were alongside the road when the threshing combine on its way to Rossa's came rattling through town and stopped for Denny. Men aboard the last rig gave him a hand up, and all of them waved at Norah and Mary, who watched until the blinding sunrise washed them out of sight. Children, up at dawn to follow the caravan through town, went home to breakfast and the sisters turned into their own walkways. Mary resented Norah's being there, but it was not in her heart to part without a word.

"Will you have a cup of tea? The kettle's on the back of the stove."

Norah would rather have gone home. More and more she felt the presence of Dennis to be everywhere in Mary's house. She even avoided seeing the cot where he slept in the back kitchen. But what she said was, "Let me close the front door and I'll be over."

"Oh, for the love of God," Mary said. Doors were anathema to her.

Norah pulled a chair out from the kitchen table.

"I'm leery of that one," Mary said from the stove. "I can't break him of the habit of teetering on the back legs of a chair. You'd think they were rockers."

"I won't teeter," Norah said. The chair creaked when she sat down. "And I won't be staying more than a minute."

Mary brought the teapot and swirled the tea before she poured it. It was on the tip of her tongue to say *This'll put hair on your chest*, but she held it back. She was trying to cure herself of saying the common things like it she had picked up God only knew from where.

Norah helped herself to sugar. Whatever milk Mary had was always on the turn in summer. She could have kept it in the well like the couple used to. "Did you want the old trunk in the storeroom badly, Mary? I could empty it out."

"What would I be putting in it?"

"And what will you put in the cupboard when you get it over?"

"Won't he be getting clothes one of these days and needing a place to hang them?"

Norah was sure now she shouldn't have come. She felt hurt, pushed out. She wanted to push back. "I've been going through the things I've kept in the trunk all these years—I was thinking I'd make a rag rug of them someday but I never did—her petticoats and his flannel shirts. The shirts would fit Denny, you know. I could shorten the sleeves for him."

Mary's face shriveled up like an old woman's and the spittle sprayed from her mouth before she could speak. "Keep his filthy shirts to yourself. They're all yours. Do you think I'd let him put them on his back?"

"It was a long time ago, Mary."

"If it was forever, would I forget it?"

"I know how you feel."

"You know how I feel! There's more feeling in this teapot than in you."

Norah struggled to get up. "I don't have to take this from you, Mary. I could turn you out if I wanted and nobody'd say I did wrong. It wasn't my fault he made a strumpet out of you. Didn't you beg them to bring you over? 'I'll do anything that wants doing,' you wrote. I read them your letters—she couldn't read—and I remember him sitting there laughing to himself. 'Isn't she the lively one now?' he'd say. He treated me like dirt from the day you arrived. The two of you making fun of me behind my back. I never told on you. I never complained to her, but she knew. She'd sit at the sewing machine and cry to herself."

At the mention of tears her own eyes filled, not at what she remembered, but at the feeling of emptiness building inside her. "I'm trying to help you if only you'd let me. I've tried ever since the day you came back. Even Father Conway says I could not have done more."

"Nor cared less," Mary said. "Will you go home out of here, Norah? You're like a great, fat hen, scratching everything into your nest. Cluck, cluck, cluck. Can't you leave him and me alone?"

"You think you own him body and soul," Norah blurted out. "You'd hire him out to your bootlegger friend, but you wouldn't let him wash a window in my house."

Mary put her hand up to shield her face. Norah looked about to strike her. And Norah had never wanted more to hit her across the mouth. But she pulled back and made her way toward the door. She stopped and looked round at a burst of laughter from Mary.

"Oh, my God," Mary shouted. "You're in love with him!"

Norah quick-smiled. "You can't say that, Mary. Haven't you always said, 'Poor Norah. She can't love anybody except herself'?"

Rossa stopped for a word with Mary when he brought Denny back on his way into town. "I was wrong about him, Mary. He's not all muscle. He's got a brain up there. And get him to sing 'Home on the Range' for you."

"Aren't you the one," Mary said, sparing herself having to thank him.

Christopher Columbus could not have had more to tell returning from America than Denny coming back from Donel Rossa's farm.

"Did you learn how to milk a cow?" Mary asked.

"And how to squirt milk in the cat's mouth," Denny said.

Mary remembered learning to milk and the kick of the cow who didn't think much of how she went about it, and she thought of Norah's going on about how she had begged to be brought over. She'd known when she landed she'd never go back. In steerage, sick as a dog all the way.

And him threatening to send her back if she didn't give in to him. "Lie down on the bale there and turn up your arse." She'd never got over it, even with Michael. And Norah saying, "I know how you feel." Norah had gone home and pulled down the blinds on the windows that faced the barn. When she came out of the house it was by the front door and she never looked across. Nor had she hung a stitch on the clothesline.

"I didn't get to do much milking," Denny said. "It's terrible hard on the wrists, you know."

"Is it now? Would you teach your granny to milk ducks?"

Denny told things in spurts. He'd have told them better, Mary thought, if they'd had a tune to them—how the men on the wagon took the pitchfork away from him and made him load the sheaves by hand. "I couldn't get the hang of it, you see. They said I'd be murdering them." And Mrs. Rossa's pies: "The look of them made your mouth water. Only she'd made a mistake and put salt instead of sugar in them. You should've seen Donel. I thought he was going to hit her. But he put his arm around her at the last minute, and told the men, 'I'll make it up to you,' and he sure did. Two bottles. He told me after he was taking an awful chance. One of the ones he didn't know could've been a spy, a Revenue agent."

Rossa had kept Dennis a day and a night after the combine pushed on to the next farm, land to hear Denny tell it, nothing as wonderful had ever happened to him before. He discovered Rossa's collection of guns that he kept locked in the harness room. Rossa was a hunter. He showed Denny how to load and carry a shotgun, and had taken him out at dawn that very morning to shoot at the crows where they were cleaning up grain left in the harvest stubble.

"I told him about the gun in Norah's storeroom. You didn't even see it, I bet."

"I've seen it," Mary said.

"It's a shotgun, Donel says. I knew that myself when I seen his. He says if Norah would let me borrow it, he'd help me clean it up and oil it. And he'll take me hunting with him in the fall. They hunt small game with it—squirrels and rabbits. He told me you can make a better rabbit slew than Mrs. Rossa."

"Once in my life," Mary said. "Once in my life. Donel skinned it for me and I pretended it was an old rooster."

Denny pulled his chair closer to hers. He wet his lips. "Would you ask Aunt Norah for me?"

She should never have taken him over there, Mary thought, but she'd been all over that with herself. And she ought not to have made fun of Norah, blurting out that she was in love, though she didn't believe it for a minute. From the way Norah was carrying on since, Mary wasn't sure what was going on with her.

"I'll have to think about it," Mary said. She'd begun to feel sorry for her sister, the boob, the big, blubbering boob. "There's enough to do in the onion patch to keep you busy. And for God's sake take off the clothes you're wearing and soak them in the tub."

"I will," Denny said. "I sweated a lot. Donel says we should keep the gun ready just to fire off and scare the Revenue men if they come snooping around. He says they might."

"I said I'll think about it," Mary said.

How many times in those three days had Norah said, "How dare she!" and attacked with fury every chore she could put her mind to. She scoured the kitchen and bathroom sinks, the toilet bowl, the front steps. She finished the last of the schoolgirls' dresses, folded them, and called round for them to be picked up. Her anger fed on memories of one good thing after another that Mary had spoiled for her. Even the piano. The dead piano in her parlor—Mary's joke.

But her anger and her feeling of shame wore down, and that morning when she heard Rossa's truck pull up to the barn, she looked out through the crack of daylight between the blind and the window frame, and watched Denny's return. She pulled up all the blinds and boiled an egg for breakfast.

"I could have done this myself," the girl said, wanting to hand in the dress without a hello or how-are-you when Norah opened the door. Margaret surely taught her better.

"Come in and let me look at you," Norah said.

"Dad's in a terrible hurry."

"No, dear. You are." Norah smiled and backed into the house. "I know your father." Tom Dixon was a great talker. Mary got to know more about what was happening in the town from an hour with him than Norah learned reading a month of the *Hope Valley News.*

The girl had little choice but to follow her indoors.

"If you had more time," Norah said, "I'd ask you to play your latest piece for me."

"When I pick up the dress, maybe," the thirteen-year-old said. She was even less fond of Norah's piano than of the one at home. She could kick hers and the place she'd kicked wouldn't show.

"You'll have to put the dress on, dear, if I'm going to pin it up."

"Mother said . . ."

Norah stopped her. "Elaine, I know how to alter a dress."

The girl took the dress into the bathroom and put it on.

Why they named her Elaine, Norah would never know. From a poem Margaret had read, she remembered. Or was it after someone in Tom's family? He was English. She certainly wasn't Norah's notion of an Elaine. No wonder they called her Lainie.

What was her hurry? Norah wondered when she let her out of the house and watched her lope across the way. Did the girl hate her that much? Norah did know she was fonder of Mary and her ramshackle house. It struck her then: Denny.

Lainie burst into Mary's kitchen. "She's spooky!"

"That's enough," Tom said.

Mary chuckled. "I think it myself sometimes." She turned up her cheek for a kiss. "Is it you that's growing or me that's shrinking?"

"Where's Denny?" the girl asked.

"Didn't I tell you?" Tom said to Mary. He was right. The girl had reached the age where one word said it all: boys.

"I've fixed him a jar of tea. You can take it down to him in the far field and make him share it with you."

"You have the devil in you, Mary," Tom said.

She gave that rattle of a laugh. "Sure, it's broad daylight."

And the blinds were up next door. Wouldn't Norah be watching with the frozen heart of a chaperone? Mary pushed their tea things out of the way. "I've a question or two for you, Tom. You're wearing your badge, I see."

"If I didn't the sheriff would take it from me."

"I thought maybe something was up. The Revenue men going round, say. Or is Donel filling Denny's head with goblins?"

"I'm on the side of the Feds. I have to be," Tom said. "It's the law."

"Would they be after Donel, do you think?"

"I'm not in their confidence, Mary."

She let it go. "Wouldn't you think they'd have more to do in this country than put and take laws like that one?"

"It's a country for and by the people," Tom said. Scratch a veteran and find a patriot. Mary could beat time to it.

"You know Donel's put down money on a building in town," he added.

"Is that a fact?" she said, all ears.

"I've heard he'll be opening a business of some sort, a big one."

"And quitting the farm?"

"The farm's quitting a lot of us these days, Mary."

Mary envisioned the main street of Hopetown as she had last paid it attention. Vacancies galore.

"What kind of business, do you think?"

"It's a ways off," Tom said.

"He plans ahead," Mary said. She was thinking of Donel's palaver about the horse and the truck. "And he has money. Sure, that's what makes the mare go, Tom. Money makes the mare go."

"I'll put the dishes in the sink for you," Tom said, getting up.

"Leave them. There's something I'd like you to do for me while you're here: Give Denny a hand with a cupboard he's to bring over from Norah's."

She made her way to the telephone and gave it a mighty crank.


"Are you feeling better, Norah?" The very tone of Mary's voice, the purr of concern, put Norah on guard.

"I'm doing fine," Norah said.

"Ah, that's good news. I was worried about you," Mary chirped. "I was wondering if you felt up to it, while I have Tom here, could him and Denny pick up the cupboard? I can't count on Donel these days."

"I'll go down and unlock the door," Norah said.

"Would it be less trouble if I sent Denny ahead for the key?"

"I said I'll go down." She'd send Denny ahead for the key, taunting her, that's what it was, Norah thought.

She was sure of it when all four of them crowded down the cellar steps. The girl giggling and Denny coming down backwards to give her his hand. A gentleman!

"Hey! It's creepy in here," the girl squealed.

"Couldn't we have more light?" Mary called. "Tom wants to look at your furnace while he's here."

Denny opened the storeroom door for her, where she pulled the switch that lit up the whole cellar. Denny seemed to light up with it, as though she had conjured the light for his delight. She could not conceal the pleasure of looking at him, but she turned on Mary. "Is that light enough for you?"

"Ah, Norah, you're still not yourself. It's Denny made me come along and speak to you for him. I think he's afraid of you, God knows why." She gave a swipe of her hand at Lainie, who'd crept up, never wanting to miss anything. "Go there with your father, girl. He'll need your advice." And to Norah, "Can we come in for a minute?" Her stick ahead of her, she was already in the storeroom. Canny as a scavenger, she saw the gun, but didn't let on at first. Then: "There it is!" She looked up at her sister. "It's the gun, Norah. It's been on his mind ever since we were here. If I'd known at the time, I'd have said something."

Norah's brief shock of pleasure went dead. She felt let down by Denny, betrayed, him letting Mary in on the little bond she'd thought between him and herself. Afraid of her? Mary's nonsense. Nobody was afraid of her. He was shy. That's what she loved about him.

He stood there holding his breath, waiting for the next word.

"What about the gun, Denny? Can't you tell me yourself?" She didn't want to hear any more from Mary.

"Aunt Norah," he started.

"Just plain Norah, Denny."

He nodded. "Could we borrow it, Aunt Norah?"

"Who's the 'we,' Dennis?"

"Mr. Rossa and me. He'll help me clean it up and take me hunting with him in the fall."

Norah did not like Donel Rossa. She didn't trust him—all his trips to and from Chicago, and his "holy water," his "smiles" as he called them. He was in the business, she was sure. Why he coddled Mary, she never knew, but she did know how he treated her. Like she was a crook, like she'd befuddled the old lady into leaving her everything. In truth, he made her feel about herself the way she felt about him.

"Have you ever fired a gun in your life, Denny?"

"I have—in the amusement park in White City. I shot down the whole row of ducks and I took the prize. It was a kewpie doll I gave to my mother."

"Oh, my God," Mary said. "Tell her about the crows in the field this morning."

Denny repeated the story much as he'd told it to Mary. He wasn't sizzling, Mary thought, but he was holding his own. And so was Norah. Mary could see her guard going up. She was afraid of losing something, of something being taken away from her, and she didn't like Donel, Mary knew.

Tom and the girl had come to the door.

"Rossa knows guns," Tom said. "He'll teach you proper. I'm not a hunter myself, but I know one when I see the gun in his hand."

"Dad won't even shoot a fox," Lainie said. "I'm a better shot than he is."

The bold thing, Norah thought. Next she'd want to go hunting with Denny and to hide in a duck blind with him.

"Could I show you, Aunt Norah?" Not waiting for leave, he darted across the room and took the gun in hand. He brushed away the dust and broke the breech. Not easily. It needed his strength.

"Empty," he said of the cartridge chamber. "You must never take a chance." He locked the gun again and held it crosswise to himself and waited.

They were all waiting. Except Mary, who had neither patience nor use for guns, especially this one. She was determined Denny could become the apple of Donel's eye. "What good is it to you, Norah? Couldn't I have taken it the day we were in here cleaning out for you?"

"You could not," Norah said. "Shall I tell you why?"

"There's no need." She turned round to the door. "Come on, Denny, let's go home."

Norah spoke out so that all of them would hear. "You may borrow the gun, Denny, if you give me your word as a gentleman, it stays in this house when you're not out hunting with it. But you must give me your word."

"I do," Denny said with such fervor it made Mary laugh.

She laughed, but with no great pleasure. Norah had won something though she wasn't sure what. Her back was to them when Denny put the gun back from where he had taken it.

"Thank you, Norah," he said, up close to her face.

Norah thought it eloquent, that soft, rich voice. Simple and eloquent. "We'll have a key made for you, Denny."

His smile went through her.

Tom was already testing the weight of the cupboard. He had rarely visited the sisters that they did not end things with a quarrel between them. He wanted away. "Let's go, Denny. I want to get home before the cows come in."

Lainie was there first, lifting the other end of the huge pine box with its clattering doors. "Lay it down flat and you could put a couple of bodies in it," she said to her father just above a whisper.

"Never mind," he said. But he let her help. He always said she was more help to him than ever a boy would have been.

Denny wanted to telephone Donel that very night and tell him he'd be able to go hunting with him in the fall.

"When you next see him, it'll be time enough," Mary said, and when he drooped like a spent daisy, she explained, "Donel Rossa has more on his mind than teaching you how to shoot rabbits."

"I know that, but I could start working on the gun by myself. It's terrible rusty." He suddenly brightened. "I know what I'll do—I'll go in town to the hardware store and they'll tell me what I need."

"I'm sure they will," Mary said. "And maybe they'll tell you how to pay for it."

A storm blew up in the night and set the beaded curtain rustling. Old bones, she thought. That's what it was made of. She hadn't listened to it much since he had come and she had a terrible premonition that she was going to lose him. It was a new kind of pain, as though she needed it. She reached for the flask under the lumpy pillow. She was going to lose that, too.

Rain came with the wind and in the morning she knew they were not going to pick a second round of tomatoes or plough under the potato field. She also knew that one thing she had to do about Denny was keep him busy. She waited for him to come up from emptying the slops and wash the bucket at the outdoor pump. By the time he came in he was soaked to the skin. From the storage bin under the sofa she brought out a checkered wool shirt of Michael's she'd intended to wear herself someday. The someday had never come. "It'll keep you warm hunting ducks," she said. "Put it on for now."

At the first break in the weather they went out to the padlocked back door of the barn. "This is where the cows came in," Mary said, and Dennis, with his nose in the air, said, "I can tell."

Piled along the cement frames where once there had been stanchions were several sheets of beaverboard and the lumber they had not used in carving a place of her own for Mary. Donel had been generous and he dreamed big dreams. She would remind him, when the right time came, of how they'd planned a second room, and maybe a second stove off Mary's parlor. She pointed out to Denny the slit of light in the roof, a boxed vent to where a chimney pipe might be raised.

It was her dream at the moment, not Denny's. He wandered off. He was a city boy, sure, and he'd met cows for the first time in his life at Donel's, and he'd caught the smell of them here.

She was startled when he called out to her, "Aunt Mary, someone's standing in the doorway."

As she turned to see the man, he greeted her, "The top of the morning to you!"

"Oh, my God," she muttered. It could have been Donel with his make-believe Irish, but it was not.

He was holding an open wallet for her to see his identification. When she reached him she saw little except the government insignia, for her heart started to pound. She thought he was from Immigration. She'd never lost the fear of being sent back.

"What is it you want, mister?"

"My name is Spillane. I've orders to search the premises for corn whiskey, ma'am. You've nothing to fear if you're clean, Mrs. O'Hearn."

He stretched his neck to see behind and beyond her into the cavernous barn and he took a good look at Dennis when he came up. Whoever he was, his pale eyes had no warmth in them and he had stoked her fear. She disliked him on sight.

"What kind of name is Spillane?"

"It's Irish, as Irish as yours."

"And you a Revenue man," she said with scorn, the full use of her tongue restored.

He put the wallet back in his pocket. "So you're one of *those* Irish women," he said. "I have a warrant in the car if you want to see it."

"Never mind. Take him around, Denny. And be sure to show him the still."

"Where, Aunt Mary?" Denny had missed the point.

"Oh, for the love of God, go where you like, Mr. Spillane, and take care you don't miss my bedroom."

He did not miss much. He went to his car and brought a flashlight. A touring car with the windows all open to let out the stink, Mary thought. He'd be losing his authority soon. Maybe that was what ailed him. But he made Denny lift the cover from the mouth of the well. He searched its depth with the beam of the torch. He looked up at Mary where she watched from the back stoop and he'd have heard her laugh. He reached out and snatched the cup from where it hung by the pump and threw it into the well.

"May you die of thirst," Mary shouted and went into the house.

When he was gone, Mary poured herself and Denny cold tea from what was left in the breakfast pot.

"What did he mean by one of those Irish women?" Denny wanted to know.

"Why didn't you ask him?" Mary snapped. She'd known exactly what he meant: They should never have been given the vote. Not, of course, that she had ever used it.

"He didn't talk much. I didn't like him either, Mary."

"Did he say anything to you at all?"

"Yeah."

"Well, what?"

" 'Where'd you get those great, big beautiful eyes?' "

"The bastard," Mary said.

"Yeah. Now can we call Donel?"

Donel came in the afternoon. He heard them out, but he shook his head. "Did you have to make an enemy of him, Mary?"

"Was I to make a friend of him, then?"

"It's what I've been doing all my life, and I eat three square meals a day." He dropped his voice. "They're all over the place, so do me a favor, Mary, if he comes back, give him a cup of tea."

"I know what I'll put in it then, him pouring the last drop in my bottle down the sink."

"You've had worse things happen to you."

He was out of patience—short of time, she realized, and he hadn't offered to replenish her holy water. She saw a glint of anger in his eyes. She wouldn't want him for an enemy, either.

"And I've had better!" In spite of herself, she couldn't yield the last word, but she rang a good change on it with a nod toward Denny. "Till this one."

Denny grinned. "Donel," he said, "I got the loan of the gun."

Donel grunted as though to give his memory a jog.

"I plan to clean it up myself," Denny went on, "and be half-ready at least, when we can go hunting."

"That won't do at all," Donel said. "It's not a musical instrument. It's a weapon."

"I know," Denny said.

"You think you know. That's worse than not knowing at all."

"I'll learn."

Mary was proud of the way he said it.

Donel said, "That's better. Let's have a look at it while I'm here."

"I have to keep it at Norah's," Denny said, "but I'm to have a key."

Mary's eyes and Donel's met, for they shared a deep and silent association with the words. When Mary had run away to Chicago, she found a haven and employment with a friend of Donel's to whose house Donel had a key.

"He'll make friends at Murray's Hardware," Mary said. "They'll get him started."

Donel looked at his watch. "I'll take you in town with me now and introduce you to Murray. If you can bring the gun, he'll know what you're talking about."

"I will," Denny said. "I'll ask Aunt Norah. It's a single-barrel twelve-gauge shotgun."

"It'll do," Donel said without enthusiasm. It was one of the cheaper guns on the market. "And where in hell did you get the shirt you're wearing?"

Norah made a quick choice of where to hide when she saw Rossa stop and wait in the truck for Denny to come to her door. She wasn't ready yet. She listened as Denny rapped and called out her name. The note of concern was endearing. She sat on the cushioned lid of the toilet and waited to hear the truck pull away. In a snatch of memory she heard Mary's cackle: "God save the queen."

The bathtub, she thought, staring at it, was big enough for him to flop over in. He'd splash and grin. She thought of getting a bar of Lifebuoy soap.

Denny knocked on her door again late in the afternoon. He had come back on foot carrying a brand-new canvas knapsack.

"I must have heard you in my sleep," Norah lied. "I lay down with a headache after my lunch, and wasn't I dreaming of you?"

"What was I doing?"

"You were playing the piano," she said. "It's just come back to me now."

"You were dreaming, all right," Denny said.

They went down through the house to the cellar, and Norah pointed out a workbench near the coal bin he could use.

"Couldn't I take it over there to work on?"

"You could not."

While she watched him unpack the knapsack she listened for a telephone call from Mary or the rap of her stick on a window. "Isn't Mary feeling well?"

"She's all right."

Which told her nothing. "I wondered if it was a doctor I saw stopping in this morning."

"Not for Aunt Mary. She thinks they're all quacks."

He'd been given instruction, Norah thought, on what he could say and what not. She was furious, not so much at what she might be missing, but at the idea of Mary's taking advantage of his innocence. She had made up her mind from what she'd seen of Mary's visitor that morning that he was on a mission from Donel Rossa. He might even be bringing her the monthly holy water. He looked like a bootlegger and his long-nosed car suited the notion.

"Will you save your tin cans for me, Norah? Donel says I should set them up on the fence posts in the far field and practice."

"You know this is all my property, Dennis."

"Oh, I do. Donel said I should ask you."

"I'll save you the tins."

"Thank you, Norah." His smile was like honey.

It would do for the day, she thought. "You'd better go now. She'll be waiting for you."

"She will. She'll want to hear."

"To hear what, Denny?"

"About Donel's construction business. Mr. Murray shook hands with him. It's going to be great for Hopetown—for the whole valley."

Norah smiled. "How nice!" she said.

"Mary! Come outdoors quick!"

"Quick!" she mocked.

And when she got to the stoop: "Look!" he insisted.

"I can hear them," she said.

Fading fast into the morning mist even as their cries grew dimmer, the Canadian geese were going south.

"Would God they were coming back." She drew her shawl tighter. "For God's sake put your shirt on, Denny. You'll catch your death of cold."

"I won't." He still washed, naked to the waist, at the pump by the well. He shaved at the kitchen sink.

They had eggs for breakfast that morning, and though she knew he was only half listening, she told him, and probably for the second or third time, she thought, of how as children she and Norah waded in the stream at home, groping the sand with their toes for duck eggs. Whoever found one got the top when her father opened it for his breakfast the next morning.

"Did you and Norah fight over it?" He was listening after all.

Donel stopped on his way into town. He was a little early, due at the lawyer's office within the hour to sign the final papers. The teacup trembled in his hand. He put it down. "I'll be glad to get this over with," he said.

"Will you have a drop from my bottle to settle you?" Mary said.

"Not on your life, macushla."

He had brought her the last "smile."

He stretched out his hand and held it steady, but his teeth were clenched. He took up the cup again. "I'm clean, Mary." He toasted her—or himself—with the lukewarm tea: "Slainte."

Let Norah ridicule him all she liked, Mary thought, but they would never know a man more Irish.


Norah was on the lookout. She had been from the moment she heard Rossa's car drive into the yard. The family car, no less. He sometimes drove her and Mary to Sunday Mass in it. Lately he'd been driving it into Hopetown. It was more befitting a businessman than the Ford truck. She knew Denny would be going back to the farm with him— to shuck corn and then to go hunting with him in the morning.

He would come soon for the gun and take it away for the first time. And what would she have left? A bag of tin cans with holes shot through them. She caught a whiff of her cologne. She'd used too much of it. And dreamed too much. She'd worn out a paltry thrill remembering it. Only once had she come even close to telling him she loved him.

He'd been at the cellar workbench that day, his back to her, and what she told him was of her love for music and how beautiful she thought his voice was. When he seemed to stiffen, she thought it safer to talk about the piano and how she'd hoped someday to even play it herself. She'd been pleased at the moment for what she said then: "But it's my heart and not my head that's musical."

And Denny, looking around to her in the expectant silence: "Couldn't you sell the piano?"

"I don't need the money, Denny."

"Aunt Mary would have," he said.

Denny came out from the barn with Rossa. He put his knapsack and a box of Mary's preserves, no doubt, in the rear seat of the sedan. He stepped back and watched Rossa drive off. Without a glance her way, he went back in to Mary.

He would not come till the last minute, waiting for Rossa to return and hurry him away.

She watched the traffic coming into town, not a car a minute, but picking up these days. She couldn't believe it had anything to do with Donel Rossa's new enterprise, Hope County Construction. County no less.

She moved away from the window and then went back to straighten the curtain. By sheer chance she saw the black long-nosed touring car drive past the house and on into Hopetown. When she thought about it, she wasn't a bit surprised.

In the late morning she heard Dennis open the cellar doors. She called down to him to leave them open, that she would close them when the sun was gone.

"I didn't want to bother you," he said at the bottom of the kitchen stairs. "Donel didn't think he'd be this long. Mary says it's the lawyers that's holding things up."

"Ah, yes, what Mary says." He was like a silhouette between her and the shaft of daylight. "I'm coming down," she said.

"You don't need to, Aunt Norah."

He didn't want her to. He wanted to go off, gun in hand, without even a thank-you-very-much. "I'm coming down."

He lifted the storeroom door for her when she went in to switch on the lights. "I was going to fix this for you, wasn't I? When I come back from Donel's."

She followed him to the workbench. "What if Rossa doesn't come, if something happened to change his mind?"

"He'd let us know," Denny said. He took the gun from the rack he had built for it and broke it to be sure the chamber was empty.

"You are such a foolish boy, Dennis. You believe everybody. The Revenue agent in the rain that morning: I could have told you the truth about him. But Mary spat at me when I even mentioned him."

"That bastard," Denny said.

"No, Denny. He's worse. He's a gangster. I would take my oath on it. And isn't he back today for the celebration?"

"He's back?" Denny questioned as though he didn't understand her.

"You don't forget an automobile like that, Denny. When Donel left here this morning, it came by right after him. What an odd coincidence, I thought at first and then I realized: Of course, they're going to the same place."

Denny groped his jacket pocket and brought out a cartridge. He loaded it into the open gun and closed it.

She was a second or two understanding what he had done. "He doesn't need you, Denny. He's one of them."

"You're crazy," he said.

He edged her aside, when she tried to block his way to the door. "It's Mary needs me, don't you understand?"

"No, I don't understand and I never will. You can't have the gun, Denny. It's mine. I want it back."

She tried to take it from him, but he was by far the stronger. She tried to twist it free.

The explosion rocked the house. Smoke and debris clouded the air. She knew she was losing consciousness, but now she couldn't let go of the gun. It was frozen in her hands. And her hands were wet with blood, her sleeves, her breast saturated. She could taste it. So much blood.

Then nothing.

When the girl, Lainie, got home from Denny's funeral, she put the Mass card in the box of clippings she was saving from the *Hope Valley News*. It didn't belong there, and yet it did. It would always carry her remembrance of the lone high voice from the choir loft singing the "Dies Irae," Day of Wrath, and the single sob it brought from her aunt Mary.

For as long as she lived, Norah would say that she had killed Denny—in spite of the coroner's finding that his death was most probably caused by a bullet fired from the cellar doorway an instant before or an instant after the gun in her and Denny's hands exploded.

Mary swore she had seen Spillane when she started over at the sound of gunfire. So she, too, bore willing guilt. But it was Donel who could beat his breast the hardest.

Norah had been right. Spillane was a low-level member of the Chicago gang Donel had been in business with for years. He had thought he was breaking away from them that fall. "The boss" thought so, too. He suspected at first that Donel was tying in with another gang and using Mary's place for storage. Spillane investigated even the well. Donel no more than Mary doubted his claim to be a federal agent.

When the news of the construction business came out—Hope County Construction—"the boss" wanted a part of it. Donel refused. As he told Mary, he was clean. He thought he was, but Spillane caught up with him before he reached the door of the lawyer's office that morning. The boss expected him to postpone the contract signing and expand the partnership. The boss promised he would get well paid, whichever way he played it. Donel told him to go to hell.

Why Denny and not Mary if Spillane was his killer? It was probably the boss's decision. Denny was Michael O'Hearn's nephew, and Michael had been killed—in the line of duty—in an exchange of gunfire that also killed a young and promising member of the gang those many years before.

Spillane was never found, dead or alive.

# BLUES IN THE KABUL NIGHT
*By Clark Howard*

Clark Howard sold his first short story, a Western, in July 1955 to *Stag* magazine. He has since sold more than two hundred stories to a wide variety of magazines from *Twilight Zone* to *Penthouse*. He is a regular contributor to *Ellery Queen Mystery Magazine,* where he has won five Readers' Awards. He has also won Edgar and Derringer awards, and has multiple nominations for Spur, Shamus, and Anthony awards. Although he has written two dozen books, the short story has long been his favorite form.

T he old four-engine, Constellation cargo plane dropped down out of the darkening Afghanistan sky shortly after flying over the border from Pakistan, and received landing instructions from the tower at Kotubkhel Airport outside Kabul. Morgan Tenny, hunched in a jump seat behind Benny Cone, the pilot, looked down on the squalid outskirts of the Afghan city as the runway lights came into sight.

"You sure I'm not going to have any problem at the airport?" Tenny asked.

"Trust me," said Benny Cone. "I been sneaking people in and out of this country for three years and haven't lost a client yet."

"What's your secret?" Tenny asked.

"Hershey bars," Cone replied.

"Hershey bars?"

"Yeah, with almonds. Afghanis are nuts about almonds. Excuse the pun."

The old plane's landing gear bumped hard against the blacktop runway, rose, bumped again, harder, then settled roughly into a jerky, lurching landing and decreased speed as it rolled toward the cargo terminal. When it came to a stop, Morgan Tenny followed Benny Cone through a narrow aisle between large, cable-secured wooden crates, to a high, wide cargo door which Cone unbolted and slid open on ball-bearing runners. Four forklift off-loaders were already driving toward the plane. Opening a hatch next to the cargo door, Cone unfolded an aluminum ladder that reached to the ground. Swinging a carry-on over one shoulder, he climbed down.

"Hand me your duffel," he said.

Tenny lowered an ancient sea bag on which could barely be distinguished four stenciled letters: USMC.

"Ain't seen one of these in a long time," Cone said. The closure of the bag folded in quarters over a steel hasp through which a combination padlock was fastened. "Heavy, too," the pilot observed. "Whatcha carrying?"

"The usual things," Morgan Tenny said as he climbed down. "Guns, ammunition, laundered currency."

"Everything a tourist in Kabul needs," Cone said with a smile. He nodded toward the terminal. "Follow me. Keep your mouth shut and do what I say. You ever been to Kabul before?"

"No."

"Well, it's a real shit hole. It's like no place you've ever seen, man."

"I've seen a lot of places, Benny," said Morgan Tenny. "Zaire, Saigon, Nairobi, Angola—"

"Yeah, well, you ain't seen noplace like Kabul. It is a *real* shit hole. The whole place."

"I thought the UN was cleaning it up after the Taliban got bounced?"

"The UN is a joke, brother. Wait and see."

The two men entered the Customs and Immigration section of the shabby cargo terminal and found a heavyset, droopy-eyed Afghan man browsing through a U.K. edition of *Playboy*.

"Moazzah, my friend!" Cone greeted him jovially. "How are you?"

"Passports and visas," the man named Moazzah said, without looking up from the magazine.

"Moazzah, look what I have for your lovely wife," Cone announced, pulling a carton of two dozen Hershey bars, with almonds, from his carry-on.

Moazzah looked up and took the carton. "Very nice, thank you." He held out a hand. "Passports and visas."

"And," Cone further declared, "look what I have for your beautiful mistress!" He produced half a dozen packages of black pantyhose, held together by a thick rubber band.

"Such generosity I do not deserve," the Afghan official said. His free hand was still out. "Passports and visas."

"Moazzah," Cone pleaded pitifully, "you know I am a stateless person without papers. All I want is a permit to unload. I won't even be leaving the terminal."

"And your friend?" Moazzah inquired.

"A tourist, that's all. He missed his commercial flight from Karachi and out of the goodness of my heart I gave him a ride. But his passport is still at the Arabian Air desk back there. Be kind, Moazzah. He just wants to spend a few nights with the China girls at the Escalades."

"I see," said Moazzah. The Escalades was the most notorious of Kabul's brothels. It was currently being run by a White Russian woman who called herself Madam Kiev, who had the best body in the brothel but never sold it, and had two former sumo wrestlers at her side at all times to keep the peace in her busy establishment. Moazzah knew the place well. He eyed Morgan Tenny for a long, solemn moment. "Pray tell, what do you have in your duffel?" he asked.

Morgan shrugged. "The usual things: guns, ammunition, laundered currency."

For a split second Moazzah frowned, then laughed out loud and pointed a finger at Morgan. "Your friend," he said to Benny Cone, "is a very funny fellow."

"Yeah, a million laughs," Cone agreed, smiling nervously. He handed Moazzah a British fifty-pound note.

"Take him to the taxi queue," the Afghan official said. "But *you* remain in the terminal."

"Blessings on your house," Cone said as Moazzah put the candy and pantyhose into a deep desk drawer and locked it.

The pilot led Morgan outside where several rattle-trap taxis waited. "You'll find Donahue at the Dingo Club," he told Morgan. "He's partners in the joint with an Aussie ex-pat. Tell him I said cheers."

Morgan nodded. "Thanks for the help."

"Thank *you*," said Benny, "for the stack of hundreds. Good luck."

*I'll need it*, Morgan thought, getting into a taxi.

The Dingo Club was on Chicken Street, one of Kabul's main pot-holed thoroughfares. Night had fallen now and multicolored neon lit up the sidewalks and the milling people entering and exiting shops selling handicrafts, carpets, pastries, hijacked Western food, pirated DVDs, and, farther along, bars, clubs, brothels, massage parlors, fast-food joints, tattoo kiosks, and the like, all of it reminding Morgan of the last week before Saigon fell. Slim and slung Asian girls wearing purple and orange makeup plied their trade to passing mercenaries, war-zone hangers-on in combat fatigues, along with contract laborers in denims, UN workers in dress shirts with rolled-up sleeves and neckties stuck in trouser pockets, and a few young U.S. Marines on liberty. All of them were armed: automatic rifles held casually, shoulder holsters holding Walther PPKs, revolvers tucked under bullet-filled cartridge belts. It was a totally dangerous street, but no one seemed to be bothered by it.

Morgan stepped inside the entrance to the Dingo Club. During the taxi ride to town, he had unlocked and opened his sea bag, and now had a Sig P230 automatic pistol in his waistband under his coat, an extra magazine of 60-grain bullets for it in his coat pocket, and a smaller automatic, a Kahr K9, in his belt at the small of his back. Standing just inside the club door, the big sea bag slung over one shoulder, he scoped out the noisy, raucous, smoky scene before him. Like a cautious falcon in unknown woods, his eyes flicked along the packed bar, the booths lining the walls, the tables in between, looking for familiar, especially unfriendly, faces among the patrons, bar-tenders, waiters, and pimps for the China girls who were working the room. Even after he spotted Donahue, the man he was looking for, his light-blue eyes kept moving, shifting, searching, until he had satisfied himself that he had no enemies there—at least none on the surface. Only then did he make his way to a back table where Donahue sat with three other men.

"Hello, Donny," he said when he got to the table. Donahue looked up.

"Well, well, well," he said. "If it ain't the calm half of the infamous Tenny twins. I wondered when you'd get here."

"You can stop wondering now," Morgan said.

The man at the table stood up. Michaleen Donahue was a great bull of an Irishman, sixty-six years old, thick-necked, massive-chested, muscular-armed, wearing a skin-tight camo shirt over which was strapped a Roto shoulder holster and magazine rig holding a Glock 17 automatic on one side and a double magazine pack on the other. He grabbed Morgan in a grand bear hug. "How are you, boyo?"

"Good, Donny. You?"

"Never better, lad. Come on, I've an office where we can talk. 'Scuse me, mates," he said to the other men at the table, and led Morgan into a nearby hallway to an office where he closed the door behind them. It was a sparsely furnished little room, with a metal utility desk, metal chairs, and several metal ammo boxes on the floor being used for files.

"Sit, boyo, sit," Donahue said, dropping his bulk into a swivel chair behind the desk and retrieving a bottle of Gilbey's and a pair of metal canteen cups from a bottom drawer. He poured two doubles.

"Cheers," they said in unison, and took their first swallows.

The swivel chair creaked as if in pain as Donahue leaned back. "I'm afraid you've made a trip for nothing, lad. What you're here for is a lost cause."

"That doesn't sound like the Donny I've known all these years," Morgan said.

The Irishman shrugged. "As a man gets older, he gets wiser. Wiser about everything: women, drinking, killing. He tends to realize there are some things he simply can't do anymore."

"Aren't you the one who always said life was doing what couldn't he done, and the rest was just waiting around?"

"Like I said, I'm older now."

"Well, maybe I'm wasting my time with you, then," Morgan said. "Maybe I should look for someone with more grit."

Anger flashed briefly in the big Irishman's eyes, but he quickly suppressed it and leaned forward, folding his thick fingers on the desktop. "Look, Morgan, I know there's a fine edge to you right now, with your twin brother Virgil being held in the Pul-e-Charki prison. But he's been charged with the torture and killing of three Afghan citizens while attempting to get information from them as to the whereabouts of Osama bin Laden—all so he could collect the twenty-five million bucks bounty on the son of a bitch. Virgil's going to be tried before an Afghan judge named Mehmet Allawi, who is as anti-Western as they come. He has stated openly that Western influence since the fall of the Taliban is ruining his holy land, and he's the leader of a party that wants all non-Muslims thrown out of the country. Your brother is the first Westerner to be charged with a capital crime since the U.S. invasion in 2001. Allawi intends to use him to make a statement against the U.S., the UN, and all other foreigners who are here. Virgil is going to be found guilty and hanged. And that, my boy, is that."

"I intend to break him out," Morgan said simply.

"Break him out?" Donahue grimaced in disbelief. "Out of Pul-e-Charki? You're dreaming, lad. It's not possible. There's no way to spring a man from there."

"I don't plan to just spring a man. I plan to liberate the whole damned prison, Donny."

Donahue grunted. "That would take a small army."

"I want to raise a small army. A strike force of trained mercenaries."

"You're crazy. It would cost a million dollars."

"I've got a million dollars," Morgan said. Reaching down, he patted the sea bag on the floor next to him, "Right here."

"You serious?"

"Dead serious." Morgan leaned forward, elbows on knees. "I know about that prison. I know men who've been in it. I've heard stories. It's a filthy cesspool. Whips, chains, rats, vermin, slop for food—it's a nightmare. They've even got torture chambers—"

"Your brother Virgil is in there for torturing people," Donahue reminded him.

"The three men Virgil tortured—"

"Two men," Donahue corrected. "One woman."

That gave Morgan pause for thought. But only momentarily. "Makes no difference," he said. "They were all al-Qaida. No telling how many innocent people they'd killed. Whatever the case, I want to blast open Pul-e-Charki prison." He locked eyes with Donahue. "You with me or not?"

Donahue took a long sip of gin, then pursed his lips for a moment. Finally he said, "Tell you what. You and me'll go out and have us a good look at Pul-e-Charki in the morning. Then you can tell me how you'd plan to go about doing it. After I hear your plan, I'll decide. Good enough?"

"Good enough," Morgan agreed.

They toasted again and finished their gin. Then Donahue asked, "Got a place to bunk yet?"

"No."

"Down the street to the right. The Mustafa Hotel. Use my name. Tell the desk clerk to give you an upstairs room in the back, away from the street noise. I'll come by for you about ten in the morning."

With his sea bag again slung, Morgan left the Dingo Club and turned right down the busy street, his senses alert to everything around him. He knew before she got there that a young woman was hurrying up beside him.

"Excuse me. May I speak with you for a moment, please?"

"Not tonight, honey," Morgan said, thinking she was street girl. "I'm dead tired, just in from a long flight."

"I know," she said. "I followed you from the airport."

Morgan stopped, his right hand instinctively going to the automatic in his belt. "You *followed* me from the airport?"

"Yes. In my car. I wanted to talk to you."

Looking more closely, Morgan now saw that she was definitely not a street girl. She was, he guessed, Afghan; *modern* Afghan: smallish, attractive, wearing a stylish pantsuit, carrying a large purse over one shoulder. He decided to play dumb.

"Why on earth would you follow *me*?" he asked with feigned innocence.

"My name is Liban Adnan," she said. "I'm a broadcast journalist. For NKR—New Kabul Radio. I'm doing a series on mercenary soldiers in the city. I'd like to interview you."

"You've made a mistake, miss," Morgan said. "I'm not a mercenary soldier. I'm a pharmaceuticals salesman."

"Oh?" Her full, dark eyebrows went up. "When you were leaving the Dingo Club, I saw you shake hands with Michaleen Donahue, a notorious mercenary soldier. Were you selling him aspirin, perhaps?"

"I went into that club to ask directions to the Mustafa Hotel. I didn't even know the man I was talking to."

"I see." She pulled a five-by-seven black-and-white glossy photograph from her purse. "I suppose you're going to tell me you don't know this man either."

In the neon light above a lap-dance club, Morgan looked at the picture. It was his twin brother, Virgil, in handcuffs and belly chain, being held between two Afghani policemen.

Taking Liban Adnan roughly by the arm, Morgan drew her into a nearby passageway between buildings, out of the busy sidewalk traffic. Once there, he kept her arm in a grip tight enough for her to know that she could not break away. "Exactly what do you want?" he asked coldly, evenly.

"I told you. An interview. I want to explain to the citizens of Kabul why scores of heavily armed men prowl their streets at night. I want to try to make the public understand who they are and why they are here."

"If I *was* a mercenary, do you think I'd be stupid enough to let you interview me about my reason for being here?"

"It could be an anonymous interview," she said, squirming in his grip. "We could even use a vibraphone mic to disguise your voice—"

"Look, miss," Morgan said firmly, "you've got the wrong person, understand? I don't know the man back at the club, and I don't know the man in that photograph!"

"But he looks just like you. Is it you, or—or are you his *brother*?" she exclaimed, as if that had just dawned on her.

"Listen to me, lady," Morgan tightened his grip on her arm, "mind your own business or you might be very sorry."

Liban squirmed even more. "Please, you're hurting me—"

Morgan let go of her arm. "Stay away from me," he warned.

Leaving her in the passageway, Morgan stepped back onto the sidewalk and continued toward the Mustafa Hotel.

Donahue was in the hotel lobby at ten the next morning when Morgan came down. He led Morgan outside to a battered Jeep with no top. Donny was again wearing the double Roto holster, and now was carrying an AR-15 automatic rifle as well. Morgan carried his same two handguns, but also had with him a Mossberg 500 shotgun equipped with a Knoxx folding stock, which allowed him to carry and fire it as a long-barrel pistol. He again had his sea bag slung behind one shoulder, but it was noticeably lighter now.

"Unpacked everything but the money, I see," Donahue observed.

"You guessed it," Morgan replied.

"Carrying it around like that, ain't you afraid somebody might take it away from you?"

"Somebody might die trying." Morgan jacked a 12-gauge Pit Bull shell into the Mossberg's chamber and held it between his knees next to the sea bag when he got into the Jeep. As Donahue slid behind the wheel, he observed that Morgan was wearing a flak vest under his jacket.

As they pulled away from the hotel, Morgan noticed a green Volkswagen parked nearby. Liban Adnan was in the driver's seat. *Son of a bitch!* he thought angrily. But he said nothing to Donahue. He did not want to alarm him.

The two men drove out of town. As they moved past numerous destroyed buildings and out onto a vast, flat scrub plain, Morgan watched in the outside rearview mirror on the passenger side and saw that the green Volkswagen was following at a respectable enough distance behind not to be obvious. Glancing at Donahue, he concluded that the big Irishman had not noticed it. Cursing silently in his mind, Morgan decided to go with the flow of the moment; there was nothing he could do about it, not just then. But later . . .

About ten miles outside Kabul they pulled onto a gravel road that faced Pul-e-Charki Prison. From outside, the facility appeared antiquated, its walls crumbling in places, its turrets looking unsteady at best. The Russians had built the place when they occupied Afghanistan, and its upkeep had been inadequate even then. After the Afghan government took it over, maintenance deteriorated even more: the cells, plumbing, toilets, food, and prisoner treatment—all went to hell. Everything except security: That had improved.

Donahue parked where they could get a view of the main gate and outer walls. "Picture yourself looking down at it from above," he said. "There are four blocks of cells around an inside courtyard. Block One, called 'Block-e-Awal,' is there," he pointed toward one front corner. "That's for high-status prisoners, foreigners, mercenaries mostly. They've got Jack Idema in there. He ran Saber Seven, a free-lance outfit that captured and tortured Afghan nationals, just like your brother did, trying to get a lead on Osama bin Laden. Jack's doing ten years; he was smart enough not to kill anyone. Virgil's in there too, along with some journalists and photographers who wrote about and photographed some things the new government didn't approve of.

"Block Two is directly across the center courtyard, over there," Donahue pointed to the opposite corner. "It's strictly for political prisoners, nobody really worth mentioning, mostly just ex-Taliban and protesters against the U.S.

"Block Three is back there, behind Block Two. It's full of common criminals: thieves, child molesters, drunkards, dishonest merchants, people who disrespect the Koran and Muslim law."

Donahue stopped talking and looked out over the wasteland toward a hazy, indistinct horizon. Morgan waited several moments, then: "You said four blocks."

"Yes, well." Donahue cleared his throat. "Block Four is where the executions take place. Some hangings. Beheadings. Occasional lesser punishments: cutting off the hands of a thief, blinding a man who spied on another man's wife that he coveted, stoning to death of women adulterers—"

"Rough justice," Morgan commented.

"If you can call it justice at all." Donahue's voice, Morgan thought, sounded unusually soft and sympathetic. Especially for a man who had for more than forty years killed for a living.

Glancing off in the distance, Morgan saw the green Volkswagen parked where its driver could observe them. He was going to have to decide what to do about the woman. He could not let her upset his plans to save his brother.

"So what do you think, lad?" Donahue asked, interrupting Morgan's thoughts.

"You have any guard contacts inside? That can be bought?"

"Maybe." The Irishman shrugged.

"Can you get me a dozen men—*good* men—on the outside?"

"Depends. You want specialists?"

Morgan nodded. "Four explosives men, two rocket experts, six tough ground troops."

"Possibly. Weapons?"

"AR-15s for the ground troops, plus any handguns they want for backup. Thirty-seven-millimeter launchers for the rocket men. K-2 plastics, coils, and timer detonators for the explosives."

"Ammo?"

"The works. Armor-piercing, incendiary, tracers. The best available. And plenty of it."

Donahue rubbed the stubble of beard on his chin. "Vehicles?"

"One armored halftrack with dual tactical mounted .50-calibers. And a Devil's Breath with dual tanks."

"Jesus, Morgan! A flamethrower?"

"Yes. And two armored specialists to handle the whole rig."

Donahue sighed. "Anything else?"

"Two armor-plated Humvees for the rest of us, to flank the half-track when we charge the main gate." Morgan took a deep breath. "That's it."

"You're sure now?" Donahue asked, a little sarcastically. "Sure you don't want a couple of fighter jets to strafe the place ahead of time?"

"Can you get it all or not?" Morgan asked flatly.

"I'll let you know. Come see me tonight at the Dingo."

As Donahue drove them back to Kabul, Morgan watched the green Volkswagen follow them in the passenger rearview mirror.

His lean jaw clenched.

Half an hour after Morgan returned to his room, there was a soft knock at his door. Holding the Sig 230 close to his right leg, he stood to the left of the door and said, "Yes?"

"It is I," a female voice said. "Liban Adnan."

Snatching the door open, Morgan jerked her into the room and locked the door behind them.

"You've got a hell of a lot of nerve coming here after following me all morning!" he' said angrily. "Didn't I warn you to stay away from me?"

"I am not afraid of you!" she snapped.

"That's obvious. What the hell do you want now?"

"Perhaps," she said, her voice as angry as his, "I came to show you these bruises you left on my arm last night!" Pulling up the sleeve of her blouse, she held out an arm with several dark, purplish bruises on it.

"You're liable to get more than bruises if you keep meddling in my business!" Morgan threatened.

"Again I say, I am not afraid of you, Mr. Tenny. Whatever you are planning, you surely would not interrupt it to do anything foolish to me. Especially since I have a friend at my radio station who knows I've been following you. The authorities would be on you in a heartbeat."

"If I did do anything to you," Morgan said confidently, "believe me, nobody would be able to prove it."

"They could certainly prove you are in the country illegally," she retorted. "I saw how you came in at the airport with Benny Cone. That alone is enough to get you *inside* the prison you and your friend Donahue studied so closely this morning."

Turning away from her, Morgan walked across the room. She had him on that. All he could do now was figure out a way to handle her. He walked back to her.

"Look, I'm sorry about the bruises," he said as contritely as he could. "But you came on pretty aggressively and I wasn't prepared for you. Can we start over?"

"Without the rough stuff?" she asked, sounding more American than Afghani.

"Definitely without the rough stuff."

"All right. I want to talk to you. But not here. Your friend Donahue has ears all over this place. I'll pick you up out front at six and take you to a little place I know on the edge of the city. We can have supper and talk about a compromise arrangement between us. Will you agree to that?"

"Yes."

"Good." Liban Adnan nodded brusquely. "Until six, then."

Unlocking the door, she left.

Morgan stared thoughtfully at the closed door behind her. Where in hell, he wondered, was *this* going to lead?

As Morgan walked out of the Mustafa Hotel, the green Volkswagen pulled up at once and he got in. Liban swung the car back into traffic and headed out the western highway toward Jalalabad. Neither of them spoke at first, until finally Morgan asked, "Have you told anyone else about me? Besides your friend at the radio station?"

"No, of course not." She glanced at him. "I want this story for myself."

Morgan nodded. Several minutes later, he said, "I'm sorry, I've forgotten your name."

"Liban Adnan. Just call me Lee."

She drove to a small settlement just outside the city and parked in front of a surprisingly nice-looking roadside restaurant, the name of which was written in Arabic across its facade. "This is a respectable family establishment," she said, "so please don't flash your guns around."

"What guns?"

"The ones I'm sure you are carrying. Let's not play games, Mr. Tenny."

Inside, Lee selected the table she wanted, off to one far side, and they were seated. "Are you familiar with Afghan food?" she asked.

"No."

"Then let me explain what you can order. *Mourgh* is skinless chicken marinated overnight in lemon pulp and cracked black pepper, then broiled. *Aush* is chopped beef, spinach, and dark *makhud*—sorry, yellow split peas—fried in coriander and turmeric, and served with dried mint sprinkled on it. *Qabili pilau*, is lamb and yellow rice boiled with carrots and black seedless raisins." She raised her eyebrows inquiringly.

"I'll have whatever you have," Morgan said. She ordered the *aush*, with sweet red tea and pistachios to munch on while they waited.

"I'm sorry you can't get something stronger to drink," Lee apologized, "but alcohol is not served here. You see, in our faith, especially among the *Tajiks*, who are the predominant population—"

"Look," Morgan interrupted, "can we get down to the business of why we're here?"

"Well, yes, of course. I was just trying to be cordial."

"Forget cordial. Specifically, what is it you want in order to leave me alone?"

Her eyes, dark like ripe plums, fixed on him. "I want the complete story of what you and Mike Donahue are planning and how you are going to go about it—"

"You're crazy," Morgan scoffed.

"Let me finish, please. I want the complete story—to be released *after* it happens. After you've done what you're planning to do, after you've gotten away with it—*if* you get away with it—"

"We'll get away with it."

"Fine. After you get away with it and have safely escaped. When everyone is running around, pointing fingers, blaming everyone else, trying to figure out who did it, how it was done—that's when I want to reveal everything."

"What do you expect to get out of that?"

"A reputation. Stature as a broadcast journalist. A move from radio to television. Perhaps even a position with CNN International."

"I see. You want to be famous."

"I want to be successful."

"You want to be another Christiane Amanpour."

She shrugged. "Perhaps." From her expression, Morgan knew he had nailed it.

Before they could converse further, an older man entered the restaurant, followed by two younger men, an older woman, and two younger women. They walked in single file, toward a family section in the rear that was configured with larger tables. But as they started to pass the table where Morgan and Lee sat, the older man abruptly stopped, as did everyone behind him. Standing ramrod straight, he glared down at Lee. He did not speak. Lee looked down at the table. Morgan saw that the five people behind the man also had their eyes downcast.

The silent confrontation lasted perhaps forty seconds, but it somehow seemed much longer. Presently, the older man moved on, his entourage following.

"What was that all about?" Morgan asked.

"That was my family," Lee replied quietly. "My father, my two brothers, my mother, my two sisters." She looked over at him woefully. "I have been banished from my family, you see. When I took up Western ways, Western dress, got a Western job as a radio broadcaster, my father ostracized me. I am not allowed to go around any member of my family, or to communicate with them in any way, or they with me. None of them may cast eyes upon me except my father, and then only to revile me with his look."

Morgan saw a sadness in her eyes, but it did not seem to be for the painful scorn of her father and the loss of her family. Rather it was a sadness of fear, the kind Morgan had seen in the eyes of many who were about to die; it was a sadness not of something that had already happened to her, but of something that was going to happen to her, and she *knew* it.

At once, as he looked at her, she became appealing to him, her despair coupled with a longing, all of it concealed to some degree by her effervescent aggressiveness—no, not aggressiveness, he rethought it—more like assertiveness, an *anxious* assertiveness. Morgan felt something emanating from Liban Adnan that he could not define or understand. But he knew he had to respond to it.

"All right, I'll help you, Lee," he told her, suddenly deciding. "I'll give you your story."

A glimmer of a smile came tentatively to her lips. "Thank you, Mr. Tenny."

"Call me Morgan," he said.

Later that night, back in the office of the Dingo Club, Morgan again sat across the desk from Michaleen Donahue.

"I want a hundred thousand for myself," Donahue said.

"You want it now?"

The Irishman's thick black brows went up. "That would be nice."

Morgan unlocked and unzipped the bag that constantly hung from his shoulder, and from it counted out ten banded sheaves of hundred-dollar bills, fifty to a sheaf, and twenty sheaves of fifty-dollar bills, also fifty to a sheaf. "That leaves me with nine hundred thousand, Donny. Will that do us?"

"I think so. I put a pencil to it earlier—" He pushed a yellow lined pad across the desk, which Morgan picked up and began to study. "I figure twenty thousand each for the two guard contacts we'll need on the inside," he told Morgan. "Four explosives men at forty each is a hundred-sixty. Two rocket-launcher men at thirty-five apiece is seventy. Six ground troops to back up you and me at—"

"You and me?" Morgan interrupted. "You're coming along?"

"Certainly," Donahue said, taken aback slightly. "You think I took a hundred thousand just to sit on my ass?"

Morgan shrugged self-consciously. "Well, I—I mean—well—"

"Well, hell! A well's a hole in the ground, lad! Your brother's a friend of mine. And so are a few others in that hellhole of a prison. Yeah, I'm coming along. You bet your ass I am." Donahue cleared his throat. "Now, as I was saying: Six ground troops at twenty-five per is another one-fifty. The half-track, used but in good condition, will cost us two hundred thousand. And the two armored Humvees will run seventy-five each, that's one-fifty." Donahue got out a bottle and poured drinks for them while Morgan studied the figures. Taking a long sip of his own, he sat back and licked his lips appreciatively at the taste. "I make it seven-seventy," he concluded. "That leaves one-thirty for weapons and ammo."

"One-thirty will be a stretch," Morgan guessed, frowning.

"Might, might not," said Donahue. "Depends on where I have to buy. If I can run at least half of what we need from Uzbekistan, we'll be okay. If I have to deal with the Pakistanis, those bloody bastards will try to rob us blind." He paused for a moment, then said, "It might be possible to steal some ammo from the UN forces arsenal down in Qandahar. I don't know how you'd feel about that, you being a Yank and all—"

"Steal it anywhere you can," Morgan said flatly. "I don't owe the UN anything."

"Right. Well, then." Donahue rose and drained his glass. "I'll get the ball rolling first thing in the morning. You want to interview personnel?"

"Not unless you want me to."

"I'll do it meself then. How do you plan to get Virgil out of the country?"

"Same way I got in. Billy Cone."

"Billy might not be up for anything that heavy. What if he says no?"

Morgan locked eyes with the Irishman. "Then I'll kill him, take his plane, and fly it myself."

The next night, Lee invited Morgan to her apartment, where they would have the privacy to talk more openly.

Lee lived in one of the older, modest buildings in a more or less grubby section of south Kabul, but she said she liked the location because it was convenient to the traditional Afghan food markets as well as a newer, Western-style superstore that sold canned items imported from the U.S. Plus, the sparsely but comfortably furnished apartment offered a parking shed for her little green Volkswagen. Morgan noticed at once that the apartment's cracked and pitted walls were colorfully concealed with a variety of posters: Emiliano Zapata, Muhammad Ali standing over a prone Sonny Liston, Mother Teresa touching the forehead of a sick child, Roy Rogers with six-guns blazing.

"Roy Rogers?" Morgan said in surprise.

"Yes. I watch his old films on the new satellite station. They have subtitles, of course. I think his horse is nice. And I like the way he sings."

She had prepared a cold supper for them.

"*Samboosak*," she told him. "Cold meat pies with leeks and mild spices. And there are boiled eggs and a spinach-and-chickpea salad with pine nuts. And," she added proudly, "just for you—" She produced a bottle of Australian wine. "Another reason my father has disowned me: I like a glass of wine now and then."

As they ate, Morgan outlined for Lee in detail his plan to breach Pul-e-Charki prison with a small armed force, an armored vehicle, and two armed Humvees, to liberate his twin brother Virgil from Block One, where the high-profile prisoners were kept, and then how the two of them would escape the country in Benny Cone's plane.

"What about the other prisoners in Block One?" Lee wanted to know. "And in the other blocks?"

Morgan shrugged. "They'll be pretty much on their own. If they can get to the main gate, a lot of them can pile onto the half-track and the Hummers when they retreat."

"And the guards?"

"Most of them at the main gate and around Blocks One and Two will probably be killed in the initial assault."

Lee looked down at the table. "A lot of those men are just ordinary family men, working men, most of them not political at all."

"They chose to work there," Morgan said evenly. "They knew the risks involved." He paused, then continued in a softer tone. "Look, Lee, everyone makes their own choices in life. Everyone pays their own prices for those choices. That's just life."

"Or in this case, death," she amended.

They finished supper and went outside to sit on the building's back steps and drink the rest of the wine.

"I try very hard to understand you Westerners," she said. "All of you who are here in my country: Americans, British, Irish, Australians, the mixed Europeans. I try to understand the little regard you all seem to have for human life if something stands in the way of what you want."

"I've been trying to understand your people, too," Morgan said, "since I saw your own father stare so hatefully at you, and you told me how you'd been ostracized by him from your family. I don't understand that. My brother Virgil and I are twins; we were together in the womb, born together. We grew up together as dirt-poor Catholics in a steel-mill town in a place called Pennsylvania. Our father was a drunk; our mother washed other men's dirty, stinking mill clothes to feed us. We got made fun of as free students in a hard-knock Catholic school because of the shabby hand-me-down uniforms we wore. We never got invited to join school teams or clubs, or come to school parties. But we got away from all that. When we were old enough, we joined the Marine Corps. We went through boot camp together, then weapons school, where they taught us to use rifles, pistols, machine guns, flamethrowers, hand-held rocket launchers. Finally we went to sniper school together and learned to kill. We lived by the sniper motto: One shot, one kill. When we left the Corps, we both had confirmed body counts in the high twenties. The day we were discharged, we were recruited for a mercenary team to fight in Zaire. We've been fighting, and killing, ever since."

Morgan fell silent then. The two of them sat there in the shadows, the wine warming them, listening to mixed night sounds of Kabul. Someone, somewhere not too far away, was playing one of the new Western stations on the radio, and the mournful voice of a mournful woman was singing "Blues in the Night." They listened until the song ended, then Morgan spoke again.

"I know what my brother is accused of doing, and I don't condone what he's done. But he's my brother. I can't disown him like your father has disowned you. It's not in me to do that."

In the darkness, Lee reached out and took his hand.

Later, she moved close to him and he put an arm around her shoulders.

Within a week, Michaleen Donahue was almost ready to move.

"The CV-6 Russian half-track," he reported to Morgan, "is hidden under a camo tarp about five miles from the prison. The Hummers are concealed nearby; we got lucky and stole one of them from the Marines down near Ghazni, so we saved a nice piece of change there. The launchers and rockets are stowed in a house on the outskirts. The K-2 explosives are stashed in another house not far away. All weapons and ammo, including the flamethrower, are at a third location convenient to the other two. And I've got personnel all over the bloody city, paid and waiting to be summoned."

"What kind of men have we got?" Morgan asked.

"Good men, the lot of them. Three have relatives in the prison that they're going to try and spring. Those are Afghanis, of course. Then," he began to count on his fingers, "I've got two of me own Irish lads from Belfast; two Aussies who've worked together as a team for twelve years; a couple of real killers from Tajikistan who deserted the Russian army; a Pakistani, and two Turks."

"Turks, good." Morgan nodded. "I'll fight with Turks any day."

"I feel the same way," Donahue agreed. "We'll put them on the Hummers with ourselves."

"Right. Inside help?"

"Two guards have been bribed. They'll see to it that the Block One prisoners will be let into the courtyard for exercise ten minutes after our mechanized force breaks cover and heads for the prison. All the men will be armed before daybreak and rendezvous at two separate locations to be picked up by the Hummers. The K-2 will have been placed on each side of the main gate during the night; I'll carry one igniter switch and one of my Irish lads will have the other one in the second Hummer. Launcher gunners and their rockets will be in slit trenches fifty yards away on each side; they'll take out the gun turrets. The flamethrower man will be on the half-track." Donahue lighted a fat Cuban cigar. "All's left is for us to set a time."

"You said we had money left?"

"Sure. What we saved by stealing one of the Hummers. What d'you need?"

"I'm thinking some kind of diversion on the side of town far-thest from the prison, to distract the civilian law and the local army garrison."

"Good idea. Let's see what we can find here . . ." Donahue unrolled on his desk a map of the city and began tracing it with one tobacco-stained finger. "Over here we have a sugar-beet plant and a few food-processing and canning factories. There's a rather large woolen mill here. At this point here, farther out, there's an industrial district with some metalworking shops, a lumber mill, a number of woodworking businesses—"

"How big's the lumber mill?"

"It's quite a good size."

"Let's set it on fire."

Donahue frowned. "All the wood's pretty dry this time of year. The place'll go up like a tinderbox. Could spread and burn down a couple square miles of the city. Including a lot of homes."

"Too bad," Morgan said. "I don't owe these people anything. Let's set it on fire."

Donahue shrugged. "All right. It's your call."

Morgan could tell that the idea didn't sit well with Donahue. But it wasn't Donahue's brother in Pul-e-Charki. "Can you get somebody to do it?" he asked.

"Sure," the big Irishman said quietly. "I know a couple of Iranian thugs who'll do anything for a laugh."

"Okay. Set that up and then we'll decide on a time."

As Morgan started to leave, Donahue said, "Incidentally . . ."

Morgan stopped. "What?"

"One of my lads saw you in a restaurant with that radio woman, Liban Adnan."

"Yeah. She's been after me to do an interview on mercenaries. I'm just stringing her along."

"Well, you might want to be extra careful with her. She's a police informant."

That night, walking arm in arm back to Lee's apartment after a late dinner, Morgan was trying to decide how to kill her.

Breaking her neck was probably the best way; it was quick, quiet. And with the difference in their size and weight, it would be easy enough.

But he hated like hell to do it.

During the past week they had been developing—something; Morgan wasn't quite sure what. Ever since they had sat in the shadows on the back steps of her building and he had told her about himself and Virgil, and she had ended up with her head on his shoulder, they had both begun feeling—something.

It had started with casual touching, quick, spontaneous hugs, brief kisses on the cheeks, then the lips, lightly at first, barely, then, longer, more serious, urgent.

"What are we doing?" she had asked just the previous night. They had stepped into the doorway of a shop to get out of a sudden downpour. She had come into his embrace, her arms crossing behind his neck, her lips and body hungry. And then: "What are we doing?"

"I don't know," Morgan said. "Are we falling in love?"

Then it was her turn to say, "I don't know."

"I've never had feelings like this before—"

"Nor I—"

"It's a crazy thing to have happen—"

"I know. It's insane—"

"With what's going on and all. It's not rational—"

"No, not rational at all—"

Still, they had kissed some more, and when the rain stopped they had walked with their arms around each other back to her apartment. But she would not let him come in.

"Wait, Morgan, please. Until tomorrow night. Let's give ourselves a night to think about this."

"I don't have to think about it. I want you."

"And I want you—"

"Then let's go inside." Gently he took her arm.

"Please, Morgan. Not tonight. Today is Friday. There is a *khutba* tonight. A special congregational prayer. I want to go to it. To see if perhaps there will be a message in it for me. For us."

"I don't understand," Morgan said, confused. "I thought you walked away from all that. I thought you were liberated."

"I am. But I still have my own beliefs. So, please. Wait. Until tomorrow night."

So Morgan had waited.

And later that night Donahue had told him she was a police informant.

Now tomorrow night had come. And instead of thinking about making love to this pretty, sad-eyed, anxious young Afghani woman, Morgan was thinking about how to kill her.

At Lee's apartment, she led Morgan into her tiny bedroom and lighted ivory votives in each corner that threw enough flickering yellow light to illuminate a bed made up with pristine white satin hemmed in puce, stitched with gold thread.

"This is our bridal bed," Lee said softly. "At the *khutba* last night, the message I got was to follow my heart. That is what I will do." She touched Morgan's cheek. "You undress while I prepare our bath."

"Our bath?"

"Yes. Before we make love, we must cleanse ourselves together."

At that moment, Morgan desired her with an intensity he had never imagined he could feel. Through the open door to the bathroom, he watched as she ran water into a large old sunken family tub made of blue tiles. Then she began to undress. As did he.

When they stood naked in the now steamy little bathroom, Lee opened a basket and from it sprinkled small red, yellow, and white flowers onto the surface of the bathwater.

"These are wild *honisoukes*," she said. "You Westerners call them honeysuckles."

They got into the tub together.

All thoughts of killing her left Morgan's mind.

"Everything's ready when you are, lad," Donahue told Morgan the next day. "The two Iranians are straining on their leash to torch the lumber mill, God forgive us. All the men, weapons, and vehicles are in place, and we're locked and loaded. We just need to give our two inside men one day's notice."

Morgan nodded. "I'll set up our exit with Benny Cone. His Kabul contact said he's flying in with a load of hijacked cigarettes tomorrow at noon." Pausing a beat, he then added, "And just so you know, I'll be taking Liban Adnan with Virgil and me when we go."

Donahue's ruddy Irish face darkened in a scowl. "How much does she know? And don't lie to me, Morgan."

"She knows everything, except the day. And the lumber-mill fire."

"You bloody fool!"

"Listen to me. It doesn't matter. She's on our side. I guarantee it."

"You *guarantee* it! Who the hell do you think you're talking to! I warned you about her! We could be walking right into a trap, all of us!"

"That won't happen, Donny. Listen to me. I confronted her about being a police informant. She admitted that at times she had cooperated with certain police officials, but only in matters involving drug smugglers, slave traders of children, things like that. Listen, think about it. If she had informed on us, if the military or the prison authorities knew about the plan, they'd already have moved in. They wouldn't wait until we launched our attack; they'd have to take casualties and structural damage that way. They could have taken us anytime without a fight. All they'd have to do is seize our weapons stockpile and we'd be out of business." He stared down Donahue. "I'm telling you it's all right, Donny. You have my word."

"I need more than your word to risk my life!" Donahue declared.

They fell silent for a long moment. The little office was still as death, as if both of them had stopped breathing.

"I didn't have to tell you about her," Morgan pointed out.

"I know that."

"It should be easy enough for you to find out if there's been a betrayal of any kind."

Donahue nodded brusquely. "I'll do you the courtesy of checking it out. I'll meet with the two guards I've paid off. If anything's amiss, they'll know it. And if they try to lie to me, *I'll* know it." He came over to Morgan and got square in his face. "If you're wrong, lad, you'll never have a chance to be right again."

It was as clear and cold a threat as Morgan Tenny had ever heard.

On Sunday at noon, Morgan was back out at the cargo terminal of Kotubkhel Airport. He hung around the Customs area, staying well out of sight so that Moazzah, the agent who had let him into the country, would not see him. Benny Cone's old Constellation touched down an hour late, at one o'clock, and awhile later Morgan saw him come into the terminal and loiter around Moazzah's desk for a few minutes while passing along several parcels of bribery goods. There was a cafe in the passenger terminal next-door, and Morgan gave one of the shoeshine boys near the baggage kiosks a handful of Afghani dollars, equal to about one buck U.S., to take Benny a note he had prepared in advance, which read: MEET ME CAFE. TENNY.

After watching to make sure the note was delivered, Morgan went over to the passenger terminal. It was a great anthill of people, long queues trying to check in at the counters of Ariana Afghan Airlines, which consisted of several old Air India airbuses repainted and being flown by Russian contract pilots. The only uncrowded counters were where the VIPs and others were checking in at UNHAS to board one of the modern daily United Nations Humanitarian Air Service jets that served Kabul. The terminal itself was filthy and stank of every imaginable odor; its air was infested with large, aggressive flies, and was smoke-filled by many passengers standing obliviously under No Smoking signs. Security guards, all of them in British Royal Air Force uniforms, stood everywhere, armed with H&K G3 automatic weapons.

Morgan went into the grubby little cafe on the upper level, purchased a bottle of unchilled Fiji water, and found a small table in the back corner, away from pedestrian traffic. Awhile later, Benny Cone sauntered in, located him, and came over to sit down.

"Well?" Benny asked. "Was I right?"

"Right about what?"

"About Kabul. Is it a shit hole or isn't it?"

"It's a shit hole," Morgan agreed.

"Told you so." The pilot tilted his head. "You ready to get out?"

"I will be, day after tomorrow, Tuesday. Can you be on the ground ready to fly at four in the afternoon?"

"I guess. Where to?"

"Anywhere you can set us down without papers. Karachi, where we can get sea transportation, would be nice; Abu Dhabi, if the Emirates are open; Bahrain or anywhere in the Gulf of Oman. I'll leave it up to you."

"Okay. You said us. Who's us?"

"Me, my brother Virgil, a woman, maybe Donahue, if I can talk him into it."

"Who's the woman?"

"An Afghani broadcast journalist. She's clean but doesn't have a passport."

"Who the hell does these days?" Benny grunted. "Baggage?"

"Carry-ons, two or three personal weapons per man."

"What can you pay?"

"What do you want?"

"What I want is a hundred thousand per person, but what I'll take is five per. Twenty thousand."

"Deal. Payment in the air?"

"Deal." Benny bobbed his chin at the bottle of water Morgan was drinking. "You shouldn't be drinking that shit."

"Why? It's Fiji water."

"It's a Fiji water *bottle*, probably been refilled a dozen times from the tap." He took a pewter flask from his inside pocket and passed it over. "Here, gargle and rinse your mouth out with this."

Morgan took a swig, rinsed, gargled, nearly choked, and spat it on the floor behind his chair. "Jesus!" he said. "What the hell is it, cyanide?"

"You're close. It's Kazakhstan bootleg vodka. Tastes like hell, but it kills bacteria. I never leave home without it." Benny rose. "I have to get back or Moazzah will piss his pants. He's edgy today." He took back his flask and held out a hand. "See you Tuesday."

"Tuesday," Morgan said.


Back in town, late in the afternoon, Morgan looked for Donahue at the Dingo Club.

"He ain't here, mate," one of the Irishman's cronies told him.

"Know where I can find him?"

"I do. But he don't like to be bothered on Sunday afternoons."

"It's important. He'll want to see me."

The crony studied Morgan for a moment, then said, "You'll find him at the Italian Embassy, out on Great Massoud Road."

Morgan frowned. "The Italian Embassy?"

"That's what I said, mate. But don't expect him to be in a jolly mood. Like I told you, he don't like to be bothered on Sunday afternoons."

Outside, Morgan found a dilapidated taxi whose driver, incredibly, knew exactly where the Italian Embassy was located. But what in hell, Morgan wondered, would Donahue be doing there? He was an Irish Free State national traveling on Swiss and Swedish passports, none of which had anything to do with Italy. Just what, Morgan puzzled, could the old Black Irishman be up to?

When he got to the embassy grounds, Morgan found it to be casually guarded by several *carabinieri* wearing sidearms but without heavier weapons. He was courteously directed toward a small group of people congregating in a flowery ornamental garden near a small chapel. One of the people was Donahue, clean-shaven, wearing a starched white shirt, appearing unarmed, talking to two nuns. When he saw Morgan, he smiled, excused himself, and came over to him.

"What the hell are you doing here?" he asked irritably. Morgan, seeing a priest join the two nuns and go into the chapel, quickly said, "Going to Mass. You?"

"Well, I'm going to Mass too," the Irishman growled. "But I didn't expect to see you here." He squinted suspiciously. "How'd you find the place anyway? It's the only Catholic church in the whole of Afghanistan."

"Taxi driver told me."

"I've a feeling you're lying."

Morgan shrugged. "Why would I lie?"

"Well, tell me, then, Morgan Tenny, if you go to Mass, who will you pray to?"

"The usual people. Jesus. Blessed Mother Mary—"

"No, no," Donahue challenged. "I mean, who *specifically*?"

Morgan caught on quickly and outsmarted him. "St. Philomena," he said confidently.

"Ah," said Donahue, surprised, a little chagrined. "The Patroness of Desperate Causes. A good choice."

Morgan tilted his head. "And you, Donny? Who do you pray to?"

"Me?" The big Irishman shrugged. "I go straight to the top. Jesus himself. I used to pray to St. Michael the Archangel, you know, to protect me in battle. But he let me get shot by an Orangeman in Derry some years ago, so I dropped him. Now it's between me and Jesus on the Cross. My best hope at this point is to get into purgatory." He patted Morgan on the shoulder. "Yours too, I'd wager."

"I'm not even counting on purgatory," Morgan said. "I expect to go directly to hell." He put his own hand on Donahue's shoulder. "And you will, too, Donny. Neither of us will ever see heaven."

From inside the chapel, chimes sounded. The two men fell in behind others and entered, dipped a fingertip in holy water, walked down the narrow center aisle, genuflected, made the sign of the cross, and entered a pew made of hardwood where they knelt and closed their eyes in prayer.

There was nothing much different about them from the rest of the mixture of UN employees, Europeans, and Americans in the congregation, except for the few whispered words they exchanged upon entering.

"Are we set?" Morgan had asked.

"We're set," Donahue said.

"Okay," Morgan told him. "We go day after tomorrow."

"Tuesday?"

"Tuesday. At noon."

Their killing schedule was on, now firmed up in the little Catholic chapel.

Morgan spent all day Monday and Monday night with Lee.

During the day they walked around, exploring the parts of the once-great city that were being rebuilt after being pillaged, looted, and desecrated first by Russian soldiers, then by Taliban officials, finally by rogue mercenaries from around the world.

"Not all of it is the wreckage you see around you," Lee told him. They were having a Western lunch at the new Marco Polo restaurant. All the patrons were Westerners, with not an Afghani to be seen. "I will show you something very beautiful that is still intact after four centuries."

After lunch she took him there, to Babur's Gardens, a terraced hillside resplendent with flowers, leading up to a pristine white mosque and a small marble gravestone, and two others on the terraced garden just above it.

"This is the burial place of Babur, who founded the Mogul Empire—*not*," she emphasized with a pointed finger, "the dreaded *Mongol* Empire, which was something altogether different. Of course, it is true that Babur was a great warrior and led his people in overcoming Turks and Indians and many others, but he was also a very gentle man, a poet, a writer of history. Nearly everything good in our culture began under his rule. This," she drew in the gardens, the mosque, the gravestones with a sweep of her arm, "he designed him-self more than four thousand years ago as the final resting place for himself, his wife, and their daughter."

"It's very beautiful," Morgan said, impressed.

But the memory of the place became tainted in his mind later that day when they walked past the ruins of the Kabul Museum and Lee said sadly, "It was once one of Asia's greatest museums. Now see what unscrupulous men, vulgar men, have reduced it to."

Men like me, Morgan thought, oddly uncomfortable.

In the evening they had dinner at the elegant Khyber Restaurant, eating a mixture of Western and Afghan foods. They were both aware now that the hours before Tuesday were passing quickly.

"At times like this," Lee asked, "do you worry much?"

"No," Morgan said. "Worry is like thinking about a debt you may not have to pay." It was a lie. He always worried. Before a battle, he felt as if live things were crawling around in his intestines, eating away at them.

Later he told her, "Tomorrow pack only a small bag. Stay home all day. I'll come for you in the afternoon." And he asked, "You're still sure about going?"

"Yes, still sure."

"You may never see your family again."

"I never see them now."

Walking to her apartment after dinner, he admitted, "I lied to you earlier. I do worry." For some reason he felt sad. "Can we bathe together again tonight?"

Lee touched his face with both palms. "Of course, my love."

Going into her building, neither of them suspected that they were being watched.

At ten the next morning, Morgan strode into the Dingo Club, two pistols and ammo in a belt around his waist, an Uzi 9mm machine gun and web belt of extra magazines slung over one shoulder, car-rying the Mossberg shotgun in one hand.

The club, not yet open, was empty except for Donahue at his usual table. Halfway back to it, Morgan stopped cold. Donahue had a glass and bottle in front of him, telling Morgan that something was very wrong. No professional soldier drank before a fight; you didn't want alcohol in your system if you might be wounded. Walking on up to the table, Morgan stood there, waiting for Donahue to speak.

"The operation's off, lad," the Irishman finally said.

"What's happened, Donny?"

Donahue looked up at him forlornly, his expression desolate, eyes mournful.

"Your brother Virgil was put on trial at seven o'clock this morning. He was found guilty at eight. And he was hanged at nine."

Morgan was thunderstruck. "Virgil—? He's been—*hanged*?"

"I just got the news a bit ago. I'm sorrier than I can say, lad."

Shock overwhelming him, Morgan sat down heavily on one of the chairs, laying the Mossberg on the table, dropping the Uzi and web belt to the floor next to him. His lips parted wordlessly, incredulously.

"One of the guards I bribed got word to me," Donahue said. "I'm truly, truly sorry, Morgan. I really wanted to have a go at this one. With you. Your brother. I was gonna make it my last big raid. I really wanted it—" Tears came to the big Irishman's eyes. He poured a drink, but did not raise the glass. Instead he angrily propelled both glass and bottle off the table with the sweep of an arm. "Oh, damn them! God damn them to hell!"

The two men sat in silence, not looking at each other, for what seemed like a long time. Around them, club employees began to straggle in and begin making the club ready for its noon opening.

*Hanged*, Morgan thought, shaking his head dully. It was almost too heinous to imagine. Virgil, hanged.

Finally, Morgan rose from his chair. "We're set to fly out with Benny Cone at four, if you want to come along."

Donahue shook his head slightly. "Thanks anyway, lad."

Leaving the Mossberg and Uzi and ammo, Morgan walked out of the club.

At Lee's apartment, the door was ajar. Frowning, Morgan drew his Glock, thumbed the safety off, and eased inside. Lee's father was sitting on the couch, staring straight ahead as if in a stupor.

"Where is she?" Morgan asked.

The father smiled slightly. "I watched you last night," he said. "I saw you come in here with her and I waited all night until you came out this morning. I know that you have dishonored her and she has dishonored my family. Shame has been cast over me. Now that shame is erased."

Morgan's already ashen face blanched even more pallid and horror clouded his eyes. He went into the bedroom.

Lee lay on her back, still wearing the plain white cotton gown she had pulled on to say goodbye to him at her door. Her face was whiter even than Morgan's, whiter than the white cotton gown, whiter than the pristine white satin sheets on the bed. Her throat had been cut and the blood in which she lay had dried almost black under her head.

Morgan sighed a great, hollow sigh and thought: *This is my punishment for the life I've led.* He felt deep remorse that Lee had been punished too.

Walking back to where her father sat, Morgan raised the Glock and put the muzzle between the man's eyes.

"Shoot me," Lee's father said. "Kill me. I do not care. I did what was right. I face death without shame."

Morgan thumbed the safety of the Glock back on. "No," he said. "You live with it."

He left the man sitting there.

Stretched out on the empty cargo deck of the Constellation about five minutes after it was airborne, Morgan heard Benny Cone call back to him from the cockpit.

"Hey, Tenny! We got off by the skin of our teeth! They just closed the airport!"

Morgan went forward to the cockpit. "What happened?"

"It just came over the air from the tower. There's some kind of rebel army attacking Pul-e-Charki prison. The place is under siege. Prisoners are escaping like ants."

*Son of a bitch*, Morgan thought. *Donny's doing it anyway. He's getting his last big raid.*

"The radio say anything about a big fire on the other side of the city? A lumberyard?" he asked Cone.

"Nope. Just the attack on the prison."

*Good for you, Michaleen,* Morgan thought. *Just you against the prison, with no diversionary tactic. One on one. Way to go.*

Going back aft in the plane, Morgan stretched out again. For a brief moment, he felt guilty about not being there with Donahue. Then he thought of Lee and the guilt faded.

Lee would forever be with him.

And he would never kill again.

# THE PROFANE ANGEL

*By Loren D. Estleman*

Loren D. Estleman is the author of more than sixty novels. He has earned five Spur Awards from the Western Writers of America, four Shamus Awards from the Private Eye Writers of America, and three Western Heritage Awards from the National Cowboy Hall of Fame. In 2007, the Library of Michigan named his novel *American Detective*, the twentieth featuring Amos Walker, private detective, a Notable Book of the year, and *Publishers Weekly* singled it out as one of only eight mysteries on its list of 100 Best Novels of 2007. *Frames*, the first novel to feature Valentino, will appear in May 2008.

Pegasus made his majestic way down the San Diego Freeway, waiting with wings partially folded through the relatively steady stop-and-go before the morning crush and the noon rush; took brief flight on Sunset Boulevard; and settled down to wait through the standard three light changes at each intersection in West Hollywood.

The sight of the mythical beast, painstakingly worked in plaster and spray-painted all the colors of the Day-Glo rainbow, drew no more than the occasional curious glance toward its perch on the open rented trailer. L.A. had seen stranger sights on an almost daily basis.

Nevertheless, Valentino was relieved when he pulled into the alley next to the Oracle Theater and found Kyle Broadhead waiting with a pair of husky undergraduates to help him unload the sculpture. He disliked attracting attention, and had chosen the one place in America to live where it was virtually impossible.

Broadhead wrinkled his nose at the garish paint job. "What a hideous way to treat a noble creature that never existed. Where'd you find him, Fire Island?"

"Close." Valentino got out of the car and stretched. "An Armenian rug dealer in the Valley stuck it in front of his shop to attract business. Some students from State have been redecorating it once or twice a week for five years. It'll take ten gallons of mineral spirits just to get down to the original workmanship."

One of the burly UCLA students snorted. "Everybody knows you can't trust a Statie with a box of Crayolas."

"Spoken by the young man who credited *Stagecoach* to Henry Ford on his midterm." Broadhead, rumpled and dusted with pipe ash, patted Pegasus on the flank. "Welcome home, Old Paint. Your brother's missed you."

Valentino untied the ropes that lashed the statue in place, the students bent their shoulders to their task, and after much grunting, mutual accusations of sloth, and two pinched fingers, the winged horse stood at last on a pedestal opposite its twin at the base of the grand staircase in the littered lobby.

"There's teamwork." Broadhead admired the tableau.

Valentino said, "What's that make you, the coach? I missed your contribution."

The professor took his pipe out of his mouth. "Do you realize how much concentration it takes to keep one of these going?"

The student who had suffered the casualty stopped sucking his fingers. "The new one's bigger."

"It won't be when we strip off all those coats of paint," Valentino said. "It isn't any newer than the other one. They were sculpted at the same time by the same artist. If I hadn't tracked this one down by way of the Internet, duplicating it would have cost me a fortune."

"As opposed to the several you've already sunk into this dump." Broadhead nursed his pipe.

"A man has to have a hobby."

"Movies are only a hobby when your work hasn't anything to do with them. You spend all week procuring and restoring old films and all weekend rebuilding a theater to show them in. Which reminds me. Someone called while you were out riding and roping." Broadhead unpocketed a foil-lined wrapper that had contained tobacco and handed it to Valentino.

"What's it say?" He couldn't read what was scribbled on it.

"An old lady in Century City says she has something to sell. Probably a home movie of her playing jacks at Valley Forge. I told you that interview you gave the *Times* would draw more pests than genuine leads."

Valentino went up to the bachelor quarters he'd established in the projection booth and dialed a number off Caller ID. He couldn't distinguish letters from numerals in Broadhead's scrawl. A young woman told him he'd reached the residence of Jane Peters. He got as far as his name when she interrupted.

"Yes, Miss Peters is expecting your call. She's resting at the moment. Are you free to come to the apartment later today? She has a property she thinks might interest you."

"May I ask what it is?"

"A movie called *A Perfect Crime*."

"The title's kind of generic. Can you give me any details?"

Paper rustled. "It's a silent, released in nineteen twenty-one. The director's name is Dwan." She spelled it.

"*Allan* Dwan?"

"Yes, that's the name."

He steadied his voice. "What's the address?"

Broadhead was alone when he returned to the lobby. "You owe me twenty apiece for the grunts," the professor said. "I offered them extra credit instead, but any dolt can pass a film class."

"Here's fifty. I'm feeling generous."

"What's the old lady got, *The Magnificent Ambersons* uncut?"

"Almost as good. Carole Lombard's first film."

He dropped off the trailer at the rental agency and daydreamed his way across town. Carole Lombard, the slender, dazzling blond queen of screwball romantic comedy, had made an insignificant debut at age twelve, then blazed across the screen in the 1930s, reaching her peak of fame when she married Clark Gable, the King of Hollywood. Stories of her bawdy sense of humor and outrageous practical jokes were legend, and by all accounts the couple was deliriously happy. But it all ended tragically in early 1942, when the plane carrying Lombard home from a war-bond rally slammed into a mountain thirty miles from Las Vegas. She was thirty-three years old.

Valentino hadn't had cause to revisit Century City since he'd moved out of a high-rise to take up residence in the Oracle, where he awoke in the morning to the zing and chatter of the renovators' power saws and nail guns and went to bed in the evening past walls where there had been empty spaces and empty spaces where there had been walls only hours before. But in Jane Peters's building he congratulated himself on the move: A brat hit every button on his way out of the elevator, sentencing its only remaining occupant to stopping at every floor.

"Mr. Valentino? I'm Gloria Voss, Miss Peters' health-care provider. We spoke on the phone."

He shook the hand of the tall, slim brunette in a white blouse, pressed jeans, and new running shoes. The living room was clean, spacious, and decorated tastefully in shades of gray and slate blue, but smelled of many generations of cigarettes under a thin layer of air freshener.

His nose must have twitched, because she said, "She tries to fool me by flushing the butts down the toilet, but the place always smells like a smoking car. I think she bribes the nasty kid downstairs to smuggle them in. He probably shoplifts them."

"I might have met him."

"That explains why you're late. Some day he's going to try that button trick on Miss Peters and get a tongue-lashing to make him wish she'd used a paddle. She has an impressive vocabulary."

"No wonder she likes Carole Lombard. They say she had her brothers teach her every curse word they knew, to put her on level ground with every man she dealt with. They called her the Profane Angel."

"Jane told me that; and many other stories as well. I'll have to rent a Lombard film sometime. Anyone whose escapades can make a trained nurse blush is worth checking out."

"You haven't seen *A Perfect Crime*?" He had a sinking feeling he'd been lured there under false pretenses.

"No projection equipment here. But she tells me I'm not missing much. 'Child actors should be drowned, like kittens.' That's a quote."

She excused herself to knock on a door, across from the entrance. "Mr. Valentino's here." After a muffled invitation she opened the door and held it for him. As he stepped past, she lowered her voice. "Find out where she hides the cigarettes."

When the door closed behind him, he was in a large bedroom done in white and gold. There was a white four-poster bed, neatly made, a dresser and vanity table, and a sitting area made up of two reproduction Louis XIV chairs and a chaise, all upholstered in Cloth of Gold. Plastic prescription containers and over-the-counter pill bottles took up every horizontal space except one: Valentino's practiced eye went immediately to four flat aluminum film cans stacked on the vanity table.

"You look like a Valentino. Family resemblance, or plastic surgery?"

The tobacco-roughened voice came from a very old, very plump woman seated in one of the chairs. She wore a red sweater that made her look like a tomato, blue sweatpants with sharp creases, and thick socks in heelless slippers. Her hair was shorn to a white haze on her scalp. She had blue eyes.

"Neither," Valentino said. "There might be some relation way back; not enough to inherit."

"He didn't have much to leave. His career was on the skids when he died at thirty-one. 'Good career move,' someone said. It was the same with Lombard. She hadn't made a movie worth shouting about in years when that plane cracked up. She was mostly famous as Mrs. Clark Gable."

"So much for breaking the ice."

"I'm ninety-eight. I can't wait for it to melt on its own. Sit down."

As he lowered himself into the chair facing hers, she took the top off a fat pill bottle and drew out a filterless cigarette. A smaller container yielded a slim throwaway lighter. "If you tell Field Marshal von Voss about my stash, the deal's off." She blew twin jets of smoke out her nostrils.

"Trying to keep you healthy doesn't make her a Nazi."

"I gave up two breasts for the privilege years ago. Fortunately, they weren't much to begin with. It was practically out-patient surgery."

He laughed, more in response to the wicked gleam in her eye than to the black humor. His work put him in frequent contact with senior citizens, veterans of the Golden Age, and he found them more entertaining company than most of his own generation. "How did you come into possession of *A Perfect Crime*?"

"It was no feat. They hadn't invented rereleasing back then, no TV or video markets, so no one gave them any thought after the first run. But you know that. If the studios had kept better track of the inventory, we'd be up to our butts in celluloid and you'd be out of a job."

"Were you in the industry?"

"I came out here when I was eight years old. It wasn't an industry then. But it was the only factory in town, and if you wanted to work, that's where you went."

He excused himself and got up to look at the film cans. *A Perfect Crime* was stenciled on the lid of the one on top, with the year and production number. It looked genuine, but he'd been fooled before. "Silver nitrate?"

"No. I had it transferred to safety stock before you were born. I burned the original negative before it burned me. That stuff's worse than nitroglycerine."

"Were you a technician?"

"I could've joined the union if I'd wanted. I always got on with all my crews. They like to talk about their work, like everyone else."

He went back and sat down. Time had done its work on her face and figure, but essential beauty leaves a glowing memory, stubborn as embers clustered here and there. "Were you an actress?"

She laughed, coughing smoke, and deposited the smoldering stub in a water glass. It spat and died in the inch of liquid in the bottom. "The critics didn't all agree on that. I used to be Carole Lombard."

He was silent long enough for her to fish out a fresh cancer stick and set fire to it.

"Jane Peters," he said. "Lombard's real name was Jane Alice Peters. I didn't make the connection."

"I was still fooling with it until I was almost thirty, when I made it legal. I was Carol without the *e* until *Fast and Loose*; my twenty-eighth, for hell's sake, counting the Sennett shorts. Spelling mistake in the credits. That *e* made me a star."

He almost said, *It wasn't that that made you a star*, then remembered she was a fraud or delusional. "Lombard's been dead more than sixty years. Even you said so."

"I said her plane cracked up. I didn't say she was in it. I mean *I*. I've been talking about myself in the third person so long I sometimes get to thinking I'm somebody else."

"Her remains were found on the scene, along with the pilot and all the other passengers. One of them was her mother."

"I never got over that." She used the little finger of the hand holding the cigarette to sop a tear from the corner of one eye. "She was my buddy. Pa was nuts about her. Gable, I mean. We called each other Ma and Pa, not Carole and Clark. Sounds like an advertising agency." She took a long, shuddering drag and seemed to collect herself. "They found some wisps of blond hair and a mass of pulp in a section of fuselage squashed into a block ten feet long. It wasn't me. I gave up my seat to an army nurse when we landed in Albuquerque to refuel. I told Mom to stay aboard and tell Pa I'd be along later by train. I said it was my patriotic duty, but what I really wanted was to drive him so batty he'd take me right there in the station. We were always pulling pranks like that on each other."

Valentino said nothing. He'd encountered cases of Alzheimer's and senile dementia often enough to know better than to upset the afflicted party by contradicting her.

"I scrubbed off my makeup and tied a scarf around my hair before I boarded the train in Albuquerque," she said. "I was tired of signing autographs and grinning at fans. I found out about the crash when we stopped in Flagstaff, where the newsboys were shouting. 'Carole Lombard Dead,' that knocked all the tired out of me. I got out and bought a paper. I didn't make it through the first paragraph before I fainted.

"I woke up in a doctor's office. He told me I was pregnant."

"Clark Gable's child." He couldn't keep the cynicism out of his tone.

She nodded. "In the course of thirty minutes I learned I was an orphan, I was responsible for an innocent young woman's death, and that I was going to be a mother. It starts you thinking." She smiled crookedly. He wondered if she'd rehearsed the expression in front of a mirror with Lombard's picture taped to it. " 'Madcap.' 'Screwball.' Those were the words that came up most often when people talked or wrote about me. Not much of a legacy to leave your kid with. I was getting a little long in the tooth to get away with the reputation much longer before it became pathetic. The public already sensed it, and had stopped going to see my pictures. A star fades quickly under those circumstances; neither the doctor nor the people who carried me to his office nor his nurse recognized me. So what was I working so hard for?"

"You're forgetting Gable. He grieved the rest of his life."

"When I heard he'd volunteered to serve as a tailgunner in the air force, I almost came forward," she said. "It was a suicide's cry for help. But then I realized MGM would protect him if it meant bribing Hitler to send the Luftwaffe in the other direction. And later, when he remarried, he seemed happy. I kept up with him through the trades and film magazines right up until he died. I cried that day, too. But, you see, I didn't love him."

Anger flared. He tamped it down through an effort of will. "Gable and Lombard is Hollywood's greatest love story. Greater than Bogie and Betty. Greater than Pickford and Fairbanks and Garbo and Gilbert and all the rest."

"You're overlooking the fact that Garbo left Gilbert at the altar. That Pickford and Fairbanks broke up. That Bogie may have cheated on Betty and vice versa. The rest is PR. You've been around this town long enough not to judge by appearances. Russ Columbo was the love of my life."

"The bandleader. He and Lombard were seeing each other when he was killed in a hunting accident."

"For a long time after that, I expected to die any minute of a broken heart. Well, I didn't and I knew Pa wouldn't either. Deep down, under the public show of tragedy, I think he knew we couldn't have lasted. He'd been through divorce; me too, and it stinks. Drives a wedge right down through the center of your fan base. But everyone gathers around a handsome widower.

"Meanwhile," she continued, "I had someone new to love, a beautiful daughter. I raised her in Buffalo, New York, which is as far as you can get from Hollywood culture without going Amish. She died four years ago of leukemia, still thinking her father was the man I married, the owner of a fleet of Great Lakes ore carriers." She flicked away another tear, leaving a smudge of ash on her temple. "By then he was dead, too, so I moved back here, away from the Buffalo winters. The old bastard left me loaded. I never did take his name."

"Why are you telling me all this now?"

She was busy lighting a fresh cigarette from the butt of the last. She dropped the remnant among the others floating in the water glass. "I keep thinking about that poor girl, that army nurse who took my place on the plane. There's a family somewhere that doesn't know if she was murdered or ran away or if she is lying at the bottom of a well. They can identify people now by DNA. If they exhume the body interred under my name in Forest Lawn and run tests, maybe someone can be notified, even if it's a grandnephew who wasn't even born at the time of the crash. What's that word? Closure? Everyone deserves that."

"Are you telling me the film's a dummy, just to get me to listen to your story?"

"Of course not. It's the McCoy. I'll even let you take a reel with you to screen. Reel three, to guarantee you won't just run off with it. No one wants to come into a picture in the middle."

"But why now? Why not years ago, when there was a better chance some of the dead woman's immediate family was still around to hear the news?"

"Well, that's not the only reason." She blew smoke at the ceiling, tipping her head back the way actresses used to do in glamour shots to show the smooth line of a throat. Hers was festooned with loose skin. "It's part of the price for donating that turkey to UCLA. I want you to tell the world my story. You can use the campaign to promote the film as a vehicle. 'Lombard Lives!' Boffo box office."

He leaned forward, choosing his words carefully. If she wasn't just posing, his pointing out the basic inconsistency in her story could arouse paranoia and possibly violence. "I don't understand. I thought the whole point of your not coming forward was to put all that behind you."

"It was. But I miss it. I miss the fame, God help me. Gable's gone,

Bogie's gone, Jimmy and Kate and Spence and Bette. At the end they were dropping like leaves, from one Oscar telecast to the next. I'm the only name-above-the-title star left from the glory days. The last dinosaur. I want to feel flashbulbs bursting in my face one more time, put my dainty foot on the red carpet, wave at whoever knows who the hell I am sitting in the bleachers on the sidewalk. Stick my hands and feet in the cement at Grauman's. I never got to do that."

"That's your price? Fifteen minutes more in the spotlight?"

She flashed that crooked smile. "Time is relative. Gloria will tell you I haven't much longer than that."

"I can't promise anything without proof. Will you submit to a DNA test?"

"Absolutely not. Even if you can find some shirttail blood relative to provide a match, I won't open my mouth for some joker to swab around inside it. How do I know they won't clone me after I'm gone? There's only one of me; that's the selling point." She extinguished another butt. "I want to be Carole Lombard again. Who wouldn't?"

He and Kyle Broadhead screened the silent reel in the projection room where the professor showed films to his students. They sat at kidney-shaped writing tables and watched the pubescent star-to-be pretending to be Monte Blue's kid sister. She was unconvincing, even in pantomime. "Howard Hawks said she couldn't act," Broadhead said. "Getting the performance he got out of her in *Twentieth Century* proves just how great a director he was."

Valentino said, "John Barrymore told her she was the best he ever worked with. She claimed she learned more from him on that shoot than she did during her previous twelve years in pictures."

"What are you going to tell the old lady?"

"I owe her a look-see into her story just for this. Do you know anyone who could check and see if any army nurses vanished around the time of the crash?"

"If I knew my way around the Net as well as the worst of my students, I could hack into the Bank of America and finance the whole preservation program. I'll ask one. Don't tell me you're buying into this fairy tale."

"Give me a break. People who are supposed to be dead are rumored to be still alive every day, and none of them has come out of hiding yet."

"If you try trotting her out like Princess Anastasia, when it blows up in your face the scandal will do more harm to the program than if this piece of tripe stayed buried."

"I know."

"The smart thing to do is to return the reel and call it off."

"I know."

Broadhead blew through his pipe. He never lit it in a room that contained film. "So how far do you think you can string her along?"

"What makes you think I won't do the smart thing and forget all about it?"

"Ten years of daily association. Every loose frame left unaccounted for is an orphan. You'd adopt them all even if it ended in disgrace for you and the institution that keeps us off food stamps."

Valentino patted his friend's knee and stood. "Put your whiz kid to work."

Star vehicles are like peanuts, and twenty minutes of *A Perfect Crime* created a hunger that demanded satisfaction. Valentino checked out *Twentieth Century, My Man Godfrey,* and *No Man of Her Own*—her only appearance on film with Clark Gable—from the university library and watched them back-to-back at the Oracle, using the rebuilt Bell & Howell projector and state-of-the-art composition screen that had set him back two mortgage payments. He had them all on tape and disc, but preferred to watch the classics the same way they were seen back when stars still glittered like gifts from the Milky Way and ushers prowled the aisles ready to expel any atheists who wouldn't stop talking during the feature.

There in the dark he fell in love all over again with the incendiary blonde who had won the heart of America's Rhett Butler and hundreds of thousands of moviegoers in New York and San Francisco, Terre Haute and Cincinnati. He had always found her unsympathetic in *Century*, and so had most of middle America during its first run, but now he appreciated the breezy skill with which she met every challenge from John Barrymore, the prince of players. Her ditzy debutante in *Godfrey* charmed him as it had William Powell, who despite their real-life divorce had insisted upon casting her opposite his socialite-turned-tramp-turned-butler (and netting her an Academy Award nomination), and although little of the chemistry between her and Gable showed in *No Man*, it comforted Valentino to see them together again, in a medium where no catastrophe, natural or man-made, could separate them. From her golden hair to her shimmering gowns she glowed, and there was more erotic tension in the arch of her brow and the hollow of her cheek than in the most explicit NC-17 ever shot.

Gable had known that. Valentino rejected out of hand the notion that the spark between them had been just another invention of the flacks in the MGM publicity department. What if all the legends were fake? If someone else had been at the wheel of James Dean's wrecked Porsche? If Spencer Tracy and Katharine Hepburn had secretly loathed each other? If a stunt double had hung off the high clock in Harold Lloyd's place? An industry without a healthy mythos might as well churn out bottle caps.

When the last frame flapped through the gate he rewound the final reel and retired to bed and his Deco dreams.

"Well?"

Two days had passed since their conference in the projection room. Broadhead had entered Valentino's memorabilia-cluttered office in his usual fashion, without knocking, swept a stack of French film journals off a chair, and sat scraping out the bowl of his pipe with a Tom Mix penknife he found on the desk.

"Edith Jenkins," he said.

"What about her, whoever she is?"

"Was. She enlisted as a nurse just after Pearl Harbor, to escape her abusive husband. When she'd been AWOL six weeks, the husband was arrested for questioning, but without a body or any other evidence he was released. The papers lost interest after a while, as they will when the story has no conclusion. She never turned up."

Valentino started to rise. "Then that means—"

"Don't get excited. This isn't a movie, where everything ties together just before the fade-out. She was a brunette. She wouldn't have left any blond hair in any broken airplane."

"She might've dyed it when she ran away from her husband. Lombard dyed hers."

"I'm not through."

Valentino sat.

"This kid's a freshman, but Bill Gates better watch his back. He dug up a dozen unexplained disappearances involving young women within two weeks of the accident. Two showed up alive later, three dead. No information on whether any of the others were in the army, although two were nurses, a vulnerable occupation then as now. One of them might have signed up under a nom de guerre. Point is the results are inconclusive."

"Huh."

"Eloquently put." Broadhead found high C on his stem.

"We could use that."

"*You* could. I'm a publish-or-perish academic. If I start endorsing Elvis and Bigfoot, this institution will retire me on my over-upholstered laurels and I'll wind up writing paperbacks about alien autopsies and weapons of mass destruction."

"Your liberal bias is showing."

"You're right. Scratch the alien autopsies. So what are you going to do?"

"There's always DNA."

"You said the old lady turned you down flat on that."

"She wouldn't have to take part. If we found a cousin or something of Lombard's—a 'shirttail blood relative,' as she put it—exhumed the body from Forest Lawn, and compared samples, we could either settle the question or make her claim credible."

"Even if you could do that, say you proved the corpse is Lombard's, which of course would be the result. She might destroy the other three reels of *A Perfect Crime* out of spite."

"Not if she relinquishes possession first. We could stall for time, go ahead with the publicity arrangements as promised. No one could expect us to follow through with them once she's exposed as a pretender."

Broadhead put away the pipe. "Where'd you tell me you were from originally?"

"A little town called Fox Forage, Indiana. I saw my first movie there in a stuffy little box made of concrete."

"I think you should go back there for a vacation. You've been out here so long you're beginning to think like a grifter."

Valentino sat back, deflated. "I didn't like it when I heard myself saying it."

"Don't feel bad. I said, 'Even if you could' get Lombard's body exhumed. You can't. You'd need that theoretical cousin's permission or a court order, which you won't get because there's no probable cause for a search, and then you'd have to pay for it. Digging corpses out of mausoleums is ten times more expensive than putting them in. *Then* you have to pay to put them back. UCLA won't foot the bill; we're lucky it keeps us in paper clips. How's your cash?"

"Ask my contractor. He's seen it more recently."

"Well, there it is. You've got one reel of a film you can't exploit and a crazy old bat who thinks she's the Queen Mother of Hollywood."

"I liked her, though. If she isn't who she says she is, she oughta be."

Valentino was having a familiar dream. In it, he was standing on a thousand-foot cliff overlooking the ocean, arranging lemmings into an orderly herd to drive inland to safety. Suddenly a storm broke out. Thunder and lightning and lashing winds panicked the lemmings, who stampeded between his feet, dodging his grasping hands, and plunged over the edge of the cliff and down into the pitching waves, which swept them out to sea and out of sight.

He was grateful when the telephone woke him. The lemmings were a unique breed, black and glistening as the bits of film he gathered from both hemispheres to assemble and save from obscurity. Too often he failed just when success seemed at hand.

"I'm not getting any younger," said a cigarette-hoarse voice. "None of us is, but I'm moving faster than most. Do we have a deal or what?"

"I'm sorry, Miss Peters."

"I'm sorry, too, if 'Miss Peters' means what I think it means."

"It's just too risky without proof you're Carole Lombard. My reputation's one thing, but the preservation program's is another. A lot of important work has been destroyed in the past because someone failed to check his facts, deliberately or by accident."

"In other words, I'm a damn liar."

"There's just nothing to show the world you're telling the truth."

"What's *A Perfect Crime*, chopped liver?"

"The argument could be made that you don't have to have been in it to acquire a print. You said yourself the studios were careless in those days. You know a lot about Lombard, but she's been written about a lot. I'm sorry."

Silence crackled for what seemed a long time. "Well, people have been called phonies less politely. You know, you could have had what you wanted just by blowing smoke up my skirt until I kicked the bucket."

"I admit the idea was discussed, but I couldn't live with it. I'd have gotten a bad case of hives every time *Nothing Sacred* played on TCM."

"Bill Wellman directed that one at the top of his lungs. I waited until we wrapped, then got the crew to tie him up in a straitjacket." She exhaled, probably blowing smoke. "Toodle-oo, kiddo. Drop reel three by anytime." The line clicked and the dial tone came on.

Gloria Voss answered the door. She looked as trim and elegant as ever, but her eyes were red. "Jane passed early this morning, in her sleep."

"I'm sorry." He truly was, somewhat to his surprise. He gripped the film can he was holding so hard his fingers went numb.

The nurse excused herself and went into the bedroom. She came out carrying the rest of *A Perfect Crime* in a stack. "She asked me— told me—to give you these in case she missed you. 'Tell him to go to hell, and no hard feelings,' those were her words. It was the last thing she said before she went to sleep."

"But that wasn't the deal."

"I know. We had no secrets. She liked to come on as a tough old broad, but she had a heart as big as L.A. She ordered me not to see her films because they might corrupt me. Once, she said, she altered a contract with her agent so *he* owed *her* ten percent of everything he made instead of the other way around. He signed it without reading. She had him over a barrel, but she laughed and tore up the contract and had him draw up another."

"I've heard that story."

"I think she was testing you. Congratulations. You passed." She held out the stack of cans.

His cell phone rang. He apologized and answered. It was Kyle Broadhead. "Listen, my whiz kid found a great-grandniece of Lombard's in Fort Wayne, that's where Lombard was born. She's agreed to provide DNA samples."

"Kyle—"

"I'm not finished. I talked to Ted Turner's people. He'll finance an exhumation in return for distribution rights to *A Perfect Crime*. We've got the niece's permission, and Turner already owns everything Lombard did for MGM. He wants to put together a box set with her debut film included."

Valentino explained the situation.

"Doesn't change a thing," Broadhead said after a pause. "You can't buy publicity like this, but thank God Ted Turner can. People love a clever fake. The attention will bring in donations to the program like—like—"

"Lemmings," Valentino finished. "Tell Turner no deal."

"I heard some of that," Gloria Voss said, when he flipped shut the instrument. "It means you don't believe her, but it was a wonderful thing to do."

"I don't know what to believe. Whichever way it went, it would have spoiled a beautiful story."

"Grandma would say, 'Thanks, buster.' "

He reacted after a beat. "Grandma?"

"She's the one who talked me into becoming a nurse. She had a soft spot for them."

"So you're the granddaughter of—"

"Jane Peters and the owner of Buffalo Shipping. That's what it says on Mom's birth certificate." She thrust the cans into his arms, smiling with Carole Lombard's cheekbones and Clark Gable's mouth.

# BEREAVEMENT
## By Tom Piccirilli

Tom Piccirilli is the author of more than twenty novels, including *The Cold Spot*, *The Midnight Road*, *Headstone City*, and *A Choir of Ill Children*. He's a four-time winner of the Stoker Award and has been nominated for the World Fantasy Award, the International Thriller Writers Award, and Le Grand Prix de l'Imaginaire. Learn more about him and his work at www.tompiccirilli.com.

If you love, you lose. We all know it. But you also gain a heaviness of shadow and soul that will serve you throughout life in some capacity. It's as natural and inevitable as it is righteously unfair. You'll need that protection. What you welcome into your heart will eventually die or vanish without reason or acknowledgment. Your dog, your woman, your infant, your father, your flowerbed. We all know it. Your love will be swept under the wheels of a northbound Freightliner or disappear mewling in a freak blizzard in May. You'll sit at the window for weeks and months afterward trying to come to terms and make sense of your pain. You'll fail.

But perhaps your pain will make sense of you.

You'll endure because you must. You'll ponder your heartache and prod the raging areas of memory. You'll pinwheel through the world without being able to say a word to anyone. Thankfully, you will become another person by degrees. It's a small but treasured gift, your transition. You'll relish your damage and learn to love it in lieu of your dog or your father or your amputated left foot. You will replace your love with your loss and learn to adore it instead.

I was back in the hospital on a deathwatch for the ninth time in a year. I remembered my mother telling me about how, in one eighteen-month period, she and her sisters lost ninety percent of the previous generation. The parents, aunts, uncles, and friends of the family. All of the elderly hitting that age when the diseases and the cigarettes and the whiskey and all the other mistakes finally caught up with them. At the time I thought surely it couldn't be true. At the time I was young and stupid and newly engaged. Now I am older and more attuned to the ways of bereavement.

In twelve months I had buried my mother and father, two aunts, two uncles, an older brother, a much older cousin, and one long-lived great-grandfather who, by then, was the size and shape of an over-grown toddler. I often put him in a wheelchair and pushed him around the hospital grounds on sunny days. He had once been a long-shoreman on the Manhattan docks. I remembered when he used to carry four cinder blocks at a time in his massive arms, laying them out around his small tomato garden. At the end, I could've flung him across a football field one-handed. He knew it and hated me for it because he no longer even had the strength of will to despise himself.

It wasn't easy losing him or any of them. Each one was aware there would be no recovery. They would never again see their homes, enjoy a drive or a walk through the park, make love, have a night out with the boys, see a play, build a bonfire, make a pot of pasta, or even bother to curse their bills and debts. They were beyond such triviali-ties, the mundane chores of the living. Each of them made a valiant effort to beam and appear happy and confident that they'd soon be healed, even my great-grandfather with his glower boiling with more sadness than bitterness. They did so out of love for me and the rest of us who would remain behind. They, too, often failed.

You can practice smiling while making optimistic chatter. It's an art form almost everyone becomes good at very quickly. You can force yourself to ignore their yellowing skin and the rheumy crust of death forming around their mouths. You can cling to them in their beds and keep your face expressionless as you feel shock and terror at how immaterial their bodies have become.

My father, eighty pounds at the end. My mother, sixty, with no teeth, with no breasts, no eyes. My brother Joe with both his muscular arms cut off after a car accident. Hugging him was like holding on to a yardstick.

But tonight, this was so much worse.

Tonight my son lay dying in ICU, twisted beneath the sweat-stained sheets and surrounded by immense, clamorous, glowing machinery.

I had always thought that brain cancer was rare, especially in a child, but now they told me that Billy had an *atypical* form of brain cancer. The doctors tried to explain to me what was so special, so aberrant about the disease that was killing my boy, but I could only stare at their moving mouths catching every fourth or fifth word while they placed hands on my shoulders and gently patted. They all looked like murderous angels in their brilliantly white lab coats. They all looked like they were straining not to laugh in my face. They all looked like they knew the answer to a great secret they would never share.

Two night nurses on watch in the ICU unit stood by with a couple of young, freshly appointed doctors who jittered with energy, horny and smiling with perfect caps, flirting and cracking jokes. You can get used to anything. We all know it. The machinery in the patients' rooms hammered and whined a contrapuntal rhythm so powerful that I could eventually feel my pulse changing, shifting into it.

One of the nurses noticed me standing in the hall. I had ruined their little get-together. She gave me a stern expression, the kind the nuns would give us when we didn't finish our homework, when we couldn't remember all the words to our prayers. The handsome young doctors with sharply moussed hair and well-crafted mustaches pursed their lips in irritation. She approached with vigor, her hips pumping. She covered the ground between us quickly. She seemed indignant, severe, and willing to punish.

"Sir! Excuse me, sir? You can't be here. Visiting hours are restricted to—"

"Dr. August said it was all right," I told her.

"He did?"

"My son is here."

"Your son? Who is your son?"

"Ask Dr. August."

"He's not on duty right now."

"I know that, but my son is dying and I'm not leaving him."

She frowned and said, "Sir . . . ? Which room? This is . . ."

"Highly irregular, I know. So is an eleven-year-old boy dying of brain cancer. Wouldn't you goddamn agree to that?"

"Well, yes, but really, there's no need to—"

"I can't leave him, do you understand? I can't leave my boy here alone. I have to be with him. He's got to know I'm here, that I'll always be here for him. Just in case he wakes up, even for a moment."

I knew what she saw. A man in his late thirties who looked like he'd been sleeping in a bus station for a week. Unkempt, unshaven, face ashen. My hair had a shock of white up front that hadn't been there three years ago. There were smudges under my eyes that would never go away. I was as far from the beautiful doctors as a person could get. She saw me but didn't actually, did not *truly* see me. I waited.

I stared at her. I made my presence known and undeniably understood. The hospital is filled with currents of energy. The dying drain away, and the living, despite themselves, feed on it. It was no wonder the doctors all appeared so handsome and fit and vibrant. The nurses so full of force and sensuality. I was a man with nothing left to lose, balanced on a razor, and I could snatch my hand out and rip her smile from her and put it in my hip pocket.

The doctors had both begun to flirt with the other nurse. They laughed loudly and the disgusting bray reverberated through the corridors. I stared until her bottom lip quivered and she drew her hand to her throat. She averted her face as the other nurse tittered and tee-hee'd, and I walked down the hall to Billy's room.

My son had loved baseball. He had once stolen home twice in a single game and been written about in our local paper. The clipped article, tacked to the wall above his desk, snapped in the draft whenever I opened the door to his room. The picture was of him in action, headfirst in the dirt with his hand outstretched and reaching for the plate, a spray of dust rising around him and his helmet tipped back, about to fly off.

His mitt sat on his bed waiting for him like a lonely pet. Photos of his mother were framed on the dresser, on his nightstand. In one, she is standing behind him shortly after he first joined little league. He's in his uniform and they're both giving such similar know-it-all, mess-with-us-and-we'll-kick-yer-ass grins that I often try to slip into the smile myself. I make the effort but I can never get it quite right. They were two of a kind.

Since the death of my wife Katie four years ago, Billy has been all that gave my life any real significance. You hear the words and they sound trite. Everything becomes irrelevant in the brightly lit eminence of a thriving hospital. You'd think it was the other way around, that it would be a place where all matters held a much greater importance.

But no, you say "kidney failure" or "congenital birth defect" and it holds no more weight than "the doctor is unavailable this afternoon, this is his answering service." Shooting adrenaline into a stopped heart is no different from shooting a 38 on the back nine. The shriek of sirens becomes background music. The bills for chemotherapy of pancreatic cancer, the birth of twins, or having an ingrown toenail removed are printed on the same paper, with the same ink. The morgue is crammed with children, and your son won't be recognized or acknowledged.

The irrelevancies build up, preparing you for the day when the boy's bed will be empty. Or worse. When the bed will have someone else in it who looks the same as your dying boy but isn't.

My life after Katie consisted of nothing but Billy, and now even he was being pulled from me, inch by inch. He was all that had kept me rooted in the world and allowed me to fight the tide of my own emptiness which always tried to draw me from him. And it seemed now that failing to attain me, it had steadily acquired him instead.

The machinery surrounded and hunched over him, plying his flesh and murmuring. It confided and hissed. He slept on. I hoped he would hit his grin while he dreamed—if he dreamed. I wasn't sure anymore. His lips were parted as if he might be trying to say something to me. I pulled a chair close, sat, and leaned in nearer. I would give anything to hear just a word from him.

He was sweating despite the coolness of the room. I put the back

of my hand to his forehead and wiped until he was dry. Every ago-
nized breath contorted his body. I sat there for hours and watched the
sun rise. I didn't have much time left.

I whispered in Billy's ear. I told him how much I loved him. The
words sounded more inhuman than the beeps and buzzes. I said the
two prayers that I knew, the ones the nuns had beaten into me deeply
enough. The machinery continued to batter and pound the life into
and out of him.

I took his hand and pressed it to my lips and although I thought—
I always thought—that I could cry no more, when the tears came they
wouldn't stop. I had learned to sob silently so as not to disturb other
families waiting for their own children to pass. My body heaved and
I grew lightheaded. I begged his forgiveness. I begged my wife's
pardon, my father's. I hoped Billy would understand.

I tried to say more and my voice became a squeak. The thought of
this torturously slow death tore at my chest and I had to press my
teeth into his flesh to keep from letting loose the scream that was
always inside me. His blood filled my mouth.

He awoke, briefly, and said, "Dad?"

I turned and spat his blood on the floor. "I'm here."

"Dad?"

"Yes, I'm here, it's all right."

"My chest. My hand."

"Shhh, my boy . . ."

"Who are . . . ?"

"Shhh . . ."

His eyes closed again, his brow furrowed in anguish for an instant
before softening. I wedged his bleeding hand under his leg where the
wound soon tapered off.

You can get used to almost anything except the ongoing murder of
your child.

The pain and guilt rides in your veins. It rushes and burns through
your system and blasts into your skull. Sometimes your eyes roll back
in your head. Sometimes your lips skin into a bizarre leer.

Your love turns you into a junkie constantly hopped on your
own agony.

You can't go another minute without it. Even as you know, with a clarity that had previously escaped you in all other matters of your life, that you can't watch your son dying anymore.

Out in the hall, the nurses were changing shifts. It was seven A.M. The aroma of fresh coffee, bagels and donuts wafted through the corridors. There was small chatter, a bark of laughter. I fell back into the shadows of the room and watched them go by. The night nurses left without glancing into the room. I had been forgotten.

I drew the empty hypodermic needle from my jacket pocket and inserted it into one of his three IV tubes.

I repeated the two prayers I knew. I promised to learn more. I had promised the nuns to learn more and I never did. I always promise to learn more, and I never do.

I kissed his forehead and my tears dripped down his face. For an instant his lips shrugged into that amazing grin.

I whimpered, "Oh god, I'm sorry. I'm so sorry I didn't do this sooner. I love you, Billy. Rest. Sleep now, my boy. In a moment the pain will be gone. You'll be with mommy soon." I pressed down the plunger, withdrew the needle, and put it back into my pocket.

My boy's eyes shot open. They trembled in their sockets but didn't focus on me or anything. He was already gone and had been for months. The machinery began to break rhythm.

I turned and a man who looked very much like me stood in the doorway and said, "Who are you?"

He hadn't slept well in weeks, and his beard grew in wild patches, just like mine did, because he hadn't shaved in days and the last time he'd done a very poor job. His hair was windblown and dirty and hung in clumps. His wife, who visited in the afternoons, had looked even worse yesterday. Wide-eyed with splotchy cheeks. Her cheeks were hollowed, her voice strained. Her clothes hung off her bony frame badly.

He was carrying a large container of coffee, stopping in before facing the morning rush hour traffic into the city where he worked.

He repeated himself. "Who are you?"

"I'm Billy's father."

"Who's Billy?"

"Billy's my son."

"What are you doing in here?"

"Billy has an *atypical* form of brain cancer."

"What?"

"You should go. You should leave right now."

"Leave? I'm not going to leave. That's my son Roger. He's had heart surgery to correct a hole in his aorta. He's going to be fine."

The machinery began to grow louder, the numbers and lines on the screens fluctuating radically.

"You're mistaken," I said.

"What?"

"You're crazy," I told him.

*"Who the hell are you?"*

He rushed me, keyed up but holding on so much better than I ever could. He still wanted to talk. He hadn't had his coffee yet, and he was still sleepy. He continued to grip his styrofoam container. He didn't notice the machines vacillating yet, didn't realize that Billy's body was shuddering.

The man shocked me—that even now he could remain so calm and steady, so normal and sane. His rationality offended me.

I chopped him in the throat with the side of my hand, yanked him forward, and twisted him down onto the floor on the far side of the bed.

His coffee ran steaming across the casters of the IV stands. He choked and wheezed for air and I pressed his face harder into the polished tiles. I drew out the hypodermic needle and jabbed it into his throat. I missed the vein the first time. And the second. I tried once more and nicked his carotid, and then I pressed down on the plunger. He was already bleeding to death, the arterial spray sending up a thin gushing arc that shot over one of the blaring machines and painted the far corner.

He went into violent convulsions as I flattened myself over him and eventually his struggles weakened, his anguish rolling from him wave after wave the way night moves on across the world.

When he finally stopped moving, and the arterial spray had bubbled its last, I turned him over, pressing my forehead to his. I said, "Joe. It's all right, Joe, I know this is what you really wanted. I'll always help you."

You can get used to almost anything.

The sorrow and guilt fires into your skull and turns you into a junkie hopped on your own agony. You can become addicted to heartache. You will replace your love with your loss and learn to adore it instead.

The morning nurses were slow to move. They hadn't had their first cup of coffee yet either. By the time they were shouting out codes and rushing a crash cart to Billy's room, I'd slipped down the hall and was at the elevator. Soon I'd be back at the bus station.

Tomorrow night, or the maybe night after, I would visit the bright and sourly astringent room of someone else I cared for. Perhaps I would take up the deathwatch of my wife once more. Katie. Her name had been Katie, and it would be again. A name that was beautiful and burdensome, and it snagged in my throat with the sweetest bereavement every time I even thought to say it. I shut my eyes and thought about her grin.

I would find her asleep in another hospital in another city, needing me, hopefully dreaming of me—if she dreamed. She had once loved to bake cookies for Billy and his friends on the team. She liked to sing in the shower, and she did it badly. She had once enjoyed running on the beach in the rain. She had once loved to dance.

I would soon sit in another waiting room and listen to the white-coated clusters exchanging trivial information until I found her doctors. They would recognize me as one of those who did not share in their secret. I would make my presence known. They would try not to laugh in my face. They would gently pat my shoulder again. I would endure. My pain would make sense of me.

# COUNTRY MANNERS
## By Brendan DuBois

Brendan DuBois is an award-winning author of short stories and novels. His short fiction has appeared in various publications, including *Playboy*, *Ellery Queen Mystery Magazine*, and *Alfred Hitchcock Mystery Magazine*, as well as numerous anthologies, including *The Best Mystery Stories of the Century*. He has twice received a Shamus Award for his short fiction and has been nominated for three Edgar Allan Poe Awards. DuBois' long fiction includes six previous books in the Lewis Cole mystery series, as well as several other suspense thrillers, including his recent U.S. release *Final Winter*. DuBois lives in New Hampshire with his wife, Mona.

B eing the only woman private investigator within a fifty-mile radius in a rural county in upstate New Hampshire, one would think that business would be sparse. Maybe so, and maybe I was lucky, but I always had enough work to pay the bills, sock some cash away every year in my IRA, and still have enough free time to canoe the local streams, do some stargazing, and pretty much stay out of trouble.

And staying out of trouble was something I always try to do. So no deranged boyfriends looking to find their girlfriends, no young ladies looking for creative ways to eliminate their parents, and nothing else equally shady ever made my client list. Which is why I should have cuffed my visitor that late morning, tossed him out onto the sole sidewalk of Purmort, New Hampshire, and then taken the rest of the day off.

But maybe I'm getting older, or bolder, or something, for I didn't sense trouble when he first came in.

My office is small, with a desk, phone, three chairs, computer, and two three-drawer filing cabinets with good solid locks. The walls have a framed print of Mount Washington, my framed license from the N.H. Department of Safety, and an award I received in a previous life from the New England Press Association. The window behind me overlooks a set of abandoned B&M railroad tracks and some marshland, and the front glass door gives a nice view of the Purmot grass common, once you get past the gold-leaf lettering that announced K. C. Dunbar, Investigations. Next door, in the same building, is an Italian restaurant, the Colosseum, which is run by a second-generation Greek family, which is typical for New Hampshire. But don't ask me why.

So the door opened up that morning and a man came in, slim, late thirties, short, dark blond hair. He was wearing a nice black suit, light blue shirt, and red necktie, and carried a slim, black leather briefcase. I looked at him and he looked at me, and I thought, lawyer, out of town, looking for something or another from the local talent. Said local talent being me. Still, I opened the center drawer of my desk and waited. Yeah, probably just a lawyer.

And in a way, I was correct, but only correct in the manner of stating that if you loved ice, the maiden voyage of the *Titanic* was a brilliant success.

"Miss Dunbar?" he asked.

"The same," I said.

He put his briefcase on one of the two polished wooden chairs in front of my desk, held out his hand, which I promptly shook. "Stewart Carr." And then he put his hand inside his coat, pulled out a thin leather wallet, and popped it open in front of my face. "Special Agent, Federal Bureau of Investigation."

I looked at the photo and the accompanying detailed information card, and then looked up at him.

Perfect match, of course.

"Gee," I said, knowing I sounded awestruck but hoping my expression said something else.

"May I sit down?" Carr asked.

"Of course," I said, my first mistake of the day.

He sat down with a smile and looked over at me and said, "Just to clear the air, Karen Christine Dunbar, I'm not here about any of your clients or past cases. So we can get past the whole client confidentiality issue."

I leaned back in my chair, conscious of his nice suit and my own faded jeans and T-shirt advertising last year's Purmort Old Home Days. "All right. Consider it passed."

He looked around and said, "Nice office. Cozy."

"Thanks. It works."

"I would think that an investigator in your position . . . might be more comfortable working out of your home."

I smiled and decided I really didn't like Agent Carr. Tried to one-up me by knowing my whole name, and now telling me that he knew how much I made and no doubt how much I had in the bank. "Thought about that at first, but I decided that some clients, well, I didn't want some clients being in my private space where I live. Besides, the landowner gives me a break on the rent: He owns the restaurant next door, and I help keep an eye on the place during off hours now and then."

He grinned. "Really? Didn't think there'd be much crime in a place like Purmort."

"Not enough to reach the FBI statistics desk, but there's more than enough vandalism, break-ins, and the general stupid people doing stupid things to keep some of us busy."

"I see."

"And speaking of stupid . . . What can I do for the Department of Justice today?"

Ouch. That left a mark. While his grin remained, his face colored a bit as he reached over, picked up his briefcase, put it on his lap. He snapped the lid open and said, "We want to hire you."

I tried not to laugh and admired myself for succeeding. He waited for my reply, I suppose, and I said, "Go on. You've got my interest."

"Good. Glad I've succeeded, Karen."

A snippy tone but I let it pass. "For how long? And where? And why?"

"This weekend. Day after tomorrow. Friday evening to Sunday morning. The where is a farmhouse near the end of a dirt road called Dutton Hill Road. Number eighteen. Familiar with the road?"

"Road, yes. Farmhouse, no. What's the deal with the farmhouse?"

"We'd like you to conduct a surveillance on the house for that period of time, Friday evening to Sunday morning."

He pulled out a sheet of paper, examined it for a moment, and said, "Your normal rate of pay is eighty dollars an hour. The period of time we require your services is thirty-six hours, for a total of two thousand eight hundred eighty dollars. We'll offer you three thousand for that work."

Not a bad nut, I thought. Exhaustive work for thirty-six hours, but I could pull it off. And it would really help fatten up the old bank balance. Still, when the government comes calling, why not answer with enthusiasm?

"All right. Call it four thousand."

Another little bit of color was added to his face. "You seem pretty confident of yourself."

"I'm the only good P.I. within quite a distance."

"There's Roger Valliere. Out in Montcalm."

This time, I didn't succeed. I did laugh. "Roger's a retired deputy sheriff. Nice old buck, if you want a car repossessed or a lawsuit served. For a thirty-six-hour surveillance . . . he won't last, sorry."

"Thirty-five hundred."

Oh, what the heck. "Deal. What's the surveillance? Keeping an eye on who's living in the farmhouse, or who's going in and going out?"

"The place is empty. We want you to see if anyone shows up during that time frame."

"Who?"

"Anyone, that's who."

"Sounds intriguing. All right, you haven't answered the most important question."

"Which is?"

"Why?"

"Sorry?"

I shifted in my seat. "Why? I've been in business long enough to know that private work and public work rarely meet, and when they do meet, they usually don't get along. So why is the FBI wanting to hire lil' ol' me?"

"Resources."

"Really?"

"Really. You know what's been on our mind since 9/11. White-collar crime, bank robberies, computer fraud. It's all taken a back seat to counterterrorism. We don't have the manpower anymore to do routine work. Which is why we're looking to hire you for those thirty-six hours. We have information that someone of . . . someone of interest might be in the area."

"Someone bad?"

"Let's just say someone of interest and keep it at that."

"Do I get to know who he or she might be?"

Another chilly smile. "If you take the job, you'll be given a secure, prepaid cell phone. If someone shows up—even somebody delivering a package or reading a gas meter—you'll give us a call."

I thought about the job offer, thought about my bank account, and looked at Agent Carr again. His face had a mocking look about it, like he was daring me to take the gig.

"And you're saying the farmhouse is empty?"

"Quite empty," he said.

"You sure?"

"The FBI says its empty. We'll leave it that."

I tried not to show my lack of enthusiasm for the FBI's capability to determine very much unless it was presented to them wrapped up in bright red gift ribbon.

"All right," I said. "You've got me. Thirty-six hours beginning this Friday evening."

I went to a side drawer of my desk to pull out a standard client contract, but he beat me to it. A sheaf of papers came out of his briefcase and went across my desk.

"A contractor agreement," he said. "Please review and sign. And note the nondisclosure and confidentiality clauses in the last two pages."

I suppose I should have sent him on his way and then spent an hour or two with a friendly local attorney to see what I was getting myself into, but I still liked the thought of thirty-five hundred dollars for thirty-six hours of running surveillance. I skimmed through the form and signed the bottom, and Agent Carr did some magic of his own, and then passed over a cashier's check for half of the amount.

"Standard, am I correct? Half in advance."

I slipped the check into a side drawer. "Quite standard."

Two more items were now on the desk. A cell phone and a business card. "My business card, if you need to contact me. And the encrypted/prepaid cell phone, to make the contact. Any questions?"

A whole bunch, but only a couple came to mind. "This he or she. Dangerous?"

"You have to make your own judgment," he said quietly. "The fact that this someone is a person of interest to the FBI should give you the necessary guidance."

"All right," I said. "Do you want a report when the surveillance is done?"

An amused shake of his head, as if I were wasting his FBI-man time by asking such silly questions.

"No, no report necessary. If we don't hear anything from you, we assume no one showed up. And if someone shows up, you'll make the call, and we'll take it from there. Anything else?"

Well, I thought. This was sure going to be a day to remember.

"Nope, I think we're all set, Agent Carr."

He snapped his briefcase shut and stood up. I stood up as well and shook his outstretched hand. He said, "I'm pleased this went so well. Country manners, am I right?"

"Excuse me?" I asked.

"Country manners," he said. "I'm originally from Boston, got assigned to the Chicago bureau when I graduated from the Academy . . . I like the pace, like the nice country manners up here. It's a nice change."

"Glad to hear it, Mister FBI," I said, putting on my most innocent smile.

And I waited until he got out of view before looking down at my center desk drawer, open since Agent Carr had first walked into my office. And nestled there, above a checking account statement from the Purmort Cooperative Savings Bank, was my Ruger stainless steel .357 revolver. For whenever a sole male comes into my office, I always have the center drawer open, just in case.

Country manners, indeed.

So after a while, I decided it was time to leave my office and get home to see Roscoe, my male better half, to see how he was doing and to tell him about what had happened with the FBI. I got a free cheese pizza from my neighbors next door—being in a conservative small town, I leaned toward conservative eating when it comes to pizza—and a five-minute drive got me home. I parked my four-year-old Ford SUV in the dirt driveway, and apologies to all, but an SUV gets me out of trouble during rainy days, snowy days, and muddy days here in Purmort, and balancing dinner in my hand, I went home. My home, small and lovely, is a cottage of sorts on two acres of land on the Hanratty River, and belongs to me, Roscoe, and the Purmort Cooperative Savings Bank. I got the door opened and yelled out, "Honey, I'm home!"

No answer. Typical.

Through the small living room into the combo kitchen and dining room, I put the pizza box down and said, "Roscoe, come on, it's not nice to tease." Approaching footsteps. Finally.

I grabbed a Coke from the fridge and went to the countertop that served as my table, and sitting on a tall stool, washing a paw, was a black and white short-haired cat that was the size of a small raccoon.

I scratched his head as I opened the pizza box and popped open the Coke. "And how was your day, hon?"

In reply, Roscoe started purring. He's not a lap cat, not a cat over-brimming with ootchie-cootchie cuteness, but he can always be counted on to start rumbling with pleasure when on the scene.

Which meant, in my universe at least, that he beat out most male bipeds.

As I munched on the first slice, I said, "So. Get this. There I am, minding my own business, wondering what to do for the rest of the day, when the FBI shows up. A representative from one of the top law enforcement agencies comes into Purmort and requests my services. Can you believe it?"

The purrs grew louder. "No, I can't believe it either. If the FBI really wanted to do a freelance surveillance and not tie up their own resources, they'd bring in contract people, already vetted and experienced. Like retired military or FBI. Not a local yokel, as attractive and smart as she might be."

The purrs seemed to slow. I finished one slice and reached for another. "I hope your purr drop-off isn't a comment on my looks and abilities." I took a smudge of tomato sauce and let Rosoe lick it off with his raspy tongue. Our own secret, never to be shared with his vet.

"So what does that leave me?" I asked. "It means we're en route to make a nice piece of change that can get the house painted before fall . . . for doing just a bit of surveillance work. It also means we're involved with something slippery with the Feds."

I thought some more, started to reach for a third slice, hesitated.

"And, my friend," I said, rubbing his face with both of my hands, "it means we're being set up for something. I don't know what it is, but I don't like it, money or no money. This whole deal stinks, 'cause when the Feds are there, they got the bigger guns, and you know what they say. God is always on the side with those with the heaviest artillery."

Then it seemed chilly for a moment, and I picked up Roscoe and hugged him tight and said, "Lucky for me, we've got a weapon or two hidden away."

The next day was Friday, the day my surveillance was set to start, but I had a little private work to take care of before I offically clocked in on the Fed's payroll. After my morning exercise routine—roll out of bed, shower, breakfast, pet the cat—I got out and went to the Purmort Town Hall, where I had an interesting few minutes with the town clerk, Mrs. Pam Dawkins, who helped me make sense of the town's tax records.

"So," she said, looking at me over her half-spectacles from behind the waist-high counter that separated the small office from the town hall lobby, "what interest do you have in this farmhouse on Dutton Hill Road?"

"Professional, what else? And I suppose I can count on your usual discretion."

"Sure," she said, winking at me. Last year I had helped her locate Mr. Dawkins, who had skipped out of town and had a philosophical opposition to paying child support. However, after I had located him, he found a higher philosophical opposition to having his cheating butt in county jail, and since then, the child support checks have been regular and on time.

Pam flipped through a bound computerized printout, running a thick finger down the columns of names and numbers, and she said, "Ah, here it is. Eighteen Dutton Hill Road. Two bedroom home . . . owned by something called Grayson Corporation. Property tax bills paid promptly, every six months."

"How long have they owned it?"

"Hmmm . . . looks to be ten years. Before that it was owned by Muriel Higgins, she used to be the principal of Purmort Regional High School, and it'd still be owned by the Higgins family, if it weren't for her two worthless sons. Morons decided to start a business doing day trading on the Internet, and when they finally crashed and burned, they had to sell their mom's place to pay off the tax bills and penalties."

"I see," I said. "And what's Grayson Corporation?"

"Don't know," she said. "They're not local. The bills get sent to a post office box in Allentown, Pennsylvania. No phone number, no contact person. Sorry, Karen."

"No problem," I said, gathering up my bag from the countertop, but before I turned to leave, Pam said, "Want to know more?"

"Excuse me?"

"I said, do you want to know more about Grayson Corporation?"

"Sure," I said. "What do you have in mind?"

She smiled, flipped the tax book shut. "I'll give it to Stephanie."

"Steph? Your daughter?"

"Absolutely," she said. "She's not old enough to drive yet, but Karen, she knows how to dig out info from the Internet."

"Pam . . ."

She raised up her hand. "Please. Even though we settled up our bill, I still owe you. And I'd rather have Steph spend her computer hours doing something productive, instead of looking for boys to chat with. Deal?"

I smiled back at her, thought about Agent Carr. Well, he was right about one thing.

Country manners.

"Deal," I said, and I left Purmort's seat of government.

Dutton Hill Road started off paved, and after a couple of miles became a dirt road. A typical rural road out in this part of New Hampshire, there were wire fences set on each side of the road, interspersed with rock walls that were about as old as the town. Small homes and farms were set off at a bit of a distance, most of which had a few horses or cows or some chickens out there in the yards. Nothing that was really a working farm, but small homes with folks that liked to keep their hands in the rural tradition of their parents and grandparents.

Lucky for me, the mailboxes out here were numbered, and it took me about ten minutes of driving before I reached number eighteen. It was on the right side of the road, and the mailbox was black, with white numerals neatly painted on. The driveway was dirt and the home was about fifty feet away. I pulled to the side of the road, let the engine run for a bit.

"Well, Tyler," I said, speaking to an empty vehicle. "Time for you to make another appearance."

From the passenger's seat, I picked up a dog leash and a home-made flyer, showing a mournful Labrador retriever's face, with the words LOST DOG at the top, with a description, name—Tyler—and my phone number, off by one digit. I switched off the engine, got out of my SUV and went up the driveway, calling out, "Tyler! Tyler! Where are you, buddy?"

With dog leash in one hand, flyer in the other, I certainly didn't look like a P.I. checking things out; I just looked like a concerned young lady seeking her lost pooch. One of the many advantages to being a female P.I. Strange men bopping around a neighborhood tend to be observed and recorded. Odd women doing the same are usually overlooked, especially if they're women looking for a lost dog, or women conducting a door-to-door survey, or women looking for an address. Nice bit of tradecraft that gives us a slight advantage, especially since male P.I.'s, when doing sur-veillances, can usually do their business with empty soda bottles when their bladder gets too full. I, on the other hand, know the location of every rest stop, gas station, and kind motel owner within fifty miles.

So up the dirt driveway I went, calling out poor Tyler's name—a dog whose picture I had downloaded off the Internet months ago—and checking things out. The first thing I noticed was the driveway; it was dirt, which is usual for this part of the state, but this one was in very good shape, a nice mix of dirt and gravel, nice drainage off to both sides. I went up to the farmhouse.

"Tyler! You around here, buddy? Tyler!"

Quick look around the place. Two-story, maybe a hundred years old or so, with unattached garage and a barn to the rear. I went around to the outbuildings, dangling the leash. The buildings were empty. No rakes, no farm equipment, nothing.

"Tyler!"

The yard was in poor shape, with weeds and knee-high grass, but the buildings didn't reflect the landscaping. They were in okay shape. Hard to explain, but if the place hadn't been lived in for a decade or thereabouts, you'd expect things. Cracked windows. Shingles falling off. Siding cracked and worn. The place wouldn't make *Town and Country* magazine, but it was in better shape than one would expect.

"Tyler!"

Off to the house. Knocked on the door. No answer, of course. But procedures had to be followed. I made notice of the door. Nice and solid, lock and dead bolt. First class, all the way. Went to the side window, peered in. Place was empty. The big room had wide planks for a floor, and I could make out a kitchen counter off to the rear. Everything looked too clean, too neat.

I juggled the leash again. Empty house, well maintained, nice driveway up and back.

Like it was waiting for someone, someone to stop by for a quick visit on his or her way to someplace else.

The someone being my surveillance target?

Perhaps.

I went back down the driveway to my SUV. Looked at the flyer.

"Thanks again, Tyler. Can always count on you."

And I went into the SUV, closed the door, and said, "But don't tell Roscoe I said so."


Home, getting ready for my thirty-six hours. A small knapsack, digital camera, telephoto lens, cassette recorder, notebook, spotting-scope, and iPod. Looked to Roscoe, scratched his head for good luck, tried to ignore the growing feeling in my gut, like a little field mouse, busily chewing away on my innards. I was getting into something, and this something I couldn't quite figure out.

Then my phone rang.

"Hello?"

"Karen? Pam Dawkins here. How are you?"

"Doing fine," I said, scratching Roscoe's head one more time. "What's up?"

"Can I come over for a quick visit?"

I looked at my small collection of gear. "Pam, I'm about to—"

"Karen," she said firmly, "it's about Stephanie. I'll be there in ten minutes."

So ten minutes later, I was in my driveway, waiting, when Pam drove up in a battered Toyota pickup truck, colored black except for where rust had chewed up on it some. She stepped out and I said, "Pam, I really don't have that much time."

"Whatever time you have, you'll have some for me," she said, leaning back against the truck cab. "Stephanie did her magic work on the Internet this afternoon. Found some things out. Told me what she learned."

"And why did you have to come here to tell me? Why couldn't you have called?"

She frowned. "Because Stephanie told me it'd be better to tell you face to face. And not over the phone. So here I am. And none too pleased that I volunteered my daughter this morning."

"Pam, I'm sorry if I—"

She held up her hand. "Nope, my deal, not yours. And I'm sure nothing will come of it. But look, can you give me ten minutes so I can tell you the ins and outs of that farmhouse's owner?"

I checked my watch. Tight but manageable. "Ten minutes will be fine. Want to go in the house?"

"No," she said. "Let's do it here."

Which is what we did.

So, fifteen minutes after Pam arrived, I was alone again, not counting Roscoe, of course, and back into my house I went. There, amidst my pile of gear, was the special encrypted cell phone that Agent Carr had given to me. I picked it up, made sure it was on, and then dialed the number on his business card.

I also wrote the number down on a pad of paper.

I put the phone up to my ear, listened. One ring and then it was answered, "Carr."

"Karen Dunbar here."

"You're early, and you're not where you're supposed to be," he said, his voice frosty. "What the hell do you mean by calling? I said you were only to call if there was a sighting."

"You certainly did," I replied. "But I wanted to make sure the phone worked. I didn't want to be in the middle of the woods at two A.M. and have a dead phone in my hand if somebody showed up. You see, what you get for when you pay me, Agent Carr, is my professionalism. And my professionalism demanded that I check the phone before I depart. Is that all right, Agent Carr?"

His reply was crisp and to the point. "Call again only if there's a sighting."

I said, "You got it," but by that time, I was speaking into an empty phone.

No matter.

I left shortly with my gear, and left the special phone behind as well.

Surveillances.

In moderate-sized towns and cities, it takes guile and patience, and finding a nice place to hang out for a while. Preferably a parking lot, a busy street, or someplace where a car parked all day doesn't bring much attention.

Sure. Try that on some of the roads around my town and surrounding towns, and after a half hour or so, somebody will stop by—probably somebody you know—and say, "Need some help?" And within an hour, a bunch of people will know that Karen's on the job, and within another hour, the whole town will know what you're doing.

So my best friend in doing surveillances is the U.S. Geological Survey. They make wonderful topographical maps marking, among other things, roads and elevations, and with a bit of work, you can find a nice quiet spot that gives you a view of what you're looking at.

Which worked well for me this Friday afternoon. I backed my

SUV up an abandoned logging road—and thanked Detroit again for four-wheel drive—and did a small hike up to a hill that overlooked Dutton Hill Road. There was a nice large maple tree and some low brush that offered some concealment, and within twenty minutes or so, I was set. I had a low-slung and comfortable camp chair that I settled into, and with my spotting scope at a sweet angle, I had no problem keeping an eye on at least half of the house. Maybe the mysterious he or she would approach the house from the rear; if so, there wasn't much I could do about that, but at least I had the road, the driveway, the front and part of the side yard in clear view. Among my collection of stuff was a down sleeping bag, which I unrolled for later use. I had water, instant coffee, some Coke in a beverage cooler, and some freeze-dried food to cook up on a small gas stove. For a bathroom I had the woods and a well-placed log. It wouldn't be perfect, it wouldn't be luxurious, but it would work.

Probably not as exciting as working a surveillance in midtown Manhattan, but I was outdoors and I was on my own, which situated me fine. Years earlier I had been a newspaper reporter for the state's largest newspaper, and a pretty good one at that. I found I enjoyed poking around and finding things out, and after a few years suffering under some editors, I decided to go on my own. About ninety percent of what I do now—records research, tracking people down, so forth and so on—is identical to newspaper work. But for the most part, I get to choose my clients and my own schedule, and that is nice indeed.

Surveillance.

Sounds so mysterious, so sexy.

So here's what it's like.

Sitting and watching. Taking a picture of the house. Listening to music on your iPod. Watching some birds fly by, deciding they're crows: They're always crows. Looking through the spotting scope. Feeling your heart race just a bit when a vehicle approaches, the letdown when it passes the house. Yawning. Scratching. Tiring of music, trying something else. Listening to a book-on-tape, which really isn't on tape anymore, since you're using an iPod, but it's a book about FDR that sounded interesting. Drinking water. Snacking on pretzels. Pulling the sleeping bag up over your legs and lap as it gets cold. Watching again as another vehicle approaches. Another bust. Drinking a cup of coffee from a Thermos, knowing you'll have to make a fresh batch later on. Another photo of the house. Racing to the nearby log to do your business, coming back to find no lights on at the target house. Good. Listening to nature for a while. Yawning. Scratching.

It's now dark, as the stars and at least one planet slowly come into visibility. An owl hoots out there, hunting, and I think to myself, well, I'm here alone, unarmed. Maybe I should have packed the Ruger. It's too late now. I turn back to the spotting scope. Nothing. I murmur a few words into the cassette recorder, tracking the time and place of vehicles that went by. I figure on another cup of coffee in an hour, another photo of the house. It would be easier if I'd been born a pervert, for they get off on being voyeurs, but most times, surveillances are boring as hell. A vehicle approaches, my heart rate increases. Another bust. I check the time, pick up the digital camera, and take one more photo of the empty house.

Two hours have passed.

Thirty-four to go.

And so, at hour thirty-six and one minute, I stumbled back to the SUV, carrying my gear, stumbling, yawning, and feeling dirty and worn and used. No one showed up, no one at all, and if I wasn't so tired, I suppose I could have thought it through some, but no, it was time to go home.

I drove slowly, blinking my eyes, yawning hard, until I got home, and I decided the gear could stay right where it was, in my SUV. I unlocked the front door and Roscoe was there, bumping and rubbing against my legs, his meows no doubt stating, "Where in hell have you been?"

I knelt down for a moment, scratched his ears. "Later, pal. Later. Right now, Mama's gotta get some sleep."

In the kitchen I filled both his food and water bowls, and then half ran, half stumbled upstairs, where I unplugged the phone and dragged the sheets back, and I know it sounds like hyperbole, but I'm certain I fell asleep before I could even be bothered to pull the blankets up.

Oh Monday, I took a few more hours off, and I was at my office at eleven A.M. I had worked some from home, so I had my unrequired report ready, and I really wasn't surprised when Special Agent Carr came into my office, face set and reddened. For some reason his expression reminded me of something I had read once about Admiral Ernest King, head of the U.S. Navy during World War II. His daughter supposedly said that her father was the most even-tempered man she had ever known: He was always in a constant rage.

So went Agent Carr, it seemed, for the first words out of his mouth were, "We've placed a stop-payment order on the check I presented to you last Thursday."

"And good morning to you, Agent Carr," I replied. "Have a seat."

He took the seat and said, "There's a lot of fraud and abuse in government contracts, Karen, but don't think you're going to get your share by cheating us."

"Cheating you how?"

"Cheating us by not being at the farmhouse, that's why."

"But I was there," I said, looking at him steadily. "For thirty-six hours. Friday evening to Sunday morning. Just like you ordered. And I expect full payment."

"For what? Sitting at home, watching television?"

"And what makes you think I was staying at home?"

A thin little smile. "We know, that's why."

In my open side drawer, I picked up the super-dooper encrypted cell phone that he had provided me and tossed it at him. I caught him by surprise, for he used both hands and fumbled it a bit.

"There you go," I said. "Your special cell phone. Very special indeed. More than just a phone, it was an active tracking device, even when it wasn't being used. You wanted to make sure I was on the job. Well, I was. I just didn't bring your Dick Tracy piece of equipment with me."

"Karen—"

And I interrupted him, saying, "Remember last Friday morning? I tested the phone. You chewed me out for not using the phone as directed, but you also let something else slip. You said I wasn't at the farmhouse yet. How did you know that? Because a tracking device in the phone told you where I was calling from."

Well, so far the highlight of my day was this little moment, getting an FBI agent to shut up. I tossed three more things at him, which he caught this time with more ease.

"First, I know you didn't want one, but here's my report of what went on, or didn't go on, during my thirty-six hours. The highlight was when a couple of deer came by at about four P.M. on Saturday."

Thump.

"Item number two. Seventy-two photographs of an empty house, taken every half hour, proving I was there."

Little thump.

"And in this envelope, item number three. The memory card from my digital camera. I'm sure your tech boys can analyze those photos, make sure they were taken at the time I said they were taken, and that I just didn't take seventy-two photos in a row, to cheat you and Uncle Sam."

He kept quiet, looking at what I had tossed toward him, and then he looked up at me and smiled. "Very good, Karen. You passed."

"Didn't know I was being tested, and don't particularly care. I did my job, and I want the second half of my payment. Now."

A pause. Decided to cut him some slack and smiled in return. "Please."

And surprise of surprises, the second check came out of his briefcase and was slid across the desk, and I promptly squirreled it away and said, "There. Anything else?"

"Don't you want to know what you passed?"

"Of course I do," I said, "but based on prior experience, why should I trust anything you say?"

"Because what I told you was the truth," he said. "I just left some things out, that's all."

"Like what?"

"Like the fact that we are short staffed, we are underfunded, trying to do too much with too little. Which is why I was here, looking at you, to see how good you were, to see your talents at work. That was the test. To see if you would stick with a boring surveillance for that period of time."

"Really? A boring surveillance on a house that you fine fellows own, is that it?"

His face flickered a bit, like the internal battery in that brain had just gotten hit with a power surge. "What . . . how did you find that out?"

With the help of a neighbor girl, about fifteen years old, I thought, but instead I said, "We're not as dumb out here as you think. The place is supposedly owned by Grayson Corporation, out of Pennsylvania, which doesn't officially exist. The state exists, of course, but Grayson is a fake. A front for something else that's a front to something else that's a front for the Department of Justice. What's up there is a spare safehouse, to be used when you folks need it, to hide people, interview subjects, so forth and so on. That's all."

Yet one more smile. "Congratulations. You passed with honor."

"With honor, then? And what does that get me? A gold star on my check?"

"No. An offer."

"What kind of offer?"

"A job offer, that's what. And here's our offer. You work for us as a contractor, perhaps doing an assignment here and there, keeping an eye on things, reporting anything suspicious to me, or whatever contact person is set up. Retainer of, oh, say, about five hundred a month."

"Why me, and why a private investigator? Thought you'd go through local law enforcement for something like that."

"Because local law enforcement means oversight, means paperwork, means bureaucracy. Working with a P.I. makes it that much more simple. And you in particular, Karen, because you've proven your abilities, and also . . . your location. You're less than fifty miles from the Canadian border. People of interest, illegally passing across, may end up in Purmort for a bit before heading elsewhere. And you'll be our contact."

"Your snitch," I said.

He shook his head. "No. A cooperative citizen, that's all."

I thought for a moment and then crossed my legs underneath my desk. "All right. The price for this citizen's cooperation is one thousand a month. Not five hundred. And I report to you anything I think may be of interest. That's my call. Not yours. I'm not going to rat out someone because they're holding a one-person protest in the town common against the government or something like that."

The cheery Agent Carr had now been replaced by the earlier Agent Carr, the one I had gotten to know and . . . well, had gotten to know.

"Impossible."

"Nope, quite possible. One thousand a month, and my call. And that's the deal."

He gathered up the paperwork, pictures, and envelope I had sent his way, and he said, "No. There's no deal."

"Oh, yes there is. Or else."

"Or else what?"

I leaned back, pointed up to my award certificate from the New England Press Association. "Or I contact some old friends of mine in the news media. At the TV station in Manchester. Or the Associated Press bureaus in Concord and Portland. Tell them what just went on, tell them what you just told me. How does that sound, Agent Carr?"

His hand was clenched tight on his briefcase handle. "We had . . . had an agreement. With express mention of confidentiality. You signed it."

"I surely did, and under false pretenses. And you know it. Come on, Agent Carr, what are you going to do? Shoot me? Arrest me? Threaten to ruin my business? Here, in a small state that distrusts government so much that we elect our governors just for two years?"

He glowered at me, like a rabid pit bull, deciding whether to go for the throat first or the groin. I gave him my best smile, usually reserved for Roscoe. "You know it's a good deal, best you can get."

"All right," he breathed. "Deal."

I felt some tension just ease away. House painted and a new roof before winter. Not a bad deal. "Delighted to hear it."

He stood up and went to the door and then looked back at me. He stood there for what seemed to be a long time.

"You know, some would call what you just did extortion," Carr finally said.

I thought of what he had put me through, how he had lied to me from the very start. I smiled and made an expansive shrug.

"Think of it as country manners," I said.

# AND THEN SHE WAS GONE

## By Christine Matthews

Christine Matthews's short stories have appeared in *Deadly Allies II*, *Ellery Queen Mystery Magazine*, *Lethal Ladies*, *For Crime Out Loud I & II*, Mickey Spillane's *Vengeance Is Hers*, *Cat Crimes On Holiday*, and *Till Death Do Us Part*. This is her fourth appearance in a Best of the Year anthology. She is the author of the Gil and Claire Hunt trilogy, the second book of which, *The Masks of Auntie Laveau*, was called by the *L.A. Times* "a blueprint for how to write a thriller." She recently edited *Deadly Housewives*, published by Avon/Morrow in April 2006.

H igh-risk lifestyle, my ass. I supposed she thinks them dudes over to the firehouse are high-risk, too? They out there cause they bein' paid to be out there. They gets to wear them uniforms, all clean an nice, a fancy place to live for a few days a week. They don't live in them houses every day, ya know? And the food. You ever been 'roun' one of them station houses when it's dinner time?"

"No, and I know you ain't, neither," Rita shot back. Victor acted like he hadn't heard her, but she knew it was only an act.

"Well, it's like Christmas every damn day. But you think they eat leftovers after they get back from a fire? No way, they just cook them up some more."

Rita leaned back in the front seat, fishing around in her purse for the lipstick she'd bought last Saturday, waiting for Victor to finish griping. He was always carrying on about how much everyone in the world had except for him.

"An' po-lice? How can you say that's high-risk when them muthas carry guns, for Chrissake? At least they got a fightin' chance. But miners . . ." He shook his large head back and forth slowly, "Now there's some high-risk for ya. All the trouble them poor suckers havin' down in some hole in some shanty town? Goin' down into hell wearin' raggedy clothes, their lungs all black. Hardly makin' no money at all. Now that's what I consider high-risk."

"Well, every one of them jobs, every single one of them is high-risk, no matter what you think."

Victor jammed his right hand on the horn, yelled out the open window of the limousine, "Yo! Shit for brains. Ya retarded or some thin'?" then continued the conversation. "You're right, Rita, that's my point. We takin' all the risks while every asshole out there looks at your sorry ass thinkin' how dangerous ya got it when that ain't the truth, at all."

Victor and Louie lived in their own macho world, stumbling through days drunk and coked up. Somehow they had convinced themselves that the girls they sold day after day, night after night, were safe because of them. Cared for. Even loved.

"Me and the King, we knows how to work it. First we check out the johns, an' then deliver you real classy, first class in a lim-o-zeen. We always pick ya'll up later, don't we? Have you or any of my other ladies had to wait in the cold? Or the rain? No street corners, no alleys for my girls. Clean sheets, clean business, that's how I does things."

"She musta been talkin' 'bout them girls, the ones on the corners with their tits hangin' out, those girls that ain't lucky like me an' Tanya or Contrelle," Rita lied.

"Yeah, maybe."

Victor stared straight ahead and Rita looked at his profile against the tainted glass. No hat for this limo driver, he wasn't anyone's servant. Victor had what the girls all called the three B's. He was bi, black, and bald. Handsome, vain about how he looked. A large diamond stud glistened in his earlobe. It was the first thing Victor had bought himself with the first dollar he'd earned pimpin'. Only Victor didn't never call it pimpin', he considered himself a "businessman." His girls were his "staff," and the johns, they were "clients." His motto: "If ya thinks proud an' walks proud, you is proud," would have been engraved on a plaque, hanging on his office wall . . . if he had an office.

"So where are you s'posed to meet her?"

Rita put her lipstick back. "Look, I don't hafta go—"

"Oh yes, you do. I tol' you it's good PR."

"For Chrissake, PR for what? We're fuckin' breakin' the law here. We're doin' shit here that makes me an' you, both of us, lowlifes."

"Lowlifes is somethin' you're puttin' on yourself there. Now, you're gonna meet her at her hotel an' do that interview."

Rita glared out the window, wondering how the hell all the decisions she'd made in her life had led her here? Sittin' next to this jackass, ridin' in this stinkin' limousine, livin' an workin' in fuckin' Hollywood, California? Why was she bein' punished just for bein' a little stupid?

"Did you brush your teeth?"

She turned and gave him a big toothy grin.

"Ya got on that underwear I bought ya?"

"What the hell does that matter?"

"It's respectable. It'll make ya feel like a lady."

That one cracked Rita up. "Lady, my ass."

Victor squealed to a stop for a red light. "An' don't be talkin' trash like that. We want this Miss Whatzername to take notice of Victor's work force."

The light changed and he turned onto Sunset Boulevard.

"It's just that I hates that bitch. I hates everything about her."

"You don't even know her, baby."

"She comes into the diner the other day swishin' her Louis Vuitton like she owns the place and every damn thing in it. Tanya an' me sit there askin' each other just who the hell does this bitch think she is?"

Victor patted the bag in Rita's lap. "You got your own Vuitton, girl, so what you gripin' about?"

"I seen you, Victor. Me an' Giselle watched you sneakin' out of that Chink girl's apartment, buyin' this here knockoff. Who the hell you think you're foolin'?"

If he hadn't been driving he would have hauled off and smacked her. But instead, Victor just gritted his teeth. "No one knows the difference."

"I do. Giselle do. Even that stupid bitch Connie do."

"That Daisy Mae from buttfuck Nebraska? I'll have to teach that hillbilly somethin' about respect."

Shit. Now Victor was mad and Rita's big mouth would probably be the cause of Connie getting knocked around. The poor kid couldn't help being so ignorant. Rita never told anyone how much she liked the girl . . . especially Victor. She was smart enough not to let him know she had feelings for anyone or anything. And now she was even smarter, sitting back and letting his anger run its course.

He pounded the steering wheel several times, hollered about how ungrateful every single one of his whores were, until Rita couldn't stand it anymore. "Look, you want me to do this interview thing? So, tell me what to say."

That got him going. There wasn't anything Victor loved more than talkin'. Talkin' *at* her, talkin' *to* her, repeatin' every word, turning them over and inside out, sure she'd die without his expertise on everything in the whole frickin' world. That and money. Victor loved to hear himself talk and he loved money. The only thing Rita wasn't sure of was which he loved more.

Liz Petkus didn't think Rita would show. As she sipped her water she wondered if the coffee shop was too casual. She'd rethought her choice of meeting places for days. The first place she'd considered was far too formal, too intimidating. The second place, too dirty. The last thing she wanted was for the hooker to think she was treating her with contempt. Even choosing her clothes had seemed difficult. After three changes she finally settled on jeans and a blue pullover sweater. A watch was the only jewelry she wore but it was the Rolex her father had given her when she'd graduated from film school. And now here she sat, so very proud of herself, making notes for her first documentary.

She checked the clock on the wall, behind the counter. If Rita didn't show up, she would order lunch without her. She was starving.

"Are you sure I can't get you anything?" the waitress asked for the second time in ten minutes. "How about some iced tea, at least? A cocktail? Maybe some soup to start off with?"

The soup sounded good and Liz was just about to give in when she saw Rita walk through the door.

"My friend just arrived. Give us a few minutes."

The waitress was one of those too-much women. Too much bleach on her too-short hair. Too much shiny lip gloss making her lips look way too big. Too much perfume, too much cleavage, and way too much glitter on her claw-like fingernails. When she turned to look over her shoulder and saw Rita strutting toward the table, she asked Liz, "That's your friend?"

"Yes, you know her?"

"I don't associate with her kind."

"Well, it's a good thing then that I'm only asking you to bring us some lunch and not be our friend, isn't it?"

Rita smiled as the waitress huffed off. Sliding across the black plastic seat on her side of the booth, she wiggled out of her jacket. "Tiffany givin' ya trouble? cause if she is, I'll tell Victor an' he'll—"

"No, it's okay."

"If that old queen been insultin' ya, Victor'll have to have a little talk with her, know what I'm sayin'?"

"Queen? That wasn't a woman?"

Rita laughed. "Nuthin's what you think it is in movieland. This here is Oz, Dorothy, an' that bitch is the Wicked Witch."

Liz hated feeling naive. It shifted power to Rita, and she had to stay in control if the project was to get done.

Liz leafed through notes scribbled on a yellow legal pad.

Rita sat across from her, calm, hands folded on top of the table.

Liz glanced up. "Are you hungry? Should we talk now or while we eat, or after . . ."

"It don't matter to me. But I gotta be out front at two. Sharp. Victor's drivin' me to a date at LAX, some dude has a two-hour lay-over and wants to spend it with me." Rita smiled proudly.

"Okay, that gives us almost two hours."

"For what, exactly? When you made this date . . . an' it is a date . . ."

"Don't worry. I'm going to pay you for your time," Liz assured her.

"Good." Rita held out her right hand. "Two hours, two hundred."

"Now? Before we talk?" Liz asked.

"Get business outta the way first. That's how it's done."

Liz pulled out her checkbook.

"Cash," Rita said. "How dumb are you, anyway?"

Liz counted out two hundred dollars, leaving her with only thirty in her wallet.

After counting the bills again, Rita stuffed the money down inside her cowboy boot. Then she straightened up, folded her hands, and asked, "So, what you need?"

Tiffany came back and threw down two menus. After they ordered, Liz started right in. "I'm making a documentary about working girls, such as yourself. I want to find out how you got hooked up with Victor, why you . . . need him. What makes you—"

Rita played with a small pearl button on the cuff of her blouse, listening until she couldn't take anymore. "That the best you can do, girl? You tellin' me you takin' up my time askin' the same tired-ass, bullshit questions everyone been askin'?"

"I know there've been documentaries about prostitution . . ."

"Bet your sorry little self they done hundreds an' thousands of 'em. All the time showin' some bitch with her eye swelled up, dirty alleys, cars bouncin', parked on some street while they tape gruntin' and groanin'. An' every time, they say, 'never-before-seen footage, shocking, the untold story.' " For the last part Rita sounded as good as Barbara Walters ever had. "I seen 'em, you seen 'em. Everybody who's got a TV set seen 'em. They be on the news, HBO, Showtime, all over every channel. So why does a girl like you from the middle of nowhere—"

"Lincoln, Nebraska. Then on to Iowa City where I studied film. I graduated at the top of my class, with honors, I am working on a grant, now. I think I know what I'm doing just a little bit better than some—"

"Hooker? Whore? Will it make you feel smarter to think I'm not as good as you? I can be anyone you wants me to be. You wants a druggie? I'll shake all over, scream for a fix. You wants me to tell you I come from a home where my Daddy raped me? Beat me? I'll gets me some scars to show you. I can be anybody you wants. But you. Look at you." Rita sniffed like she'd just smelled a pile of shit. "Just startin' out, tryin' to make a name for yourself. For the life of me, I can't figure out why you don't wanna do somethin' better. Why you wanna waste your time an' film on the same ol' crap?"

Liz didn't get angry. How could she? The woman sitting across from her had just said everything she'd been thinking for months. But she'd kept it to herself. Her first important project and it had come too easy. Late at night, when she sat up, doubled over with doubts, a thought had started taunting her, asking her if maybe her father had pulled some strings? Her idea wasn't original. She knew it then and she knew it for sure now.

"Okay, let's suppose someone dropped a camera in your lap. What would you make a film about?" she asked Rita.

Their burgers arrived and Rita took a big bite. After a few moments of chewing and thinking, she said, "The men. I'd tell the truth about them."

"You mean pimps? It's been done."

Rita nodded. "They likes to think of theyselves as royalty, you know?"

"I've seen films about the Pimp Ball. That big party they have, all of them arriving in limos, dressed in the ugliest suits, girls catering to them, fussing over them like they're movie stars."

"An' why you think that is?"

Liz shrugged. "I don't know. I've always wondered why anyone needs them for anything."

"It's the fear. They have the fear."

"Fear of what?" Liz asked.

"Bein' nobody. They knows they can't make it without us girls an' that scares 'em. Scares 'em big time. Then they pass the fear down to us. All the time sayin' how worthless we is, how we'd be nowhere without 'em."

Liz wiped ketchup from the corner of her mouth. "Work with me, Rita," she said. "Help me. Instead of interviewing you, I'll use you behind the scenes. I'll pay you a salary, you can be my production assistant."

"Uh-oh, here come the fear again," Rita said.

"What do you mean?"

"I'm afraid you couldn't pay me enough to make it worth my while. An' Victor would never let me do anything like that. Are you crazy? He'd kill us both."

Liz tried to understand how one minute this woman could seem so educated, so self-assured, and in a heartbeat collapse into helplessness.

"You think Victor would kill someone? For real?"

"I ain't sayin'; I just knows better than to cross Victor." Rita picked up her burger and continued eating.

When Victor came to get her, King Louie was sitting in the backseat of the big black limo. The gaunt, pale pimp thought of himself as a full-time rock star and a part-time "businessman." He had a cell phone in one hand and a glass of champagne in the other. When she got into the front seat, Rita ignored their passenger.

"So, what happened? You didn't tell that bitch too much, did ya?" Victor asked.

"What kind of a fool you take me for?" Rita worked up an innocent look.

"I'm just lookin' out for you . . . an all my staff. A man can't be too careful in this line of work."

"I know," Rita assured him, "I know you is."

King Louie snapped his phone shut. "I don't like this. Not one single, tiny bit."

"Shut up, you hillbilly," Victor shouted. "We needs to show our respectability. Rita show up there all classed up, no boobage hangin' out. She look like a model. Better than any those bitches in them magazines. Good enough to be in the movies. No damaged merchandise here, just prime cut—Grade A. Did you tell that woman you went to college? Do she know that? You tell her no one makin' you do nuthin' you don't wanna do? You what they calls a free agent. I just actin' as your manager, so to speak."

"I told her," Rita lied.

"Good."

King Louie pushed himself forward, stuck his face closer to the back of Rita's head. "We gonna be in her movie, then? All of us?"

"Maybe. She still got a lot of interviewin' to do."

"You sure she's gonna make us look good?" Louie asked. "Not like some derelicts in them cheap-ass pornos. Make us look respectable. High-class?"

Rita stared straight ahead. "Sure."

"Say you love me," the john demanded as Rita spanked his fat ass.

"I loves ya, baby. I loves ya soooo much it makes me wanna hurt ya good an' hard."

"I still don't believe you."

Rita picked up the magazine spread out on the night stand. He wants Halle Berry, she thought, he gonna get her. Rolling the magazine tight, she smacked his butt until he screamed. "Does ya believe me now, sweetheart? Can ya feel the love?"

She waited for an answer but he was too busy jerking off. It was times like these that she felt so totally in charge of her life. Better than any big-shot CEO. Just this dip-shit an' her in one of the best rooms in the Beverly Hills Hotel. Five hundred dollars stuffed deep in her bag. Thirty minutes of workin' off the anger. That same anger those Botox wives carried with 'em to their fancy psychiatrists. It don't get much better, she thought.

Lifting herself off the bed, she stood in front of her date, letting him take in her nudity. "Are we done or do ya wanna fuck me?"

As he lay there, she could see where the sprayed-on tan had dripped down his left thigh. "No, baby, we're done. That was great. I'll call Victor next time I'm in the neighborhood."

"You do that."

She slowly walked across the room to the glorious bathroom. After emptying a bottle of bath salts into the tub she lowered herself into the hot water and settled in for a leisurely soak.

Winter in Hollywood. Plastic Christmas trees, plastic snow, plastic credit cards makin' everybody nice an happy.

It was always about the money. She mentally calculated. The money she'd taken from that Petkus chick topped off her private account at fifty grand. Victim, my ass, she laughed. Victor an' his idiot friend might scare the other girls but Rita was different. Rita had a plan and stayed focused. Rita was goin' to Paris. Get herself a little place, buy some new paints, study real hard. They liked black girls over there. Color didn't matter in Gay Paree.

She looked out the window at the lush surroundings. Everything seemed to be washed with gold today. The jasmine-scented room made her feel as though she were on an island planted in the middle of a sea bluer than blue. No need to rush. The dirtbag in the other room had an appointment and the room was hers for the rest of the day . . . or until Victor called.

She was thinking how she needed a pedicure when her cell phone rang. Then a knock.

"Should I answer it?" he asked from the other side of the door.

"Would you be sweet an' bring it in to me?"

Half dressed, he skittered across the tiled floor with the phone held at arm's length like it was a snake. "Cool ring tone. Prince rules."

What a dipwad, she thought. "Thanks."

He stood there for a moment, waiting for her to flip the phone open. Before speaking she dismissed him, watching him practically skip out of the room.

"Hello, Victor."

"I'm comin' for ya. Be out front in five."

She laughed. "Hell, I'm not even dressed here. You're gonna hafta give me—"

"Get your bony ass downstairs or I'll give ya up ta the cops. Does ya want that? Does ya wanna end up in fuckin' prison?"

"Is this another one of your lame jokes?"

"Listen up. That white girl? The one makin' the movie?"

"What about her?"

"She got herself killed, stupid bitch."

"What that gotta do with me?"

"They found her in your crib, spread out on your bed. Dressed in your Gucci."

"Goddamn."

"Why'd ya'll go an' tell that cunt anything? Anything at all?" King Louie whined. "She was our ticket, man. Our free pass."

"What the hell you talkin' 'bout?"

"The cops have her for the crime, let her put in the damn time. How dumb are ya, man?" Louie reached up to rap his partner on his shiny skull.

Victor grabbed the man's wrist, nearly snapping it in two. "How many times I gotta tell ya? Never touch me. Never!"

"All's I'm sayin' is we don't owe that bitch nuthin'. Not one fuckin' thing."

"She's one of my girls an' I takes care of my girls. That's what Victor do. Besides, she innocent. You knows that as well as I do."

"Who the fuck cares?" Louie smiled, wiping at his nose. The doper was always wet somewhere. "She takes the heat off us, keeps the cops off our ass."

"How do you figure?"

"What the hell do ya mean, how do I figure? What's wrong with you, man?"

"Rita knows lots of stuff that could get both of us locked up for a long time. Stuff worser that some murder. Stuff that gets ya killed in the joint."

Louie squinted up at his partner, "Murder's the worse. Dude, ain't nuthin' worse than that."

"Ya think?"

Rita was waiting in front of the hotel when Victor pulled up. Her hair, limp on her head, damp; she held a pair of gold metallic stilettos in her right hand. In her left she swung the tote bag containing her bra and panties as well as the usual. When she saw the limo pull up she ran, beating the doorman to open a back door.

Trying to be calm, Victor waved. "Fuck."

"What?" Rita asked from the back seat. "What now?"

"That's Freddie. You know, Four-Way Freddie?"

"From Glendale?" Louie asked. "So what?"

"So he seen Rita, all undone. An' he gonna remember, 'specially when he looks at TV, sees the news. Make him put two an two together, know what I'm sayin?"

"I ain't done nuthin', Victor. Ya believe me, dontcha?" Rita asked, trying to hold it together.

" 'Course I do, baby."

"So where we goin', then?"

Louie looked up, suddenly aware he was in a moving car. "Yeah, man, where we goin'?"

"We gotta stash Rita someplace safe."

"But Victor . . . I—"

"Shut up, girl, I knows what's best. Just trust me."

Now he'd gone and done it. Asked for the one thing she'd used up long ago. The one thing she didn't have to give. Not to him—not to anyone. Trust.

He braked for a red light and that's when she jerked open the back door.

Louie opened his door, unsure of what to do.

As Rita cut through a parking lot she could hear Victor shouting for her to come back.

The good thing was, Rita didn't have any friends. She hung out with Victor's girls, but they didn't count. And she liked it that way. No family, no friends. No one cryin' or bitchin'. No guilt, no waitin' 'roun' for some half-assed promises to be kept that tender lovin' relatives or best friends passed out like they was free samples down at the grocery. She considered herself smart and lucky. Most the time. But now . . . well . . . she wasn't feelin' neither. There was no one to trust. Nowhere to go. No one to help her out. An' that sucked royally.

Her hair had dried and now stood out all kinky. Ducking into a gas station bathroom, she washed her face, pulled off her skirt, took a pair of shorts out of her bag and yanked them on. She'd left her shoes in the limo but always kept a pair of Nikes with her. Bending, she hastily tied the laces. Without makeup she could pass for someone at least five years younger than her twenty-four years.

Now what?

She stood there, listening to voices outside, traffic, stood there just wondering. Then a knock at the door.

"Are you almost done? My kid's gotta go."

She'd have to leave sometime. Might as well be now.

A cab rolled by and she waved for it to stop. The driver, a burned-out hippie type, smiled. When she got in, he turned down the music coming from some Moldy Oldie station. "Where to?"

She had no idea.

He patiently waited for her to say something but after a full minute he asked, "Just get into town?"

What was wrong with her? Lying was her business. If they gave out trophies she'd be in the fuckin' Hall of Fame.

A car honked but the driver ignored it, still waiting. "I bet you're an actress," he finally said. "We get busloads of 'em every day. Come to La-La Land to get a million-dollar contract. Right?"

"No."

"Then you gotta be a tourist. Here to look at all the stars."

"You're good. Damn good." The bullshit kicked in and she smiled. Thank you, Jesus.

"So, what do you wanna see first, then? I can be your guide." He leered at her from the front seat. "Show you what's what, if you know what I mean."

She watched him lick his fat, ugly lips and POW! Just like that, she was back in charge. "Sure." This could buy her time till she figured something out. "Maybe I can show you a few things, too." Flash them pearly whites, she told herself, an' keep movin'. Use the dude to hide behind. Douchebag wanna play the big man, let 'im.

He must have heard her stomach growl. "How about some lunch for starters? There's a great place over 'round Hollywood and Vine called Joseph's Café. Greek food. Sound great?"

"Let's do it."

Rita expected it to be like in one of them black-an'-white movies Victor was watchin' all the time. She really thought when she walked into the restaurant there'd be a newspaper on the counter with them big ol' black headlines. And those headlines would be about that Petkus chick gettin' murdered. And there'd be a TV up over the bar or in a corner. They'd shoot a close-up of an anchorman, lookin' real serious, talkin' 'bout the murder. An' neighbors she might recognize from her building. All sayin' what a surprise it was they didn't hear nuthin', considerin' a woman was bein' murdered.

But it wasn't like that, at all.

"By the way," the cabbie extended his hand, "name's Perry."

"Rita," she said as he held the chair out for her. Before the waiter could say anything Perry waved him off. "The lady and I will need a few minutes. But while we're decidin', you can bring us a couple of beers."

"Ain't you drivin'?"

"It's okay," he said. Then to the waiter, "Two Buds."

He started tellin' her about every fuckin' thing on the menu like he had the damn thing memorized. While she pretended to be listening her eyes kept track of every part of the room. How long did she have? was all she could wonder. How long until Victor or Louie went to the cops to cover their own be-hinds?

Perry was still yappin' when the waiter came back. She just nodded when he asked if it was okay for him to order somethin' foreign.

Then he stood up. "I gotta go wash my hands. This town's a cesspool, know what I mean?"

"Sure do."

He hadn't even cleared the dining area when she heard a rapping on the window near her. Then another, until she was curious enough to walk over to have a look.

"Yo, Rita."

The sun was bouncing off the glass and she couldn't get a really good look.

"Come outside."

A lot of men in Hollywood had long hair but not like his. The Beatle cut was his trademark.

She tried shushing him through the glass, but he kept calling for her to come out. Jumpin' up an' down like a fool idiot. The waiters outnumbered the customers, and those not in the kitchen were real busy ignoring her. So, she grabbed her stuff an' took off. Weird as he was, Rita knew she could trust Crazy John Lennon.

But by the time she hit the sidewalk, he was gone.

"Over here."

Rushing past the large window of the café, Rita ducked behind the bushes where Crazy John was hiding.

"You're in big trouble, Rita."

"No shit. Tell me somethin' I don't know, fool."

"That's why I ran over here soon as I saw you go in there. Don't worry—I'm gonna take you home. To my house. You'll be safe, an' I got something really, really important to show you."

She'd never thought he had a home—well, not a real one. Now she tried picturing him in a regular house with furniture an' shit. Hell, the only time she ever saw him was on Hollywood an' Vine, where he was all the time cleanin' an' polishin' that star they laid down in the sidewalk for John Lennon. She and some of the girls had even started calling him Crazy John Lennon after a while 'cause that's all he ever talked about. A crazy fan but nice enough. Just some poor bastard with nuthin' better to do, who'd never done nuthin' worse than smile at her. Soon she started looking for him when she had a date nearby. She'd even make Victor stop so she could bring him coffee or a taco every now and then, thinking poor ol' Crazy was homeless.

"How far is it?"

"Long Beach."

He had to be kiddin'. "How the hell we suppose to get there? That's all the fuckin' way over there somewhere."

"Don't worry. I have a car."

A car? Who the hell was this maniac? "You got a car? I'm supposed to believe you got a house an' a car? All to yourself?"

Before she had a chance to get an answer he was slinking off toward a parking lot.

What else could she do but follow? Hell, man had wheels an' a place to crash. Best offer she'd had all day.

Then Crazy John Lennon all of a sudden straightened up all proud like an' took a set of keys out of a front pocket of his bell-bottoms. Three keys, all attached to a chain with a small guitar made up of letters spelling out the word IMAGINE. Then he put the biggest one of them keys into the lock of the whitest, sleekest sports car Rita had ever seen.

"Oh man," she whispered, "you gotta be shittin' me."

"Here we are." He pulled into a circular driveway.

"I still don't get it," Rita said. "You live all the way out here? You got beach right outside your back door an' you get in your fine car an' drive all the way to Hollywood for some ol' piece of sidewalk?"

"No, I do it to honor the greatest human being to have lived in my lifetime. I owe him that, at least."

"You don't owe no one nuthin', baby."

Crazy John unlocked the front door and Rita felt like she was in one of them magazines all 'bout style the movie stars have in their houses an' clothes—shit like that.

"Come on, Lovely Rita Meter Maid, I'll give you the tour."

"How many times I tol' you not to call me that?"

"Eight times. You told me eight times."

"So why you still call me that, then?"

"It fits."

The formal living room was painted white. A white piano was the only piece of furniture and it stood in the middle of the room.

"John Lennon once owned this," he told her.

Dumbest thing she'd ever seen. A whole room just for one lousy piano. She was not impressed.

They walked down a long hallway and then he stopped.

"Before I open this door, I have to tell you I've never shown this part of my collection to anyone. Ever. You're the first."

She didn't know how to feel about any of it.

He took out the keychain again and inserted a small gold key into the lock. When he opened the door, Rita couldn't help but be impressed. Even if she didn't know what the hell she was lookin' at. The room was huge. And like everything she'd seen so far, it was white. Walls, carpet, every shelf, even the two leather chairs. Glass had been mounted in front of every shelf. Dude lived in a fuckin' museum.

"Let me get this right so's I understand what's happenin' here. You drive me all the way out to fuckin' Long Beach to show me all this very important shit while I'm runnin' for my life. My fuckin' life! You get that? Tell me I have this wrong. Tell me you're not standin' there in them raggedy old clothes—"

"Vintage, they're vintage clothes. From the sixties. And they cost a hell of a lot more than any of the knock-offs you wear."

"Well, excuse me all to hell." She shook her head, still not believin' all this crap. "So, you're standin' like an idiot in some vintage clothes, expectin' me to cream my pants because you showin' me a buncha posters an ol' records? Shit, I wasn't even borned when that Lennon dude got hisself shot. Am I supposed to care? You crazy, man. Really crazy if you think I care 'bout any of this shit."

His hands started to shake. "No, you're crazy," he said. "You're looking at a collection any museum would kill to have. You're standing in a house worth more than two million dollars that you got to in a car driven by a genius. A brilliant man who would have been kind and loving to you, like I'm trying to be."

He walked over to the other side of the room. Behind a portrait of John Lennon and Paul McCartney was a safe. Crazy John twisted the dial and reached in. After closing it back up he walked over to her and handed her a plastic bag.

"What's this? More of your sixties shit?" She could tell she was pissin' him off and didn't care one bit.

He bit his lip, trying to hold back anger caused by her disrespect. "No, it's a present . . . it's your freedom."

She held the plastic bag up and immediately recognized the Rolex. The one that Petkus bitch had been wearing. It wasn't easy to forget somethin' as big and expensive as that. No way.

When she started to open the bag he jumped at her. "Don't touch it! It's got prints on it. I bagged it—like they do on *CSI*. You can take it to the police."

Rita didn't like what she was thinkin'. Backing away, she threw the watch to the floor. "You killed her?"

"No, listen, that's not what happened. Why would I kill someone I don't even know? I'm a pacifist . . . like John was . . . like he wanted the world to be. Love, baby. Peace and love." He made that dumb-ass peace sign. It was the first time she realized how small his hands were. How gay he looked.

Bending to pick up the watch, still sealed in the sandwich bag, he took her arm and led her out of the room.

"Where ya takin' me?"

"To the kitchen. I'm thirsty."

"So you saw Victor? You saw him kill that dumb bitch?"

Crazy John poured her another glass of iced tea. Carefully, up to the top line of the design on the crystal. Then he put a slice of lemon in the glass, carefully, so as not to splash on the white countertop.

"Like I said, I was down, cleaning the star, and I saw Victor and that friend of his—"

"King Louie?"

"Skinny? Sounds like a real shit-kicker."

"Yeah, that's him."

"They were talking real loud. I couldn't help but hear. And then that woman shows up. I didn't recognize her. Figured her for a tourist until I saw her holding up a recorder, asking questions like she was interviewing him."

"Bet Victor ate that up."

"No," he seemed upset. Louie tried calming him down but Victor got angrier, especially when she kept calling him a pimp.

"It was getting dark and they started pushing her. Louie on one side, Victor on the other. I looked down for a minute, one tiny minute . . . and then she was gone. They all were. Victor came back after about five minutes; Louie was running after him, brushing his pants off."

"An' they was nowheres near my apartment?"

"What's your apartment got to do with anything?"

"Victor says they found her in my place. In my fuckin' bed, for Chrissake."

"You must've heard wrong. After I was sure they were gone I went down the alley. First I spotted her watch by the Dumpster and then I see her foot sticking up. Carefully, I picked up the Rolex, figuring it would nail those bastards.

"You see the news?"

"Yeah. Why?"

"An' they don't say she was found in my place?"

"Rita, Lovely Rita, where are you getting all this from?"

"So Victor lied. Why he do that?"

" 'Cause you're holding out on him. Something about you cheating him out of money that belonged to him. 'Cause he wants to teach you and the other girls a lesson."

Rita hugged her bag close. It never left her side. It held her life, her fortune, her fifty grand. How the hell had Victor found out?

Crazy John asked if she wanted another glass of tea.

"No. I gots ta figure this out."

"What's to figure? You take the watch to the police, they have Victor's prints on it—"

"How do you know that for sure?"

"I watched them grab her, the way they led her down the street—they have to be there."

"You go, then, you so sure. Why I have to be involved at all? You go, Victor don't know you. You just a witness. A rich, white witness. Everybody believe you."

A phone rang from somewhere in another room. Crazy John held up a finger, cutting her off. "I gotta get that."

After he left, Rita crept behind, listening, trying to figure out who was tellin' the truth an' who the hell was jerkin' her around.

There was an office at the end of a long hallway, carpeted in white shag. That ugly shit oughtta be burned, she thought. As she stood close to the doorway she heard Crazy John yelling something about money an' promises. Rita leaned in closer.

"I delivered—you owe me, man. I'm not takin' no more crap from you, understand? I've carried you long enough. You an' Victor better be nice to me cause I got something here that can put both of you away. All I gotta do is make one call to the cops."

Liar. So he did know Louie. Was there one fuckin' man alive who didn't lie?

"That's better. You want the big rush—you pay. Good. I'll bring the stuff by around six."

Drugs. That was the only thing she wasn't into. King Louie was all the time tryin' ta get her high, but she told him to blow the blow out his ass.

Rita didn't move fast enough. The door opened and she stood, frozen. "You dealin', an' you dealin' ta Louie? Is that what's happenin' here?"

"Come on, whose side are you on? I keep you safe—"

"An' just why you be doin' all this for me? Just cause you queer for some dead Beatle? Is that it?"

His fist went into her face before he realized what happened. Just a reflex. But when her head banged against the wall, she dropped hard. Blood spattered across the glass of his autographed White album, hanging beneath a single spotlight.


The sun was shining brightly, making John Lennon's star at Hollywood and Vine almost glow. But then, he was one of God's favorites.

A grubby family of tourists walked over the star, Crazy John swore as they left dirty marks behind. "Have some respect, here!" Bending down, he squirted Windex across the metal and rubbed.

"Calm down." It was a cop. "We've been getting complaints. You harassing the tourists again, John?"

"No, man, I wouldn't do that. Love and peace. That's what I'm about. You know that, Pete."

"Yeah, I know what you're about. I heard you were down at the station yesterday. Word is you had some evidence regarding that girl found in the Dumpster. Better watch out or Geraldo will be coming out here, making you famous." Pete laughed.

Look at him, one of the little piggies they sang about. And now ol' Crazy John was their hero. Brilliant. Bringing that watch in himself really made him look like a concerned citizen. John Lennon would have approved big-time of the way he tried to help Rita out. No kissing up to the establishment, just one on one. Love and peace. But maybe this one time, just to get the piggies looking the other way so he could keep his sources from drying up.

"Have you seen this girl?" Pete held up a picture of Lovely Rita.

"Rita. Wow, I used to see her around here almost every night. Then all of a sudden—nothing. One minute here, and then she was gone."

"Well, if you see anything, hear something, let me know, will you? Some of Victor's girls got together a reward for information. They're scared. You know how dangerous their line of work is. Hookers get thrown away all the time."

"Yeah, I'll let you know, Pete."

As the cop walked away, Crazy John looked at the flyer the cop had given him. Ten thousand dollars. Shit, he'd made more than that just yesterday. But it wouldn't last long. No one had any idea how much money it took to keep up the house, the collection . . . his life's work.

Love, love, love. All you need is love.

And Lovely Rita's fifty grand.

# THE GUARDIANS
*By Jim Fusilli*

Jim Fusilli is the author of four novels, including *Hard, Hard City*, which was named Best Novel of 2004 by *Mystery Ink* magazine. In 2007, he edited and contributed a chapter to *The Chopin Manuscript*, a serial thriller featuring a dream team of top-selling authors of crime and suspense. His short story "Chellini's Solution" appeared in the 2007 edition of *The Best American Mystery Stories*. This year, his first novel for young adults, *Marley Z and the Bloodstained Violin*, will be published by Dutton. Jim also is the rock and pop critic for the *Wall Street Journal*. His book on Brian Wilson and the Beach Boys' album "Pet Sounds" was published in 2006 by Continuum.

H is stepfather was a cop, and Luther Addison became one, too, determined to address the indignities the old man suffered. A prideful shell now—racking coughs led to finding a dark spot on his lung—W. E. Addison was fading rapidly, down to a fragile hundred and six pounds from a rock-hard one eighty-five. So the burly young cop chose to keep his plan a secret from his loving family.

But as he entered the living room of his parents' little colonial in Cambria Heights, Queens, he found his stepfather already knew. Same as it ever was: No corner of his mind escaped the man's insight since he began courting Lucy Addison when Luther was five years old.

"Running for president?" W. E. Addison asked. The stereo was off, and his rocking chair didn't move.

"Organization needs a president," the son replied lightly, trying to cut the tension. He'd already given the Entenmann's to his mother, kissing her plump cheek as she prepared the cassoulet.

"We don't need the organization," W. E. said, staring ahead, shoulders high, his elbows on the chair's curved arms.

Luther removed his blue clip-on tie. "Come on, Pop. Let's not—"

"That's Sergeant," he replied sharply. "Given the topic, it's Sergeant Addison."

The son sat in his mother's seat, lifting the *TV Guide* from the soft cushion and dropping it on the coffee table next to his eight-point service hat.

He clasped his stepfather's frail forearm. "Should've been Lieutenant Addison. Precinct Commander Addison."

"Maybe so," the old man said. "But NYPD doesn't need—"

"Levels the playing field, Pop," he said softly.

"Says you're black, not blue."

No, Luther thought, as he stood to turn on a Hank Jones album. Says we're black *and* blue.

The *Times* placed it inside the Metro section, but the *Post* allowed the story to scream on page one: "Activist Cop in Teen Shooting."

Her Anthony was a sweet child who took his sister to Saint Helen's every Sunday morning, cried Rose Ciccanti, near collapse in the picture the tabloid ran next to her son's junior prom photo. "How could they do this to my Anthony?" she wailed. "My only son."

According to the *Post*, Philip Altomonte, a cousin, said, "They want everything, and they'll kill you to get it."

What Altomonte, who was known throughout the neighborhood as Fat Philly, actually said was, "These spooks want everything, and now they got cops who'll kill you to get it."

On the day the story broke, neither paper, nor the *Daily News* for that matter, mentioned that Anthony Ciccanti Jr., a k a Little Flaps, spent eighteen months in Bridges Juvenile Center in the Bronx for his role in a scheme to rob winners in the parking lot at Aqueduct. Could've been worse: Their third victim was a cop who skipped duty to hit the track with a tip. The cop was carrying, but he let the crew lift his eight hundred dollars so he wouldn't have to explain why he wasn't on patrol.

In January, jug-eared Ciccanti was released to the bosom of Howard Beach, where the Gambino crime family reigned.

Three months later, he was dead near a Dumpster at the United Postal Service facility in Brooklyn, a short drive from his parents' white brick house on 160th Street.

TV crews descended on the Ciccanti home, where flowers were stacked against a plaster Madonna behind an ornate fence. Their reports, which led the news at six o'clock and again at eleven, featured an ID photo of a light-skinned black man with green eyes and a smattering of freckles across and around his nose. He was identified as Luther Addison, president of the Guardians Association, a fraternal organization for black cops.

No photos of the other three policemen at the scene, all of whom were white, were provided to media. By the following morning, when the *Post* ran the charmless picture on its front page, it was widely believed that Patrolman Addison shot young Ciccanti, though his department-issued Glock 19 hadn't been fired. The victim had been struck three times by rounds from a Cobra FS-32, a classical throw-down piece. Addison didn't carry one.

Two patrol cars had responded to the call to the UPS site, which sat on the Brooklyn-Queens border. One rolled from the 1-0-6 in Howard Beach, the other from the 7-5 in Brooklyn's East New York neighborhood.

Andy Hill, an oily, permanent-boil-on-his-butt cop, was behind the wheel of the car out of Howard Beach. The other car was driven by Joe Dalrymple, who graduated with Hill from the Academy when his "always by the book, college boy, Malcolm XYZ" partner was still in high school, back when W. E. Addison was walking a beat in oven-hot Crown Heights or directing traffic at JFK, yellow slicker doing little to ward off waves of freezing rain.

In a moment of candor, Dalrymple once told his young black partner that Andy Hill was an opportunist, and connected. "His pockets never don't jingle," he explained with a knowing wink.

Though they'd been all over the 7-5, Internal Affairs wanted him at 1PP. Addison knew there would be photographers—Mayor Koch was holding hands in Howard Beach and calling the black activist cop on the rug would play big—so to dodge the gauntlet, he took the R train to below City Hall, stayed underground, and entered One Police Plaza via its loading dock, where two Guardians Association members were in the doghouse, along with a redhead named Restovich who discharged his firearm into a Pac-Man machine at a bar in Bensonhurst.

IAD seemed surprised he looked so composed, his polyester blues pressed to a guillotine blade's edge.

Addison studied the stuffy, wood-paneled conference room as he dropped a manila envelope on the long table. He'd half expected they would do it in a box at the First Precinct, maybe cuff him to a soldered-on ring. The other half of his expectations was that this was all foolishness that would pass with an insincere apology after the real shooter was revealed.

"Luther Addison," he said, adding his badge number as he sat.

On the way in, he passed framed photos of President Reagan, Mayor Koch, and Commissioner McGuire, bracketed by the Stars and Stripes and the flag of the State of New York.

The two IAD detectives were white too.

"Where's your union rep?" asked Alderman.

"Maybe the Guardians don't provide a rep or a lawyer," said Zachary.

Addison looked at his wristwatch. "Eight seconds," he said. "Took you eight seconds to flip the card."

"Yeah, well, you knew Ciccanti was white when you shot him," Zachary said. He was good looking, boyish with sandy brown hair and crisp-cut jaw; an unlikely choice for the bad-cop role. Maybe he wasn't ready for any part of it: Slamming the Guardians confirmed IAD wasn't recording the interview.

"Check my ten card," Addison said. "I don't carry a Cobra."

Zachary, again: "You the kind of guy who puts everything on the ten card, Addison?"

"That's Officer Addison," he said sharply. "Given the topic, it's Officer Addison. And, yes, every gun I own is listed on my ten card."

"Hard case," Zachary muttered as he left his chair.

"Officer, we're just trying to piece it together," Alderman said, tapping his middle finger on an accordion folder. "I mean, it's a tough one, right?"

"It became tough when someone went to the media," Addison

replied. "You're going to have to undo that and face the cover-up charges."

"Not if we make you for it." Zachary.

"I don't throw down," Addison said. "I don't shoot unarmed kids."

"Says . . ."

"Anyone you interview."

"Long as he's black."

Addison shook his head and, quoting Reagan, said, "There you go again."

Alderman said, "You told your CO you didn't draw—"

"No I didn't. I drew," Addison said. "I didn't fire."

"The Glock," Zachary said, his back to the table.

Addison opened the manila envelope and withdrew a notarized document. He passed it to Alderman, who read it with care.

Hearing silence, Zachary turned and looked over his partner's shoulder. After a moment, he said, "What makes a man do something like this?"

"People like you," Addison replied.

"*Two* tests," Alderman muttered as he reread the report. "Overkill."

After the lengthy interview at the 7-5 following the Ciccanti shooting, Addison arranged for tests that proved he hadn't fired a gun, making him the first to use the resource at City College he proposed and helped develop for the Guardians.

"That's going to the press," Addison said, nodding.

"Why's that?" Alderman asked, suddenly agitated.

Addison slid the front page of this morning's *Post* from the envelope. "IAD set that in motion."

Someone inside NYPD told the *Post* the investigation would be guided by a respect for Office Addison's "civil rights," a phrase that meant one thing to blacks and another to certain whites, including many in Howard Beach.

The *Post* headline: "Where's My Brother's Civil Rights?" Nine-year-old Angela Ciccanti in her Saint Helen's uniform. Meanwhile, Fat Philly's crew and their families marched Cross Bay Boulevard, signs in fists, demanding the medical examiner release Ciccanti's body.

Alderman asked, "Got friends in the press, do you?"

Addison stared at Alderman's face, the blond mustache that didn't work, the clenching at the corners of his eyes. He was the one, not Zachary. Alderman wanted this black versus white, the easiest way for IAD to make it disappear.

"No friends in the press," Addison replied. But his wife's sister knew the principals at D. Parke Gibson Associates, an influential public relations firm. "We're just going to make certain that—"

"Who's 'we,' Addison?" Alderman asked sharply.

" 'We' is me and anyone in NYPD, the D.A.'s, and the Justice Department that wants to find out what happened to Little Flaps, who was breaking into the UPS depot last Thursday night with a Philips head, a box cutter, an Instamatic, and a duffel bag."

Alderman said, "The D.A. being your friend Sharon Knight. Sister is bucking for chief of the Homicide Bureau, isn't she?"

" *'Sister'?*" Addison held back a laugh.

Zachary put his palms on the table. "Officer," he said, "I'm guessing you know nothing you do is going to wash this away."

"And I'm thinking you've got two days, maybe three, to hook this where it belongs," Addison replied. "Once we get it off me, it'll go where it goes. Which could be IAD, could be the mayor's office, could be whoever shot the boy."

He looked at Alderman.

"A lot of heads for your plate, Detective," Addison said, "but the black one is up and leaving."

He sat back satisfied, the Guardians and Sharon Knight on his shoulder.

Alderman smiled dark as he leaned in.

"Let me tell you how *we* see it," he said. "Kid made you run your lazy black ass. Dalrymple told you to cool down, but you wouldn't have it, not after Flaps dropped a couple of N-bombs on you."

"Ciccanti was at least sixty feet—"

Alderman brought up his index finger. "You pull your throw down—hell, half the 7-5 will say you carried it—and you shot him. Three times. Then you stonewalled your CO, ran to your black-ass friends at City College to kick off the cover-up, and you went out and hired some PR firm to work the press. You'll ask the D.A.'s office to dump this on a white cop 'cause blue ain't good enough for you. You'll say anything to tear us down."

Addison stared at him.

"And that's the way it plays," Alderman said. "It's 1982 and you shot a white boy in Howard Beach. You know what's up and leaving, Officer? Your career, your freedom. Your freedom and your career."

Steele and August were at a table in the corner near the garbage bin and a stack of orange trays. They'd pretended they hadn't seen Lucy helping W. E. out of the cab on Ninth, leading him by the elbow and then hanging back as he made his way alone along the haphazard aisle of Formica tables and yellow plastic chairs. But when they stood to greet their old colleague, they nodded discreetly to her, gestures she returned with a pained smile.

"Mr. Man," August said with forced cheer. The stout, coffee-light-skinned man took Addison's hands in his. "Bony but beautiful."

Steele said, "W. E."

They waited until Addison angled into a seat.

"Started without me," W. E. said when his grimace subsided.

August had been dipping a finger into a small plastic cup of bar-becue sauce. "Never."

"Hammer tied you down?"

Henry Steele smiled.

Three men old before their time, though Steele, with his shaved head and impossible taut skin, looked like he might still be dogging the Genovese family's black lieutenants across Brooklyn and Queens. Cookie August, on the other hand, had put on twenty-five additional pounds since he left a stretch as the only black man in the Anti-Crime Unit. He was showing his age: The curly hair above his ears had gone from peppery gray to powder-wig white.

Good men, W. E. Addison knew, dedicated cops. Thank God nei-ther of them was on the clock with stage-three non-small-cell lung cancer that was no longer treatable by chemo or radiation.

Savoring the mesquite-wood scent, Addison looked toward the pit. Not quite noon, which meant Smokey's was still serving last night's ribs. The tender meat would fall off the bone.

"Same old?" August asked as he went for trays.

Addison nodded, knowing it might be the last time.

Luther Addison was on modified desk duty until someone leaked which phone he'd answer, so NYPD sent him home. After food shopping at Zabar's for his Giselle and their baby son, he rented a black Buick Century, waited until dark, and drove the Williamsburg Bridge to Myrtle Avenue, making his way to Howard Beach. The funeral home was on 159th Avenue.

Fat Philly was working the front door, shaking hands like he was running for office. Red shirt open at the collar under a black suit, heavy gold chain on his wrist, red carnation in his lapel, gray patent leather loafers: His idea of appropriately somber for the photographers and TV crews.

One of the Guardians out of the 1-13 in nearby Jamaica told him a snitch reported Fat Philly behind the scheme that landed Little Flaps in Bridges. Addison wondered if Philly was making some kind of move, knowing the TV lights would keep the real mobsters at bay.

To dodge a tail, Addison drove the Belt Parkway and over to Rockaway Boulevard to circle Aqueduct before doubling back to 159th. Then he did it again. And again, driving past the funeral home, using the mirrors to see who was coming and going.

Shortly after ten o'clock, he returned to find Fat Philly putting Mrs. Ciccanti and her daughter Angela in a limo; the fat man went inside, where he stayed even after the funeral home shut down. The crowd gone, Addison parked up the block and cut the engine.

His partner Joe Dalrymple arrived shortly before midnight.

Frowning in confusion, Addison took off his baseball cap and ran his hand across his close-cropped hair. Running no more than thirty feet behind him when a weapon was discharged, Dalrymple knew Addison hadn't taken down Little Flaps, and Addison was fairly sure Dalrymple, who'd bent left coming out of the patrol car, hadn't shot him either.

Then why a visit to pay respects, especially after the widowed mother had gone?

Sharon Knight said, "If he did it, if he's lying and playing us for fools, I'll take him down myself."

In the cafeteria at 100 Centre Street, white faces nodded. Who didn't know Knight was angling to become the first African American Homicide Bureau chief in the D.A.'s office? Breaking a black cop in Reagan's America would look good on her résumé.

She knew they'd think her ambition would help make it go away on that she'd allow it to land on Addison to curry favor with NYPD and the right-wing media. Maybe they figured they'd let her choose whether to bring it to the grand jury, and then they couldn't lose. If she got an indictment, fine. If she didn't, it'd be a public failure by an African American. Or worse, it'd been seen as a refusal by a black woman to bring a black cop to justice.

She didn't care what they thought as long as they turned over the files on Little Flaps and Fat Philly, and IAD's jackets on Hill and Dalrymple.

She told Luther Addison they would.

She didn't expect they'd be delivered by Sarah Tolchinsky, the Homicide Bureau's deputy chief.

Tolchinsky, a tall Hassid with skin that seemed translucent, appeared at Knight's cubicle and waved for her to follow. They returned to her office where musty blinds prevented a view of the Woolworth Building.

The files were on her desk. She'd requested them before she learned of Knight's interest. Twenty-nine years in the District Attorney's office allowed her to recognize an IAD cover-up the moment it began. The photo in the *Post* told her they saw Addison as an easy mark for a frame, a patsy.

"What's more important to you? Your career or seeing this through?" Tolchinsky asked, as she closed her door.

Knight suppressed an inadvertent grin.

"Your career. You're young. Fine," Tolchinsky waved, "but let's see if we can help you *and* him."

She allowed Knight to use the files at a table in the corner.

An hour or so later, lost in a confusing brief crafted by one of Knight's peers, Tolchinsky heard a voice.

"*Damn*," Knight repeated. She quickly double-checked the dates she'd scribbled on a yellow pad, and then stared at her boss.

"What?" Tolchinsky stood.

"I— *We've* got it," Knight replied, wisely.


Fat Philly was relegated to page seven of the *Post*, bounced from the front page when an oil truck flipped and burned on the George Washington Bridge.

"This guy's a moron," said August, tapping the paper.

Lucy Addison had put up coffee and sliced a pound cake her son brought.

W. E. wore a bathrobe over his pajamas. His stepson, in brown slacks and sienna turtleneck, sat in his mother's seat at the table in a sunny kitchen that could barely accommodate two.

Steele leaned against the refrigerator. "He said . . . ?"

"He told me not to worry," August replied. "About . . . ?"

August shrugged. "I shook his hand and told him it was a terrible thing. He said 'Don't worry. It's gonna be fine.' "

"Think he made you?" W. E. asked.

"You forget I'm half Sicilian," August said. "We spoke Italian."

Luther Addison managed a smile. The three old men came up through NYPD when black men comprised about two percent of the force. They knew how to use what little they had.

"As for you, Luther," August said, "you run about the worse sit I've ever seen." He reached for another slice of the pound cake. "I wouldn't be surprised if you turn up in some TV footage. Circling, circling . . ."

" 'It's gonna be fine,' " Hammer Steele repeated. "Meaning it falls on Luther?"

"Oh yeah. Especially since Joey Dalrymple showed up."

Steele looked down at Luther. "Your partner."

"And Andy Hill's running buddy since the Academy," August added.

"Andy Hill." The dark-skinned Steele grimaced his distaste.

W. E. watched his friends. Marrying Hill and Dalrymple told him they were building to something.

"Somebody says Hill's got history with Little Flaps," August said.

"Who?" W. E. asked, his voice frail.

"Hammer."

The Addison men turned to Henry Steele.

"The Genoveses say," said Steele, who tapped an old source. "Little Flaps Ciccanti ripped off Hill."

Luther let out a little cough. He said, "August 19, 1978. Aqueduct. Fat Philly's crew, including Flaps, took down fourteen hundred dollars from a sixty-nine-year-old man who hit the trifecta for the first time in his life. Same afternoon Andy Hill claimed someone stole his wife's mink out of the trunk of his car, which she parked at . . . Aqueduct."

"No coincidence," said August, who couldn't decide if he found Addison's thoroughness annoying or amusing.

W. E. said, "If the UPS facility in Howard Beach gets ripped off, the Feds will think the Gambinos backed it." He shook his head. "Fat Philly went to the Genoveses for protection?"

Steele nodded.

August said, "What a mook."

Steele turned to young Addison. "Stand down," he said. "This thing plays out. Fat Philly will flip any way he has to."

Addison hesitated.

"Go ahead," his stepfather whispered.

Leaning over his coffee cup, Luther Addison told them what else Knight delivered and how tests City College ran cleared him. "I think we can do this by the book," he added.

"Whose book?" August asked.

Rosemary Barone worked as a secretary at Christ Hospital, a sprawling brick complex across the Hudson in downtown Jersey City. Addison was told he'd find her sooner or later in sunlight, smoking two Newports at a time and cursing ex-husbands. Imagine a rusty nail come to life, Addison was advised. That's Rosemary Flanagan Hill Barone.

"Yeah, and?" she said when Addison identified himself. He wore a gray turtleneck under a forest green corduroy jacket with gray elbow patches.

He went gentle. Jersey City had a huge African American population and he was betting she didn't much like that: All the other smokers around her were white too. The black smokers were gathered at the curb maybe thirty feet away. "I was wondering if I might have a word . . ."

" 'Have a word'? One? What kind?"

The white smokers tittered, their condescension sprinkled with uncertainty and quavering defiance.

He said, "It's about your husband Andy."

"Tell me he's dead," she said, scowling under a blond bouffant some twenty years out of date.

"No, he's not—"

"*Not?* Wrong word."

"It's about your mink coat," Addison continued. "The one that was stolen at Aqueduct."

She let loose an ugly rattle Addison took for her laugh. "You think I look like I ever had a mink stole?"

"Andy said you did. He said you left in it your trunk—"

"I left a mink stole in the trunk of my car at the racetrack? Me?" She spit. "How much did he get for it?"

"The stole you never had?"

"From insurance, wise guy."

Addison replied, and then she started spewing.

Twenty-five minutes later, her supervisor came looking for her.

"Call me," she told Addison, as she followed the hardy black woman back inside. "I'm just getting started on that miserable pimple."

Addison shot up in bed, certain the ringing phone meant his stepfather had passed. But someone had gotten his unlisted number, which he'd given only to his family, the Guardians, a couple of college buddies, and NYPD. Racial epithets mixed with profanity told him where the caller got it.

Wrapped in a robe, he went to his chair in the living room and listened to the traffic below on Columbus Avenue, trying to quell his anger. One o'clock and he knew he wasn't going back to sleep. He checked on the baby, looked over the notes he made after talking to

Hill's ex, and then replayed the conversation he'd had with the old cops—the taciturn Steele, the jovial but vaguely dangerous August, and his stepfather, the reasoned, reliable W. E.

The original Guardians, he thought, as he started looking at it through their eyes.

No sense telling IAD or his CO what he'd learned about Hill.

Two hours later, he was knocking on Joe Dalrymple's apartment door.

"You shouldn't be here," Dalrymple said. Rousted from bed, he was wearing boxer shorts and a Yankees T-shirt.

Addison encouraged his partner to step onto his fourteenth-floor balcony, which overlooked downtown Forest Hills.

"Cut your losses while you can, Joe."

Dalrymple didn't know Addison had a temper. "I don't—"

Addison held up his hand.

"What?" Dalrymple said. "What do you think you know?"

"I know Andy Hill worked a deal with Fat Philly and held a grudge against Ciccanti."

"Oh. You *know*?" he sneered.

"Little Flaps jacked him in the Aqueduct lot, and he gave up eight hundred dollars."

"Never. Andy wouldn't give up a dime, especially if he was carrying."

Addison said, "Easier to get Fat Philly to return the eight hundred and then double dip through insurance."

"You don't—"

"And Hill lets Fat Philly stay in business as long as he kicks back."

Dalrymple frowned.

"We've seen his jacket, Joe. IAD looked at him. The insurance company called on the mink claim. He didn't tell you?"

Dalrymple hesitated. "Take it up with Andy," he said finally.

"Hill is tight with the Gambinos, and Fat Philly going to the Genoveses puts him in the middle. Maybe you too."

That was out-of-the air conjecture, but both cops knew Hill was dirty. Killing Fat Philly's Little Flaps told the Gambinos Hill was still their boy; at the same time, it kept Fat Philly's business in Hill's pocket.

As for setting up a fellow member of NYPD . . .

"Black man bothers you so much, Joe, you want to take his career?"

"Get lost."

"That's it, isn't it? Hate owns your soul, Joe."

"Listen to yourself," Dalrymple said. "Black this, black that, and I'm riding with you. You're a pain in the tail, Luther, and you don't get it. There's no room for you. None."

"In what? No room for me in what?"

Shivering in the late-night air, Dalrymple said, "Nobody's going to stand by and let it happen. NYPD ain't going equal opportunity, Luther. Your father knew to shut up, but you . . ." He stopped. "Hell, Luther, you know this."

"So I'm a killer, Joe? I killed that kid?"

"It is what it is—"

"Hill knows I'm riding with you," Addison said. "He remembers all the times you told him what I said. He figures two birds: He gets Ciccanti and you get rid of your partner—"

Suddenly, Addison's heart crashed, his stomach jolted, and he understood it as clear as if his stepfather had told him what had happened.

He grabbed Dalrymple and rushed him to the balcony's edge, bending him back over the rail.

"Luther!"

"Hill pulled the throw down to shoot me, didn't he?"

"Luther, wait—" Dalrymple was halfway into the night, dangling a few hundred feet above the concrete, parked cars, and prickly bushes below.

"I go down, you take out Ciccanti and the Cobra throw down winds up in his hand."

"For God's sake, Luther—"

"To kill off the Guardians," Addison barked. "To keep it— Say it's so."

"Luther, Jesus—"

"Say it!"

"Luther," he screamed, "Luther, yeah, all right. But I saved your life, Luther. Andy set you up. You and Ciccanti. Two dead, but when I heard, Luther—"

Addison spun his partner and tossed him to the balcony floor.

"Luther, listen. I told him, we can't shoot a cop. I told—I mean, I didn't want you *dead*." He scrambled to his feet. "I wanted you gone. Shut up, gone, not dead. You're ruining this good thing, you and your other nig—"

Addison stepped hard and slapped Dalrymple across the face. Panting, he stared as his partner crashed into the sliding-glass window and tumbled back into the apartment, pulling a curtain off its rods.

"That story about Hill and Little Flaps at the track back in '78 is in this morning's *Times*," Addison said. "So you have a choice. You call IAD now and make good. Or you take a few steps back and get a running start on a dive off this balcony."

Dalrymple stared up at Addison, who glowered, spittle flying with each word, chest heaving.

As Dalrymple crawled backward toward his bed, Addison said, "Pick up the phone, Joe. Pick it up before I think better of it and toss you off the balcony myself."


Steele and August couldn't decide, so they both went, and they found Fat Philly solo in a booth in a diner on Cross Bay Boulevard.

Little Flaps Ciccanti's funeral mass at Saint Helen's was due to begin in two hours.

"What?"

Steele and August knew how to walk it so no badge was required. They eased in across from Fat Philly, his three eggs over easy and home fries in marinara sauce.

Luther told them Flaps was carrying an Instamatic, so they knew the kid went in for more than he could carry in a duffel bag.

"The Gambinos can't decide whether to pull off your head first or just stick it up your butt while it's still on your shoulders," August said.

"As for the Genovese family . . ." Steele had learned it was often better to let a worm's imagination complete his sentences.

"Andy Hill is talking," August said. It wasn't true—W. E.'s kid said it was Dalrymple who rolled over—but a plausible lie well told was at least as good as fact. "You want the Genoveses to back your move on the Gambinos' turf, and they're supposed to do it for a couple hundred Gs' worth of mink stoles?"

"You don't know what you're talking about," Fat Philly scoffed as he pushed a butter-laden piece of toast into a yolk. "Flaps was on his own, looking for baseball cards or something. Who don't know that?"

"Flaps cases the plant and he can keep anything he can carry," Steele said. "You and the crew go back a couple days later when everyone relaxes. At least that's what you told the Genoveses: UPS is moving stoles—sable, lynx, and upper-end mink from Russia and Finland."

"You got nothing," Fat Philly said unconvincingly. "Mink stoles, Russia . . ."

"You believe they won't hit you in church," Steele asked.

"Who?" Fat Philly said.

"That is the question, isn't it?" Steele.

"No, I mean who is—"

August said, "Both. They'll kill you twice."

"Or three times," Steele added. "Once the Ciccantis find out you tipped Hill that Little Flaps was alone."

"Whoa. You're saying I set up Flaps—"

August said, "You set up Flaps. Yeah."

Fat Philly slammed his palm on the table, sending coffee over the cup's side. "I knew it. I knew it," he said. "This is our thing, not your thing. *Our* th—"

Without breaking eye contact, August drove a fork an inch into the back of Fat Philly's hand.

Handcuffed and perp-walked. Andy Hill's photo was on the front page of the *News*. The *Post* had turned its attention to a meeting between Reagan and the pope.

Addison drove out to Cambria Heights, retrieved his stepfather, and brought him all but round-trip. He had considered taking him late to a jazz club, the Vanguard, maybe, or Sweet Basil's, but they were both tired of being the only black men in the room minus the musicians on the bandstand. He wanted their time together to be nothing but contentment. So back to Smokey's.

Over fall-off-the-bone ribs, W. E. Addison said, "Luther, it's time for me to say good-bye to my grandson."

Addison tapped his stepfather's hand. "I know, Pop. Next stop." Once again, he tried to make it light. "First we've got to wipe that barbecue sauce off your face."

The old man looked at his stepson, who he couldn't have loved more had he been his own blood. His tired old heart still swelled from the pride of knowing he could do right by him one last time.

They sat quiet, surrounded by the chatter of students and suits on hand for an early lunch. W. E. sipped tart lemonade from tall Styrofoam.

"Got what you need, Pop?" He hadn't told him about Hill's murderous plan. Steele might've figured it, since he told him to stand down, but there was no reason for W. E. to know there were cops who wanted his stepson dead.

But W. E. knew, of course he did. Same as it ever was.

"It's a good thing, son. The Guardians. If a man like you is at the top."

Luther tilted his head. He'd begun to think otherwise—Dalrymple told him his advocacy put a wall between the two of them when they should've worked to be as close as any two partners; and Sarah Tolchinsky, white and a devout Jew, chaperoned his cause through the D.A.'s office. Sharon Knight said Tolchinsky was the one who made the call to the mayor's office to set him straight.

Hell, even Steele's snitch was white.

"Pop," Addison sighed, "I'm thinking I've got to look deep before I decide."

"You get yourself good people like Hammer and Cookie and you'll be all right."

As Luther Addison nodded, W. E. ran a paper napkin across his lips, hiding from his stepson a smile of everlasting satisfaction.

# I KILLED

## By Nancy Pickard

Nancy Pickard, creator of the Jenny Cain series and the Marie Lightfoot series, has won Agatha, Anthony, Barry, Shamus, and Macavity awards. She is a four-time Edgar Award nominee, most recently for her novel *The Virgin of Small Plains*, which was named a Notable Kansas Book of 2006. Several of her stories have appeared in previous editions of the year's best mystery and suspense. She lives in the Kansas City area.

W hen the second man sat down, the green metal park bench groaned and sank into the dirt. He took the left side, leaving a polite foot and a half between his arthritic, spreading hips and the wide hips of the man leaning on the armrest on the other side of the bench.

They glanced at each other. Nodded heavily, like two old bulls acknowledging one another's right to be there. Then they turned their beefy faces back to the view. Each man inhaled deeply, as if his worn-out senses could still detect the burnt-grass, baked-dirt scent of autumn.

They both wore baggy gym suits that looked as if nobody had ever run in them.

Behind them stretched an expanse of golden grass, and then the elegance of Fifty-fifth Street. On the opposite side of Fifty-fifth, the big windows of large, well-maintained houses looked out over the same beautiful vista the two men faced. In front of them, there was a cement path, then trees, then the golden-green, rolling acreage of Jacob L. Loose Park. If they'd hoisted their aching bodies up, and limped to the right, they'd have come to a pond where swans paddled in bad-tempered glory all summer, but which Canada geese owned now that it was late November. If they'd hobbled left, instead, they'd have come to tennis courts, wading pool, rose garden, playground. Mansions and high-rise, high-priced condos ringed the big park in the middle of Kansas City, Missouri. To the north was a private school, then the Country Club Plaza shopping center; to the south were the neighborhoods of Brookside, Waldo, and a short drive to the suburbs.

It was a tranquil, wealthy, civilized scene in the heart of the city.

The man on the right side of the bench said, in a voice made gravelly from time and the cigars he no longer smoked, "You come here often?"

After a long moment, as if he hadn't much liked being spoken to and was considering ignoring it, the second man said, "No."

His voice sounded as if he, too, had been a heavy smoker in his day.

"I do." The first man coughed, deep, racking, phlegmy. "I come here every day." When he was finished hacking, he said, without apologizing for the spasm, "This bench, every afternoon, regular as clockwork."

"That right." His bench companion looked away, sounding bored.

"Yes, it is. You know the history of this park?"

"History?" Now the second man looked where the first man was pointing him, with a finger that looked like a fat, manicured sausage. He saw a black cannon, a pyramid of cannonballs, and what looked like a semicircle of signs for tourists. "No, I don't know it."

*And don't care to,* his tone implied.

"This was the scene of the last big Missouri battle in the Civil War. October twenty-third, 1864. The Feds had chased the Rebs all across the state from Saint Louis, but the Rebs kept getting away. Finally, they took a stand here. Right here, in this spot. Picture it. It was cold, not like today. They were tired, hungry. There was a Confederate general right here, where that big old tree is. It's still called the General's Tree. His graycoats were standing here, cannons facing across the green. Then the bluecoats suddenly came charging up over that rise, horses on the run, sabers glinting, guns blazing."

He paused, but there was no response.

"Thirty thousand men in the battle that day."

Again, he paused, and again there was no response.

"There was a mass grave dug afterwards, only a few blocks west of here."

Finally, the second man said, "That right?"

A corner of the historian's mouth quirked up. "Mass graves always get people's attention. Saddam would still be alive without 'em. You just can't kill too many people without somebody noticing."

"Who won?"

"Feds, of course. Battle of Westport." Abruptly, he changed the subject. "So what'd you do?"

"What did I *do*?"

The question rumbled out like thunder from a kettledrum.

"Yeah. Before you got here to this park bench. I'm assuming you're retired. You look around my age. You'll pardon my saying so, but we both got that look of being twenty years older than maybe we are. And not to mention, you're sitting here in the middle of a weekday afternoon, like me."

"Almost."

"Almost what? My age, or retired?"

"Both, probably."

"I figured. You always think so long before you speak?"

There was a moment's silence which seemed to confirm it, and then, "Sometimes."

"Well, retire quick, is my advice. I was a salesman."

The other man finally looked over at him, but skeptically. A slight breeze picked up a few strands of his thin hair, dyed black, and waved it around like insect antennae before releasing it to fall back onto his pale skull again.

"You weren't," he said, flatly.

"Yeah, I was. I don't look it, I know. You expect somebody smooth-looking, somebody in a nice suit, not some fat goombah in a baby blue nylon gym suit. Baby blue. My daughter picked it out. Appearances are deceiving. I don't go to any gym, either. But ask anybody who knows me, they'll tell you, I was a salesman."

"If you say so."

"I do say so. So what were you? In your working days?"

Instead of answering, his park bench companion smiled for the first time, a crooked arrangement at one corner of his mouth. "Were you good at selling stuff?"

"You look like you think that's funny. It's serious, the sales business, and supporting your family. Serious stuff. Yeah, I was good. How about you?"

"I killed."

"No kidding. Doing what?"

The other man placed his left arm over the back of the park bench. His big chest rose and fell as he inhaled, then exhaled, through his large, pockmarked nose. "Let me think how to put this," he said, finally, in his rumbling voice. "I never know what to tell people. You'd think I'd have an answer by now." He was silent for a few moments. "Okay. I was a performance artist, you might say."

"Really. I'm not sure what that is. Comedian?"

"Sometimes."

"No kidding! Where'd you appear?"

"Anywhere they paid me."

"Ha. I know how that is. Would I have heard of you?"

"You might. I hope not."

"You didn't want to be *famous*?"

"Hell no." For the first time, the answer came fast. "That's the last thing I'd ever want."

"But—"

"Fame can be . . . confining."

"I get you." The first man nodded, his big, fleshy face looking sage. "Paparazzi, and all that. Can't go anyplace without having flash-bulbs go off in your face."

"I hate cameras of any kind. Don't want none of them around, no."

"Imagine if reporters had been here *that* day . . ."

"What day?"

"The Battle of Westport."

"Oh."

"Embedded with the troops, like in Iraq. Interviews with the generals. Shots of the wounded. What a mess."

"And no TVs to show it on."

The first man let out a laugh, a booming *ha*. "That's right."

His companion took them back to their other topic, as if he'd warmed up to it. "Lotsa people with lotsa money aren't famous. You'd be surprised. They're rich as Bill Gates, and nobody's ever heard of them."

"I wouldn't be so surprised."

"Yeah, probably not. You look like a wise guy."

"You wouldn't think I was so wise, not if you'd ask my son."

"What's the matter with him?" The second man was talking faster now, now that he was asking questions, instead of answering them. They were getting into a rhythm, a pace, a patter. "He think you're an idiot?"

"He says I'm a fool, ought to mind my own business."

"But you retired from that, didn't you?"

"From what?"

"Minding your own business."

That earned another explosive *ha*, followed by some coughing. "That's right, I did."

"So the only business you got left to mind is his."

"Ha! You're right. That's pretty funny."

"But he doesn't think so. Your son, he's not so amused by you?"

"A serious guy, my son." The man in the baby blue gym suit sniffed, the corners of his mouth dropped into a frown. He settled his body more heavily into the bench. If he still smoked, it was a moment when he'd have puffed reflectively, resentfully, on his cigar. After a moment, he pulled himself up and alert again. "So. Tell me. You make any money being a comedian who didn't want to get famous?"

"I made plenty."

"Clubs?"

"I did some of those. And private jobs."

"That's how you got to know the rich people who aren't famous?"

"Some were famous. Some got famous after I met them. I'd see their pictures and their names in the papers."

"Those ones—they ever call you again after they got famous?"

"No." He smiled slightly. "They were beyond me by then."

"Really. Stupid shits. People get big heads, that's what fame'll do. They think they're too good—"

"They're dead to me now." He smiled to himself again, as at a private joke.

"Sure. So what was your act?"

"My act?" He frowned.

"Your shtick. You know, your routine."

"I didn't have no set routine. That's dangerous, to be too predictable like that. You don't want people to know what's coming, you want to keep your edge, keep *them* on edge, so you take them by surprise, startle them, come at them out of the blue where they're not expecting it. It's intimidating that way. You shock 'em. Knock 'em off balance and never let 'em get back up straight again. Then you just keep knocking 'em down—"

"Knockin' the jokes down—"

"Until they're bent over, pleading and gasping for you to stop, 'cause it hurts so bad."

"Been a long time since I laughed like that. That's as good as sex. If I recall."

The second man smiled at that. "Yeah, it's real satisfying. I guess you'd say I have a talent for shocking people. And for improvisation."

"Like George Carlin? Or that black kid with the mouth on him, Chris Rock? Not everybody can get away with stuff like that."

"I've gotten away with it for a long time."

"Good for you. So that was your act? Improv?"

"Sometimes. It varied."

"Depended on the venue, I suppose. You're smiling. Did I say something naive?"

"No, no, you're right. A lot depends on the venue, whether it's in the open air—like this, like a park, for instance. Or maybe it's inside. Could be a great big room, even as big as a stadium, or could be as small as a bathroom. Size of the audience makes a difference, too, now that you mention it, now that you've got me talking about it. Some things will go over well in a big crowd that are just overkill when there's nobody around. And vice versa. That was part of the improvisation."

"You get hecklers?"

"If I did, I took them out."

"Pretty good audiences, though?"

"I had very attentive audiences. Very."

"What's your secret?"

"You want to get their full attention immediately. Don't give them any time to adjust to your appearance. Hit 'em upside the head."

"A big joke right off the bat, huh?"

"A two-by-four. A baseball bat. *Bam*. Get their undivided attention. I'm not a subtle guy."

"Pretty broad comedy, huh?"

"Pretty broad . . . there was one of those in Pittsburgh."

"Ha ha. Vaudeville, like. Slapstick. That you?"

"Slapstick. I coulda used one of those."

"Ha ha. Borscht belt comedy. You Jewish?"

"Me? No way. I was circumspect, not circumcised."

"Ha! You're a wise guy, too."

"That I am."

"What about costumes? You ever wear costumes?"

"Yeah. Hairpieces. Teeth. Mustaches. Canes, crutches. I got a closet full of them, or I would have if I'd kept any of it."

"Your own mother wouldn't have recognized you?"

"My mother's dead."

"Oh, I'm sorry."

"It was a long time ago. I killed her, too."

"That's nice, that she appreciated your humor. Your dad, you get your funny bone from him?"

"Oh, yeah, he was hilarious." It sounded bitter, as if there was jealousy. "He killed me. Nearly."

"Is that unusual?"

"What?"

"A comic from a happy family? I thought all comedians came from bad families, like they had to laugh to keep from cryin', that kind of thing."

"I don't know about that."

"Not much of a philosopher, like you're not much of a historian?"

"Hey." Defensive. "When I was workin', I knew what I believed, and what I didn't. That's philosophy, ain't it?"

"Like, what did you believe?"

"I believed in doing my job, and not cryin' over it."

"Me, too."

"That right?"

"Yeah, do your job and fuck the regrets."

"Or fuck the pretty broads in Pittsburgh."

"I think maybe we're kind of alike, you and me."

"A salesman and a comedian."

"You still don't buy it that I was a salesman, do you?"

"You said it yourself, you don't look the part."

"I look the part as much as you look like a comedian."

"You bought it. Askin' me all about it."

"I was sellin' you. You think I'm no salesman, but I sold people down the river all the time. But you already know that, don't you? What? Gone silent again? Nothin' to say? So who sent you? One of those wise guys I ratted out? My son? Somebody else in the Family? And where's your two-by-four? You got a reputation for takin' 'em by surprise, knocking 'em flat first thing, you said so yourself. So why the conversation first before you take me out?"

"The conversation was your idea."

"What about the two-by-four?"

"Not as quick as the gun in my pocket."

"What about the noise?"

"Silencer."

"Witnesses?"

They both looked around, both of them taking note of the two young women with baby carriages over by the historical markers, of the middle-aged male jogger moving their way from the west, of the young couple leaning up against a tree.

"Witnesses to what? I get up and stand in front of you to continue our conversation. You slump over, but nobody sees past me. I grab your shoulder to say good-bye. When I leave, you're an old man in a baby-blue tracksuit, asleep on a park bench, and I'm an old man walkin' back to my car."

"And then what?"

"Then you go to hell. I go home and retire."

"You're retiring, all right. See this wire on my baby blue jacket? And see those young women and that jogger coming our way? They're FBI. If you looked behind you, you'd see a few more, including a sniper in the bedroom window of that nice house back there. He's aiming at your head, so don't think you can take a shot at mine. I just made my last sale, Mr. Comedian. And you're the product."

He stood up, slowly, heavily, and then turned and looked down at the fat man with the gun in his pocket.

"You should have paid more attention to history when I was trying to tell you.

"You want to know why the Confederates lost? Because the greedy fuckers stole a farmer's old gray mare, which pissed him off, and so he told the Feds where they could sneak over that ridge." He pointed north and a little west, as the first two agents laid hands on the shoulders of the other man. "It took the Rebs completely by surprise. Then they got surrounded, and they never had a chance." The agents hoisted his audience to his feet. "Just like you were going to steal my life, which pissed me off, so I told the Feds how to sneak up on you, so they could surround you, and you wouldn't stand a chance. You know the old song? 'The old gray mare, she ain't what she used to be'? Your life and mine, they ain't what they used to be, but my life is still mine." He banged his meaty right thumb on his chest. "I'm hanging on to it, like that farmer and his old gray mare.

"You know what they say about history," he called out, raising his voice to make sure the other man heard as they led him away. "If you don't pay attention to it, you're bound to repeat it!"

# SUBSTITUTIONS
*By Kristine Kathryn Rusch*

Kristine Kathryn Rusch is an award-winning mystery, science fiction, romance, and mainstream author. Her latest mystery novel, written as Kris Nelscott, is *Days of Rage*. Her latest science fiction novel is a mystery called *The Recovery Man*. To find out more about her, look at her website, www.kristinekathrynrusch.com.

S ilas sat at the blackjack table, a plastic glass of whiskey in his left hand, and a small pile of hundred-dollar chips in his right. His banjo rested against his boot, the embroidered strap wrapped around his calf. He had a pair of aces to the dealer's six, so he split them—a thousand dollars riding on each—and watched as she covered them with the expected tens.

He couldn't lose. He'd been trying to all night. The casino was empty except for five gambling addicts hunkered over the blackjack table, one old woman playing slots with the rhythm of an assembly worker, and one young man in black leather who was getting drunk at the casino's sorry excuse for a bar. The employees showed no sign of holiday cheer: no happy holiday pins, no little Santa hats, only the stark black and white of their uniforms against the casino's fading glitter.

He had chosen the Paradise because it was one of the few remaining fifties-style casinos in Nevada, still thick with flocked wallpaper and cigarette smoke, craps tables worn by dice and elbows, and the roulette wheel creaking with age. It was also only a few hours from Reno, and in thirty hours, he would have to make the tortuous drive up there. Along the way, he would visit an old man who had a bad heart; a young girl who would cross the road at the wrong time and meet an oncoming semi; and a baby boy who was born with his lungs not yet fully formed. Silas also suspected a few surprises along the way; nothing was ever as it seemed any longer. Life was moving too fast, even for him.

But he had Christmas Eve and Christmas Day off, the two days he had chosen when he had been picked to work Nevada 150 years before. In those days, he would go home for Christmas, see his friends, spend time with his family. His parents welcomed him, even though they didn't see him for most of the year. He felt like a boy again, like someone cherished and loved, instead of the drifter he had become.

All of that stopped in 1878. December 26, 1878. He wasn't yet sophisticated enough to know that the day was a holiday in England. Boxing Day. Not quite appropriate, but close.

He had to take his father that day. The old man had looked pale and tired throughout the holiday, but no one thought it serious. When he took to his bed Christmas night, everyone had simply thought him tired from the festivities.

It was only after midnight, when Silas got his orders, that he knew what was coming next. He begged off—something he had never tried before (he wasn't even sure who he had been begging with)—but had received the feeling (that was all he ever got: a firm feeling, so strong he couldn't avoid it) that if he didn't do it, death would come another way—from Idaho or California or New Mexico. It would come another way, his father would be in agony for days, and the end, when it came, would be uglier than it had to be.

Silas had taken his banjo to the old man's room. His mother slept on her side, like she always had, her back to his father. His father's eyes had opened, and he knew. Somehow he knew.

They always did.

Silas couldn't remember what he said. Something—a bit of an apology, maybe, or just an explanation: *You always wanted to know what I did.* And then, the moment. First he touched his father's forehead, clammy with the illness that would claim him, and then Silas said, "You wanted to know why I carry the banjo," and strummed.

But the sound did not soothe his father like it had so many before him. As his spirit rose, his body struggled to hold it, and he looked at Silas with such a mix of fear and betrayal that Silas still saw it whenever he thought of his father.

The old man died, but not quickly and not easily, and Silas tried to resign, only to get sent to the place that passed for headquarters, a small shack that resembled an out-of-the-way railroad terminal. There, a man who looked no more than thirty but who had to be three hundred or more, told him that the more he complained, the longer his service would last.

Silas never complained again, and he had been on the job for 150 years. Almost 55,000 days spent in the service of Death, with only Christmas Eve and Christmas off, tainted holidays for a man in a tainted position.

He scooped up his winnings, piled them on his already-high stack of chips, and then placed his next bet. The dealer had just given him a queen and a jack when a boy sat down beside him.

"Boy" wasn't entirely accurate. He was old enough to get into the casino. But he had rain on his cheap jacket, and hair that hadn't been cut in a long time. iPod headphones stuck out of his breast pocket, and he had a cell phone against his hip the way that old sheriffs used to wear their guns.

His hands were callused and the nails had dirt beneath them. He looked tired, and a little frightened.

He watched as the dealer busted, then set chips in front of Silas and the four remaining players. Silas swept the chips into his stack, grabbed five of the hundred-dollar chips, and placed the bet.

The dealer swept her hand along the semicircle, silently asking the players to place their bets.

"You Silas?" the boy asked. He hadn't put any money on the table or placed any chips before him.

Silas sighed. Only once before had someone interrupted his Christmas festivities—if festivities was what the last century plus could be called.

The dealer peered at the boy. "You gonna play?"

The boy looked at her, startled. He didn't seem to know what to say.

"I got it." Silas put twenty dollars in chips in front of the boy.

"I don't know . . ."

"Just do what I tell you," Silas said.

The woman dealt, face-up. Silas got an ace. The boy, an eight. The woman dealt herself a ten. Then she went around again. Silas got his twenty-one—his weird holiday luck holding—but the boy got another eight.

"Split them," Silas said.

The boy looked at him, his fear almost palpable.

Silas sighed again, then grabbed another twenty in chips, and placed it next to the boy's first twenty.

"Jeez, mister, that's a lot of money," the boy whispered.

"Splitting," Silas said to the dealer.

She separated the cards and placed the bets behind them. Then she dealt the boy two cards—a ten and another eight.

The boy looked at Silas. Looked like the boy had peculiar luck as well.

"Split again," Silas said, more to the dealer than to the boy. He added the bet, let her separate the cards, and watched as she dealt the boy two more tens. Three eighteens. Not quite as good as Silas's twenties to twenty-ones, but just as statistically uncomfortable.

The dealer finished her round, then dealt herself a three, then a nine, busting again. She paid in order. When she reached the boy, she set sixty dollars in chips before him, each in its own twenty-dollar pile.

"Take it," Silas said.

"It's yours," the boy said, barely speaking above a whisper.

"I gave it to you."

"I don't gamble," the boy said.

"Well, for someone who doesn't gamble, you did pretty well. Take your winnings."

The boy looked at them as if they'd bite him. "I . . ."

"Are you leaving them for the next round?" the dealer asked.

The boy's eyes widened. He was clearly horrified at the very thought. With shaking fingers, he collected the chips, then leaned into Silas. The boy smelled of sweat and wet wool.

"Can I talk to you?" he whispered.

Silas nodded, then cashed in his chips. He'd racked up ten thousand dollars in three hours. He wasn't even having fun at it anymore. He liked losing, felt that it was appropriate—part of the game, part of his life—but the losses had become fewer and farther between the more he played.

The more he lived. A hundred years ago, there were women and a few adopted children. But watching them grow old, helping three of them die, had taken the desire out of that, too.

"Mr. Silas," the boy whispered.

"If you're not going to bet," the dealer said, "please move so someone can have your seats."

People had gathered behind Silas, and he hadn't even noticed. He really didn't care tonight. Normally, he would have noticed anyone around him—noticed who they were, how and when they would die.

"Come on," he said, gathering the bills the dealer had given him. The boy's eyes went to the money like a hungry man's went to food. His one hundred and twenty dollars remained on the table, and Silas had to remind him to pick it up.

The boy used a forefinger and a thumb to carry it, as if it would burn him.

"At least put it in your pocket," Silas snapped.

"But it's yours," the boy said.

"It's a damn gift. Appreciate it."

The boy blinked, then stuffed the money into the front of his unwashed jeans. Silas led him around banks and banks of slot machines, all pinging and ponging and making little musical come-ons, to the steakhouse in the back.

The steakhouse was the reason Silas came back year after year. The place opened at five, closed at three A.M., and served the best steaks in Vegas. They weren't arty or too small. One big slab of meat, expensive cut, charred on the outside and red as Christmas on the inside. Beside the steak they served french-fried onions, and sides that no self-respecting Strip restaurant would prepare—creamed corn, au gratin potatoes, popovers—the kind of stuff that Silas always associated with the modern Las Vegas—modern, to him, meaning 1950s–1960s Vegas. Sin city. A place for grownups to gamble and smoke and drink and have affairs. The Vegas of Sinatra and the mob, not the Vegas of Steve Wynn and his ilk, who prettified everything and made it all seem upscale and oh-so-right.

Silas still worked Vegas a lot more than any other Nevada city, which made sense, considering how many millions of people lived there now, but millions of people lived all over. Even sparsely settled Nevada, one of the least populated states in the Union, had ten full-time Death employees. They tried to unionize a few years ago, but Silas, with the most seniority, refused to join. Then they tried to limit the routes—one would get Reno, another Sparks, another Elko and that region, and a few would split Vegas—but Silas wouldn't agree to that either.

He loved the travel part of the job. It was the only part he still liked, the ability to go from place to place to place, see the changes, understand how time affected everything.

Everything except him.

The maitre d' sat them in the back, probably because of the boy. Even in this modern era, where people wore blue jeans to funerals, this steakhouse preferred its customers in a suit and tie.

The booth was made of wood and rose so high that Silas couldn't see anything but the boy and the table across from them. A single lamp reflected against the wall, revealing cloth napkins and real silver utensils.

The boy stared at them with the same kind of fear he had shown at the blackjack table. "I can't."

The maitre d' gave them leather-bound menus, said something about a special, and then handed Silas a wine list. Silas ordered a bottle of burgundy. He didn't know a lot about wines, just that the more expensive ones tasted a lot better than the rest of them. So he ordered the most expensive burgundy on the menu.

The maitre d' nodded crisply, almost militarily, and then left. The boy leaned forward.

"I can't stay. I'm your substitute."

Silas smiled. A waiter came by with a bread basket—hard rolls, still warm—and relish trays filled with sliced carrots, celery, and radishes, and candied beets, things people now would call old-fashioned.

Modern, to him. Just as modern as always.

The boy squirmed, his jeans squeaking on the leather booth.

"I know," Silas said. "You'll be fine."

"I got—"

"A big one, probably," Silas said. "It's Christmas Eve. Traffic, right? A shooting in a church? Too many suicides?"

"No," the boy said, distressed. "Not like that."

"When's it scheduled for?" Silas asked. He really wanted his dinner, and he didn't mind sharing it. The boy looked like he needed a good meal.

"Tonight," the boy said. "No specific time. See?"

He put a crumpled piece of paper between them, but Silas didn't pick it up.

"Means you have until midnight," Silas said. "It's only seven. You can eat."

"They said at orientation—"

Silas had forgotten; they all got orientation now. The expectations of generations. He'd been thrown into the pool feet first, fumbling his way for six months before someone told him that he could actually ask questions.

"—the longer you wait, the more they suffer."

Silas glanced at the paper. "If it's big, it's a surprise. They won't suffer. They'll just finish when you get there. That's all."

The boy bit his lip. "How do you know?"

Because he'd had big. He'd had grisly. He'd had disgusting. He'd overseen more deaths than the boy could imagine.

The head waiter arrived, took Silas's order, and then turned to the boy.

"I don't got money," the boy said.

"You have one hundred and twenty dollars," Silas said. "But I'm buying, so don't worry."

The boy opened the menu, saw the prices, and closed it again. He shook his head.

The waiter started to leave when Silas stopped him. "Give him what I'm having. Medium well."

Since the kid didn't look like he ate many steaks, he wouldn't like his rare. Rare was an acquired taste, just like burgundy wine and the cigar that Silas wished he could light up. Not everything in the modern era was an improvement.

"You don't have to keep paying for me," the kid said.

Silas waved the waiter away, then leaned back. The back of the booth, made of wood, was rigid against his spine. "After a while in this business," he said, "money is all you have."

The kid bit his lower lip. "Look at the paper. Make sure I'm not screwing up. Please."

But Silas didn't look.

"You're supposed to handle all of this on your own," Silas said gently.

"I know," the boy said. "I know. But this one, he's scary. And I don't think anything I do will make it right."

After he finished his steak and had his first sip of coffee, about the time he would have lit up his cigar, Silas picked up the paper. The boy had devoured the steak like he hadn't eaten in weeks. He ate all the bread and everything from his relish tray.

He was very, very new.

Silas wondered how someone that young had gotten into the death business, but he was determined not to ask. It would be some variation on his own story. Silas had begged for the life of his wife who should have died in the delivery of their second child. Begged, and begged, and begged, and somehow, in his befogged state, he actually saw the woman whom he then called the Angel of Death.

Now he knew better—none of them were angels, just working stiffs waiting for retirement—but then, she had seemed perfect and terrifying, all at the same time.

He'd asked for his wife, saying he didn't want to raise his daughters alone.

The angel had tilted her head. "Would you die for her?"

"Of course," Silas said.

"Leaving her to raise the children alone?" the angel asked.

His breath caught. "Is that my only choice?"

She shrugged, as if she didn't care. Later, when he reflected, he realized she didn't know.

"Yes," he said into her silence. "She would raise better people than I will. She's good. I'm . . . not."

He wasn't bad, he later realized, just lost, as so many were. His wife had been a God-fearing woman with strict ideas about morality. She had raised two marvelous girls, who became two strong women, mothers of large broods who all went on to do good works. In that, he hadn't been wrong. But his wife hadn't remarried either, and she had cried for him for the rest of her days.

They had lived in Texas. He had made his bargain, got assigned Nevada, and had to swear never to head east, not while his wife and children lived. His parents saw him, but they couldn't tell anyone. They thought he ran out on his wife and children, and oddly, they had supported him in it. Remnants of his family still lived. Great-grand-children generations removed. He still couldn't head east, and he no longer wanted to.

Silas touched the paper, and it burned his fingers. A sign, a warning, a remembrance that he wasn't supposed to work these two days. Two days out of an entire year. He slid the paper back to the boy. "I can't open it. I'm not allowed. You tell me."

So the boy did.

And Silas, in wonderment that they had sent a rookie into a situation a veteran might not be able to handle, settled his tab, took the boy by the arm, and led him into the night.

Every city has pockets of evil. Vegas had fewer than most, despite the things the television lied about. So many people worked in law enforcement or security, so many others were bonded so that they could work in casinos or high-end jewelry stores or banks that Vegas' serious crime was lower than most comparable cities of its size.

Silas appreciated that. Most of the time, it meant that the deaths he attended in Vegas were natural or easy or just plain silly. He got a lot of silly deaths in that city. Some he even found time to laugh over.

But not this one.

As they drove from the very edge of town, past the rows and rows of similar houses, past the stink and desperation of complete poverty, he finally asked, "How long've you been doing this?"

"Six months," the boy said softly, as if that were forever.

Silas looked at him, looked at the young face reflecting the Christmas lights that filled the neighborhood, and shook his head. "All substitutes?"

The boy shrugged. "They didn't have any open routes."

"What about the guy you replaced?"

"He'd been subbing, waiting to retire. They say you could retire, too, but you show no signs of it. Working too hard, even for a younger man."

He wasn't older. He was the same age he had been when his wife struggled with her labor—a breech birth that would be no problem in 2006, but had been deadly if not handled right in 1856. The midwife's hands hadn't been clean—not that anyone knew better in those days—and the infection had started even before the baby got turned.

He shuddered, that night alive in him. The night he'd made his bargain.

"I don't work hard," he said. "I work less than I did when I started."

The boy looked at him, surprised. "Why don't you retire?"

"And do what?" Silas asked. He hadn't planned to speak up. He normally shrugged off that question.

"I dunno," the boy said. "Relax. Live off your savings. Have a family again."

They could all have families again when they retired. Families and a good, rich life, albeit short. Silas would age when he retired. He would age and have no special powers. He would watch a new wife die in childbirth and not be able to see his former colleague sitting beside the bed. He would watch his children squirm after a car accident, blood on their faces, knowing that they would live poorly if they lived at all, and not be able to find out the future from the death dealer hovering near the scene.

Better to continue. Better to keep this half-life, this half-future, time without end.

"Families are overrated," Silas said. They look at you with betrayal and loss when you do what was right.

But the boy didn't know that yet. He didn't know a lot.

"You ever get scared?" the boy asked.

"Of what?" Silas asked. Then gave the standard answer. "They can't kill you. They can't harm you. You just move from place to place, doing your job. There's nothing to be scared of."

The boy grunted, sighed, and looked out the window.

Silas knew what he had asked, and hadn't answered it. Of course he got scared. All the time. And not of dying—even though he still wasn't sure what happened to the souls he freed. He wasn't scared of that, or of the people he occasionally faced down, the drug addicts with their knives, the gangsters with their guns, the wannabe outlaws with blood all over their hands.

No, the boy had asked about the one thing to be afraid of, the one thing they couldn't change.

Was he scared of being alone? Of remaining alone, for the rest of his days? Was he scared of being unknown and nearly invisible, having no ties and no dreams?

It was too late to be scared of that.

He'd lived it. He lived it every single day.

The house was one of those square adobe things that filled Vegas. It was probably pink in the sunlight. In the half-light that passed for nighttime in this perpetually alive city, it looked gray and foreboding.

The bars on the windows—standard in this neighborhood—didn't help.

Places like this always astounded him. They seemed so normal, so incorruptible, just another building on another street, like all the other buildings on all the other streets. Sometimes he got to go into those buildings. Very few of them were different from what he expected. Oh, the art changed or the furniture. The smells differed—sometimes unwashed diapers, sometimes perfume, sometimes the heavy scent of meals eaten long ago—but the rest remained the same: the television in the main room, the kitchen with its square table (sometimes decorated with flowers, sometimes nothing but trash), the double bed in the second bedroom down the hall, the one with its own shower and toilet. The room across from the main bathroom was sometimes an office, sometimes a den, sometimes a child's bedroom.

If it was a child's bedroom, there were pictures on the wall, studio portraits from the local mall, done up in cheap frames, showing the passing years. The pictures were never straight, and always dusty, except for the most recent, hung with pride in the only remaining empty space.

He had a hunch this house would have none of those things. If anything, it would have an overly neat interior. The television would be in the kitchen or the bedroom or both. The front room would have a sofa set designed for looks, not for comfort. And one of the rooms would be blocked off, maybe even marked private, and in it, he would find (if he looked) trophies of a kind that made even his cast-iron stomach turn.

These houses had no attic. Most didn't have a basement. So the scene would be the garage. The car would be parked outside of it, blocking the door, and the neighbors would assume that the garage was simply a workspace—not that far off, if the truth be told.

He'd been to places like this before. More times than he wanted to think about, especially in the smaller communities out in the desert, the communities that had no names, or once had a name and did no longer. The communities sometimes made up of cheap trailers and empty storefronts, with a whorehouse a few miles off the main highway, and a casino in the center of town, a casino so old it made the one that the boy found him in look like it had been built just the week before.

He hated these jobs. He wasn't sure what made him come with the boy. A moment of compassion? The prospect of yet another long Christmas Eve with nothing to punctuate it except the bong-bong of nearby slots?

He couldn't go to church anymore. It didn't feel right, with as many lives as he had taken. He couldn't go to church or listen to the singing or look at the families and wonder which of them he'd be standing beside in thirty years.

Maybe he belonged here more than the boy did. Maybe he belonged here more than anyone else.

They parked a block away, not because anyone would see their car—if asked, hours later, the neighbors would deny seeing anything to do with Silas or the boy. Maybe they never saw, maybe their memories vanished. Silas had never been clear on that either.

As they got out, Silas asked, "What do you use?"

The boy reached into the breast pocket. For a moment, Silas thought he'd remove the iPod, and Silas wasn't sure how a device that used headphones would work. Then the boy removed a harmonica—expensive, the kind sold at high-end music stores.

"You play that before all this?" Silas asked.

The boy nodded. "They got me a better one, though."

Silas' banjo had been all his own. They'd let him take it, and nothing else. The banjo, the clothes he wore that night, his hat.

He had different clothes now. He never wore a hat. But his banjo was the same as it had always been—new and pure with a sound that he still loved.

It was in the trunk. He doubted it could get stolen, but he took precautions just in case.

He couldn't bring it on this job. This wasn't his job. He'd learned the hard way that the banjo didn't work except in assigned cases. When he'd wanted to help, to put someone out of their misery, to step in where another death dealer had failed, he couldn't. He could only watch, like normal people did, and hope that things got better, even though he knew it wouldn't.

The boy clutched the harmonica in his right hand. The dry desert air was cold. Silas could see his breath. The tourists down on the Strip, with their short skirts and short sleeves, probably felt betrayed by the normal winter chill. He wished he were there with them, instead of walking through this quiet neighborhood, filled with dark houses, dirt-ridden yards, and silence.

So much silence. You'd think there'd be at least one barking dog.

When they reached the house, the boy headed to the garage, just like Silas expected. A car was parked on the road—a 1980s sedan that looked like it had seen better days. In the driveway, a brand-new van with tinted windows, custom-made for bad deeds.

In spite of himself, Silas shuddered.

The boy stopped outside and steeled himself, then he looked at Silas with sadness in his eyes. Silas nodded. The boy extended a hand—Silas couldn't get in without the boy's momentary magic—and then they were inside, near the stench of old gasoline, urine, and fear.

The kids sat in a dimly lit corner, chained together like the slaves on ships in the nineteenth century. The windows were covered with dirty cardboard, the concrete floor was empty except for stains as old as time. It felt bad in here, a recognizable bad, one Silas had encountered before.

The boy was shaking. He wasn't out of place here, his old wool jacket and his dirty jeans making him a cousin to the kids on the floor. Silas had a momentary flash: they were homeless. Runaways, lost, children without borders, without someone looking for them.

"You've been here before," Silas whispered to the boy, and the boy's eyes filled with tears.

Been here, negotiated here, moved on here—didn't quite die, but no longer quite lived—and for who? A group of kids like this one? A group that had somehow escaped, but hadn't reported what had happened?

Then he felt the chill grow worse. Of course they hadn't reported it. Who would believe them? A neat homeowner kidnaps a group of homeless kids for his own personal playthings, and the cops believe the kids? Kids who steal and sell drugs and themselves just for survival.

People like the one who owned this house were cautious. They were smart. They rarely got caught unless they went public with letters or phone calls or both.

They had to prepare for contingencies like losing a plaything now and then. They probably had all the answers planned.

A side door opened. It was attached to the house. The man who came in was everything Silas had expected—white, thin, balding, a bit too intense.

What surprised Silas was the look the man gave him. Measuring, calculating.

Pleased.

The man wasn't supposed to see Silas or the boy. Not until the last moment.

Not until the end.

Silas had heard that some of these creatures could see the death dealers. A few of Silas's colleagues speculated that these men continued to kill so that they could continue to see death in all its forms, collecting images the way they collected trophies.

After seeing the momentary victory in that man's eyes, Silas believed it.

The man picked up the kid at the end of the chain. Too weak to stand, the kid staggered a bit, then had to lean into the man.

"You have to beat me," the man said to Silas. "I slice her first, and you have to leave."

The boy was still shivering. The man hadn't noticed him. The man thought Silas was here for him, not the boy. Silas had no powers, except the ones that humans normally had—not on this night, and not in this way.

If he were here alone, he'd start playing, and praying he'd get the right one. If there was a right one. He couldn't tell. They all seemed to have the mark of death over them.

No wonder the boy needed him.

It was a fluid situation, one that could go in any direction.

"Start playing," Silas said under his breath.

But the man heard him, not the boy. The man pulled the kid's head back, exposing a smooth white throat with the heartbeat visible in a vein.

"Play!" Silas shouted, and ran forward, shoving the man aside, hoping that would be enough.

It saved the girl's neck, for a moment anyway. She fell, and landed on the other kid next to her. The kid moved away, as if proximity to her would cause the kid to die.

The boy started blowing on his harmonica. The notes were faint, barely notes, more like bleats of terror.

The man laughed. He saw the boy now. "So you're back to rob me again," he said.

The boy's playing grew wispier.

"Ignore him," Silas said to the boy.

"Who're you? His coach?" The man approached him. "I know your rules. I destroy you, I get to take your place."

The steak rolled in Silas's stomach. The man was half right. He destroyed Silas, and he would get a chance to take the job. He destroyed both of them, and he would get the job, by old magic not new. Silas had forgotten this danger. No wonder these creatures liked to see death—what better for them than to be the facilitator for the hundreds of people who died in Nevada every day?

The man brandished his knife. "Lessee," he said. "What do I do? Destroy the instrument, deface the man. Right? And send him to hell."

Get him fired, Silas fought. It wasn't really hell, although it seemed like it. He became a ghost, existing forever, but not allowed to interact with anything. He was fired. He lost the right to die.

The man reached for the harmonica. Silas shoved again.

"Play!" Silas shouted.

And miraculously, the boy played. "Home on the Range," a silly song for these circumstances, but probably the first tune the boy had ever learned. He played it with spirit as he backed away from the fight.

But the kids weren't rebelling. They sat on the cold concrete floor, already half dead, probably tortured into submission. If they didn't rise up and kill this monster, no one would.

Silas looked at the boy. Tears streamed down his face, and he nodded toward the kids. Souls hovered above them, as if they couldn't decide whether or not to leave.

Damn the ones in charge: they'd sent the kid here as his final test. Could he take the kind of lives he had given his life for? Was he that strong?

The man reached for the harmonica again, and this time Silas grabbed his knife. It was heavier than Silas expected. He had never wielded a real instrument of death. His banjo eased people into forever. It didn't force them out of their lives a moment too early.

The boy kept playing and the man—the creature—laughed. One of the kids looked up, and Silas thought the kid was staring straight at the boy.

Only a moment, then. Only a moment to decide.

Silas shoved the knife into the man's belly. It went in deep, and the man let out an oof of pain. He stumbled, reached for the knife, and then glared at Silas.

Silas hadn't killed him, maybe hadn't even mortally wounded him.

No soul appeared above him, and even these creatures had souls—dark and tainted as they were.

The boy's playing broke in places as if he were trying to catch his breath. The kid at the end of the chain, the girl, managed to get up. She looked at the knife, then at the man, then around the room. She couldn't see Silas or the boy.

Which was good.

The man was pulling on the knife. He would get it free in a moment. He would use it, would destroy these children, the ones no one cared about except the boy who was here to take their souls.

The girl kicked the kid beside her. "Stand up," she said.

The kid looked at her, bleary. Silas couldn't tell if these kids were male or female. He wasn't sure it mattered.

"Stand up," the girl said again.

In a rattle of chains, the kid did. The man didn't notice. He was working the knife, grunting as he tried to dislodge it. Silas stepped back, wondering if he had already interfered too much.

The music got louder, more intense, almost violent. The girl stood beside the man and stared at him for a moment.

He raised his head, saw her, and grinned.

Then she reached down with that chain, wrapped it around his neck, and pulled. "Help me," she said to the others. "Help me."

The music became a live thing, wrapping them all, filling the smelly garage, and reaching deep, deep into the darkness. The soul did rise up—half a soul, broken and burned. It looked at Silas, then flared at the boy, who—bless him—didn't stop playing.

Then the soul floated toward the growing darkness in the corner, a blackness Silas had seen only a handful of times before, a blackness that felt as cold and dark as any empty desert night, and somehow much more permanent.

The music faded. The girl kept pulling, until another kid, farther down the line, convinced her to let go.

"We have to find the key," the other kid—a boy—said.

"On the wall," a third kid said. "Behind the electric box."

They shuffled as a group toward the box. They walked through Silas, and he felt them, alive and vibrant. For a moment, he worried that he had been fired, but he knew he had too many years for that. Too many years of perfect service—and he hadn't killed the man. He had just injured him, took away the threat to the boy.

That was allowed, just barely.

No wonder the boy had brought him. No wonder the boy had asked him if he was scared. Not of being alone or being lonely. But of certain jobs, of the things now asked of them as the no-longer-quite-human beings that they were.

Silas turned to the boy. His face was shiny with tears, but his eyes were clear. He stuffed the harmonica back into his breast pocket.

"You knew he'd beat you without me," Silas said.

The boy nodded.

"You knew this wasn't a substitution. You would have had this job, even without me."

"It's not cheating to bring in help," the boy said.

"But it's nearly impossible to find it," Silas said. "How did you find me?"

"It's Christmas Eve," the boy said. "Everyone knows where you'd be."

Everyone. His colleagues. People on the job. The only folks who even knew his name anymore.

Silas sighed. The boy reached out with his stubby dirty hand. Silas took it, and then, suddenly, they were out of that fetid garage. They stood next to the van and watched as the cardboard came off one of the windows, as glass shattered outward.

Kids, homeless kids, injured and alone, poured out of that window like water.

"Thanks," the boy said. "I can't tell you how much it means."

But Silas knew. The boy didn't yet, but Silas did. When he retired—no longer if. When—this boy would see him again. This boy would take him, gently and with some kind of majestic harmonica music, to a beyond Silas could not imagine.

The boy waved at him, and joined the kids, heading into the dark Vegas night. Those kids couldn't see him, but they had to know he was there, like a guardian angel, saving them from horrors that would haunt their dreams for the rest of their lives.

Silas watched them go. Then he headed in the opposite direction, toward his car. What had those kids seen? The man—the creature—with his knife out, raving at nothing. Then stumbling backward, once, twice, the second time with a knife in his belly. They'd think that he tripped, that he stabbed himself. None of them had seen Silas or the boy.

They wouldn't for another sixty years.

If they were lucky.

The neighborhood remained dark, although a dog barked in the distance. His car was cold. Cold and empty.

He let himself in, started it, warmed his fingers against the still-hot air blowing out of the vents. Only a few minutes gone. A few minutes to take away a nasty, horrible lifetime. He wondered what was in the rest of these houses, and hoped he'd never have to find out.

The clock on the dash read 10:45. As he drove out of the neighborhood, he passed a small adobe church. Outside, candles burned in candleholders made of baked sand. Almost like the churches of his childhood.

Almost, but not quite.

He watched the people thread inside. They wore fancy clothing—dresses on the women, suits on the men, the children dressing like their parents, faces alive with anticipation.

They believed in something.

They had hope.

He wondered if hope was something a man could recapture, if it came with time, relaxation, and the slow inevitable march toward death.

He wondered, if he retired, whether he could spend his Christmas Eves inside, smelling the mix of incense and candlewax, the evergreen bows, and the light dusting of ladies' perfume.

He wondered . . .

Then shook his head.

And drove back to the casino, to spend the rest of his time off in peace.

# PICKPOCKET
*By Marcia Muller*

Marcia Muller is the author of more than twenty novels and many short mystery stories. She has also established a brilliant reputation as an anthologist and critic of mystery fiction. In 1993 she was awarded the Private Eye Writers of America Life Achievement Award, and *Wolf in the Shadows* was nominated for the 1994 Edgar Allan Poe Award for Best Crime Novel and won the Anthony Boucher Award. She lives with her husband, the mystery writer Bill Pronzini, in northern California.

S abina Carpenter put on her straw picture hat and contemplated the hatpins in the velvet cushion on her bureau. After a moment she selected a Charles Horner design of silver and coral and skewered the hat to her upswept dark hair. The hatpin, a gift on her last birthday, was one of two she owned by the famed British designer. The other, a butterfly with an onyx body and diamond-chip wings, was a gift from her late husband and much too ornate—to say nothing of valuable—to wear during the day.

Momentarily she recalled Stephen's face: thin, with prominent cheekbones and chin. Brilliant blue eyes below dark brown hair. A face that could radiate tenderness—and danger. Like herself, a Pinkerton detective in Denver, he had been working on a land-fraud case when he was shot to death in a raid. It troubled Sabina that over the past few years his features had become less distinct in her memory, as had those of her deceased parents, but she assumed that was human nature. One's memories blur; one goes on.

She scrutinized her reflection in the mirror and concluded that she

looked more like a respectable young matron than a private detective
setting out to trap a pickpocket. Satisfied, she left her second-story
Russian Hill flat, passed through the iron picket fence, and entered a
hansom cab that she had earlier engaged. It took her down Van Ness
Avenue and south on Haight Street.

The journey was a lengthy one, passing through sparsely settled
areas of the city, and it gave Sabina time to reflect upon the job ahead.
Charles Ackerman, owner of the Haight Street Chutes amusement
park and an attorney for the Southern Pacific and the Market Street
and Sutter Street Railroads, had come to the offices of Carpenter and
Quincannon, Professional Detective Services, the previous morning.
Sabina's partner, John Quincannon, had been out of sorts because she
had just refused his invitation to dinner at Marchand's French restaurant. Sabina, a practical woman, refused many of John's frequent invi-
tations. Mixing business with pleasure was a dangerous proposition; it
could imperil their partnership, an arrangement she was very happy
with as it stood. . . .

And yet, she did not find John unattractive. Quite the opposite—
Sternly, Sabina turned her thoughts to the business at hand.

Charles Ackerman had a problem at his newly opened amusement
park, on Haight Street near the southern edge of Golden Gate Park.
Patrons had complained that a pickpocket was operating in the park,
yet neither his employees nor the police had yet to observe any of the
more notorious dips and cutpurses who worked the San Francisco
streets. A clever woman, Ackerman said with a nod at Sabina, might
be able to succeed where they had failed. John bristled at being
excluded, then lapsed into a grumpy silence. Sabina and Ackerman
concluded the conversation and agreed she would come to the park
the next morning, after she had finished with another bit of pressing
business.

The hack pulled to the curb between Cole and Clayton Streets.
Sabina paid the driver and alighted, then turned toward the park. Its
most prominent feature was a 300-foot-long Shoot-the-Chutes: a
double-trestled track that rose seventy feet into the air. Passengers
would ascend to a room at the top of the slides, where they would board
boats for a swift descent to an artificial lake at the bottom. Sabina had

heard that the ride was quite thrilling—or frightening, according to the person's perspective. She herself would enjoy trying it.

In addition to the water slide, the park contained a scenic railway, a merry-go-round, various carnival-like establishments, and a refreshment stand. Ackerman had told Sabina she would find his manager, Lester Sweeney, in the office beyond the ticket booth. She crossed the street, holding up her slim flowered skirt so the hem wouldn't get dusty, and asked at the booth for Mr. Sweeney. The man collecting admissions motioned her inside and through a door behind him.

Sweeney was at a desk that seemed too large for the cramped space, adding a column of figures. He was a big man, possibly in his late forties, with thinning red hair and a complexion that spoke of a fondness for strong drink. When he looked up at Sabina, his eyes, reddened and surrounded by pouched flesh, gleamed in appreciation. Quickly she presented her card, and the gleam faded.

"Please sit down, Mrs. Carpenter," he said. "Mr. Ackerman told me you'd be coming this morning."

"Thank you." Sabina sat on the single wooden chair sandwiched between the desk and the wall. "What can you tell me about these pickpocketing incidents?"

"They have occurred over the past two weeks, at different times of day. Eight in all. Word is spreading. We're bound to lose customers."

"You spoke with the victims?"

"Yes, and there may have been others who didn't report the incidents."

"Was there anything in common that was reported?"

Sweeney frowned, thinking: The frown had an alarming effect on his face, making it look like something that had softened and spread after being left out in the rain. In a moment he shook his head. "Nothing that I can recall."

"Do you have the victims' names and addresses?"

"Somewhere here." He began to shuffle through the many papers on his desk.

Sabina held up a hand and stood. "I'll return to collect the list later. In the meantime, I trust I may have full access to the park?"

"Certainly, Mrs. Carpenter."

Several hours later Sabina, who was familiar with most of San Francisco's dips and cutpurses, had ascertained that none of them was working the Chutes. Notably absent were Fanny Spigott, dubbed "Queen of the Pickpockets," and her husband Joe, "King of the Pickpockets," who recently had plotted—unsuccessfully—to steal the two-thousand-pound statue of *Venus de Milo* from the Louvre Museum in Paris. Also among the absent were Lil Hamlin ("Fainting Lil"), whose ploy was to pass out in the arms of her victims; Jane O'Leary ("Weeping Jane"), who lured her marks in by enlisting them in the hunt for her missing six-year-old, then relieved them of their valuables while hugging them when the precocious and well-trained child was "found"; "Fingers" McCoy, who claimed to have the fastest reach in town; and Lovely Lena, true name unknown, a blonde so captivating that it was said she blinded her victims.

While searching for her pickpocket, Sabina had toured the park on the scenic railway, eaten an ice cream, ridden the merry-go-round, and taken a boat ride down the Chutes—which was indeed thrilling. So thrilling that she rewarded her bravery with a German sausage on a sourdough roll. It was early afternoon and she was leaving Lester Sweeney's office with the list of the pickpocket's victims when she saw an unaccompanied woman intensely watching the crowd around the merry-go-round. The woman moved foward, next to a man in a straw bowler, but when he turned and nodded to her she stepped a few paces away.

Sabina moved closer.

The woman had light-brown hair, upswept under a wide-brimmed straw picture hat similar to Sabina's. She was slender, outfitted in a white shirtwaist and cornflower blue skirt. The hat shaded her features, and the only distinctive thing about her attire was the pin that held the hat to her head. Sabina—a connoisseur of hatpins—recognized it as a Charles Horner of blue glass overlaid with a gold pattern.

The woman must have felt Sabina's gaze. She looked around, and Sabina saw she had blue eyes and rather plain features, except for a small white scar on her chin. Her gaze slid over Sabina, focused on a man to her right, but moved away when he reached down to pick up a fretting child. After a moment the woman turned and walked slowly toward the exit.

A pickpocket, for certain; Sabina had seen how they operated many

times. She followed, keeping her eyes on the distinctive hatpin. Fortunately there was a row of hansom cabs waiting outside the gates of the
park. The woman with the distinctive hatpin claimed the first of these,
and Sabina took another, asking the driver to follow the other hack. He
regarded her curiously, no doubt unused to gentlewomen making such
requests; but the new century was rapidly approaching, and with it
what the press had dubbed the New Woman. Very often these days the
female sex did not think or act as they once had.

The brown-haired woman's cab led them north on Haight and
finally to Market Street, the city's main artery. There she disem-
barked near the Palace Hotel—as did Sabina—and crossed Market to
Montgomery. It was five o'clock, and businessmen of all kinds were
pouring out of their downtown offices to travel the Cocktail Route,
as the Gay Nineties' young blades termed it.

From the Reception Saloon on Sutter Street to Haquette's Palace of
Art on Post Street to the Palace Hotel Bar, the influential men of San
Francisco trekked daily, partaking of fine liquor and lavish free ban-
quet spreads. Women—at least respectable ones—were not admitted
to these establishments, but Sabina had ample knowledge of them
from John's tales of the days when he was a drinking man. He had been
an operative with the U.S. Secret Service, until the accidental death by
his hand of a pregnant woman turned him into a drunkard; those were
the days before he met Sabina and embarked on a new, sober life. . . .

Once again she forced her thoughts away from John Quincannon.

The woman she had followed from the amusement park was now
well into the crowd on Montgomery Street—known as the Ambrosial
Path to cocktail-hour revelers. Street characters and vendors, beggars
and ad-carriers for the various saloons' free lunches, temperance
speakers and the Salvation Army band—all mingled with well-dressed
bankers and attorneys, politicians and physicians. Sabina made her way
through the throng, keeping her eye on the woman's hat, brushing aside
the opportunings of a match peddler. The woman moved along unhur-
riedly and after two blocks turned left and walked over to Kearney.

There the street scene was even livelier: palm readers, shooting
galleries, and auction houses had their quarters there. Ever present
were the shouting vendors and pitchmen of all sorts; fakirs and touters

of Marxism; snake charmers and speech makers of all persuasions. It seemed every type of individual in the world had come to Kearney Street for the start of the evening. Sabina kept her eyes on the woman as she moved at a leisurely pace, stopping to finger a bolt of Indian fabric and then to listen to a speaker extol the virtues of phrenology. She moved deeper into the crowd, and Sabina momentarily lost her; seconds later she heard a faint cry and pushed her way forward.

A gent in a frock coat was bent over, his silk hat having fallen to the sidewalk. As he straightened, his face frozen in a grimace of pain, he reached inside his coat. Sudden anger replaced pain and he shouted, "Stop, thief!"

But no one was fleeing. The crowd murmured, heads swiveling, faces curious and alarmed. The man again shouted, "My watch! I've been robbed!"

Sabina moved forward. "What happened?"

The man stared at her, open-mouthed.

She hurriedly removed one of her cards from her reticule and gave it to him. "I am investigating a series of thefts. Please tell me what happened."

He examined the card. "Will you find the person who took my watch? It is very old and rare—"

"Was it you who cried out earlier?"

"Yes. I suffered a sharp pain in my side. Here." He indicated his lower left ribcage. "I have had such discomfort before, and I've just come from the Bank Exchange, where, I'm afraid, I consumed an overlarge quantity of oysters on the half shell. I suppose the thief took advantage of my distress."

"Did you not notice anyone close to you? A woman, perhaps?"

The gent shook his head. "I saw no one."

Sabina turned to the ring of people surrounding them, asked the same question of them, and received the same answer.

The woman she'd followed from the amusement park had found her mark, struck, and swiftly vanished.

It was near on to seven o'clock, an inconvenient time to go calling, but over the course of her years as a Pinkerton operative and a self-employed detective, Sabina had become accustomed to calling on people at inconvenient times.

At her flat on Russian Hill, she changed into a heavy black skirt and shirtwaist and, in deference to the foggy San Francisco evening, a long cape. Once again she left in a hansom cab, one she'd hired to wait for her at her stops along the way. She had studied the list of names of the pickpocket's victims that Lester Sweeney had given her, and mapped out a convenient and easy route.

Her first destination was the home of Mr. William Buchanan on Green Street near Van Ness Avenue. Mr. Buchanan was not at home, the maid who answered the door told her. He and Mrs. Buchanan had gone to their country house on the Peninsula for two weeks.

In the cab again, Sabina crossed Mr. Buchanan's name off the list, and instructed the driver to take her to an address on Webster Street in the Western Addition.

The house there was large and elegant, and Mr. John Greenway resembled many of the well-attired gentlemen Sabina had earlier seen parading on the Cocktail Route. He greeted her cordially, taking her into the front parlor and introducing her to his attractive wife, who looked to be expecting a child.

"A note from Mr. Sweeney at the Chutes was delivered this afternoon," he told Sabina. "It said you wish to speak with me concerning the theft of my diamond stickpin. I hope I can help you."

"As do I. What were the circumstances of the theft?"

Greenway glanced at his auburn-haired wife, who smiled encouragingly. "We had ridden the water slide and stopped at the refreshment stand for a glass of lemonade," he said. "The ride had made me feel unwell, so we decided to come home. There was a large crowd watching a juggler near the gates, and we were separated in it. I felt a sharp pain in my side—the result of the ride, I suppose—and momentarily became disoriented. When I recovered and my wife rejoined me, she saw that my stickpin was missing."

Men in distress, Sabina thought. A clever pickpocket noting this and taking advantage of their momentary confusion.

She thanked the Greenways and took her leave.

No one came to the door at either of the next two victims' residences, but at a small Eastlake-style Victorian near Lafayette Square, Sabina was greeted by the plump young daughter of Mr. George Anderson. Her parents, the daughter said, were at the Orpheum, a vaudeville house on O'Farrell Street. Could she reveal anything about the distressing incident at the amusement park? Sabina asked. Certainly; the daughter had witnessed it.

In the small front parlor, Ellen Anderson rang for the housekeeper and ordered tea. It came quickly, accompanied by a plate of ginger cookies. Sabina took one as Miss Anderson poured and prattled on about her excitement about meeting a lady detective. Then she proceeded with her questioning.

"You were with your father at the amusement park when his purse was stolen?"

"My mother, my brother, and I."

"Tell me what you saw, please."

"We were near the merry-go-round. It was very crowded, children waiting to board and parents watching their children on the ride. Allen, my brother, was trying to persuade me to ride with him. He's only ten years old, so a merry-go-round is a thrill for him, but I'm sixteen, and it seems so very childish. . . ."

"Did you ride anyway?"

"No. But Allen did. We were watching him when suddenly my father groaned. He took hold of his side, slued around, and staggered a few paces. Mother and I caught him before he could fall. When we'd righted him, he found all his money was gone."

"What caused this sudden pain?

"A gastric distress, apparently."

"Does your father normally suffer from digestive problems?"

"No, but earlier we'd had hot sausages at the refreshment stand. We assumed they were what affected him and then a thief had taken advantage of the moment."

Every thief has his or her own method, Sabina thought, and evidently this one's was to seek out people who had fallen ill and were therefore vulnerable.

"Did your father talk about the incident afterwards?"

Ellen Anderson shook her dark-curled head. "He seemed ashamed of being robbed. In fact, Mother had to insist he report the theft to the park manager."

"Did his distress continue afterwards?"

"I don't think so, but he's never been one to talk about his ailments."

Two more fruitless stops left her with a final name on the list: Henry Holbrooke, on South Park. The oval-shaped park, an exact copy of London's Berkeley Square, had once been home to the reigning society of San Francisco, but now its grandeur, and that of neighboring Rincon Hill, was fading. Most of the powerful millionaires and their families who had resided there had moved to more fashionable venues such as Nob Hill, and many of the elegant homes looked somewhat shopworn. Henry Holbrooke's was one of the latter, its paint peeling and small front garden unkempt: a grand old lady slipping into genteel poverty.

A light was burning behind heavy velvet curtains in a bay window, but when Sabina knocked, no one answered. She knocked again, and after a moment the door opened. The inner hallway was so dark that she could scarcely make out the person standing there. Then she saw it was a woman dressed entirely in black. She said, "Mrs. Holbrooke?"

"Yes." The woman's voice cracked, as if rusty from disuse.

Sabina gave her name and explained her mission. The woman made no move to take the card she extended.

"May I speak with your husband?" Sabina asked.

"My husband is dead."

". . . My condolences. May I ask when he passed on?"

"Two weeks ago."

That would have been a week after he was robbed of his money belt at the Chutes.

"May I come in?" Sabina asked.

"I'd rather you didn't. I've been . . . tearful. I don't wish for anyone to see me after I've been weeping."

"I understand. What was the cause of your husband's death?"

"An infection and internal bleeding."

"Had he been ill long?"

"He had never been ill. Not a day in his life."

"What did his physician say?"

The widow laughed harshly. "We couldn't afford a physician, not after his money belt was stolen. He died at home, in my arms, and the coroner came and took him away. I had to sell my jewelry—what was left of it—so he could have a decent burial."

"I'm sorry. Why did he have so much money on his person during an afternoon at the amusement park?"

"My husband never went anywhere without that belt. He was afraid to leave it at home. This neighborhood is not what it once was."

Sabina glanced at the neighboring homes in their fading glory. Henry Holbrooke would have been better advised to keep his money in a bank.

"Did the coroner tell you what might have caused your husband's infection?" she asked.

Mrs. Holbrooke leaned heavily on the doorjamb; like South Park, she was slowly deteriorating. "No. Only that it resulted in internal bleeding." The woman reached out and placed a hand on Sabina's arm. "If you apprehend the thief, will you recover my husband's money?"

Most likely it had already been spent, but Sabina said, "Perhaps."

"Will you return it to me? I'd like to buy him a good gravemarker."

"Of course."

If the money had indeed been spent, Sabina resolved that Carpenter & Quincannon would supply the gravemarker, out of the handsome fee Charles Ackerman would pay them—whether John liked it or not.

Sabina returned to the hansom, but asked the driver to wait. A pickpocket, she thought, rarely works the same territory in a single day. The woman she had followed was unlikely to return to the Chutes in the near future; she'd seen Sabina eyeing her suspiciously. The Ambrosial Path would be similarly off limits, since she'd had success there and word would by now have spread among the habitués of the area. Where else would a pickpocket who preyed on the infirm go to ply her trade?

After a moment, Sabina said to the hack driver, "Take me to Market and Fourth Streets, please."

The open field at Market and Fourth was brightly lit by lanterns and torchlights, and dotted with tents and wagons. Music filled the air from many sources, each competing with the other; barkers shouted, and a group of Negro minstrels sang "Swing Low, Sweet Chariot." Sabina stood at the field's perimeter, surveying the medicine show.

From the wagons men hawked well-known remedies: Tiger Balm, Snake Dust, aconite, Pain Begone, Miracle Wort. Others offered services on the spot: painless dentistry spinal realignment, Chinese herbs brewed to the taste, head massages. Sabina, who had attended the medicine show with John after moving to San Francisco—a must, he'd said, for new residents—recognized several of the participants: Pawnee Bill, The Great Ferndon, Doctor Jekyll, Herman the Healer, Rodney Strongheart.

The din rose as a shill for Doctor Wallmann's Nerve and Brain Salts stood in his red coach—six black horses stamping and snorting—to extol the product. Sabina smiled; John had frequently posed as a drummer for Doctor Wallmann's, and said the salts were nothing more than table salt mixed with borax.

Someone nearby shouted, "The show is on!" A top-hatted magician and his sultry, robed assistant emerged from a striped tent; another show—Indians in dancing regalia—began to compete, the thump of tom-toms drowning out a banjo player. The entertainment quickly ended when the selling began.

Sabina continued to scan the scene before her. The crowd was mostly men; the few women she judged to be of the lower classes by their worn clothing and roughened faces and hands. Not a lady—fancy or fine—in the lot. And no one with a picture hat and unusual pin. However, the woman she sought could have changed her clothing as she herself had. Sabina moved into the crowd.

A snake charmer's flute caught her attention, and she watched the pathetic defanged creature rise haltingly from its shabby basket. She turned away, spied under the wide brim of a battered straw hat. The woman had dark eyes and gray hair—not the person she was looking for.

On a platform at the back of a wagon, a dancer was performing, draped in filmy veils. Unfortunately, the veils slipped and fell to the ground, revealing her scarlet long johns. A man with an ostrich-feather-bedecked hat began expounding upon the virtues of Sydney's Cough Syrup, only to fall into a fit of coughing. Sabina glanced at the face under the brim of an old-fashioned bonnet and saw the woman was elderly.

Wide-brimmed hat with bedraggled feathers: a badly scarred young woman whose plight made Sabina flinch. Toque draped in fading tulle: red hair and freckles. Another bonnet: white hair and fine wrinkles.

As Sabina was approaching a model of France's infamous guillotine, a cry rang out. She soon saw that the ostrich feathers of the spokesman for Sydney's Cough Syrup had caught fire from one of the torches. A nearby man rushed to throw the hat to the ground and stomp the flames out.

A freak show was starting. The barker urged Sabina to enter the tent and view the dwarf and deformed baby in a bottle. She declined—not at all respectfully.

Extravagant hat with many layers of feathers and a stuffed bird's head protruding at the front: long blond hair.

Temperance speakers, exhibiting jars containing diseased kidneys. No, thank you.

Another bird hat. What *was* the fascination with wearing dead avian creatures on one's head? The woman beneath the brim looked not much healthier than the bird that had died to grace her headpiece.

A barker tried to entice Sabina into a wax display of a hanging. No to that also.

Worn blue velvet wide-brimmed hat, secured by . . . a Charles Horner hatpin, blue glass overlaid with a gold pattern. Ah!

The woman moved through the crowd, head swiveling from side to side.

Sabina waited until her quarry was several yards ahead of her, then followed.

The woman pretended interest in a miraculous electrified belt filled with cayenne pepper whose purveyor claimed would cure any debilitation. She stopped to listen to the Negro minstrels and clapped appreciatively when their music ended. Considered a temperance pamphlet, but shook her head. Accepted a flier from the seller of White's Female Complaint Cure.

All the time, as Sabina covertly watched, her, the pickpocket's head continued to move from side to side—looking for someone in distress. Someone whom she could rob.

Sabina seldom had difficulty controlling her temper. True, it rose swiftly, but just as swiftly it turned from hot outrage to cold resolve. She, too, began looking for someone in distress. Someone whom she could save from the woman's thievery.

Before long, she saw him, nearly ten yards away: humped over, leaning on a cane, walking haltingly. She poised to move in, but the woman, who obviously had seen him too, surprised her by turning the other way.

Another old man: limping, forehead shiny with perspiration in spite of the chill temperature.

The woman passed him by.

Had Sabina been wrong about the pickpocket's method? No, this dip was clever. She was waiting for the ideal victim.

More wandering. More pretending interest in the shows and wares. No indication that the pickpocket had spied her.

In front of the bright red coach belonging to the purveyor of Doctor Wallmann's Nerve and Brain Salts, the woman stopped. She spoke to the vendor, examined the bottle, then shook her head. A crowd had pressed in behind her. She stretched her arms up behind her head, then dropped them and angled through the people.

And in that moment Sabina knew her method.

She pushed forward into the crowd, keeping her eyes on the blue velvet picture hat. It moved diagonally, toward the Chinese herbalist's wagon. Now, after ten o'clock, most of the women had departed, their places taken by Cocktail Route travelers on a postprandial stroll, after which many would visit the establishments of the wicked Barbary Coast. The woman in the blue hat would be there too, plying her trade upon the unsuspecting—unless Sabina could stop her.

The blue hat now brushed against the shoulder of a tall blond man clad in an elegant broadloom suit. The perfect victim.

Sabina weaved her way through men who had stopped to hear Rodney Strongheart sing in a loud baritone about how his elixir would keep one's heart beating forever. A few gave her disapproving glances: She should not be here at this hour, and she certainly shouldn't be elbowing them aside.

Sabina continued to use her elbows.

Now she was beside the woman. She reached for her arm and missed it just as the man in broadloom groaned and clutched his side. Sabina saw the dip's right hand move to his inner pocket; she was quick, and the man's purse was soon in her grasp.

But not soon enough to make her escape.

Sabina grasped the woman's right hand, which held the purse, and pinned the dip's arm behind her back. The pickpocket struggled, and Sabina pulled the arm higher until she cried out and then was still.

The victim had recovered from his pain. He stared at Sabina, then at the thief. Sabina reached down and wrested the blue-and-gold Charles Horner hatpin from the woman's hand.

"And that," John Quincannon said, "was the last of the Carville Ghost." He looked pleased with himself, sitting at his desk, smiling and stroking his freebooter's beard—a feature that made him appear rakish, and dangerous. He fancied himself the world's finest detective and he always preened a bit when he brought an investigation to a successful conclusion.

"And," he added, "I have collected the fee. A not inconsiderable twenty-five hundred dollars. I would say that justifies dinner for two at Marchand's and perhaps—"

Sabina interrupted his description of his evening's plans for them. "I, too, have collected a handsome fee. From Charles Ackerman."

"Ah, you solved the pickpocketing case."

"Yes." She proceeded to tell him about it, including the man who had died, Henry Holbrooke, finishing, "I thought the woman— Sarah Wilds—was preying upon infirm men, perhaps men in gastric distress. It turned out she was stealing from perfectly healthy men, stabbing them in the side with her needle-thin hatpin to distract them while she picked their pockets."

"Needle-thin?" John frowned. "I presented you with a silver-and-coral Charles Horner hatpin on your last birthday. As I recall, it was fairly thick."

"Sarah Wilds had altered hers so the pin would pass through clothing and flesh but not cause the victim to bleed much, if at all. Just a painful prick, and she'd withdraw it while reaching for her victim's valuables."

"But the man who died—Harry Holbrooke?"

"Henry. The police assume he was unlucky. The pin went in too deeply, punctured an organ, and caused bleeding and an infection. You must remember—Sarah Wilds was using the same pin over and over; think of the bacteria it carried."

John nodded. "Another job well done, my dear. Now, about Marchand's and perhaps—"

"I accept your invitation upon one condition."

"And that is?"

"You will pay for your evening from the proceeds of your Carville investigation, and I will pay for mine from my proceeds."

John, as Sabina had known he would, bristled. "A lady paying her own way on a celebratory evening—unthinkable!"

"You had best think about it, because those are my terms."

He sighed—a long exhalation—and scowled fiercely. But as she knew he would, he said, "An evening out with you, my dear, is acceptable under any terms or conditions."

As was an evening out with him.

# THE WINNING TICKET

*By Bill Pronzini*

A full-time professional writer since 1969, Bill Pronzini has published close to seventy novels, including three in collaboration with his wife, the novelist Marcia Muller, and thirty-two in his popular "Nameless Detective" series. He is also the author of four nonfiction books, twenty collections of short stories, and scores of uncollected stories, articles, essays, and book reviews; and he has edited or coedited numerous anthologies. His work has been translated into eighteen languages and published in nearly thirty countries. He has received three Shamus Awards, two for Best Novel, and the Lifetime Achievement Award (presented in 1987) from the Private Eye Writers of America; and six nominations for the Mystery Writers of America Edgar Allan Poe award. His suspense novel *Snowbound* was the recipient of the Grand Prix de la Littérature Policiére as the best crime novel published in France in 1988. *A Wasteland of Strangers* was nominated for best crime novel of 1997 by both the Mystery Writers of America and the International Crime Writers' Association. Another mainstream suspense novel, *The Crimes of Jordan Wise*, was nominated by the International Crime Writers' Association for the Hammett Award for best crime novel of 2006.

J ake Runyon and I were hunched over mugs of coffee and tea in an all-night diner near the Cow Palace when the man and woman blew in out of the rain.

Blew in is the right phrase. They came fast through the door, leaning forward, prodded by the howling wind. Nasty night out there. One of the hard-rain, big-wind storms that sometimes hammer the California coast during an El Niño winter.

The man shook himself dog-like, shedding rainwater off a shaved head and a threadbare topcoat, before the two of them slid into one of the side-wall booths. That was as much attention as I paid to them at first. He wasn't the man we were waiting for.

"After eleven," I said to Runyon. "Looks like Maxwell's a no-show again tonight."

"Weather like this, he'll probably stay holed up."

"And so we get to do it all over again tomorrow night."

"You want to give it a few more minutes?"

"Might as well. At least until the rain lets up a little."

Floyd Maxwell was a deadbeat dad, the worst kind. Spousal abuser who owed his ex more than thirty thousand dollars in unpaid child support for their two kids; hard to catch because he kept moving around in and out of the city, never staying in one place longer than a couple of months, and because he had the kind of job—small-business computer consultant—that allowed him to work from any location. Our agency had been hired by the ex's father and we'd tracked Maxwell to this neighborhood, but we'd been unable to pinpoint an exact address; all we knew was that since he'd moved here, he ate in the Twenty-Four/Seven Diner most evenings after ten o'clock, when there were few customers. Bracing him was a two-man job because of his size and his history of violent behavior. Runyon was twenty years younger than me, a former Seattle cop with a working knowledge of judo; Tamara and I couldn't have hired a tougher or more experienced field operative when we'd decided to expand the agency.

This was our third night staked out here and so far all we had to show for it were sour stomachs from too much caffeine. I had mixed feelings about the job anyway.

On the one hand, I don't like deadbeat dads or spousal abusers and nailing one was always a source of satisfaction. On the other hand, it amounted to a bounty hunt, the two of us sitting here with handcuffs in our pockets waiting to make a citizen's arrest of a fugitive, and I've never much cared for that kind of strong-arm work. Or the type of people who do it for a living.

The new couple were the only other customers right now. The

counterman, a thin young guy with a long neck and not much chin, leaned over the counter and called out to them, "What can I get you folks?"

"Coffee," the man said. He was about forty, well set-up, pasty-faced and hard-eyed. Some kind of tattoo crawled up the side of his neck; another covered the back of one hand. He glanced at the woman. "You want anything, Lila?"

"No."

"Couple of hamburgers to go," he said to the counterman. "One with everything, one with just the meat. Side of fries."

"Anything to drink with that?"

"More coffee, biggest you got. Milk."

"For the coffee?"

"In a carton. For drinking."

The counterman said, "Coming up," and turned to the grill.

The tattooed guy said to the woman, "You better have something. We got a long drive ahead of us."

"I couldn't eat, Kyle." She was maybe thirty, a washed-out, purse-lipped blonde who might have been pretty once—the type who perpetually makes the wrong choices with the wrong people and shows the effects. "I feel kind of sick."

"Yeah? Why didn't you stay in the car?"

"You know why. I couldn't listen to it anymore."

"Well, you better get used to it."

"It breaks my heart. I still think—"

"I don't care what you think. Just shut up."

Lila subsided, slouching down in the booth so that her head rested against the low back. Runyon and I were both watching them now, without being obvious about it. Eye-corner studies with our heads held still.

Pretty soon the woman said, "Why'd we have to stop here, so close? Why couldn't we just keep going?"

"It's a lousy night and I'm hungry."

"Hungry. After what just happened I don't see how you—"

"Didn't I just tell you to shut up?"

The counterman set a mug of steaming coffee on the counter. "You'll have to come get it," he said. "I got to watch the burgers."

Neither of the pair made a move to leave the booth. Kyle leaned forward and snapped at her in a low voice, "Well? Don't just sit there like a dummy. Get the coffee."

Grimacing, she slid out and fetched the coffee for him. She didn't sit down again. "I don't feel so good," she said.

"So go outside, get some air."

"No. I think I'm gonna be sick."

"Yeah, well, don't do it here."

She turned away from him, putting a hand up to cover her mouth, and half ran into the areaway that led to the restrooms. A door slammed back there. Kyle loaded sugar into his coffee, made slurping sounds as he drank it.

"Hurry up with the food," he called to the counterman.

"Almost ready."

It got quiet in there, except for the meat-sizzle on the grill, the French fries cooking in their basket of hot oil. Outside, the wind continued to beat at the front of the diner, but the rain seemed to have slacked off some.

Runyon and I watched Kyle finish his coffee. For a few seconds he sat drumming on the tabletop. Then he smacked it with his palm, slid out, and came up to the counter two stools down from where we were sitting. He stood watching the counterman wrap the burgers in waxed paper, put them into a sack with the fries; pour coffee into one container, milk into another.

"How much?" he said.

"Just a second while I ring it up."

Kyle looked over toward the areaway, scowling. Lila still hadn't reappeared.

"Hope your friend's okay," the counterman said.

"Just mind your own business, pal."

The total for the food was twelve dollars. Kyle dragged a worn wallet out of his pocket, slapped three bills down next to the two bags. When he did that I had a clear look at the tattoo on his wrist—Odin's cross. There were bloody scrapes across the knuckles on that hand, crimson spots on the sleeve of his topcoat; the blood hadn't completely coagulated yet. Under the open coat, on the left side at the belt, I had a glimpse of wood and metal.

I was closest to him and he caught me paying attention. "What the hell you looking at?"

I didn't say anything.

"Keep your eyes to yourself, you know what's good for you."

I let that pass too.

Lila came out of the restroom looking pale. "About damn time," Kyle said to her.

"I couldn't help it. I told you I was sick."

"Take those sacks and let's go."

She picked up the sacks and they started for the door. As far as Lila was concerned, the rest of us weren't even there; she was focused on Kyle and her own misery. Otherwise she might've been more careful about what she said on the way.

"Kyle . . . you won't hurt him, will you?"

"Don't be stupid."

"You hit him twice already . . ."

"A couple of slaps, big deal. He's not hurt."

"You get crazy sometimes. What you did to his mother—"

"Dammit, keep your voice down."

"But what if she calls the—"

"She won't. She knows better. Now shut up!"

They were at the door by then. And out into the gibbering night.

I glanced at Runyon. "Who's the plain burger and milk for, if she's too sick to eat?"

"Yeah," he said, and we were both off our stools and moving. Trust your instincts.

At the door I said, "Watch yourself. He's armed."

"I know, I saw it too."

Outside the rain had eased up to a fine drizzle, but the wind was still beating the night in bone-chilling gusts. The slick black street and sidewalks were empty except for the two of them off to our right, their backs to us, Kyle moving around to the driver's door of a Subaru Outback parked two car-lengths away. There was a beeping sound as he used the remote on his key chain to unlock the doors.

Runyon and I made our approach in long silent strides, not too fast. You don't want to run or make noise in a situation like this; it only invites a panic reaction. What we did once Kyle saw us depended on what he did. The one thing we wouldn't do was to give chase if he jumped into the car, locked the doors, and drove away; that kind of nonsense is strictly Hollywood. In that scenario we'd back off and call it in and let the police handle it.

The woman, Lila, opened the passenger-side door. The dome light came on, providing a vague lumpish view of a rear cargo space packed with suitcases and the like. But it was what spilled out from inside, identifiable in the wind-lull that followed, that tightened muscles all through my body. A child crying—broken, frightened sobs that went on and on.

We were nearing the Outback by then, off the curb and into the street. Close enough to make out the rain-spattered license plate. 5QQX700—an easy one to remember. But I didn't need to remember it. The way things went down, the plate number was irrelevent.

Lila saw us first. She called, "Kyle!" and jerked back from the open passenger door.

He was just opening the driver's side. He came around fast, but he didn't do anything else for a handful of seconds. Just stood there staring at us as we advanced, still at the measured pace, Runyon a couple of steps to my left so we both had a clear path to him.

Runyon put up a hand, making it look nonthreatening, and said in neutral tones, "Talk to you for a minute?"

No. It wasn't going to go down that way—reasonable, nonviolent.

At just that moment a car swung around the corner up ahead, throwing mist-smeared headlight glare over the four of us and the Outback. The light seemed to jump-start Kyle. He didn't try to get inside; he jammed the door shut and went for the weapon he had under his coat.

Runyon got to him first, just as the gun came out, and knocked his arm back.

A beat or two later I shouldered into him, hard, pinning the left side of his body against the wet metal. That gave Runyon time to judo-chop his wrist and loosen his grip on the gun. A second chop drove it right out of his hand, sent it clattering along the pavement.

Things got a little wild then. Kyle fought us, snarling; he was big and angry and even though there were two of us, just as big, he was no easy handful. The woman stood off from the Outback, yelling like a banshee. The other car, the one with the lights, skidded to a stop across the street. The wind howled, the child shrieked. I had a vague aural impression of running footsteps, someone else yelling.

It took maybe a minute's worth of teamwork to put an end to the struggle. I managed finally to get a two-handed hold on Kyle's arms, which allowed Runyon to step free and slam the edge of his hand down on the exposed joining of neck and shoulder. The blow paralyzed the right side of Kyle's body. After that we were able to wrestle him to the wet pavement, stretch him out belly down. I pulled his arms back and held them while Runyon knelt in the middle of his back, snapped handcuffs around his wrists.

I stood up first, breathing hard—and a white, scared face was peering at me through the rear window. A little boy, six or seven, wrapped in a blanket, his cheeks streaked with tears. Past him, on the other side of the car, I could see Lila standing, quiet now, with both hands fisted against her mouth.

Runyon said, "Where's the gun?"

"I don't know. I heard it hit the pavement—"

"I've got it."

I turned around. It was the guy from the car that had pulled up across the street; he'd come running over to rubberneck. He stood a short distance away, holding the revolver in one hand, loosely, as if he didn't know what to do with it. Heavyset and bald, I saw as I went up to him. Eyebrows like miniature tumbleweeds.

"What's going on?" he said.

"Police business."

"Yeah? You guys cops?"

"Making an arrest." I held out my hand, palm up. "Let's have the gun."

He hesitated, but just briefly. Then he said, "Sure, sure," and laid it on my palm.

And I backed up a step and pointed it at a spot two inches below his chin.

"Hey!" He gawped at me in disbelief. "Hey, what's the idea?"

"The idea," I said, "is for you to turn around, slow, and clasp your hands together behind you. Do it—now!"

He did it. He didn't have any choice.

I gave the gun to Runyon. And then, shaking my head, smiling a little, I snapped my set of handcuffs around Floyd Maxwell's wrists.

Funny business, detective work. Crazy business sometimes. Mostly it's a lot of dull routine, with small triumphs and as much frustration as satisfaction. But once in a great while something happens that not only makes it all worthwhile but defies the laws of probability. Call it whatever you like—random accident, multiple coincidence, star-and-planet convergence, fate, blind luck, divine intervention. It happens. It happened to Jake Runyon and me that stormy February night.

An ex-con named Kyle Franklin, fresh out of San Quentin after serving six years for armed robbery, decides he wants sole custody of his seven-year-old son. He drags his girlfriend to San Francisco, where his former wife is raising the boy as a single mom, and beats and threatens the ex-wife and kidnaps the child. Rather than leave the city quick, he decides he needs some sustenance for the long drive to Lila's place in L.A. and stops at the first diner he sees, less than a quarter-mile from the ex-wife's apartment building—a diner where two case-hardened private detectives happen to be staked out.

We overhear part of his conversation with Lila and it sounds wrong to us. We notice the blood on his coat sleeve, the scraped knuckles, his prison pallor, the Odin's cross—a prison tattoo and racist symbol—on his wrist, and the fact that he's carrying a concealed weapon. So we follow him outside and brace him, he pulls the gun, and while we're struggling, our deadbeat dad chooses that moment to show up. The smart thing for Maxwell to have done was to drive off, avoid trouble; instead he lets his curiosity and arrogance get the best of him, and comes over to watch, and then picks up Franklin's gun and hands it to me nice as you please. And so we foil a kidnapping and put the arm on not one but two violent, abusive fathers in the space of about three minutes.

What are the odds? Astronomical. You could live three or four lifetimes and nothing like it would ever happen again.

It's a little like hitting the Megabucks state lottery.

That night, Runyon and I were the ones holding the winning ticket.

# VALENTINE, JULY HEAT WAVE

*By Joyce Carol Oates*

Joyce Carol Oates is the author most recently of *The Gravedigger's Daughter* and *The Museum of Dr. Moses, Tales of Mystery and Suspense*. She is a member of the American Academy of Arts and Letters and is the Roger S. Berlind Distinguished Professor in Humanities at Princeton University.

M y calculated estimate is *Eight days should be about right.* Not that I am a pathologist, or any kind of "naturalist." My title at the university is professor of humanities. Yet a little research has made me fairly confident *Eight days during this heat should be about right.*

Because I have loved you, I will not cease to love you. It is not my way (as I believe you must know) to alter. As you vowed to be *my wife*, I vowed to be *your husband*. There can be no alteration of such vows. This, you know.

You will return to our house, you will return to our bedroom. When I beckon you inside you will step inside. When I beckon you to me you will come to me. You will judge if my estimate has been correct.

*Eight days! My valentine.*

The paradox is: Love is a live thing, and live things must die.

Sometimes abruptly, and sometimes over time.

Live things lose life: vitality, animation, the pulse of a beating heart and coursing blood carrying oxygen to the brain, the ability to withstand invasion by predatory organisms that devour them. Live things become, in the most elemental, crudest way of speaking, dead things.

And yet, the paradox remains: In the very body of death, in the very corpse of love, an astonishing new life breeds.

*This valentine I have prepared for you, out of the very body of love.*

You will arrive at the house alone, for that is your promise. Though you have ceased to love me (as you claim) you have not ceased to be an individual of integrity and so I know that you would not violate that promise. I believe you when you've claimed that there is no other man in your life: no other "love." And so, you will return to our house alone.

Your flight from Denver is due to arrive at 3:22 P.M. You've asked me not to meet you at the airport and so I have honored that wish. You've said that you prefer to rent a car at the airport and drive to the house by yourself and after you have emptied your closets, drawers, shelves of those items of yours you care to take away with you, you prefer to drive away alone, and to spend the night at an airport hotel where you've made a reservation. (Eight days ago when I called every airport hotel and motel to see if you'd made the reservation yet, you had not. At least, not under your married name.) When you arrive at the house, you will not turn into the driveway but park on the street. You will stare at the house. You will feel very tired. You will feel like a woman in a trance of—what?

Guilt, surely. Dread. That sick sense of imminent justice when we realize we must be punished, we will get what we "deserve."

Or maybe you will simply think: *Within the hour it will be ended. At last, I will be free!*

Sometime before 4 P.M. you will arrive at the house, assuming the flight from Denver isn't delayed. You had not known you were flying into a Midwestern heat wave and now you are reluctant to leave the air-conditioned interior of the car. For five weeks you've been away and now, staring at the house set back some distance from the street, amid tall, aging oaks and evergreens, you will wish to think *Nothing seems to have changed.* As if you have not noticed that, at the windows, downstairs and upstairs, Venetian blinds seem to have been drawn tightly shut. As if you have not noticed that the grass in the front lawn is overgrown and gone to seed and in the glaring heat of the summer sun patches of lawn have begun to burn out.

On the flagstone walk leading to the front door, a scattering of newspapers, fliers. The mailbox is stuffed with mail no one seems to have taken in for several days though you will not have registered *Eight days!* at this time.

Perhaps by this time you will concede that, yes, you are feeling uneasy. Guilty, and uneasy.

Knowing how particular your husband is about such things as the maintenance of the house and grounds: the maintenance of neatness, orderliness. The exterior of the house no less than the interior. Recognizing that appearances are trivial, and yet: Appearances can be signals that a fundamental principle of order has been violated.

At the margins of order is anarchy. What is anarchy but brute stupidity!

And so, seeing uneasily that the house seems to be showing signs of neglect, quickly you wish to tell yourself *But it can have nothing to do with me!* Five weeks you've been away and only twice, each time briefly, you have called me, and spoken with me. Pleading with me *Let me go, please let me go* as if I, of all people, required pleading-with.

*My valentine! My love.*

You will have seen: my car parked in the driveway, beside the house. And so you know (with a sinking heart? with a thrill of anticipation?) that I am home. (For I might have departed, as sometimes, admittedly, in our marriage I did depart, to work in my office at the university for long, utterly absorbed and delirious hours, with no awareness of time.) Not only is the car in the driveway, but I have promised you that I would be here, at this time; that we might make our final arrangements together, preparatory to divorce.

The car in the driveway is in fact "our" car. As the house is "our" house. For our property is jointly owned. Though you brought no financial resources to our marriage and it has been entirely my university income that has supported us yet our property is jointly owned, for this was my wish.

As you are *my wife*, so I am *your husband*. Symmetry, sanctity.

This valentine I've designed for you, in homage to the sanctity of marriage.

On the drive from the airport, you will have had time to think: to rehearse. You will repeat what you've told me and I will try to appeal to you to change your mind but of course you will not change your mind *Can't return, not for more than an hour* for that is the point of your returning: to go away again. You are adamant, you have made up your mind. *So sorry please forgive if you can* you are genuine in your regret and yet adamant.

The house, our house: 119 Worth Avenue. Five years ago when we were first married you'd thought that this house was "beautiful"— "special." Like the old residential neighborhood of similarly large houses on wooded lots, built on a hill overlooking the university arboretum. In this neighborhood known as University Heights most of the houses are solidly built brick with here and there a sprawling white colonial, dating back to the early decades of the twentieth century. Our house is dark-red brick and stucco, two stories and a third part-story between steep shingled roofs. Perhaps it is not a beautiful house but certainly it is an attractive, dignified house with black shutters, leaded-glass windows, a screened veranda, and lifting from the right-hand front corner of the second floor a quaint Victorian structure like a turret. You'd hurried to see this room when the real-estate agent showed us the house but were disappointed when it turned out to be little more than an architectural ornament, impractical even as a child's bedroom.

On the phone you'd murmured *Thank God no children.*

Since you've turned off the car's motor, the air-conditioning has ceased and you will begin to feel a prickling of heat. As if a gigantic breath is being exhaled that is warm, stale, humid, and will envelop you.

*So proud of your promotion, Daryll. So young!*

How you embarrassed me in the presence of others. How in your sweetly oblivious way you insulted me. Of course you had no idea. Of course you meant well. As if the fact that I was the youngest "senior" professor in the humanities division of the university at the time of my promotion was a matter of significance to me.

As my special field is Philosophy of Mind so it's "mind" that is valued, not trivial attributes like age, personality. All of philosophy is an effort of the mental faculties to discriminate between the trivial and the profound, the fleeting and the permanent, the many and the One. Pride is not only to be rejected on an ethical basis but on an epistemological basis, for how to "take pride" in one's self?—in one's physical being, in which the brain is encased? (Brain being the mysterious yet clearly organic repository of "mind.") And how to "take pride" in what is surely no more than an accident of birth?

You spoke impulsively, you had no idea of the crudeness of your words. Though in naiveté there is a kind of subtle aggression. Your artless blunders made me wince in the presence of my older colleagues (for whom references to youth, as to age, were surely unwelcome) and in the presence of my family (who disapproved of my marrying you, not on the grounds that you were too young, but that you were but a departmental secretary, "no match" intellectually for me which provoked me to a rare, stinging reply *But who would be an intellectual match for me? Who, and also female?*)

Yet I never blamed you. I never accused you. Perhaps in my reticence. My silences. My long interludes of utter absorption in my work. Never did I speak of the flaws of your character and if I speak of them now it is belatedly and without condemnation. Almost, with a kind of nostalgia. A kind of melancholy affection. Though you came to believe that I was "judgmental"—"hypercritical"—truly you had no idea how I spared you. Many times.

Here is the first shock: the heat.

As you leave the car, headed up the flagstone path to the front door. This wall of heat, waves of heat shimmering and nearly visible rushing at you. "Oh! My God." Several weeks away in mile-high Denver have lulled you into forgetting what a midsummer heat wave in this sea-level Midwestern city can be. Stale humid heat. Like a cloud of heavy, inert gas. The heat of my wrath. The heat of my hurt. As you are my wife I spared you, rarely did I speak harshly to you even when you seemed to lose all control and screamed at me *Let me go! Let me go! I am sorry I never loved you please let me go!*

That hour, the first time I saw your face so stricken with repugnance for me. Always, I will remember that hour.

As if, for the five years of our cohabitation, you'd been in disguise, you'd been playing a role, and now, abruptly and without warning, as if you hadn't known what you would say as you began to scream at me, you'd cast aside the disguise, tore off the mask and confronted me. *Don't love you. It was a mistake. Can't stay here. Can't breathe. Let me go!*

I was stunned. I had never imagined such words. I saw your mouth moving, I heard not words but sounds, strangulated sounds, you backed away from me, your face was contorted with dislike.

I told you then: I could not let you go. Would not let you go. For how could I, you are *my wife*.

Remembering how on a snowy morning some months before, in late winter, you'd entered my study in my absence and propped up a valentine on the window sill facing my desk. For often you did such things, playful, childlike, not seeming to mind if I scarcely noticed, or, noticing, paid much attention. The valentine came in a bright red envelope, absorbed in my work somehow I hadn't noticed. Days passed and I did not notice (evidently) and at last you came into my study to open the envelope for me laughing in your light rippling way (that did not sound accusing, only perhaps just slightly wounded) and you drew out of the red envelope a card of a kind that might be given to a child, a kitten peeking out of a watering can and inside a bright red TO MY VALENTINE. And your name. And I stared at this card not seeming to grasp for a moment what it was, a "valentine," thrust into my face for me to admire.

Perhaps I was abrupt with you then. Or perhaps I simply turned away. Whereof one cannot speak, there one must be silent. The maddened buzzing of flies is a kind of silence, I think. Like all of nature: the blind devouring force to which Schopenhauer gave the name *will*.

Your promise was, at the time of our marriage, you would not be hurt. You would not be jealous of my work, though knowing that my work, as it is the best part of me, must always take priority over my personal life. Freely you'd given this promise, if perhaps recklessly. You would not be jealous of my life apart from you, and you would not be hurt. Bravely pledging *I can love enough for both of us!*

And yet, you never grasped the most elemental logistics of my work. The most elemental principles of philosophy: the quest for truth. Of course, I hardly expected you, lacking even a bachelor's degree from a mediocre land-grant university, to understand my work which is understood by very few in my profession, but I did expect you, as my wife, to understand that there can be no work more exacting, exhausting, and heroic.

But now we are beyond even broken promises. Inside our house, your valentine is waiting.

As a younger man only just embarked upon the quest of truth, I'd imagined that the great work of my life would be a definitive refutation of Descartes, who so bluntly separated "mind" and "body" at the very start of modern philosophy, but unexpectedly in my early thirties my most original work has become a corroboration and a clarification of the Cartesian position: that "mind" inhabits "body" but is not subsumed in "body." For the principles of logic, as I have demonstrated by logical argument, in a systematic geometry in the mode of Spinoza, transcend all merely "bodily" limitations. All this, transmuted into the most precise symbols.

When love dies, can it be revived? We will see.

On the front stoop you will ring the doorbell. Like any visitor.

Not wishing to enter the house by the side door, as you'd done when you lived here.

Calling in a low voice my name: "Daryll?"

How strange, *Daryll* is my name. My given name. Yet I am hardly identical with *Daryll* and in the language of logic it might even be claimed that I am *no thing* that is *Daryll* though I am simultaneously *no thing* that is *not-Daryll*. Rather, *Daryll* is irrelevant to what I am, or what I have become.

No answer. You will try the door knocker. And no answer.

How quiet! Almost, you might think that no one is home.

You will take out your house key, carried inside your wallet, in your purse. Fitting the key into the lock you will experience a moment's vertigo, wishing to think that the key no longer fits the lock; that your furious husband has changed the locks on the doors, and expelled you from his life, as you wish to be expelled from his life. But no, the lock does fit. Of course.

Pushing open the door. A heavy oak door, painted black.

Unconsciously you will have expected the interior of the stolid old dark-brick house to be coolly air-conditioned and so the shock of over-warm, stale air, a rancid-smelling air seems to strike you full in the face. "Hello? Daryll? Are you . . ."

How weak and faltering, your voice in your own ears. And how your nostrils are pinching at this strange, unexpected smell.

Rancid-ripe. Sweet as rotted fruit, yet more virulent. Rotted flesh?

*Please forgive!*

*Can't return. Not for more than an hour.*

*It was my fault, I had no idea . . .*

*. . . from the start, I think I knew. What a mistake we'd both made.*

*Yes I admit: I was flattered.*

*. . . young, and ignorant. And vain.*

*That you, the most brilliant of the younger professors in the department . . .*

*Tried to love you. To be a wife to you. But . . .*

*Just to pack my things. And what I can't take with me, you can give to Goodwill. Or throw out with the trash.*

*. . . the way they spoke of you, in the department. Your integrity, your genius. And stubborn, and strong . . .*

*If I'd known more! More about men. Like you I was shy, I'd been afraid of men, I think. A virgin at twenty-five . . .*

*No. I don't think so.*

*Even at the beginning, no. Looking back at it now, I don't think I ever did, Daryll. It was a kind of . . .*

*. . . like a masquerade, a pretense. When you said you thought you loved me. Wanting so badly to believe . . .*

*Please, Daryll? Can you? Forgive?*

*. . . only just time enough to pack a few things. The divorce can be final-*
*ized by our lawyers, we won't need to meet again.*

*The most brilliant young philosopher of his generation, they said of you.*
*And he is ours . . .*

*This masquerade. "Marriage."*

*So badly I wanted to be your wife. I am so ashamed!*

*Daryll? Can you forgive me?*

Standing in the doorway of the living room you will see to your
astonishment that sheets—bedsheets?—have been carefully drawn
over the furniture, like shrouds. One of the smaller Oriental rugs has
been rolled up and secured with twine as if in preparation for being
hauled away. Books have been removed from the shelves that cover
most of two walls of the living room and these books have been
neatly placed in cardboard boxes. At the windows, blinds have been
tightly drawn shut. Flies buzz and bat against the slats. There's a
green twilit cast to the air as if the house has sunk beneath the surface of the sea.

The smell: What is it? You think *Something that has spoiled, in the*
*kitchen?*

You will not venture into the kitchen at the rear of the house.

Though you enter the dining room, hesitantly. Seeing on the long
oaken table a row of manila folders each neatly marked in black ink:
FINANCES, BANK RECORDS, IRS & RECEIPTS, LAST WILL
AND TESTAMENT.

You will begin now to be frightened. Panic like flames begins to
lick at you.

And that sound: murmurous and buzzing as of muffled voices
behind a shut door.

"Daryll? Are you—upstairs?"

Telling yourself *Run! Escape!*

*Not too late. Turn back. Hurry!*

Yet somehow you will make your way to the stairs. The broad front
staircase with the dark-cranberry carpeting, worn in the center from
years of footsteps predating your own. Like a sleepwalker you grip
the banister, to steady your climb.

Is it guilt drawing you upstairs? A sick, excited sense of what you will discover? What it is your duty, as *my wife*, to discover?

You will be smiling, a small fixed smile. Your eyes opened wide yet glassy as if unseeing. And your heart rapidly beating as the wings of a trapped bird.

If you faint . . . Must not faint! Blood is draining from your brain, almost you can feel darkness encroaching at the edges of your vision; and your vision is narrowing, like a tunnel.

At the top of the stairs you pause, to clear your head. Except you can't seem to clear your head. Here, the smell is very strong. A smell confused with heat, shimmering waves of heat. You begin to gag, you feel nausea. Yet you can't turn back, you must make your way to the bedroom at the end of the corridor.

Past the charming little turret-room with the bay window and cushioned window seat. The room you'd imagined might somehow have been yours, or a child's room, but which proved to be impracticably small.

The door to the bedroom is shut. You press the flat of your hand against it feeling its heat. Even now thinking almost calmly *No. I will not. I am strong enough to resist.*

You dare to grasp the doorknob. Dare to open the door. Slowly.

How loud the buzzing is! A crackling sound like flame. And the rancid-rot smell, overwhelming as sound that is deafening, passing beyond your capacity to comprehend.

Something brushes against your face. Lips, eyes. You wave it away, panicked. "Daryll? Are you—here?"

For there is motion in the room. A plane of something shifting, fluid, alive and iridescent-glittering: yet not human.

In the master bedroom, too, venetian blinds have been drawn at every window. There's the greeny undersea light. It takes you several seconds to realize that the room is covered in flies. The buzzing noise you've been hearing is flies. Thousands, millions?—flies covering the ceiling, the walls. And the carpet, which appears to be badly stained with something dark. And on the bed, a handsome four-poster bed that came with the house, a Victorian antique, there is a seething blanket of flies over a humanoid figure that seems to have partly melted into the bedclothes. Is this—who is this? The face, or what had been the face, is no longer recognizable. The skin has swollen to bursting like a burnt sausage and its hue is blackened and no longer does it have the texture of skin but of something pulpy, liquefied. Like the manic glittering flies that crawl over everything, this skin exudes a dark iridescence. The body has become a bloated balloon-body, fought over by masses of flies. Here and there, in crevices that had once been the mouth, the nostrils, the ears, there are writhing white patches, maggots like churning frenzied kernels of white rice. The throat of the humanoid figure seems to have been slashed. The bloodied steak knife lies close beside the figure, where it has been dropped. The figure's arms, covered in flies, are outstretched on the bed as if quivering, about to lift in an embrace of welcome. Everywhere, dark, coagulated blood has soaked the figure's clothing, the bedclothes, the bed, the carpet. The rot-smell is overwhelming. The carrion-smell. Yet you can't seem to turn away. Whatever has drawn you here has not yet released you. The entire room is a crimson wound, a place of the most exquisite mystery, seething with its own inner, secret life. *Your husband* has not died, has not vanished but has been transmogrified into another dimension of being, observing you through a galaxy of tiny unblinking eyes: the buzzing is his voice, multiplied by millions. Flies brush against your face. Flies brush against your lips, your eyelashes. You wave them away, you step forward, to approach the figure on the bed. *My valentine! My love.*

# ONLINE MYSTERY FICTION IN 2007

## By Sarah Weinman

I f 2006 was a year of expansion and growth for online crime fiction outlets, 2007 was all about flux. Several venues, like Crime Scene Scotland and SHOTS, hung up their fiction shingles and now devote themselves almost exclusively to reviews and nonfiction content. Longtime stalwart Thrilling Detective's future, as of this writing, is very much up in the air, which would be a very sad thing for enthusiasts of the private investigator subgenre. Shred of Evidence, which appeared to be in the grip of permafrost, resurrected itself in blog format—and a more frequent story posting schedule. And on the flash fiction front (for stories no longer than a thousand words, and preferably less) even though we said goodbye to Tribe's groundbreaking site Flashing in the Gutters, others picked up the flash slack in the form of Muzzle Flash (http://dzallen.blogspot.com/) Powder Burn Flash (http://powderburnflash.blogspot.com/) and Flash Pan Alley (http://flashpanalley.wordpress.com/)

But once again, the good news far outweighs the bad. Online crime fiction adopted a decidedly international flavor with the introduction of UK-based Pulp Pusher (http://www.pulp pusher.com), edited by Tony Black and The Outpost (http://www. crimedownunder.com/TheOutpost.html) Damien Gay's Australia-based fiction-centric e-zine. Todd Robinson, proprietor of *ThugLit* (http://www.thuglit.com) secured a three-book deal with Kensington for yearly anthologies of the magazine's best stories interspersed with original offerings from some of the genre's brightest stars of noir. Look for anthology number one, *Hardcore Hardboiled*, in May 2008.

The exposure of online markets also catapulted several writers to current and upcoming debut publication. Craig McDonald, who graced the pages of last year's edition of *Year's Finest*, took the bones of his story to craft his auspicious debut crime novel *Head Games*, which Bleak House Books published last fall. Keith Gilman, the most recent winner of the St. Martin's Press/Private Eye Writers of America contest (his novel will be released in fall 2008) appeared almost exclusively online. Editing *Spinetingler* (http://www.spinetinglermag.com) helped Sandra Ruttan find a publishing home with Dorchester for her Canadian-based police procedural series, which begins in May 2008 with *What Burns Within*. And Scott Wolven continues to be online fiction's poster child, garnering his sixth straight *Best American Mystery Stories* selection and publication of his debut novel with Otto Penzler's imprint at Harcourt sometime in 2008.

Now, on to the four stories I've selected for this volume. With so many outlets to choose from, it was hard to narrow the list down to just four—but in the end, these were the ones that grabbed me with their opening lines and stuck with me long after I finished the endings.

In a little over a year, Patricia Abbott has become a welcome fixture on the online crime fiction magazine circuit. Chances are likely that if you peruse any of the major 'zines, you'll find one of her stories, each of them displaying the deep psychological acuity formed from earlier literary efforts and a natural affinity for crime fiction's major concerns. The standout, however, is "A Saving Grace," contorting the private eye story into a deeper examination of accountability, crumbling relationships and whether to stay and fight—or cut and run.

Toronto native Hilary Davidson is a veteran freelance writer with over a dozen travel guidebooks and hundreds of articles for the likes of the *Globe and Mail*, *Reader's Digest*, *Discover*, and *Working Mother*. "Anniversary" is her first published short story, but all those years of writing to deadline pay off in the form of a tightly wound psychological chiller that shocks not with what is said but what is only implied.

Kerry Ashwin hails from Australia, where she recently collaborated to write a radio play for ABC North Queensland and writes for magazines with a boating theme. "Something Out of the Ordinary" may appear to give the game away with its title, but trust me—the lengths its protagonist goes to preserve his wife's memory go far beyond what the title even dares to hint at.

Finally, Bryon Quertermous has been discussed often in the pages of *Year's Finest*, first for his co-creation (along with Dave White) of the Blog Short Story Project, and then after he moved on to create *Demolition*. Disclosure requires me to note that a story of mine appeared in one of the magazine's themed issues, and one of his appeared in *SHOTS* during my tenure as its short fiction editor, but even if there was no connection whatsoever, I'd still select "Cadaver Dog" for inclusion here. With echoes of the blues, what seems to be a tale of lost love gradually reveals its darker motives—and you'll never think of a dog's plaintive looks and cries quite the same way again.

If, for whatever reason, the world of online crime fiction seems to be a roadblock for those wedded to the print medium, consider these stories a taste of what the Internet has to offer. And once ingested, you'll definitely want to take multiple bites.

## LINKS TO CHOSEN STORIES

**"A Saving Grace" by Patti Abbott**
*Thrilling Detective*, Summer 2007
http://www.thrillingdetective.com/fiction/07_06_01.html

**"Cadaver Dog" by Bryon Quertermous**
*Hardluck Stories*, Spring 2007
http://www.hardluckstories.com/Spring2007/Dog-Quertermous.htm

**"Anniversary" by Hilary Davidson**
*ThugLit*, July 2007
http://www.thuglit.com/zine/thugl7/docs/anniversaiy.pdf

**"Something Out of the Ordinary" by Kerry Ashwin**
*The Outpost*, April 2007
http://www.crimedownunder.com/Outpost/iss3_something_ashwin.html